Inner Fears

by

M.F. King

COSCOM ENTERTAINMENT
WINNIPEG

COSCOM ENTERTAINMENT
Suite 2, 317 Edison Avenue
Winnipeg, MB R2G 0L9

ISBN 1-897217-18-8

PUBLISHED BY COSCOM ENTERTAINMENT
www.coscomentertainment.com

Library and Archives Canada Cataloguing in Publication

King, M. F., 1958-
    Inner fears / M.F. King.

ISBN 1-897217-18-8

    I. Title.

PS3611.I57I56 2005   813'.6   C2005-905031-4

Cover art and design by Michele Free and A.P. Fuchs
Text set in Garamond
Printed and bound in the USA

This book is dedicated to all my friends and family who
have encouraged me. You know who you are.

Thanks to Debbie McRill, Diane Holloway, Paul Cromwell,
Craig Arny and Marge & Bob Murray for their writing expertise.

Special thanks to J.D. Reza, without whom this book would not exist.

I'd like to send thanks and happy thoughts to Dean R. Koontz,
whose stories have enriched my life and given me many hours of
enjoyment. Mr. Koontz, you are my inspiration.

Inner Fears

Prologue

Deep within the black caverns, a crack stretched from floor to ceiling like a frozen bolt of lightning. A form, wedged within the damp crevasse, stirred. Its temperature, only two degrees higher than the surrounding coolness in the cave, suddenly began to rise. The hibernating body trembled, shuddered and shook so violently it erupted from the crevasse, falling to the floor in a heap of white flesh and bones. Its heart kick-started. The internal metabolic motor rumbled.

A screech shot through the cave and raced through each surface. Writhing in agony, the skeletal hands groped at its snow-white hair. Its temperature shot up and its bowels emptied. As the thrashing continued, it became covered in insect-ridden guano. Unable to control the twitching of the atrophied muscles, its neck snapped back and its head crashed repeatedly against the wet rock.

Finally able to turn over, it crawled on claw-like hands and bony knees, snatching crickets and crayfish eggs. It smashed them into its dry mouth, crunching their shells. Creeping to stalactites, its bleached tongue flicked out, stealing drops of moisture.

After many hours, the frontal lobe pulsed and his first thought in three hundred years exhumed itself. "I am Stars in White Cloud, here to summon the demons of Wahatoya. It is finally time, time to fulfill my destiny."

1

A whirlwind of leaves and sand crashed against the window then sank to the pavement for a fleeting moment before sweeping back into a restless dance. The wind dashed and pummeled nature's litter like puppets on a swirling string, striking brick and cement. There would be no respite, not until the snows of winter diverted the wind's attention and gave it a new frozen toy to batter.

From behind his desk, Dr. Jeffrey Clinton watched the autumn show, mesmerized. *To be so free.*

He heard a knock at the door. With a sigh, he snapped off his Jackson Browne tape, tossed a pile of ungraded papers and a granola bar into the middle drawer and brushed crumbs from his desk.

Pulling off his reading glasses, he pivoted his chair toward the door, but didn't get up. Only noon, and he already had four hours of grading under his belt. Now would come the endless stream of students, all wanting his help with something they were either too lazy or too stupid to do by themselves.

Same old, same old. What he wouldn't give for some excitement, something that would give him the adrenaline rush that surgery had held for him. The synchronicity of mind and body; the feeling of being in complete command. His grand operating-room entrance, the smooth slap of the scalpel on his palm, the adoring eyes, the tension before the initial incision and how the flesh fell away under his hand when he was committed to finish because there was no going back. The smell of anticipation and antiseptic and blood.

And blood.

He fought back the nausea that shot up from the base of his spine and engulfed him. Now, the scent of blood was fear. Fear that disabled. Fear that had murdered his career and his family and his life. Fear that had chased him from his prominent Eastern practice to this teaching job in the middle of nowhere.

The knock sounded again, this time more insistent.

"Come in." His eyes snapped up as the door opened. A woman stood in the doorway.

His heart skipped.

He might have called her beautiful if he didn't know her so well. He no longer found anything pretty about Professor Vanguard— except those long, trim legs and the silky skin that lay beneath the prim suit. Except the memory of her soft whimpers when she forgot to contain herself, when she forgot who she wanted to be and allowed herself to be who she was. "Eleanor," he said. He swallowed.

"Jeffrey." She lifted her chin.

"This is a surprise."

"I'm sure it is. Believe me, I don't want to be here."

"So I guess that rules out a tearful, passionate reunion." He couldn't keep the sarcasm out of his voice. "University business, then?"

"Not exactly."

She remained silent, and for the first time he noticed the lines of anxiety around her eyes. Although she projected an air of undauntable confidence, something troubled her.

"Well, come in, then. Take a load off."

She pulled the door closed. With military precision, she marched to the metal folding chair across from his desk and perched on the edge like a nervous crow, her large purse balanced on her knees. Her mouth clamped shut, as if she wanted no secrets to drop from it.

Although she'd disguised it with makeup, the evidence of stress was easier to see close up. Dark circles ringed her puffy eyes. Her skin looked pale and blotchy, like stone-washed jeans. Her mouth hinted at a frown, as if she had to fight against gravity pulling the edges down. He'd never seen her like this. "How are you feeling?"

"Terrific," she said in a voice that made the word sound more like "shitty."

He waited for her to inquire about him.

She didn't, of course. Never had. Instead, she glanced around at the empty Chinese takeout containers spilling over the edge of the waste can, at the stacks of unanswered correspondence in his in-basket, at the tomato sauce stain on his shirt.

She was playing her old games, all right. He'd always started the conversations and kept them going. Before, when he'd cared, when he'd needed her.

Now that she'd come to him, he wasn't going to make it easy. He rocked back in his chair, enjoying her obvious anxiety. "As you so succinctly told me a few weeks ago, you have no need for my interference in your life. Or in your career. So why are you here?"

Silence. She kept the strap of her giant purse tight in her grip.

"Let's see," he ventured, staring at the ceiling as he rocked in his chair. "Why are you here? Money? I doubt it. You keep track of every cent the way most women look after their children."

She opened her mouth to speak.

"No. Don't tell me." He waved a hand at her. "After thinking it over, you've decided that you really love me, and want me back." Leaning forward, he placed his elbows on the desk, and stared right into her face. "I'm going to have to refuse the offer. Reptiles don't make the best lovers."

"Damn it!" she snapped through her teeth. "Why do you insist on being so sarcastic?"

He shrugged, relishing his temporary position of power. "I have to do something. You come in here and sit and don't say a word. You look around my office as if germs are going to spring out and strangle you, or a rat is going to run across your feet."

His heart raced, and he cursed his rising anger. Why did he have to react to her? She knew how to get to him, instantly. "Just get to the point, would you? I have important things to do."

She took a deep breath. Stared at her hands. "I'm pregnant."

It was like a bowling ball to the chest. He expected maybe she'd gone over her bills and realized he drank six instead of five beers at her house, and that he still owed her fifty-nine cents. He expected her to ask him to never, ever, tell anyone about their brief affair, as it could damage her ability to become Dean of Engineering. But pregnant?

A gust of wind rattled the window, and for a moment leaves pressed up against the glass, like tiny faces watching them. "I see," he managed to say. "So why come to me?"

"You're the father."

He stood so fast his chair rolled back and knocked into the wall. "Now hold on," he said with an ironic laugh. "There's no way—"

She stood and pointed at him. "Don't try to deny it, Jeffrey Clinton. I know it's your baby."

He opened his arms toward heaven. "No way! There is no way."

She stood, her mouth set in an angry line. "Oh, yes there is. We were…together."

He laughed inwardly. She still couldn't say the *F-word*. "I used a condom. Every single time, remember? You kept them in the drawer by the bed, alphabetized and sorted by color."

"One of them obviously leaked, or you used it improperly."

"Look at these hands. I'd like to remind you that I used to be a top-notch surgeon. I can handle a condom!"

"The key phrase there is *used to be*."

His anger flared further. He never should have told her, or shared anything about his past with her. As their brief relationship had drawn to an end, she'd never tired of reminding him of his descent from grace. She judged people by their stock portfolio, and once she'd decided he was a fallen star instead of rising one, she'd dropped him like a worm-ridden apple.

"Look," he said, biting back well-deserved but vulgar words he wanted to throw at her, "I'm not in the mood for this." He moved over to the door and opened it. "Your little plan didn't work on me. So go pick one of your other lovers to be your baby's father."

She stayed her ground, still clutching her purse. "There were no others, and you know it."

"I can't be the father," he said.

"Why are you denying it?"

He slammed the door and turned back toward her. He struggled for control, lowering his voice. "Because I'm sterile, okay? I can't father a child."

Her eyebrows lowered. Her eyes narrowed. Red patches spread over her face. Throwing the strap over her shoulder, she fumbled in her purse with shaking hands. She withdrew a white tablet and shoved it into her mouth. "You never...I didn't..."

"I got a vasectomy for my first wife. After the divorce, she had a baby eight months later. Imagine that. She married the father. That's probably what you should do, too."

Bewilderment enlarged her bright green eyes. "You can't be serious."

He nodded. "It's true."

"But you used a condom as if you needed it. You never said a thing!"

"I did need it. Besides, sharing the personal details of my life was never number one in your Daytimer. And I made the mistake of telling you about how I ended up in this desert. I wasn't about to make the same mistake twice."

"What do you mean by that?"

"I didn't tell you about my vasectomy, but you never asked, either. You never asked anything about me. Our relationship was like an orchestrated event. You probably wrote everything out on your damned computer before we ever did it. Every date, every kiss, every time we fucked!" He emphasized the last word.

She turned a deep shade of red and looked toward the door.

"What? Are you worried someone will hear us?" He turned back toward the door and cupped his hands around his mouth. "We fucked!"

"Stop that!" she stage whispered, leaning toward him, gripping her purse with both hands.

"Go ahead," he yelled, feeling his own face heat. "Tell me what to do. But I'm not going to become Daddy for your child."

"No, that's not what I'm here for." She threw another nervous glance toward the door. "Please, sit down. Hear me out."

"No."

"Jeff." She swallowed. "I need you."

He'd never heard those words from her before. Eleanor Vanguard didn't need anyone. "Okay then." He dropped back into his chair, and she lowered herself carefully back onto hers.

She set the purse on her lap and wrapped the straps round and round her hands, like handcuffs. "I know you don't believe this, but there's no way...I mean...there was no one else," she said. "You're the only one who could be the father." Her face washed out to a chalky white.

He studied her eyes. They were dark, and deadly serious. She wasn't lying.

"But I've told you," he repeated. "That's not possible."

"Then the results of the test I took must not be right."

He changed positions in the chair, his curiosity building. He picked up a pencil and tapped it on the desk. "What made you take the test in the first place?"

"I haven't felt...right...for a while. You know, nauseated. Faint. I have strange feelings, nightmares." She shivered.

"Could be hormonal," he suggested.

"That's what I thought. Then, I missed my period."

He nodded. "When did you take the test?"

"Two days ago. Yesterday. This morning."

"Three positives?"

She nodded. "I need you to verify the results of the home pregnancy test I took. If it's positive, I want you to give me something to make sure I abort."

He tossed the pencil on the desk and threw up his hands. "Oh, God, Eleanor," he complained. "Why me?"

"You're a medical doctor, as well as a Ph.D."

"Why not go to the clinic here? Or go to someone else? *Anyone* else?"

"I don't want any records. Nothing in my medical history. These things can be discovered."

He rubbed his neck, the tension spreading through his bones. "You want it kept quiet. To not hurt your chance at becoming Dean."

She hesitated. "Yes. You know that becoming Dean of Engineering is the most important thing in the world to me."

"I know." He sighed. "Okay. There are conditions that can cause a fake positive test. When is the last time you had a pap smear or a gynecological checkup?"

"Before the pregnancy test, a couple of months ago. Actually, the doctor suspected uterine cancer and had to take an endometrial biopsy. Everything was normal."

"Did you have that done at the university clinic? The one in this building?"

"Of course."

"Everything was completely normal?"

"Completely."

Wondering what the pill she'd taken a moment ago was for, he stood and walked to the window. The wind still leaped and ran, playing with the leaves. Tree branches heaved back and forth, their leaves shuddering.

"You must understand how important this is to me," she continued. "My career is the only thing I've ever cared about, ever wanted."

He turned and leaned against the wall. "How well I know."

"Now I'm up for Dean, and this," she placed her palm on her belly, "could ruin everything for me."

He looked at her slim fingers laid against her abdomen and realized the pregnancy itself was not her real problem—it was the haunting knowledge that something else had taken control of her life, even if it was only a baby. To not be in control would be the definition of hell for Eleanor Vanguard.

She hoisted the purse back onto her shoulder and approached him. Her bottom lip trembled. "I need to know. I need to know today."

Her anxiety had thoroughly infected him, as if an airborne bacteria had piggybacked her words. He, too, felt the intense need to know. Was she pregnant? If so, how? "Shit. I can't believe I'm doing this."

She exhaled heavily, visibly relaxing. "Thank you."

He walked back to his chair, in action again. "Give me a urine sample. I'll take it over to the lab tonight, and do the test myself. If it's positive, which I doubt, we'll talk about the…you know."

She glanced around the room.

"Now what?" he asked, wondering what else she would demand from him. *His foreskin?*

"What do I put the sample in?"

His eyes fell on a bouquet of old flowers in a vase on his desk, given to him by a doting young coed. He removed the dried remains, the ends dripping, and dropped them into the trash can, followed by the green, smelly water. He handed her the vase.

She turned up her nose. "You've got to be kidding."

"Unless you have a urine-sample cup in that suitcase of yours, this is it."

She accepted it with a sigh. "Where's the bathroom?"

"Down the hall. Oh, and wash the thing first, so the tests don't come back showing a paramecium infection."

After flashing him a disgusted look, she left and returned with the vase, half-full of yellow liquid. He wondered where he would stash it until that evening, when he'd have time to run the test. In the faculty refrigerator?

She stuck out her hand. "Thanks again, Jeff."

He took her hand.

Her warm fingers curled around his. He liked the feel of her soft skin and her strong grip. Their eyes held for a moment. "Eleanor."

He watched her hips move under the fitted suit as she left his office. Although she looked like a page from Fortune Magazine, beneath were all the warm curves of humanity. He'd run his hand over her waist, her hips, and held the woman. But he'd been battered by the coldhearted executive.

He walked to the window and stared out at the unceasing Albuquerque wind. It seemed symbolic, somehow. As if the remains of the past lessened the value of the present; just as the sand, thrown against paint and stucco, eventually wore it away.

A dark chill passed through him. For some reason, Eleanor had spooked him. He'd been tested as sterile many times. Had that changed? Was she lying? Or was the cause of her condition something neither of them had considered?

He couldn't shake his growing sense of foreboding.

2

Felipe Jojola adjusted his white lab coat, picked up his clipboard, and started down the even rows of cages. Everything was in order. Clean. Not a straw on the floor or the smell of feces anywhere. He ran a tight ship. At first, he'd disliked the endless hours of cleaning and organizing and logging every detail, even when one of the animals farted. But now he took pride in his meticulousness and wouldn't have it any other way. The best. Only the best. Although Caesar Bossidy was a stuck-up bastard, he paid well. Better than any job Felipe could find on the reservation.

A chimp's animated greetings stopped him in front of the fourth cage. "*Hóla*, Monica!" he said to the pregnant animal. "Look at that belly, *Mamasíta. Qué linda!*" He reached into his pocket and took out some Fruit Loops cereal he kept for her. She grabbed them through the bars and downed them hungrily, giving him an adoring look.

Caesar's strict researchers probably watched him over the security cameras. They would have a fit if they saw him offer the sweets, but Felipe didn't care. As a Pueblo Indian, a member of the P'ónin tribe, he respected all of his animal brothers. Whether used for food or to discover new ways to help mankind, their offering should be acknowledged, the animals thanked, their lives improved. But Caesar had abandoned the ways of his people years ago, and had proven repeatedly he had no feeling for Earth's creatures.

Felipe threw his long dark braid over his shoulder and watched Monica lick her fingers, searching for sugar. He shared much with the chimp, he realized, more than a sweet tooth. The mountain imprisoned them both. At least the company allowed him to send money and news through letters, though they opened and inspected everything that left the mountain, personal or not.

What could be so damned secret about a bunch of pregnant chimps, anyway? The only thing he found uncommon was their disappearance. For some reason, just as one of them neared delivery, she would vanish. The scientists refused to answer questions about where the mamas and their offspring had gone. There should be almost a dozen little furry chimps in the lab somewhere, but he'd never found any trace of them. Of course, he wasn't allowed everywhere in the sprawling company, just in his quarters, the offices and the main animal lab.

He eased his hand back between the bars with more of the brightly colored cereal. Monica greedily snatched it from his palm and sang out in joy. His face stretched into a smile. "You better tell me, girl, when you go into labor. I'll supervise it personally so that nothing happens to you. I delivered three of my own, you know."

Delighted, she tipped her face up and sang.

Her voice quieted and she cocked her head, listening. Felipe heard it too—the sound of a distant flute. It decorated the air with a haunting melody, winding through the lab. "What's that?" Felipe scanned the room. The tune was familiar, yet strange. Beckoning. "You like that, *Hijita*? That's a flute. Pretty, huh?"

Her eyes glazed. She rocked back and forth. Her hand opened and the Fruit Loops rolled across the cage floor in all directions. She doubled over. A fierce cry erupted from her throat.

"What? What is it?" Felipe dropped his clipboard and fumbled in his pockets for the cage's keys. They shouldn't lock the cages. *Unnecessary. Stupid.*

"Help me, here!" he called to the cameras. "I need help!"

He pulled the key-ring from his pocket with shaking hands. The keys jingled as he searched for the right one. They fell from his trembling grasp. "Damn it. Hold on, girl!" he yelled, bending to pick them up. His heart pounded like the ceremonial drums at the festival of St. Jerome.

She howled, a piercing shriek of agony. A strong odor gagged him and something splashed against face. He wiped it away and saw blood on his fingers. He looked up at Monica and gasped. His eyes grew wide. He backed up against the cage behind him.

Madre de Diós! Her distended abdomen had taken on a life of its own, poking out one way, then the other. Blood gushed down her crotch and over her legs, splattering into the air. Something squirmed around inside her. It appeared to be chewing her up from the inside out. Her baby? *Impossible.* A monster.

Her eyes rolled up and she fell onto her back in the cage. Dead. At least now whatever squirmed like a snake within her would suffocate. He took a hesitant step toward the cage and froze.

The thing still lived. He stared with growing terror as the rolling and pitching in her belly continued. Abruptly, something shot out from the dead chimp's abdomen. A sharp bony claw. It sliced along the skin of her gut, opening it like a zipper.

A head emerged, with a sweet baby's face. Immersed in blood and slimy liquid, the thing climbed from its mother's carcass and walked-slithered-crawled to the cage bars.

Felipe couldn't breathe, couldn't avert his eyes. Couldn't move. *Run, damn it, run!* But the vision paralyzed him. Like a terrified fly in a sticky web, the newborn's face trapped his gaze.

A demon's face.

The monster reached the bars and placed its claw around one of the thin metal posts. The bar snapped easily. The creature repeated the action on another bar, and then another. It used its chimp hand to bend them back, making a hole to crawl through.

Raising its head, it crowed.

The cry, unmistakably that of a newborn baby, halted Felipe's racing heart. The sound seemed so innocent, so vulnerable, but the creature making the sound was not either one.

It stared at him, oozing with Monica's fluids, rocking back and forth to the music of the flute. The eyes moved independently, as if two brains coexisted within the thing. Then, without warning, it vaulted from the cage and landed on Felipe's face.

"No, no!" The single claw buried deep into his neck, snipping. Intense pain melted into a warm wet gush. Grabbing at the slimy beast, he fought to drag it from the death grasp. He couldn't break its powerful grip.

The horrible nightmare face looked at him one last time then sunk its teeth into his Adam's apple, swallowing his dying scream.

3

The wind gusted past Jeff's window and carried the September colors to the university clinic a couple of windows down, rattling the frame and howling like a lost soul.

The unholy sound sent an ominous chill through Dr. Randall Meaks. He stood beside the table and talked to the young blonde student who lay on the table in nothing but a white hospital gown. "As I said, we're going to perform an endometrial biopsy today."

"What are you going to do, exactly?" Donna asked shyly.

"First, I'll insert the scapula. Then, using a long instrument like a spoon, I'll pass it through the cervix, which should be slightly dilated right now, and remove some tissue from the endometrium."

"That sounds like it's going to hurt."

"You'll feel a little cramping, that's all." He smiled and patted her arm with his fleshy hand. "Hopefully, we'll have the results by tomorrow."

"Let's do it. I've got Biology class in an hour."

"Oh, I'm afraid you'll have to stay off your feet for almost four hours after the procedure. Didn't I tell you that?"

"Four hours?" the patient complained. "But the pamphlet didn't mention—"

"Yours is a special case," he lied, putting his hand on her shoulder reassuringly. "I'm worried about excess bleeding."

"Okay, I guess…"

"Good. Megan, are you ready?" he asked the nurse.

She nodded and pulled an army-green mask over her mouth.

Dr. Meaks pulled his mask up also and walked to the end of the table where he helped the girl plant her feet in the cold metal stirrups. She slid to the end of the table. He snapped on the light, which bathed her pelvic area with warmth.

Tension gripped his chest. He didn't want to do this one after the news from the mountain. All the experimental chimp babies had disappeared, one of them right from the mother's womb. But what could he do? It was either her or him. He ran his hand over his bald head nervously before he slipped on his gloves and lifted the first instrument from the stainless tray.

Why had he ever responded to Caesar Bossidy's offer? Good money, they had said. Research opportunities. *Ha!* He was nothing more than a lab technician. The company bastards didn't listen to him at all. They just told him what to do and he was expected to follow the orders mindlessly. A flunky. He hadn't braved college and medical school, barely passing, hanging on by a thread, to let this cultish group, led by a crazed, criminal scientist, order him around.

He wanted out. Way out. But it was too late. He was up to his neck in it, and wasn't sure how far they'd go to protect their operation. He didn't want to find out.

"Okay. This is the scapula. It's going to feel a bit cold." He placed the instrument next to the girl's vagina. Too bad they picked this one. Such a pretty girl. "Close your eyes and relax." He recited the litany of OB/GYNs as he inserted the device. The shiny bullet-shaped instrument slid in. He left it hanging while he walked to the corner of the room, out of her vision.

He opened an airtight silver canister. It breathed as he broke the seal. White steam flowed out of it like fog in a television graveyard. From inside he extracted a glass tube. Opening the top, he stuck a metal wire inside and pulled out a small frozen culture. He placed it on the end of the wire whip, inside a scoop.

He hesitated. Dear God, he shouldn't do it.

The nurse narrowed her dark eyes and watched his movements carefully. She was almost certainly a spy from the mountain. They were everywhere, looking for hesitation, signs of remorse, or a change of heart. If Meaks wasn't careful, he'd wind up in one of the numerous caverns in the mountain, dead and forgotten. At first he had worried about exposure, and a loss of his tenure and practice. Now he feared for his life. He would have to go through with this procedure, whether he wanted to or not.

The company took too many risks, was in too much of a hurry. They had no proven track record, no excuse to begin tests on human subjects. Money. That's all they thought about.

Unfortunately, until last night's events at the mountain complex, money had been all Meaks had thought about, too. Now suddenly everything seemed different. Everything he'd worked for all his life was at risk. His neck was in a noose, and the rope was tightening.

He sat back down on his stool and pushed the wire through the scapula. "This is going to sting a little. I'm passing the spoon through the cervix now."

Donna grasped the edges of the table and hissed through her teeth.

He opened the scoop to release the culture he'd taken from the tube, then twisted the wire and took a sample of the uterine lining. The metal length slid back out and dropped the sample into a small tube the nurse held ready.

The instruments clanged against the tray when he dropped them back onto it. He nodded to the nurse, the spy. "Take that culture to the lab immediately."

She took the tray and left the room, glancing back at him. *Don't try to get out of this*, her eyes warned. *Don't mess up.*

He sank onto the stool. Now he'd done it, and it was too late. Nothing short of ordering a Dilatation and Cutterage would change the fate of the girl on the table now, unless she was lucky and it didn't take. Otherwise, he may as well have just cut out her heart with his scalpel.

"You're done." He helped her move back on the table, out of the stirrups. "Lay on your back. Megan will come back and help you move to a bed where you can rest."

He dragged his feet back to his office, closed the door and fell into his chair. Opening the bottom drawer, he withdrew a flask and took a long pull from the lip.

Two files for the girl lay ready on his desk. In one, he wrote:

Culture taken for uterine cancer, sent to lab, 9/23

In the other he wrote:

Implanted, 9/23

Closing both files, he dropped one into the drawer where he kept the flask, and left the other on his desk. He leaned back in his chair and took a large swallow, the fiery liquid burning his throat on the way down.

Disaster struck the project last night and had taken a human life, one of the interns attending the animals. Even the twenty-four hour guards and cameras hadn't been able to prevent it. The son of a bitch who ran the program claimed that using human mothers was the next inevitable step, that the experiment's success depended on the limited use of young women. Perhaps he was right. Dr. Meaks hoped to God he was right.

On the other hand, maybe women all over campus were going to start showing up dead, and the carnage would lead a trail right back to his office.

He had to find a way to save himself before it was too late.

4

The windy day faded to blustery dusk, gusts hinting of approaching winter. First a tepid breeze, then a cold finger of air lifted the leaves from the ground then dumped them when touched by the exploring hands of winter.

Eleanor Vanguard sat at home balancing her checkbook and paying bills. In the dark, and unaware of the approaching rain, she wore nothing but boxer shorts and a T-shirt. The seventeen-inch screen of her PC lit her face a light blue. Entering the rows of numbers relaxed her, helped reassure her that her mind remained intact, that her sanity had not slipped away. She remembered every check and charge.

After she chose *Pie Chart* from the menu, a full-color circular graph of her expenditures over the last six months blossomed on the screen. She couldn't help smiling. This graph depicted her control over every penny she spent—she knew exactly the amount coming in and going out. There were no surprises. Maybe she wasn't as emotionally bad off as she thought.

Returning to the main menu, she chose *Print,* and her laser jet kicked to life, spitting out checks. The special paper she bought to print them was more expensive than the traditional checkbook, but she felt it was worth it. This way she created a flawless record of every cent. *Like most women look after their children,* Jeff had said.

She took a deep breath and settled even further into the chair. No software existed that could help her now. Damn Jeff, anyway. He made her laugh. He made her cry. He made her feel almost human.

Judging from his behavior today, he would never forgive her for the way she broke off their relationship, and was going to relish giving her trouble over this pregnancy. Although she knew he must be the father, she didn't blame him for his reluctance. She'd purposely been cold and hurtful to keep him at a distance. Because she didn't want to feel. And because she didn't want him to know about the other strange feelings that had been bombarding her—the intense need to head to the hills, to throw herself to the wind. Like a voice from the wild, it teased her, called her. Distracted her. It had called her south to Albuquerque, where she thought the voice would stop.

Now this.

Nothing could have foretold this pregnancy, this situation that could not be solved by logic or pure force of will.

A court official who had claimed to care about her, who had tried to counsel her between each new foster home, had tried to tell Eleanor that everyone needed someone eventually.

Apparently, Eleanor's time had come.

She stared blankly at the pages of filled-in checks, spilling out of the printer.

Pregnancy would ruin her life. The conservative university would frown on a single, pregnant professor on the faculty. If news of her pregnancy got out, it would crush her chance at the Dean's position.

Her hand rested on her abdomen, then traced a line up to her heart. An emptiness, a heavy sadness had lodged itself there.

She had no option. Tomorrow, after Jeff had verified her pregnancy, he would give her something to terminate it. Then, she could return to important things and let go of the strange feelings.

The thought sent a desperate ache through her. Recognizing the sensation, she stiffened. Her heart sped, pounding in her temples. Her ears rang, changing tone, as if someone stood in her living room playing a flute. Her knee bounced and she shook with the need to run, as if she were a hunted deer. The episodes—she didn't know what else to call them—always started this way. Then sometimes she'd feel mesmerized, and take long, pointless drives in the desert, as if looking for something she'd lost.

She reached for her purse. Dr. Meaks had told her to down a pill anytime the feelings began, promising they'd help.

The shrill squeal of the remote phone startled her and she jumped. Momentary panic scurried down her spine. She plucked the receiver up nervously, hoping it was Jeff with news. "What?"

"Ms. Vanguard?" asked a shaky voice.

"Yes?" A finger of fear tickled her neck.

"This is Doctor Meaks." He slurred his speech.

The doctor from the clinic. What could he want? Had Jeff spoken to him? "Dr. Meaks? What's wrong?"

"No time. Just listen. You must get away. They're coming."

Her blood turned cold. "Dr. Meaks, have you been drinking?" The alcoholic fumes almost wafted through the phone line.

"They won't let you go."

"Who?"

"The men. In the mountain."

"Where?" she asked, confused.

"Get to a hospital. Abort the monster. Otherwise, you will certainly die."

She stifled a cry. *Run,* the voice inside her demanded. *Run.* With a shaking hand, she grabbed her purse. She needed a pill. Badly. "What are you talking about?"

"I did something bad. Very bad. Please—no time."

"What are you talking about? Please, Doctor," she pleaded. "Please explain."

The pill melted under her tongue. The line went dead.

Her mouth felt dry. A chill wafted over her skin. What did he mean, *the monster?*

The baby?

A warning rumbled deep in her gut, in the part of her that was still wild, still animal, still primitive.

Run.

Filling her lungs with air, she tried to calm down. Dr. Meaks was just inebriated, probably just wanting to annoy a woman for entertainment, just getting his rocks off. She'd report him to the university authorities, and the problem would be taken care of.

Run.

Her logic didn't boost her confidence like it used to. Instead, the walls pressed in on her from all sides. The doors and windows seemed to scream, *Lock us!* She felt the way she had in that first foster home, in that small room, all alone, where dark, evil forces had seemed to press against the windows.

She still held the phone. Heart pounding, she used the plastic-coated antenna to push aside the draperies and peek outside. She needed to reassure herself that her imagination was working overtime, that her hormones ran amuck, that the episode was controlling her emotions, that the call had just spooked her.

A small cry escaped from her throat. She saw no dark, evil forces, but while she watched, a brown van pulled up and two large men jumped out. They bolted toward her house, and they didn't look like vacuum salesmen. They trampled her pansies with no backward glance.

She gasped, barely believing what she saw. Should she call the police? No, they'd never get here in time.

A weapon. Her .22 Caliber EAA, bought on a whim, lay disassembled on her top closet shelf, no help to her now.

How about a butcher knife? *Right.* She remembered her year of self-defense classes she'd taken to refine her street fighting techniques. The teacher has always said that in any close-in fight, a knife would undoubtedly end up in her own chest. The teacher had taught her that the best defense was a quick escape.

Run. She would have to run.

Lifting the phone in her hand, she pressed *911,* but didn't wait for an answer. She tucked it under a pillow on the couch. They would send someone out. Even if no one was on the other end, a patrol car would cruise by the house.

That done, she dashed for the sliding glass doors that led to the patio.

Loud knocking sounded from in front. "Professor Vanguard?" a loud male voice sounded. "Are you there? Open up!"

She shoved open the back door and a whoosh of chilled air hit her. Football weather, Jeff used to call it. Refreshing in a wool sweater and jeans, but damn cold in boxer shorts and bare feet. It smelled like rain was coming.

She ran across the cool slate toward the back wall, grimacing. Each crack and crevice dug at her tender feet. Rushing to the wall, she put her hands on top of the stucco and pushed, lifting herself up to a sitting position. She dove over it into the gravel alleyway, landing on her knees. Pain shot through her joints. "Shit!" she cursed under her breath. The dry sound of splintering wood came from the house, and she risked a peek over the wall. Shadows moved in the living room. *They were inside!*

Lined by high stucco walls, the alley was empty and dark. Too dark. Blind fear sent her scampering down it, adrenaline coursing through her veins. She passed an iron gate on her right, a dog snarled and charged the fence on her left. Still, she ran.

Their voices were outside now. Her heart spiked. She trembled. Cold wound around her.

Keeping her head down, she forced her feet down onto the gravel again and again. Sharp rocks pierced her feet, but she couldn't cry out. They'd hear her.

"There she is. The alley!"

Stealing a glance over her shoulder, she saw a form in the darkness, silhouetted by a flashlight's yellow light from behind. Two men. Close.

She poured on the steam. Her feet screamed with pain.

Heavy breathing moved up close behind her, almost in her ear. An menacing aura seemed to reach out and touch her. She cried out and stumbled, then one foot found blacktop and she regained her balance.

The road! Emerging from the alley, she ran toward a lighted intersection. The street rose at a sharp incline. A woman walked her dog along the flat crossroad, too far away. A few cars' dark, empty forms were parked along the curb. One cruised past her with bright lights, full of life, but moving too fast to flag down.

She saw it all in a moment, then turned toward the campus at a dead run. From nowhere, someone blocked out the light in front of her, casting a shadow across her escape path. Fear came alive within her as she glanced desperately around for a way out. There had to be a way around him. *End of the road.* He held out his hands, sneering, ready to move in either direction.

She paused in a moment of indecision and a heavy hand grabbed her shoulder from behind. Instinctively, she threw her elbow back, catching him in the gut. The air escaped his lungs in an audible rush and he dropped his hands.

The sound of his pain was familiar, and her fear began to transform to something sharper. Anger. Street fighting was something she understood. She ducked her head and ran at Godzilla. If she couldn't get around him, maybe she could surprise him by hitting him head on. The top of her head struck him in the gut full force. He felt like iron, not flesh. Her neck bent painfully.

He put both arms around her in a bone-crushing embrace. "You're a wild little mule, eh?" he said with a heavy accent, then laughed.

Anger surged through her. He was stronger than the girls she'd dealt with in the foster homes, but she was smarter. Gritting her teeth, she forced her knee into his crotch, propelled by a childhood of anger. She heard a satisfying crunch.

"Ah! Son of a beetch!" he cried, dropping both arms from her. She slipped from his grasp and bulleted down the hill toward the campus, not looking back for a second. She heard their angry curses as they stumbled after her.

* * *

Dr. Meaks heard the phone disconnect and knew immediately that the company must have bugged the phone. Throwing the receiver down, he raced toward the clinic's front doors as fast as his large bulk would allow him to go. His stomach churned and whiskey backed up into his throat. He choked it down. *Escape.* He had to get away.

He heard the door burst open in the outer room and froze. His heart boomed in his ears. Shock waves crashed through his chest. *What now?* He was trapped. There was no way out except straight through the front door, and that meant passing whoever had just broken in.

Ever since he'd finished the implant on the girl this afternoon, he'd been stuck in his chair downing shots, trying to figure out how to get out of the pile of shit he'd dug himself into. The answer came to him on the wings of Jack Daniels. He'd call his patients and warn them, confess, empty his bank accounts and leave the country, pronto. After securing a morning flight to Brussels, he'd called two of the three implanted women before someone killed the line. Only one of them had been home.

Unfortunately, his mouth had felt stuffed with cotton and he wasn't sure he'd made any sense to her. It would have to be good enough, because he was out of time. He turned and stumbled back to his office, his legs quivering with exertion.

How stupid! He'd made a fatal mistake. He should've called from somewhere else—of course they had tapped the clinic's line, and sent someone after him when they heard him make the reservations to leave. They were everywhere.

He only had seconds to act. His stomach clenched as if grabbed by a fist, and he bent over in a dry heave. Trembling uncontrollably, he backed against the wall and gasped for breath.

"Meaks! You might as well come out. There's no place to hide."

The confidence in the calm voice scared him more than anything else. He was finished. No escape. They would never let him go, not now. Another wave of nausea folded him in half.

He should, in his last moments, do something good. Maybe God would have some mercy on him if He knew that he'd tried to make amends.

He had to hide the files. He'd created them against orders, because he wanted records of what he was doing. *Maybe there was more of the doctor left in him than he realized.* If he could hide the files, then maybe someone who understood could find them, and stop the company. Stop the madness.

He lurched to where the files lay on his desk, under the empty bottle. His hands spasmed and he couldn't pick them up. He let go a scream of frustration.

"Meaks," said a deep voice. The owner of the voice filled the doorway, a brutal giant. Black hair streamed to his shoulders and a bandanna was tied across his forehead. An Uzi rested in his grip. His eyes stayed locked on Meaks as he called over his shoulder to someone else, "Did you find the cylinder?"

"*Sí*, I got it," came a voice from the other room.

"Get the drugs, *también*," the giant ordered.

Dr. Meaks heard the glass to the locked drug cabinet shatter. "Let me go," he begged, his tongue feeling swollen and dry. "I won't tell anyone anything, I swear."

The giant smiled, revealing several missing teeth.

Dr. Meaks couldn't take his eyes off the black holes in the man's mouth. They seemed like the most important thing he'd ever seen.

"This is from Cesár. He says to tell you he doesn't like traitors."

Dr. Meaks felt his body jerk and dance as the Uzi emptied, each bullet warmer, hot, hotter, until blood boiled into his throat and he drowned.

5

The desert surrounding Caesar Bossidy was dark as a sea of ink. Headlights carved out two long triangles ahead of his Jeep, where thick dust swirled. He hit the gas too hard and the Jeep spun its wheels. He cursed. No hurrying on this dry road.

The unpaved road was not the only thing that annoyed him. The wild countryside was useless, just miles and miles of tumbleweeds, scrubby plants, dust and dumb animals. No wonder they picked New Mexico as a testing sight for the atom bomb. It was nothing but desolate wasteland and backward people.

Caesar was one-half Native American. The relatives on his mother's side lived in the Pueblo of Isleta, on the land bordering his own. He didn't look P'ónin—a pueblo native—not really, and had spent most of his life denying any connection to the ignorants who continued to maintain their backward way of life. His mother was a fanatic, naming him what roughly translated to Little Creeping Lizard. What a name. He'd legally changed it, taking his father's last name and the first name of a mighty conqueror. After that, he'd never gone back to the pueblo where he'd been forced to live as a child. He didn't miss it a bit.

From his first memories, he knew that he was meant for greater things than feathered pipes and old legends, dust and clay. He would be a scientist. Work with educated men in glass offices with the best in cutting-edge equipment. Things of the future, because the future was strong, the past weak. His mother's people lived in the past. It was no wonder his father had abandoned them both.

The hills in front of him became black shadows against the dark sky as he raced toward them. He banged his palms on the wheel and cursed his slow progress. All it took was one weekend away for his project to fall into chaos. Their university contact had turned traitor and had made plans to leave the country, but not before he'd managed to alert a human subject, Number Two, Professor Eleanor Vanguard. They'd cut him off before he could attempt to contact anyone else, but Caesar had ordered the coward's termination anyway. He'd also sent men to pick up Number Two, so she wouldn't have the chance to act on Meaks's warning.

This just added complications. The disappearance of a college professor would be noticed, especially when accompanied by the murder of a doctor at the same school. At least he had some of the local law enforcement on his payroll.

Within the complex, they'd lost a dedicated lab assistant and an intern who'd been watching the nursery. And the most devastating news—in one night, all of the Cybers had disappeared—all of his altered, transgenic chimps. Only one Cyber still remained in his grasp, because it hadn't been born yet.

Thirteen Cybers would be born by chimp or human host. Thirteen superior creatures created through nanotechnology, the first generation of his new race. The Cybers were his crowning achievement, his life's work, and now all that had been in his possession were gone.

He approached the turn that would take him to the perimeter fence. He'd told Bruce Jawoski to beef up security, and it looked like he'd followed orders and added an extra checkpoint. Through the whirling dust, Caesar's headlights found a parked Aerostar van, blocking the road. He slowed and pulled up to it cautiously. An Apache, armed with a large rifle, jumped from the passenger side and came to his window. Caesar gave the man's knee-high moccasins a disdainful scowl.

"Clearance please," the man said.

Caesar handed over his card.

"Thank you, Mr. Bossidy," the guard said, giving back the card. "Have a good night." He waved his arms and the mahogany van pulled off the road to give Caesar's Jeep access.

Ahead, the perimeter fence stretched out in front of him like a silvery spider's web, waiting to catch unwary intruders. As he approached, an alligator-size iguana appeared in front of him, stopping for a moment to stare into the lights before scurrying off into the darkness.

Little Creeping Lizard. Caesar shook his head in disgust.

Another van, the color of rare steak, sat at the gate. A shack stood right beyond the fence where a guard was stationed twenty-four hours a day. He pulled up and read the sign. *TransGenesis, Incorporated. Restricted access. Do not enter. Dangerous substances in use.*

The vehicle switched on its lights when he approached the gate, and this time the driver clambered from it. Caesar recognized the man as one of the small-framed Puebloans he'd hired from Isleta. He wore a white Stetson with no crease and a straight brim. A hand-woven sash formed a belt, tied at his right side, beside the holster. Instead of a rifle, a double-action Colt hung on his hip western-style. As he jogged toward the Jeep, the breeze lifted his long braids and the fringes of his belt. The van's lights lit the Indian from behind, making him look like an apparition from the past. "Mr. Bossidy, I'm sorry for this inconvenience," he said, a trace of accent from his native tongue, Tiwa, coming through. "Please get out and open the back of the Jeep."

"Don't you know who I am?" Caesar asked as he climbed from the Jeep. The lights shone on its metal surface. He hated the sound of Tiwa. So primitive. He was careful to never let it slip through in his own speech.

"Yes, sir, I do. But my instructions were to stop every vehicle both coming and going from the complex for a thorough search." The man opened the back of the Jeep and began rummaging through it.

Caesar fumed. Every delay meant his company fell further into ruin.

"Your weapons will be returned on your way out, sir." Concluding the search, the guard returned carrying a rifle and a 9mm semiautomatic.

Caesar didn't like giving up his firearms. They were his only protection out here in the wild.

The guard backed away and waved toward the watch shack. There was a hum and the wire door slid open mechanically. Grudgingly, Caesar climbed back into the Jeep and drove through the gate. He would have to talk to his head of security. For all the delay they'd caused him, he'd still made it through with a small .22 Derringer in his pocket.

He parked and passed through the company's sliding glass doors on foot. Crossing the lobby, ignoring the law-office type decor, he entered a keypad code that allowed him into the part of the company built within the mountain itself. His mother's people had used the huge natural cave as refuge from the invading Spaniards, then for centuries as a meeting place for holy ceremonies. He'd decided it was a perfect place for his business—secure, close to the university, and easy to heat and cool. TransGenesis had managed to buy it from the pueblo, gutting part of the inside and building within the mountain.

For awhile, P'ónin protesters had tried to halt construction, swearing that the company invaded holy ground or some such nonsense. But of course, his company won in court. No contest. TransGenesis had emerged with all rights to the mountain and nothing but a curse from his mother's people. Although they now employed more Puebloans, Hopi and Apache than any other company in the area, the traditionalists still fought them.

The structure actually occupied only a small section of the caverns. Not unusual in New Mexico, an entire network of caves stretched throughout and under the mountain, and if he made as much money as he expected to on this project, he would expand back into the mountain and delve into other aspects of transgenics using nanotechnology. He would soon be the most renowned scientist in his field in the world. He smiled. Every day they prospered within the mountain was a slap against his mother's people, who claimed all invaders of their sacred Wahatoya would be driven away by the demons. Because he'd prove their stupid legend to be untrue, the taste of success would be twice as sweet.

He stepped into his office and closed the door. The small area contained his living quarters as well, a bed and small kitchen, and a bathroom off to the side. In the very back of the room was something only he knew about. A small unmarked door led out to the caverns, connecting with a passageway to the surface. If anything ever happened that should require escape, he was assured of a way out.

He pressed a button on his phone, and his voice reverberated throughout the complex. "This is Bossidy. I want a meeting with everyone who worked with Monica in the main conference room in ten minutes."

In the bathroom, he brushed his teeth and ran a comb through his ashen hair. He scowled at how thin and straight it had become; he used to be the envy of women with his thick wavy hair and vivid blue eyes. He raised his chin in the mirror. He still presented a compelling figure, even though the frame was a bit withered. Now everything about him seemed muted and gray. His hair had lost its shine, his eyes seemed misted over and cloudy, his skin smoked and leathery. His nose, the only Puebloan feature he'd received from his mother, seemed flatter. His eyes formed a permanent squint from years of driving in the New Mexico sun and dust, and a frown curled down the edges of his mouth.

The scowl was not his fault. No one could make his brilliant ideas work. He chased idiots around way too often, trying to get them to do something, anything, right. He'd overseen every position from janitor to CEO, but could not possibly keep that pace. He needed to find a competent partner, an equal. That was his motivation for creating the new creatures, the Cybers. They alone held the promise of his glory, because they would be the only creatures on Earth that could understand his exalted plans, and have the intelligence and strength to help him execute them.

He entered the conference room. Small, beige, stuffy. The table was cheap, the chairs hard. Other than in the lobby, meant to impress visitors and investors, Caesar spent his money where it mattered—in the lab. A florescent light flickered above the table like police lights at an accident scene, casting a surreal glow on the grim faces of the men gathered there.

They all hunkered around the table: Dr. Claus, geneticist, his thick paw curled around the ever-present Coke can, with an appropriate nickname, Santa. Next to him sat the willowy employee relations manager, Hog, with his stoic features and stupid Isleta braids. Stark looked like a thick-necked linebacker but was the IT manager, and Dr. Chung served as chief veterinarian, in his thick glasses and white coat. Angry determination warmed Caesar's gut as he spotted Bruce Jawoski, the man who had allowed all hell to break loose during Caesar's two-day absence. Bruce's eyelids were blinking heavy and fast, meaning that he was aware of how much trouble he was in.

Caesar nodded to them and took his chair at the head of the table.

Bruce squinted at the VCR and then pushed a button, starting a tape. His mouth mimicked a tight grin as he blinked at the screen. "This is the footage from the lab's surveillance camera, this morning at approximately 2:00 a.m.," he explained, then paused to watch the footage with the rest of them. "As you can see, Felipe Jojola stopped at Monica's cage, talked with her, and gave her some Fruit Loops. Then...this."

Caesar sat in silence. A vise squeezed his temples and a cold sweat broke out on his back as he watched the gruesome record of Felipe's death.

"Run it back. Replay it," Caesar ordered, making circles in the air with his finger.

He watched it again. Bruce's eyelids were working rapid-fire, matching the strobe effect of the bluish light overhead. A dull pain pumped in Caesar's head. "Okay, stop," Caesar ordered, leaning over the table. "Could the Fruit Loops have anything to do with it?"

"No," answered Dr. Chung, pushing up his black-framed glasses. "Absolutely not."

"Was she due? When was Monica's Cyber due?"

Claus cleared his throat. "Next week." His voice sounded sticky, and Caesar tried to not visualize the thick syrup lodged in the man's throat from the never-ending stream of Coke.

Caesar thought fast. It would take a signal from their hand-held palm controllers to activate the nanochip inside the Cyber's brain and force it to emerge on its own. "Let's say that someone used a palm controller and commanded the Cyber within Monica to come to him. It would be possible for the Cyber to receive that signal within the womb and respond to it, wouldn't it? We send the nanochip other signals—to regulate the fetus' growth and development."

"It's possible, of course," Stark said in his high nasal voice, leaning back in his chair and crossing his legs. "But we don't know. The only palm controller in regular use is kept by the nursery worker, and he's had no need to use it—"

"Until last night," Caesar finished for him. "Did he use it last night?"

The engineer's eyes widened, his lips tightened. He rubbed his nose with the back of his hand and it made a gooey, fleshy sound. "Actually, it was the night shift." He paused, as if he'd explained everything. He wiped his hand, the one he'd used on his nose, on something under the table.

Caesar waited, gritting his teeth until pain shot through his jaw. Getting information from these men was like pulling weeds from cement.

Stark finally met Caesar's eyes and realized he was still waiting. "Oh. Well, everything has been running smoothly, so we put one of the new interns in the nursery last night."

"Yes, I know. Did he use the palm controller to try to call the Cybers back? Put them to sleep? Anything?" Caesar bit out each word one by one, between his teeth.

"We're not even sure the kid knew how to use it." Stark's finger went back to his nose.

Caesar wanted to reach out and strangle his stump of a neck. They'd assigned an inexperienced intern to watch over his creations, someone who didn't even know how to use a palm controller. "You imbeciles."

Two roses bloomed on Stark's cheeks. His eyes shined with foolish guilt, like those of an adolescent caught with his pants down. Caesar raised his voice. "Why are we not watching the tape of what happened in the nursery, where we were keeping the babies? And if we have the tape, why don't we know what happened?"

"The Cybers went ape," Bruce said.

Caesar scowled, daring anyone to smile at Bruce's unwitting pun.

"They tore apart the nursery," he continued. "One of them pulled the camera right out of the wall. We have no footage."

"How did this happen?"

The group remained silent.

Caesar took a deep breath, letting the oxygen flow to his lungs and exhaling slowly, calming himself. He spoke quietly, pulling the anger back inside. "So let me get this straight. Tell me if I'm wrong. Monica's Cyber cut out of her, killed Felipe and disappeared. Meanwhile, the previously docile Cybers in the nursery went ape," he frowned at Stark, "killed the intern, broke the camera, and disappeared. Poof!" He snapped his fingers above his head. "And no one has the slightest idea as to why this occurred?"

He drilled his eyes at each man individually. None but Hog could meet his gaze. "Well? Is this what you're telling me?" Frustration balled into an explosive mass in his gut. These men were the best in their fields, but seemed only a few IQ points above the chimps and several hygiene points below. This was why he needed the Cybers, they were life forms he could command, with minds that could match the genius of his own. The nanochips in their brains ensured that. "So where are the goddamned Cybers now? Do any of you fools want to make a guess?"

"Something activated the emergency exit system," Bruce said, glancing around the table for help.

A droplet of sweat appeared on Claus's forehead and rolled down his cheek. He wiped it away with the back of his hand and slurped the Coke. "The system did what it's supposed to do. Lock all the inner doors and open the emergency cavern exit."

"But that can only be triggered by one of us, with a key, while standing by the exit door inside the cave room."

Stark cleared his throat. "Let me add to that. It can also be triggered by the computer, from one of the terminals."

Air as thick as water filled Caesar's chest.

Silence permeated the air.

The men glanced across the table at each other, daring someone to speak.

The ticking bomb in Caesar's chest threatened to explode.

Hog took his turn to speak. His accent seemed thicker than usual, full of sputters and coughs. "We believe that the Cybers escaped when the emergency doors were triggered. By themselves."

Caesar guffawed and leaned back in his chair. "Now I've heard it all. A bunch of babies just got up, all at once, killed their guard, activated the emergency exit system, found the cave room and escaped into the caverns." He glanced around at his staff members. Their faces remained stony. A chill ran up his spine. *No. It couldn't be.* It wasn't possible these idiots really believed such an outrageous hypothesis. "So you're saying they just walked out the emergency exit?" He turned to Chung. "Would a Cyber be able to walk at birth?"

Dr. Chung cleared his throat. "They weren't designed to be commanded as infants, so we don't know. We haven't ever tried it."

"But if a Cyber was commanded to, would it have the necessary muscle development to get around on its own?"

"The nanochip increases brain density and muscle tone during the fetus's development, as well as speeding up its incubation period," Chung rattled off. "The bones are lightened, made more flexible. The fetus is essentially a genius-gymnast. But it would still have to practice," he continued. "Crawl for awhile, it seems. We haven't seen any kind of behavior like this, previous to the birth of Monica's Cyber."

Claus took a large, noisy gulp of his Coke. Caesar looked over in time to watch it pass down his throat. Caesar's own mouth was dry.

"We've never tried the palm controllers on them," Santa said, a whine in his voice, "so we don't know how they would react to a command. We treated them like normal infants. They were bottle fed, in diapers—which are now all over the nursery. We were allowing them to grow naturally. The chip speeds up their learning processes and we were already seeing evidence of language development. We planned to begin testing the palm controllers very soon."

"So what do you think?" Caesar asked. "What does this soliloquy mean?"

After a moment, Bruce said, "It's possible that someone else beat us to the test."

Someone else! Felipe's grisly murder flashed through Caesar's mind. Could someone have ordered it? It made more sense than the idea that the Cyber had done it of its own free will. "There is a control for violent behavior," he said.

"Yes." Bruce nodded, eager to please. "Several. But they're not random. An ordered violent act would be specific. Someone would have to know the palm controller and how it works to match the frequency."

"So this is an inside job."

"It appears so."

Caesar frowned. "From now on, only those cleared for the palm controllers tend the animal labs."

"No problem."

"Get those controllers out of storage, or wherever the hell they are, and make sure the lab technicians and each of us have one. And by God, make sure everyone knows how to use them."

"I've passed them out to cleared personnel already," Bruce said.

"And did you attempt to order the Cybers' return?" Caesar asked, looking around the table.

"Yes, we did," Stark answered, nodding. "We're still trying. Must be dead or out of range."

"Have you gone into the caverns? Attempted to bring them within range?"

The corner of Stark's mouth twitched. "Most of the men will not pass into the caverns, sir. Because of that Waha-whatever Indian legend. That demon mountain thing."

"You mean you haven't gone after the Cybers in all this time because of that idiot legend?" He stood and leaned on his hands, his anger in full tilt now. "In case you don't care about your own careers, let me remind you that those Cybers are everything. Everything! Without them, we have no experiment, no product, no proof, no way to continue our funding. If we don't find them, we're ruined."

Hog spoke, his expression never changing. It irritated Caesar no end that he couldn't tell what the man was thinking. "I will take a group into the caverns to find the Cybers."

"Good." Caesar slapped the table. "Take Bruce and Stark with you. Also take the palm controllers along, but first try to find a way to boost the signal . We must have the Cybers back. We can't afford to let them fall into someone else's hands." He sat back down. "Report back here in ten hours with all of the Cybers, alive or dead. And I want to know if there is anyone in this mountain trying to sabotage us."

Silence pressed on the group. A heavy stillness, the calm before a storm.

"Don't let anyone work near the animals alone," Caesar ordered. "Sunflower is the last chimp due. Put her in an isolation booth. Something no one can get in or out of. Wave-proof. So no one from the outside can send any kind of signal to the fetus. Place two people on guard around the clock. We can't afford to lose another Cyber." He gritted his teeth. An extreme headache welled up in his head, brought on by anger. "Now, run the tape again."

Caesar sat down and watched carefully. There was a clue in this video, somewhere. "There." He pointed toward the screen. "At the beginning. It looks like he's listening to something. Stop. Stop it there. Do we have audio?"

Bruce nodded. "I'll turn it up and run it again."

"I still don't hear anything. Louder."

"Okay, it's at max.."

The tape played, and this time soft tendrils of flute music wove through the action on the tape. A chill went down Caesar's spine. A feeling of childhood mystery, like when legends were told around the campfire, before the chanting began. The sound was somehow familiar, yet indefinable, buried too deep. "What the hell is that?"

"I don't know," Bruce answered, shaking his head. "Probably just one of the natives practicing on break."

"Find him, bring him to me. I want to see his flute. I want to question him."

"I'll find him," Hog said.

Caesar nodded. "Now, what is the status on the incidents at the university?"

"We sent out people to take care of Meaks," Bruce said, seeming more confident on this subject.

"And Number Two?"

In silence, eyes met around the table.

"Well?" Caesar said, raising his voice.

"She escaped."

Caesar stood, bracing himself on the table, hanging his head. He took a deep breath before speaking. "I want her here by morning." He looked up, hammering Bruce with a glare. "Is that clear?"

Bruce swallowed hard then nodded. "Okay."

"Hog. I'm counting on you to retrieve the Cybers. Go now. All of you report back to me as soon as you return."

The men filtered slowly from the room, talking in subdued tones.

Caesar banged his fists against the table. Pain shot up his arms, but he didn't care. *Superstition.* The Cybers hadn't been found because of superstition. *Demon mountain, Wahatoya, my ass.* When were his mother's people going to grow up and realize that they were sealing themselves in the past by their insistence to follow their stupid traditions? Technology had already taken over their superstitious world, and they were too blind to see it.

His men had better be back with those Cybers soon, or he would go get them himself. No P'ónin legend could stop Caesar Bossidy.

6

Stars in White Cloud sat cross-legged on a broken stalactite as wide as a ceremonial drum, naked. His eyes had sealed shut long ago, not needed in the total darkness of the caverns. He chanted quietly as visions filled his mind. The gods had always been good to him, telling him much.

He knew that in the caverns color abounded, because long ago he'd seen it with the wide eyes of a child. Light from unknown sources filtered through occasionally, but was so dim that only he, with his special eyes, could see the beautiful stalagmites and molds, the decorations of Wahatoya, The Mother of the Earth.

He'd been here since he was a child, in the innermost cave. Upon his birth, he'd screamed at the intensity of the light, cramped his pink eyes shut and not opened them again until darkness had fallen. His mother had packed his skin with red clay, which had protected it until he found his true home.

He'd been told that his skin was whiter than the white man's, his hair like the brightest snow. The gods had formed his hair from the clouds, his skin from the great white sands, his eyes from two jewels snatched from the night sky. Certainly he had come as a warning to the people of the pueblo, a foreshadowing of the foreign invasion.

Here, he'd found a beautiful world only he could see, and he became the cavern guide. When the invaders had come, he'd led his people to safety through the inner caves, occupied by bears and mountain lions, to the middle caves, with the strange birds, countless bats, and deep guano. In the innermost hidden caverns, deep under the mountain, only creatures like the blind white fish, crayfish and translucent water bugs could scrape out life. No human could see anything except the luminous glowworms hanging from the ceiling, mimicking the star-studded sky.

But he'd learned how to glide his way between the rock formations, some sharp as pointed arrows, through meditation and chanting. The vibrations he emitted allowed him to see the cave through sound. He stayed to live under the sacred ground the rest of his life, the elders coming to him with sustenance, news, and teachings. There, through meditation, he slowly changed and became a creature of the caverns, doomed to remain within the cave-island, surrounded by an ocean of stone. But he had also become a great shaman. Now if he left, the desert air would cook his skin as if he squatted within a *horno*, and he would certainly die.

His people came to him for many years to teach him. And then they came for answers, for blessings, for curses, for calls. He conducted special ceremonies of cleansing never before known in the villages. He'd become the bird messenger during the uprising, carrying news between the tribes when they'd overthrown the invaders.

But for many years he'd seen none of his people. In their absence he'd fallen into a deep trance, hibernating like his spirit guide, the bat. Although he'd now fully revived, weakness still weighed him down as if the hands of the Earth reached up and grasped him, trying to pull him through the cave's floor into its bowels. When the great fatigue struck hardest, it forced him to his knees to forage for food.

Every time his mind drifted back to his tormenting emergence from hibernation, he shuddered. He longed to leave his aching body and go to the sky-fields beyond, where he could run with his ascended brothers through the countryside of the gods, giving up his life of service, of solitude, buried beneath the earth.

But he could not die until he called all twelve demons and taught them all of the P'ónin legends. They were the New that would marry the Old.

He'd been waiting here in the darkness for their arrival since he first came and the spirit of the bat had told him of his destiny. His youth had turned to thick middle-age, then to the sticks of an old man, and now he was but a wisp of bone and hair.

The time was soon.

He rose from the pillar and stepped back into the long abandoned cavern, deftly avoiding each spike stretching from the floor or the ceiling. He knew each feature of the caves, and did not want to change anything. As he moved through the caverns toward the innermost room, small rat-sized bodies chittered from the deep shadows and then emerged, following at his ankles.

Now there were nine. He knew these were the demons his spirit guide had foretold. This was his destiny. He'd drawn the images of them on the walls of the caverns and called them with his courting flute, carved with the image of his guide. If the others did not arrive soon, he would have to take another form, and go out into the world to bring them home.

After meeting them, he finally understood why he'd been chosen to rule the demons of the mountain. Like him, they were ugly. They could see in the dark. They fit nowhere. But what he had most in common with the demon children was that modern man had made them both into freaks. He'd heard the men inside the lighted cave speak of the reservations and knew that now his people, and their natural spirits, were tethered like horses. That's why they no longer visited him. The demons, too, were controlled by these men. If the little ones left the caverns, they would probably be locked in cages or sacrificed. White Cloud knew this was wrong.

These creatures were born of beasts, never before seen by the eyes of the Earth. But he was certain of one thing—within each demon lived the spark of a human spirit.

7

As the wind huffed and circled in the darkness outside his window, Jeff sat at his desk, his brass lamp casting a warm circle of yellow light onto Eleanor's lab results. The report had come back in a matter of hours.

She was pregnant, all right. And she appeared to have some kind of infection, although he couldn't recognize the type from this simple test. If he were an obstetrician, he would bring her into the office for an examination to confirm her pregnancy, give her an antibiotic, and offer his congratulations.

He sighed and leaned back in his chair, unable to shake the uneasy feeling that had settled over him like a wool blanket since seeing Eleanor. It was a black mood, the anxiousness that arises from deep inside the animal part of a man, the instinct to take cover before an approaching storm.

Probably because this kid was his. It was more likely that he had impregnated Eleanor with one renegade sperm than she'd jumped in bed with another man. She certainly hadn't come willingly with him, even after months of dating. It was more like she'd crawled, covered with spermicide, her eyes tightly closed, her skin recoiling at every touch. She would have pulled a giant condom down over her head if she'd had one.

Not that she didn't have potential to be a good lover, *oh no*. His hands and skin and whispered words had been so close to freeing her caged lioness. She'd almost relaxed, given in, let go. He'd been able to tell that she'd almost allowed herself to lose control and just be a woman in his arms.

The familiar glow kindled again, warmth that spread up from his groin and through his body like warm honey.

Sometimes he wondered what kind of woman she must be, to have locked herself away so securely. If they'd had a little more time together, she would have drowned in the flood of her own humanity, and he would have been a witness. Perhaps that was what scared her off, why she'd brushed him off like a speck on her tie.

Eleanor was a woman in charge. Except now, her humanity had taken over without her permission. She was becoming a mother. And that meant he would be...

A father. Dr. Jeffrey Clinton, Dad.

Daddy, would you help me with my homework?

He shook his head, a dull ache starting behind his eyes. He didn't know the first thing about being a decent father. As a child, his parents could not be depended on. Wait, take that back—he could depend on endless nights of drunken chaos. A slamming door was the shot signaling the race's start. Then came sudden bone-jarring crashes as glasses broke against the wall, sharp slapping sounds followed by muffled screams that brought tears of anger bubbling up into his chest until he couldn't breathe, the TV on too loud but not loud enough to cover the yelling that pierced his temples like the glass shards he knew covered the kitchen floor. The sharp pieces his bruise-faced saggy-eyed mother would sweep up after his shoes had crunched over them getting his own breakfast, after he walked to school alone, after she had her first beer to calm the shakes in her hands.

Father? He'd left his far, far away.

Hard work and success had been his ticket-to-ride. Getting A's in school, working two jobs, applying for scholarships, even residency, had been easier than one night with his father.

Reaching beneath his glasses, he rubbed the bridge of his nose. He'd been Eleanor's only lover, he was sure of it. That meant he was the father. And now, he didn't even have success to float him through this. Along with the woman he'd almost killed by the botched surgery, he'd lost his insurance so he couldn't practice anymore, lost his self respect, lost everything it seemed, and for some reason, it made the echoes of those hellish childhood nights grow louder every day. He was already afraid he was becoming more like his father.

Now he was going to be one.

But even with all his doubts, he'd already decided. He would never help abort his own child.

A muffled sound drew his attention. He sat straighter in his seat and looked up from his desk, listening. A thump. A deep voice. Glass breaking.

He waited for a roar of laughter. Loud jovial talking, something that would say it was all right. Just an accident. No problem.

Then he listened for a scream.

The wind howled, and sand brushed the window. His desk clock ticked, a lonely, nighttime sound.

Grabbing the corner of his wire-rimmed glasses, he pulled them off and combed his hair back with his fingers. He went to the window, his heart banging against his ribs like a jailed madman.

Outside, sand and leaves played under the street lamp. A dark van idled by the curb, its lights on.

He moved to the hallway door, pushed it open and peered out. The hall was empty in both directions. He took a hesitant step and started toward the noises he'd heard. The gray, utilitarian carpet and white walls echoed silence.

Deafening, rapid-fire gunshots shattered the air and he stumbled to the wall in surprise. The clinic door flew open. Two brown-skinned behemoths emerged, armed with huge guns on shoulder straps. The first man carried a silver cylinder the size of a baseball bat. Behind him, the other had a bulging pillowcase slung over his shoulder.

The big man in front saw Jeff, and their eyes locked.

Sweat ran under Jeff's collar. His heart stopped. He held his breath.

The man's eyes glowed, swam with fire and seemed to say, "I just killed someone and I liked it. How about you next?"

Jeff stepped back, unable to look away. The man heaved his weapon into place. On pure instinct, Jeff turned his back and dove to the floor. His elbows burned across the carpet.

Gunshots rang out, like land mines bursting near his ears.

The walls around him exploded into tiny chalk-dust bombs, raining down on him from all directions. He scampered on his forearms, combat-style crawled, back toward his office door.

It was open.

A powerful impact ripped the carpet to his right. His arm blew out in front of him, on fire. He fell on his face. With a huge effort, he rolled himself through the door and kicked it closed and scrambled to his feet. He threw the bolt lock with his good hand.

His body shook. Ice flowed through his veins. His arm throbbed and felt wet.

But he was alive.

What now? Fighting down a sickening wave of terror, his eyes made a desperate search of the office. There was nowhere to go, nowhere to hide, except the closet. If they came after him, he was dead.

The chair where Eleanor had sat this morning. He grabbed it and lifted it over his head. He'd break the glass, dive out the window, go for help. He saw something move outside.

The assholes were on the lawn, running to the van, two dark figures, getting in. The van screeched away, leaving rubber on the pavement. He lowered the chair, still holding it, not letting go.

A warm trickle ran down his arm. A wave of nausea washed over him. Dark blobs swirled in front of his eyes. Raw pain shot up his arm, but that wasn't the reason for his light-headedness, and the fear angered him far more than the pain. It was the same old haunting fear, like a curse. He wouldn't yield to his weakness, not now. The men who'd come after him had already shot someone before they'd materialized in front of him in the hallway. The smell of death had been on them, the predatory gleam shining in their eyes.

I'm a doctor. In medical school, it hadn't bothered him to be elbow-deep in a corpse. He'd focus on that. The way he felt then. Right now, someone back there in that clinic needed him.

I'm a doctor. He repeated it like a mantra.

This time, he ran down the hall to the clinic. The door stood open. He stopped. Fear again. Sharp, shameful. "Hello?" he called. "Anyone in there?"

No answer.

He stepped inside. He stopped. He continued on.

Broken glass. The drug cabinet. The doors were ripped off the hinges as if mauled by a bear. A prescription bottle lay by his feet. He reached down, picked it up, read the label. Diazepam. The pillowcase must have been filled with drugs. Jeff placed the bottle back in the cabinet. Glass crunched under his shoes.

A light shone through a cracked door.

He stopped. He continued on. Of its own will, his hand pushed on the door.

Blood.

His brain didn't comprehend it all at once. Couldn't. Smeared over the slumped figure in the chair, matting his hair, soaking his shirt. Rolling down the wall behind him, dripping from the ceiling, splattered across the bookcase. Drop by red drop, he saw it. He gagged.

Red lights, blue, flashed through the window. Police cars.

He gritted his teeth, holding back the threat of warm vomit, of cool blackness, of suffocating fear. No need to examine the body, he knew, the man was beyond hope. Still, in case of a miracle, Jeff crept to the shredded form and pressed a finger against his neck. Instead of a pulse, he pulled his finger away sticky and red.

He looked over the desk to find something to wipe it on. He just wanted it off his skin, it seemed to burn him. He searched the desk for a napkin and his eyes fell on a familiar name. A chill shot up his spine.

Eleanor Vanguard. He picked up the file, and a couple more underneath it.

The police charged into the office, gun barrels first. Their lips moved. Their eyes flashed.

Jeff's ears rang. He couldn't hear them. "I'm a doctor," he blurted out. He could barely hear his own words, as if they were spoken under water. His injury pulsed, his own blood mingling with the corpse's. "I work next door. I heard shots." He motioned to the body. "He's dead," Jeff said, then bent over and began throwing up.

* * *

Overhead, clouds rushed in from the west, as if they didn't want to miss the action below. Eleanor ran downhill in the middle of the street. Her feet pounded against the blacktop, faster and faster until she was sure she'd end up sprawled out on the pavement. Her lungs clenched, tight, tighter, thirsting for oxygen, and a sharp pain stuck in her side, as if someone had left a scissors lodged there. The men yelled to each other behind her, coming closer.

She whimpered. Tried to go faster.

Sirens howled in the distance. Were they responding to her 911 call? Maybe her neighbors had heard the commotion and called the police. She could only hope.

Coming to a cross street, she took a quick right and dashed down the first driveway she came to. She ripped open a tall gate and stumbled into someone's backyard. She shut and secured the gate just as the men came tearing around the corner.

She tried to quiet her gasping breaths. She couldn't run another step. This was her limit. If they discovered her here, she'd have to fight.

She peered out through the slats of the fence. The men's footsteps dragged. They stopped under the street light, talked to each other, pointed. Their heads whipped back and forth, looking for her.

Eleanor examined their faces. The police would ask for a detailed description, and she wanted these men to be caught. No one invaded her space without paying a price.

Their eyes were bright, intense. One was a short but muscular Native American. His straight black hair hung to his shoulders in the traditional style, and he wore a head band. The other man was a well built Hispanic, maybe even a Mexican Indian with a big Mayan nose. Wide shoulders stretched his shirt and his neck bulged with muscles.

Her desperation flared. She fought against the urge to run—they'd see her. She must remain still, hidden from view. But all of her instincts called for flight.

The wide-shoulthat man threw suspicious glances around. Seemingly satisfied, they split up. The gym rat jogged down the street while his buddy headed back in the direction they'd come.

A group of students passed, talking loudly. More students would arrive soon, heading to different Friday night activities on campus. *Good.* She wouldn't be alone.

She leaned against the stucco wall of the house. A wave of fear trembled over her. Now that she'd stopped running, the cool air blew across her moist skin and chilled her. The desperate need to run seemed to lessen with every drop of sweat surrendered to the thirsty ground.

Slowing her breath, she forced herself to think logically. She couldn't go home, not until these men were caught. Too dangerous. But how about her clothes, and her classes? Her lecture notes lay on the table at home—how would she teach? She didn't even have her purse. No money, no credit cards.

No medication.

She shivered. For the first time in years, she felt totally out of control. Panicked. Like when the police had come to her house that evening and told her about her parents. No, they weren't going to her piano recital.

They were dead.

No, Mama wouldn't make her a late dinner after she got home.

She was dead.

No, Dad wouldn't drive her to the mall this weekend.

He was dead.

She shook her head, trying to dislodge the memories, the fears she thought she'd overcome. The episodes she'd been having brought it all back. The uncertainty, the terror. She clenched her fists willed her strength to return, the strength that had kept her alive and strong. Independent. The strength that had maintained her when her third foster father had raped her, and she'd had to run away.

Though she crossed her arms over her chest and shivered, anger girded her up and stoked her energy. How bad were bloody feet and knees, anyway? How bad could anything be compared to what she'd already come through?

A plan. She needed a plan. She'd go to the police. They'd escort her back into her house and give her a guard. Then she'd hire someone to find out what this was all about.

Renewed, she lifted the latch and took her first step out of hiding. Her feet throbbed, her knees bled, her bones were cold. Blood rushed through her veins and her breath came fast, but at least the sharp sense of warning she'd felt earlier was gone.

She sneaked back around the front of the house and looked up and down the street. No dangerous-looking men, just students walking to and from campus. A crowd of five or so coeds passed her and she fell in behind, trying to fit in. They took some sidelong glances at her knees, whispered and giggled a little, but at least she was safe. No sign of her pursuers.

She turned the corner and circus-like activity stopped her in her tracks. Campus cops, local police and fire trucks were parked haphazardly near the building that housed the student clinic, lights flashing. Officers acted as sentries along a string of yellow tape, draped across the entrance of the building. Curious onlookers swarmed around the ambulance, all trying to get a look at whom its gaping mouth would swallow up.

Grateful to be surrounded by law enforcement, she wandered over to a woman holding a small child. At least Eleanor felt safe for the time being. "What happened?" she asked, her gaze traveling over the crowd.

The woman turned, her dark eyes wide. "Someone got murdered, can you believe it? Right here on campus."

"Murdered?" Jeff's office was in the building, and he planned to work late to give her the test results. *Oh God, no.* "Do...do you know who?"

She shook her head. "Nope. Won't tell us a thing. I think it's one of the doctors, though."

Eleanor's heart jumped into her throat. She pushed her way through the crowd up to the police line, intending to pass through.

A young cop grabbed her arm and pulled her to a stop. "I'm sorry, lady, but you can't go in there."

"I'm a member of the faculty," she announced, jerking her arm away. "And one of my friends is in there."

The policeman lifted the bill of his hat and looked her up and down, from her bare feet and skinned knees to her boxer shorts, to her low cut T-shirt, to her tousled hair. "What happened to you?"

Her cheeks heated. "I was gardening," she snapped. She rubbed her crossed arms, shivering.

His concerned eyes melted into irritation. "Look, we are not allowed to let anyone behind this line, faculty or otherwise. This is a crime scene, lady, do you know what that means?"

"Of course I know." She tried to calm herself. "Can you just tell me what happened?"

"What happened to you?" he repeated, pointing to her feet.

"It's part of my ninja training. Had to walk over hot coals," she said.

The policeman's eyes narrowed.

"Just tell me what happened, please!" Eleanor snapped.

He crossed his arms. "Looks like someone went in after drugs and a doctor got in the way."

"What doctor?" Her heart pounded. "Who?"

The cop sighed. "Guy named Meaks."

Shock tore through her. The call. He said they'd kill her. Now he was dead. "Dr. Meaks?" she asked, her voice cracking. "That's impossible. He called me just minutes ago." Another wave of trembling overtook her.

"He's dead, lady."

"I was just on the phone with him, I swear. Then two men—"
She broke off, sensing she shouldn't tell this man anything more.

The cop straightened up. "The investigating officers are going to want to know all about your talk with Meaks. Go inside and report to Sgt. Chavez. Tell him what you just told me." He stepped aside and let her through. "And have someone look at your..." He pointed to her knees. "You know."

She hesitated. She knew, all right. And her injuries were sure to make them ask all kinds of questions, like why was she seeing Dr. Meaks, and what he had said on the phone. And why was she in boxer shorts in such cold weather? And what was her tie to Dr. Meaks?

Only moments ago, she'd been eager to talk to the police. But now she wasn't sure she wanted anyone to know that somehow, she was deeply involved.

8

The sludge that clung to Jeff's teeth matched the unshakable vision in his mind; he tasted evil, fear, and his infinitely vulnerable mortality. When his eyes fell on the unfixable mistake that had been Dr. Meaks, his mind had connected the vision to his own bloody mistake, the woman he'd cut and sewn and never listened to until she'd screamed with the agony of the filth running through her veins and the waste that had seeped through her colon, poisoning her body.

Jeff grabbed his stomach as it wretched, in vain it spasmed, trying to rid his being of the universal reality, that all people were nothing but blood and guts and thin membranes held in such a delicate balance that one mistake could burst the organs that formed the costume of life. The acid on his tongue was proof of his own vulnerability and the blood on the walls inside was inevitable corruption. He couldn't change it, couldn't stop it, couldn't... The violence of the convulsion bent him in two, his body trying to expel the medical knowledge he'd worked so hard to earn, and now would give anything to forget.

But nothing came up. He couldn't throw up his humanity. He couldn't rid himself of what he'd seen. His gut could not reverse the moil of a human and his gun.

Through the haze of his misery, he felt the paramedics drag him out to the ambulance. They told him the bullet had passed right through the fleshy part of his tricep, and he tried to keep from visualizing the inside of his own arm. The flash of his medical credentials and a promise to get his arm stitched at the hospital gained his release. He wanted to be whole again, and the cursory bandage they wrapped his arm in was like a blanket that concealed a naked child, something that should not be visible to the prying eyes of the night.

Within a few minutes, the paramedics released him and turned their attention to Dr. Meaks. Jeff planned to call one of his sympathetic friends at the medical center who knew about his phobia. Daniel would come out and stitch his arm, no questions asked, and save him the trip to the hospital.

As Jeff started to recover, he felt a great sense of relief. He'd been shot but he was still alive, all of his bones and organs in one piece and in the right place. The police were here, with their flashing lights and shiny badges. Right now, he saw each officer as a sort of super hero, fighting for truth, justice, and all that. For the time being, at least, he was safe.

Jeff stumbled back into the building and found himself amid a crowd of bustling police. Hoping he could skip any questioning tonight, he headed toward his office. Unfortunately, the officers' questions flew at him like a swarm of black flies. He answered as best he could through a sense of unreality and a surreal haze of pain as thick as crematorium ashes. When they asked him if he'd touched anything in Meaks's office, it was as if thin lips had covered his mouth and blown him full of the hot breath of horrible remembrance. He said, "Yes," and held up a finger. "I touched Dr. Meaks."

Past his finger, Jeff spotted a middle aged Hispanic man approaching, his short, stubby legs and a barrel chest plowing through the crowd. His brown three piece suit hugged him like a shell on a turtle, and he gripped a cellphone. A blonde young man the size of a basketball center followed close at his heels. The group parted to let them through, making Jeff guess these were the head honchos. He hoped they would tell him he could go home.

They stopped in front of him and the seven-footer stuck out his hand. "Dr. Clinton?"

"That's right."

"I'm Murray," he said, smiling. He pointed down at the frowning Hispanic man. "This is Sergeant Chavez. He's in charge here."

Jeff shook left-handed. "Murray," he said in greeting, and nodded to Chavez, who didn't offer his hand or his gaze.

"We have a few more questions for you." Murray stared at his arm. "You doing okay?"

"Yeah. I guess." Jeff breathed out heavily. One of the men wore aftershave that smelled like dead fish.

Chavez raised his cellphone and poked at the screen with a small wand. Jeff realized what he thought was a phone was actually a thin PDA. "Nice little gadget you have there," Jeff said, ready to talk about anything but the murder. "A wireless PDA?"

"Yup," said the younger officer. He flashed playful blue eyes at Jeff. "And it ain't no Palm Pilot. It can call reports in from anywhere right to home base. Keeps us all connected. And Sgt. Chavez, here, is the only fish in our stream big enough to get one. Won't let us guppies near it, either." He opened his mouth in a silent laugh, obviously teasing Chavez about his short stature.

Chavez wiped a dry, sandpaper glance across the younger officer, who stopped his rambling and reddened.

Jeff noticed a logo on the computer: a *T* and a *G*, wrapped around each other in an Escher-like pattern. "That's the thinnest PDA I've ever seen. Who makes it?"

Pressing keys, the Sergeant kept his eyes on the computer. "Don't know. Some company the department has a deal with, I guess." Chavez talked so quietly Jeff had to lean in to hear him. "We're trying them out." He finished entering something and looked up, his bulbous eyes focusing on Jeff. "Okay. So you said you got a good look at the shooter."

"Shooters. There were two."

His eyebrows knit together. "Two?"

"Yeah. They were Native American or Hispanic, I think. Big men."

"Could you pick them out of a line up?"

"I don't know. I think so. Do you think you're going to catch them?"

The Sergeant's eyes flashed toward the front doors, then back to the computer, then back to the front doors. "We're doing our best. We have people out looking for a dark van in the area right now. With luck, we'll apprehend them soon."

Although salt looks like sugar, it doesn't sweeten Kool-Aid. And the weak assurances in Chavez's voice seemed just as bitter. Chavez didn't think they were going to find the men in the brown van, that was obvious enough. Jeff's stomach gave another squeeze. There were murderers out there, and they were now personal acquaintances who had an open invitation to come by and kill him anytime.

"So you witnessed the doctor's shooting?" Murray asked.

Jeff let out a nervous laugh. Why hadn't this guy talked to the other officers before interviewing him? "No. I heard something, left my office to see what was up, then heard shots. The men came out of the clinic holding big guns." He formed his hands over an invisible rifle to show them the size. "Oh, and a cylinder. And a sack. Full of drugs, I guess."

"You guess?" Chavez asked without looking up.

"I didn't see inside it, but that's what was missing from the clinic, right?" He lifted his injured arm. "Then one of the assholes shot me."

Someone called to Murray from down the hall, near the clinic doors. Murray looked up and trotted in that direction. Jeff's instincts rebelled at Chavez's individual attention.

"How did you get away?" Chavez asked.

"Well, I managed to get back inside my office and they didn't follow me."

"Why?"

Jeff frowned at the sergeant. Most people would at least say something like, *Bet you're happy about that,* or *Thank God.* This guy seemed irritated the men had left a witness he had to interview. "I heard sirens," Jeff said. "They must have, too."

Chavez's mouth pursed so tight it resembled the asshole he seemed to be. His eyebrows raised skeptically, and he took a long moment to enter something into his computer.

Each pump of Jeff's heart flushed pain through his arm, pounding with each beat of his heart, counting off each button Chavez pressed on his palm-sized computer. Why did he have to record that they'd left him alive? That they'd been frightened off by sirens? Who cared?

"This...van. Remember the plates?"

Finally, a question that made sense. "No. Didn't see them. Sorry."

"The model?"

"A minivan. Nissan or Mercury, maybe. Dark color."

Chavez typed some more, then leveled a stare at Jeff. The folds of his drooping eyelids looked like two glistening fish caught in eyelash nets. "Dr. Clinton, what were you doing here so late? Is it normal for you to be working at this hour?"

"Normal? I don't punch a time clock, Sergeant, I'm a professor. My hours are different every day."

"Why were you here tonight?"

Jeff sighed in objection and cradled his arm. This wasn't any of Chavez's business, and it had nothing to do with Meaks's shooting. "I was doing a favor for a friend."

"Who?"

Eleanor the Terrible. The woman whose name was on the files Meaks held in his death grip. You know, the files I stole from the crime scene? The files resting in his palm seemed to scream, STO-len STO-len STO-len. He adjusted the files and hoped Chavez didn't notice his discomfort. "I don't see what this has to do with your case."

"Just answer the question, Dr. Clinton."

"I'm sorry. I can't." He shook his head. "Doctor-patient privilege, confidentiality, all that. You see what I mean," he mumbled.

The Sergeant kept typing on the damn machine in his palm, his face impassive. Ignoring him, but demanding his presence anyway. Jeff was developing a keen dislike for the little turtle man.

"Look, can I go now? I need to get my arm stitched up."

"Yes. I'll have someone escort you to the hospital."

His stomach clenched as if a fist tightened around it. He wasn't going to the hospital and he didn't want to explain why. Especially to this short, wide, droopy, rude, son of a bitch with aftershave that smelled like swamp water. "Thank you. But I'm not going to the hospital. One of my friends, who is also a doctor, is going to take care of it right here in the clinic." He pointed down the hall.

"I see. Your friend is a medical doctor?"

Jeff shrugged, trying to look casual, although his heart still beat double time. "Yeah. He's first rate."

"How do you know him?"

"I worked with him at one time."

"I see."

If the Sergeant said, *I see*, one more time, Jeff would spit.

"You're also a medical doctor, aren't you?"

Chavez might as well have lifted a red flag and waved it in Jeff's face. He resisted the urge to lower his horns and charge. "Yes, I am. Why does that matter? Why all these questions about me? I want to help, but I have to admit, you're starting to piss me off."

Chavez ignored him, again. "So why are you teaching freshman Biology at a small university? Couldn't you make a lot more money practicing medicine?"

"Sgt. Chavez, I don't have my resume with me, but I do have a hole in my arm and a hell of a lot more things I'd rather do than stand here and spout my biography to you. If you think of any relevant questions, I'll be in my office." Jeff turned and walked away, his pounding heart increasing the pain in his arm and the tightness in his gut. *Screw this guy.* They'd never find the murderers by asking about his own sorry background. He was the victim here. *What an idiot.*

As he approached the oasis of his office, he heard the sergeant's voice call to him. "We'll need to talk to you again. Don't leave the building."

Before closing the door, Jeff glanced out long enough to see that Chavez had posted a uniformed guard outside his office. At least the offensive sergeant was making sure the witness was safe.

He plopped wearily at his desk to look at the files he'd lifted from the crime scene, the warm guilt circling within him. After careful examination, he'd return the lifted files and explain that the shock of the murder had made him forget he'd picked them up. But he had to see first, for himself, why Dr. Meaks had held Eleanor's file in his death grip.

He put on his glasses and began to read. Her name, Eleanor Vanguard, was shaded with a red smear. The writing underneath seemed shaky, no more than a frightened scribble. Jeff's stomach churned. He adjusted his posture, took a deep breath and opened the file.

Nothing jumped from it. Just a regular medical file.

At the top, Meaks had written Eleanor's age, blood-type, and physical information, like blood pressure and temperature. Then he'd listed a pap smear, and several tests noted in a way Jeff didn't understand. They were sent to *T.G.*

He stopped and lifted his eyes toward the window. Where had he seen a *TG?* Must be a lab he'd used before, because the initials rang a bell.

His eyes fell upon a scrawl that caused his heart to speed up and thud wildly in his aching arm.

> *TG says she is perfect for test subject 2. Is sexually active, no family, likely to hide preg. from others. Will want abortion, can put her off until extraction. On campus, easy observation. Implanted 8/13. Extraction due: 11/5.*

Jeff looked at the date on his watch. This was September 23. The "extraction" was scheduled for six weeks from today. What did that mean? *Extraction.* It wasn't a normal gynecological term, and the word had a suspicious smell. It couldn't possibly be referring to a Cesarean—Eleanor wasn't anywhere near term. If it was an abortion, he wouldn't wait six weeks.

Scribbled at the bottom of the page was one more hasty note:

> *Anxiety episodes still occurring. Have increased necessary medication. Ask Big Chief if this is expected.*

The other two files said the same sort of thing. *TG* chose clinic patients for implantation, and one of them, Rita Frederickson, was due for extraction in only a week. The other girl had been implanted today. Coincidence?

When he closed the files, his eyes fell upon a logo in the bottom front corner. The *TG* again, this time in a shape that sent recognition spinning into his brain. He knew where he'd seen the logo before, and it wasn't from some lab report. This logo had been on Chavez's PDA.

Jeff hurriedly slipped the file folders into his drawer. The police would have to wait a little longer. Until he talked to Eleanor, he didn't want to show them to anyone. And until he figured out who this *TG* was, he didn't want to give them back to the police. If the company was supplying the police with computers and the murdered doctor with lab assistance, Jeff had to tread lightly.

He was a witness, and now he'd found an even stranger fact, another thing he probably shouldn't know. The last thing he wanted to do was connect himself to Dr. Meaks's murder in any more ways. That could lead to an investigation that would turn up his background, and his New Mexican oasis would become a memory.

After Daniel stitched his arm, he'd head over to Eleanor's for a long talk. He needed to tell her about Dr. Meaks, give her the test results, and ask her about these files. Maybe she knew something that could help alleviate his suspicions. Certainly, there was no connection between Dr. Meaks's murder and the strange notes in the files, but he just wanted to make sure before he gave them back. Why not just call? It would be a relief to hear her voice—to listen to her clipped, ordered, predictable manner after all this chaos.

He dialed the phone, feeling awkward with the left-handed, left-eared hold on the receiver. He let his right arm relax on the armchair. His mouth tasted like the bottom of a pond. The phone rang several times before it was picked up. Silence hung on the line.

"Eleanor? Is that you?" he asked. Maybe his left ear, like his left hand, didn't work so well.

He heard someone on the other end clear his throat. Someone male. Deep voice. "No, not here." Accented speech. "What do you want?"

Jeff slammed the receiver down as familiar outrage tightened around him. *Lies.* Here he was, the idiot, starting to warm up to Eleanor again, thinking about how nice it would be to hear her voice. He'd been playing the big man, protecting her from the bad guys while she'd been lying to him. Playing him for a sucker, she'd come to him for a quiet, off-the-record abortion, swearing he was the father.

Hadn't slept with anyone else?

Ha.

Mysterious pregnancy?

Ha.

Doesn't form attachments easily?

Oh, yeah. But Mr. Deep Voice is answering the phone.

When was he going to learn to stop caring for Eleanor? There was obviously a man in the picture, and that man was probably the father of her mysterious baby. Jeff smacked his hand against the desk, and cried out as pain shot up his arm. *Stupid, stupid.* She'd just used him. Again.

He sighed, ripped off his glasses and leaned back in his chair, the sense of dread he'd felt since Eleanor's visit increasing. The world seemed out of alignment, things weren't clicking along properly. Besides, there were indications that this wasn't just one of Eleanor's tricks. For instance, how about the strange notes in the files? The murder? The logo? The lines around her eyes? The feelings she'd spoken to him about?

The files could be logically explained if he knew the whole, truthful, story. The lines around her eyes he'd mistaken for stress were probably just lack of sleep, due to sharing her bed with Mr. Deep Voice.

Another shooting pain passed through his arm, and he groaned. Time to call Daniel and ask him to stitch it up. To hell with Eleanor and her problems. To hell with Sergeant Turtle and his inane questions. He should be concentrating on getting stitched up, and staying out of shotgun range until the bad guys were caught.

Jeff called Daniel and explained the situation. Leaning back in his chair, Jeff cradled his injured arm and waited for his friend to show up. A few more minutes, and there would be smooth sailing.

He couldn't save the world. Couldn't save Eleanor.

It wasn't his responsibility to check out connections between files and computers with the same logo. It wasn't his responsibility to handle Eleanor's pregnancy. It wasn't his responsibility to protect her image.

She went and got herself pregnant. That wasn't his problem. If she was connected to Dr. Meaks's murder, well, let *her* explain it to the police.

He stared at the files, then jerked them off the desk, turned off the lights, and went in search of the sergeant. Who cared if the world found out about Eleanor's pregnancy? Connected her to the murder? So what if she lost her chance at becoming Dean? Why should he care? He had a duty to turn over these files to the police, and tell them everything he knew. Which wasn't much. Letting go of this thing would give him great relief.

He pushed out of the office and into the hallway. The guard took up steps behind him. As he turned the corner to head for the crowd of police, he saw it. At first he couldn't quite understand what he was seeing, as if he'd found a tree growing out of the linoleum in the lobby.

Eleanor Vanguard. What was she doing here?

9

Eleanor stood with her arms crossed, shivering, talking at a uniformed officer. Wearing nothing but boxer shorts and a T-shirt, she hugged her bare arms and rubbed her hands over them. Mud caked her skinned knees. Her feet were packed with dirt and blood, her hair askew.

Jeff stopped in his tracks. Seeing Eleanor in anything but a business suit and pumps was like sighting a rare bird. Seeing her in nothing but her underwear was like sighting the Lochness Monster. Yet here she was, in public, baring all.

He blinked. Was it really her, or was he becoming so obsessed with the woman that he was just having nightmares while still awake? Maybe this was some other woman, a normal woman.

Her mouth flapped. Her finger pointed accusingly at the officer. Her stance was threatening, like an IRS worker gearing up to do an audit.

This was Eleanor, all right. Her human disguise could not hide her mainframe personality.

Jeff felt like buying some popcorn and pulling up a chair to see how the young officer would deal with her. As irritated as Jeff felt, he couldn't help being amused. The poor officer had no idea who he was dealing with. The man quietly stared at her clothing, her knees, her feet.

"They broke into my house. Chased me," she insisted, a slight tremor in her voice.

"Two men in a brown van?" the officer repeated. He scratched an itch under his hat. "Are you sure?"

"Yes, I'm sure. Do I look like an imbecile? They were men. The van was brown. Men...brown. What part of this aren't you getting?"

At hearing her words, Jeff's amusement suddenly vanished. "Excuse me, officer," he said, stepping up to them. "This is a friend of mine." He rested his uninjured arm around her shoulders. Her skin was cold, her hair smelled like fresh air and lilacs.

"Jeff," she said with great relief in her voice. "I was so worried about you." Her eyes fell on his bandaged arm. "What happened?"

A pleasant warmth spread through his chest. Eleanor seemed glad to see him. She'd actually been worried about him. "We have to talk," he said quietly in her ear. Over her shoulder, he saw Chavez, his puffy eyes glued to them. His expression sent a chill down Jeff's back.

Jeff gave the officer Eleanor had been lecturing a tight-lipped imitation of a smile. "Do you mind if I talk to this woman?" he asked. "Calm her down for a minute?"

The policeman shrugged. "Sure," he muttered. "I've got enough to do around here already." He wandered off towards the other officers still working at the murder scene, glancing back at Eleanor once, over his shoulder. His expression would normally have made Jeff laugh out loud, but right now he was too worried.

Eleanor's face twisted. "I don't need calming down," she snapped. She pushed his arm off her shoulder. "I need these people to do their job. They should get out to my house and—"

Before she could say more, Jeff gripped her arm and tugged her into his office, shutting the door behind them. He tossed the files on his desk and shoved her into a chair.

Her protests continued rapid-fire, but he ignored them for the moment. He took a multicolored Indian blanket from his closet and draped it over her. She pulled the soft folds tightly around her shoulders.

Jeff planted himself in front of her. "What are you doing here?"

Her eyes squinted, her chin lifted. "I was in the neighborhood. Saw all the cars and thought you were having a party."

"This is nothing to joke about. A man was killed here tonight."

"You know why I'm here. You heard what I said to the officer out there. I was almost killed tonight, too."

"By two men in a brown van."

She lifted her brows, pursed her lips, and gave him a challenging stare.

He lifted a hand in defeat. "Okay. I believe you, and want to hear all about it. But first, let me examine your feet." He dragged a folding chair in front of her and patted the seat. "Prop your feet up here. Let me have a look."

She shifted her weight carefully and laid her legs on the chair, hanging her feet off the end. He grasped one of her heels and lifted it. It was bleeding in several places, and a long gash ran down the side. Gravel stuck in the skin like a raised rash.

"I feel like Bruce Willis at the end of Die Hard," she moaned.

"You definitely have his hairdo."

She shot him a killing look and wiped a dirty hand over her head.

"That looks awful," he said, getting a closer view of her badly damaged feet. "You didn't even have time to grab your shoes?"

"Obviously not," she snapped. She hissed in pain. "They hurt a lot more now than when I was running over here."

"Adrenaline. I have a substitute." He walked around his desk and brought out a bottle of Grand Marnier from the bottom drawer. "This is my favorite. Like to sip it while I go over the next day's lectures."

"No wonder your classes are so well liked."

He ignored her sarcasm. There was a more important subject to fight about, and he could wait. "Now, for glasses." Opening another drawer, he pulled out a stack of plastic urine cups. He filled one, and handed her the brandy. "Sip this. It should calm your nerves. You're shaking."

She took the cup and examined it with a frown. "Did you have these in your drawer this morning?"

"Yes."

Her eyes squinted again, matching her down-turned mouth. "You son of a...you mean you had these cups and you made me pee in that vase?"

"This is my good china. I save it for guests and holidays. Cheers," he said, and touched the rim of the glass to hers. Satisfaction ran through him like cool mountain spring water.

He downed his shot. Grabbing his medical bag from the same drawer, he sat across from her on the edge of his desk.

She looked ten years younger than she had at her visit earlier in the day, her scrubbed face blushed by the cool outside air and exercise, the stiff spray washed from her hair. The windblown auburn hair cascading about her face looked unprofessional, and incredibly sexy. Even the smeared mud couldn't hide the swell of her breasts, her muscular legs, her flawless skin. All obvious in her scant clothing.

He liked the change.

"Okay, now let's get busy on your feet. You've got half of Albuquerque in there." He opened his bag and grabbed tweezers. "This is going to smart. Just relax."

"Shouldn't you wash your hands first?" she asked.

"I just spent a half-hour in the ambulance. Believe me, I'm sterile." He ignored the double meaning of his words and on his knees, he sidled up to her and focused on a piece of gravel near her heel. He grabbed it and pulled.

"Yow! Be careful."

"I'm trying," he said.

She shivered and pulled the blanket around her tighter. "Please do. You wouldn't believe what I've just been through."

"Maybe I would. I got shot tonight," he said, nodding toward his arm. "By two men in a dark van. Sound familiar?"

Her eyes opened wide. Her bottom lip shook. "That's who was chasing me."

"You said that. Why would they be chasing you?" The pain in his arm grew steadily, and his head was beginning to pound.

Shit. He couldn't ignore his suspicions about her involvement any longer. She had to be up to her nose in this drama. *What kind of hell had she dumped in his lap this time?*

"Do you think I just went out for a jog? Jesus, Clinton, wake up!" She kept her features pulled taut and her voice steady, even though he knew he was hurting her. "Right after the call, they stormed my house. Broke my door in. Bastards," she hissed.

"Wait." Jeff shook his head, not wanting to believe this. He'd almost been out of Eleanor's mess. Just another few minutes, and he'd have been home in a warm bath, free of the whole damn thing. Well, most of it, anyway. "Go back. Tell me the whole story."

"Dr. Meaks called me tonight. Right before he was murdered."

Jeff worked the tweezers around a small piece of glass and plucked it out.

So that was why Meaks was holding her file. He'd called her. *Why?*

"He sounded...strange," she continued.

"What did he say? Why did he call you?"

"He told me that I must abort the monster." She said the words in a low, mysterious voice.

Jeff frowned at an imbedded piece of glass, trying to ignore the threatening feeling settling over him like thick smog. The words in the file were starting to make sense. A strange, sci-fi kind of sense he didn't want to think about. *Monster. Extraction.*

"And that they were coming for me."

"They did."

"Yes, instantly."

"Maybe your phone was tapped."

She laughed, her voice filled with sarcasm. "Oh yeah, that makes sense. The KGB wanted to know if my doctor called."

He unwrapped some sterile gauze, soaked it with disinfectant and wiped off the bottom of her foot. "There's one foot done."

"Hooray," she said in a flat voice, raising her glass again.

A vision of the shredded doctor holding Eleanor's file flooded Jeff's mind. He narrowed his eyes and looked at her other foot. "Could he have been killed because of this call he made to you?"

"That makes absolutely no sense."

Not unless you've read the file, Jeff thought.

"He called me because he was out of his mind. Stinking drunk. So loaded he could barely talk."

"Those were his exact words?"

"What words?"

"Abort the monster."

"Yes. Ouch!" She jerked and pulled her foot away reflexively.

"Relax."

"I'm trying to. It's not everyday I get crank calls from dead men and goons try to kill me."

"Thank God for that."

"Are you about finished?"

"Yes," he said, exhaling loudly and standing. He poured another drink, sniffed the sweet orange scent and took a sip. It warmed him, all the way down to his belly. He hoped it would relieve some of the pain in his arm, too. "All I gotta do now is slime and wrap, and treat your knees."

"Ooh. That's sounds nice."

"It'll feel great. It's still gonna hurt like hell to walk, though." He pulled a tube of Neosporin from the drawer and rubbed it all over her feet, wound gauze over the salve then wrapped them with Ace bandages—a difficult process using only one arm.

"Here, these will match your outfit," he said with a smirk, handing her some of his athletic socks he kept for lunchtime racquetball. He enjoyed her indignant expression.

She shrugged off the blanket and pulled the socks on gingerly. "Next time I'm just sitting around the house," she mumbled to herself, "I'm going to wear my best Armani. No more boxer shorts."

"Now, just one more thing," he said, pulling a syringe from his bag. "Turn around and drop your pants."

"Absolutely not."

"Look, this is an antibiotic shot, and without it, you've got all of the germs between your house and my office swimming in your blood stream, unabated." He decided not to mention the signs of infection he'd found in her test. Not yet. He didn't want to continue as her doctor, and didn't want to give her the impression that he would.

She frowned and stood up carefully, wincing. "I'll just pull down the waistband a little bit. That okay?"

"Just need some fat, that's all." He buried the needle with pleasure and emptied the syringe. "There, you're done."

"Great. Then I've got to go to the police, now, and tell them about this. Obviously, the attack on me is connected with the attack on the doctor. I need an escort back to my house, and—"

He shoved her back into the chair. "I don't think so. We got problems, and we need to talk."

She looked surprised. A shadow of fear crossed her face. "All right then. Talk."

"Those men from the van, the ones I saw, were the ones who killed Dr. Meaks."

She gave him a withering look. "I assumed so."

"I saw them. I'm an eye witness."

"Did they see you?"

"Unfortunately, yes. Very clearly." He remembered the savage look in the eyes of the man who opened fire on him. He wouldn't feel safe for a long time to come.

"And they came after you, as well. Since this happened simultaneously, we have to assume that there were two vans. Four men. Who are they? Why do they want to kill you and Dr. Meaks?"

"How the hell should I know?" She moved uncomfortably in her seat. "Can I go now?"

His anger flared. Couldn't she even discuss this without talking down to him? "Look. What ever kind of trouble you're in, which you seem to be in up to your neck, you've dragged me in, too. The least you could do is try to be civil. Because of you, I have a gunshot wound and two murderers—maybe four, after me."

"Now wait a minute," she said, her face reddening. "All I did is visit you. Professionally." She shifted in her chair. "I didn't come and kill someone and tell you to watch. It's not my fault."

"No." He paced to the window, remembering the voice on the phone, trying to dampen his anger before he spoke. "You just came to me as a friend in trouble and told me the absolute truth about everything. You opened your heart to me and asked me for help. There's nothing wrong with that, is there?"

She lifted her chin. "Absolutely not."

He made a buzzer sound. "Wrong!" he said, throwing one arm out and pointing at her. "You lied from the first word out of your mouth. Should I be surprised? No! And now, because of your lies, I've been shot. My life is in danger." He stopped right in front of her chair, leaned on an arm rest awkwardly with his good hand, and spoke into her face. "And there is something wrong with that. It's fraud. It's misrepresentation. It's using me, it's dangerous, and it's just not very nice."

"What the hell are you talking about?" she asked, shaking her head. "I didn't lie to you."

"Oh? What about your boyfriend?"

"My what?"

"That Cro-Magnon man at your house."

She stared at him blankly.

"The big burly-man you left manning your phones?"

Her eyes widened with terror. Her nostrils flared. "He's still there?"

"Well, at least you admit it," he said, pushing off from her chair and pointing at the tip of her nose.

She slapped his finger away. "I admit nothing!" she insisted, rising carefully to her feet. "The men who chased me. They must be waiting at the house for me."

He ignored the fear in her voice. "What, they're just hanging around on your leather couch, eating carrot sticks and watching CNN?"

"Damn you, Clinton," she said. "This is serious. They were going to kill me. I called 911, left the phone connected and stuffed it under a pillow. If he answered the phone, he must have found it. I left the computer on, printing my checks. My God. Anyone could delete my account, or mess up my entire month's bills." A sob escaped her throat.

"Oh, God, Eleanor." He pulled her to him, carefully wrapped both arms around her, and softened his voice.

She laid her face on his shoulder. Her whole body trembled.

"I had no idea. Here we are, wasting our time talking about Dr. Meaks's murder when something really serious has happened." He patted her back. "I'm such an insensitive jerk, wanting you to explain why I got shot tonight, when right now someone could be changing the balance in your checking account."

She stiffened. "You bastard. I can see your bedside manner hasn't improved a bit."

He dropped his arms and turned away. "I can't believe I ever let you through my door this morning. And I really can't believe I ever agreed to help you." He wanted this whole business out of his hands. It would be much better to hand Eleanor, the files, her pregnancy, and this whole incredible mess over to the little turtle man, the charming sergeant. Then he could concentrate on covering his butt until someone caught the murderers.

"I dragged you away from that officer because I was actually concerned about you saying the wrong thing to him, and connecting yourself with Dr. Meaks's murder. I thought being a murder suspect might be worse for your reputation than pregnancy." He turned and walked toward the door. "I was actually feeling protective of you, and the child, but with your attitude..." He threw open the door. "Go. Tell them everything."

"Wait," she said, putting up her hand to stop him. She stood. The color drained from her face. When she put pressure on her feet, she grimaced, but she shut the door and leaned against it. "The child. You said, 'And the child.' Are you telling me that I'm pregnant? That you verified I'm pregnant?"

He exhaled heavily. "That's why I was here. Getting shot at."

Pink roses bloomed on her cheeks. "This is important. Why in the hell didn't you tell me right away?"

"You were busy fucking up my life."

She slapped him across the face.

His cheek stung. A fresh pain. Like sweet frosting on an old, moldering mix of aches.

He stared at her narrowed eyes, furious dipped brow, tight lips. He willed her to soften, to cry. To drop the crap and just connect with him. Somehow.

He heaved a sigh.

Eleanor was the definition of tough. She wasn't going to care about him, no matter how much he needed her to. She wasn't going to realign her priorities because of a little thing like a murder. She wasn't going to change. Ever.

Unfortunately, as he mumbled the words, "I'm sorry," he realized that he was not going to change, either. He cared about her, damn his heart, and he wanted to help her. And the child.

He was in this mess for the duration.

He watched as Eleanor pulled back her palm and laid it over her abdomen. The protective gesture conflicted with her outraged expression. "How dare you accuse me of hurting you?" she spat. "I'm the one who's hurt here. I'm pregnant. And it's not my fault. It's your fault." She closed her eyes and when she opened them again, they had darkened to an army green. "And it's too late to apologize. The damage has been done. To me, to my career. To my life."

Jeff fought back his own anger. "As far as I can tell, you don't have much of a life to damage."

"I was going to become Dean," she said. "Now, I might become just another single mother."

"My God." He couldn't believe what he was hearing. "Where is this coming from? You're the same person you were before you got pregnant. Nothing has changed! You're still in one piece, unlike myself," he said, gesturing to his bandaged arm. "You haven't lost any friends or family members. Of course, you didn't have any to begin with."

"Go on. Insult me. I don't care. If you expect me to act like a pregnant woman and blubber and cry and fall to pieces so you can step in and save the day, you're going to be disappointed." She lifted her chin. "Maybe I don't have friends. But that's because I can't count on people, can't count on feelings. And you need both to have friends. But I can rely on myself, and my money and my logic, my education, my…"

She stopped in mid-sentence, lowered her head, and set her fingertips against her forehead. When she finally dropped her hand, he saw tears glistening on her palm, on her cheeks. When she raised her gaze to his, he saw them pooling in her eyes. "It's no use," she said. "It's just no use."

The evening had brought fatherhood, murder and a slug in the arm. But Eleanor's tears were the first thing that made him start questioning his reality. Was he actually dreaming? Perhaps he'd been mortally wounded by the bullet, and was in a hospital somewhere, unconscious. Over the last year, whether or not he liked her actions, Eleanor's consistency had been his guiding force. He could always count on her attitude, her selfishness, secretiveness, her complete control of emotion.

Eleanor Vanguard did not cry. Could not cry. The foundation of his world fell away piece by piece, as each tear dropped from her eyes.

10

Instinctively, hesitantly, Jeff reached out his arms and drew Eleanor into an embrace. She stiffened then relaxed into him, and the flow of tears became a torrent. He held her against him as she emptied herself, rid herself of whatever she couldn't hold back, as he had done only minutes ago. Her shoulders shook. She gasped for air. She cried, almost silently.

His heart clenched, as much from guilt as anything else. He had become so callused to her abrasive personality that he'd almost forgotten she had feelings. He'd been hoping that she would break down, so he could step in and play macho man. Now it was time to play, and he didn't feel macho. Not at all. The good thing about her strength was it had increased his own courage.

"Elly." He cleared his throat. "What is going on? What's no use?" He backed her away only far enough to peer into her eyes, now red and swollen. "Come on, you have to trust me. I'm the closest thing you have to a friend."

She raised her eyes. They were wide, like a frightened child's. "I don't know." She sniffled. "I have these feelings, these God-awful strange feelings."

"What kind?"

She shook her head and rubbed her nose. "I don't know. They're like nothing I've ever had before."

She tried to draw away, but he tightened his hold. She looked away, but he raised his injured arm, grasped her chin and turned her face to his. "Tell me."

Her lips pressed together and she took a deep breath through her nose. "I...know things. I hear things. I feel things." Her voice squeezed with tension. "I never wanted to be a mother. Not after, you know, what happened to me in the foster homes. But now..." She shook her head. "Everything in the dream is so real, I'd swear I was awake. Except for the baby." Her gaze darted away, then back. "I can't quite see what it is, but I hear it. I really do. But it has a strange voice, harsh, tinny." Fear flashed in her eyes, and her voice fell to a whisper. "Jeff. I don't love the baby. I'm scared to death of it."

"That's only natural, considering your situation. You feel the pregnancy has taken over your life. You're an electrical engineer, so you dream with symbols of machines and computers."

"No." She paused, as if to consider whether to go on. "This started before the pregnancy."

Cold feet stepped up his spine. He stared, uncomprehending.

"And there's more."

"You're pregnant, Eleanor. Hormones are powerful things." Although he reassured her, his gut said something else. It repeated the contents of the files, the strange questions the police had asked, the chaos that she'd injected into his life.

Her body stiffened and she pushed away from him. Stoically, her mouth in a firm line, she grabbed a tissue from his desk, dabbed at her eyes, and strolled to the window. She stood and stared out into the darkness with an unfocused gaze, as if she had raised her face to the sun and was soaking up rays. "Don't you hear it?" she asked softly.

She's insane, he thought. *Totally 'round the bend. One strand short of a double helix.*

Ignoring the goose flesh on his arms, he joined her at the window. She still shivered.

Outside, the wind-tossed branches threw ghostly shadows across the lawn. The scattered clouds had drawn together, holding hands, forming a police-line in the sky. Chavez stood by the curb, talking with one of the ambulance attendants.

"Who is that man?" she asked.

Just looking at the turtle man spiked Jeff's anxiety. "That's none other than Sgt. Chavez. He's the jerk who interviewed me, and told me to stay here and wait. Why?"

"I don't like him."

"Nobody ever mistook that guy for Mother Teresa," he said, watching her from the corner of his eye.

Her eyes widened with a caged-monkey glare and she whirled toward him. "We have to get out of here." She talked in a monotone, her gaze soft and distant.

"We can't," he answered, startled by her sudden change in attitude. "I mean, I can't go. I've got to stay and talk to Chavez again."

She placed her hand back over her abdomen, almost as if she listened to some silent voice deep inside herself.

The hair prickled on the back of his neck.

"No," she said. "We have to go. Don't you hear it?"

"Come on. Cut the crap. I'm waiting for Daniel to come and stitch up my arm."

"I'm leaving now. With or without you."

Jeff smirked. "Now that's friendship for you."

She turned and walked toward the door.

"And where are you going to go?" Desperation seized him. She couldn't go. Not now. Not by herself. "Back home, to cozy up to the guys who tried to kill you? Or out to talk to the sergeant you don't like?"

She grabbed the doorknob and froze.

"Eleanor?" he asked, watching her closely.

"Not this way," she said in that monotone. Her glazed stare wandered and found him. "We have to go out a different way."

"We could break the window, but I think it might draw attention to us. I don't know. What do you think?"

She glanced around the room until her eyes fell on the corner of his office. "The closet."

"What about it?"

"There's a door in the back. A wooden staircase leads to the cellar. It's the old service stairway they blocked off when they renovated this wing."

"You're kidding. How convenient." He remembered back to the shooters chasing him and his intense panic at being trapped in his office, thinking there was no escape. "It sure would have been nice to know that before."

She pushed past him, into the walk-in closet.

Jeff had never used the thing, it had always been possessed by an intense, bad smell. Only a few crates of old textbooks, displays from Biology lectures and a forgotten plastic air freshener huddled in the darkness.

He went in after her. He wrinkled his nose; the closet still stank. One by one, she moved aside a cardboard display of mitosis, a flow chart of the nitrogen cycle and a huge map entitled The Process of Photosynthesis. *What was she doing?* Sure enough, she revealed a shoulder-high door, set in the back wall.

She crawled her fingers along the frame and settled them on a small, iron handle. "It's probably locked," she said. "From the other side." She tugged harder. The door shifted and white dust rained from the ceiling, but it remained jammed. She pounded the door with her fist. "We have to get out of here. Please. Help me!"

She sounded close to hysterics. "Okay, okay," he said. "Stand back."

Grabbing the handle, he placed his foot on the wall alongside the door and heaved. He swallowed a cry of pain—his arm again—and the door popped open. He drew back. The air, if he could call it that, smelled like Dracula's exhale. Stale. Mold spores and dust and rodent droppings and only God knew what else filled his nostrils. Now he knew where the stench came from. No wonder an entire bottle of Febreeze hadn't helped.

A steep wooden staircase descended. Below waited silence, and a darkness so hungry it swallowed everything it touched. Eleanor took one look and started down the stairway.

"Wait." He was worried about her in earnest now. He'd better go along and make sure she didn't hurt herself. When he got her calmed down and settled somewhere, he'd come back and tie things up with the sergeant.

He grabbed the files off his desk, retrieved his medicine bag, and hurriedly searched his desk drawers for the small flashlight shaped like a Prozac capsule he'd received in the mail last week. *Shit!* When was he going to get organized? He couldn't find it. They'd have to go in blind. He darted back into the closet, making sure to secure the door behind him. Taking a deep breath, he ducked through the opening onto the staircase. *One small step for man,* he thought, *a giant leap for the sucker.*

"Close the door," she called up to him.

"It's our only source of light."

"Close it!"

Against all sensibility, he turned and closed the door, the mystery door, plunging them into complete blackness.

He stood still on the staircase, listening for Eleanor, waiting for his eyes to adjust. He could hear her footsteps as she descended below him. And then another sound, from his office.

"Where the hell are they?" demanded an angry voice.

It was Sgt. Chavez. Automatically, Jeff reached to push open the door and answer, then pulled it back. He remembered Eleanor's words as she'd touched the door to his office. *Not this way.*

"I don't know," another, meeker voice answered. "I swear, they didn't leave."

"Find them, damn it! Take Clinton into custody. With his record, he'll be easy enough to take down."

"How about the woman?"

"You know what to do with her. Make sure no one sees you." Their steps retreated from the office.

Jeff's heart raced. It was all a setup. He and Eleanor were blind mice, dropped into a dangerous maze.

He peered into the darkness. Realizing it would get no lighter, he took his first tentative step down.

They had better get the hell outta Dodge. Then, he'd try to figure out how in God's name Eleanor had known. About the cops, about the door.

About everything.

11

Mark groaned in pleasure and ran his hands over the full breasts, the bulging abdomen. "I can't believe you're this big already, it doesn't seem possible," he whispered to Rita.

"I know, I know. Maybe it's twins."

"Two little Marks. What a concept."

"Or two little Ritas."

"Or one of each."

"Kiss me."

He rolled towards her and planted his lips on hers, holding her arms back above her head, pressing them into the mattress. The length of his muscular, nude body covered hers. He withdrew his mouth and scattered small kisses over her cheeks. "Are you sure it won't hurt the baby?"

"Positive. Women have been making love while they're pregnant since the beginning of time."

"Well, I guess you should know. You're taking anthro."

"Sexual habits of early man. The chapter I just finished."

"So sexy," he slurred, moving his mouth down her neck.

"Mark, I can't take it."

"What?"

"Please, put it in. I'm going to die if you don't put it in."

"Me too."

"Then what's stopping you?"

"I'm trying to make you suffer, make you beg."

She laughed. A deep, throaty laugh. "So naughty, Mark. I promise you, I'm suffering."

He raised his head and looked her in the face. "The baby won't...won't grab it or anything, will it?"

"No! We've talked about this."

"And I can't, like, bang it on the head or anything?"

"Oh, Mark, you oughta take a few less engineering classes and do some Biology. You're hopelessly ignorant."

"I know how your body works just fine. Well enough to get along, anyway." He punctuated his statement with penetration.

She gasped. "You sure do get along."

"Get along, get along," he sang as he moved within her, "get along little doggies. You know that Wyomin' will be your new home."

Another groan interrupted his song. "Oh, Rita, you are magnificent."

"Mark?"

"What, my love, oh, my lover?"

"Did you leave the stereo on? Listen."

Pausing, he rested inside of her, and listened as the haunted sound of a flute floated through the room. "Where is that coming from?"

"I...don't know. Outside?"

"It sounds like it's right in the room," he said, looking around.

He withdrew and rolled to her side, keeping his hands busy, running them up and down her body. "It's kind of beautiful, isn't it? Like a love song." His hand met her belly, and he felt movement. "Rita. The baby is moving."

"Maybe he's dancing to the music." She pulled Mark back on top of her. "Let's finish what we've started. Let's dance, too."

He entered her again, and they moved in silence, the movement of the child within entrancing them both. Rita called out, loud and earnestly. "Oh my God!"

"Coming already, dear? I don't think you've ever beaten me!"

88

"No, oh God, the pain, help me, Mark, oh my God!"

He pushed up to arm's length and stared into her eyes. "Are you kidding? What's wrong?"

Her eyes were wide, her mouth open. She arched her back. Her knees jerked up, then down again. She shrieked and writhed beneath him.

His heart beat wildly. "What? What is it?"

As he examined her tormented face, a claw clamped down on his penis. Inside her. He screamed. Hot agony shot through his groin and up into his chest. He tried to pull out, but any attempt to withdraw stretched his penis beyond pain.

Rita screeched and went limp, but her abdomen still moved beneath his chest, each horrifying motion tearing him.

Then the pressure, the horrible, intense, torturing pressure was gone. He fell back on his haunches and looked down. Blood flowed where his penis used to be.

A ripping, a gurgling, pulled his fading attention back to Rita. A stench wafted over him. The face of a baby, dripping and bloody, shoved its head out from her swollen belly, showed him impossible teeth, and cried out like a newborn baby.

The monster turned its head and fixed its eyes him. Mark knew it was the last thing he'd ever see.

12

Relieved, Stars in White Cloud took a deep breath, filling his lungs with stale air. His flute had instructed one of his demons to emerge and begin its trip to the holy mountain, and had warned the mother of demons to run. She was safe, at least temporarily, within the womb of the earth. Evil forces were at work out in the world, but as long as the demon mother continued to respond to his flute, she would soon be with him—perhaps in time for White Cloud to witness the child's holy birth.

Letting go of the demon mother, he concentrated within, sending his spirit high into the innermost cavern, searching. His people, the P'ónin, used this ceremony to bond with the massive buffalo, enter the powerful eagle of the sky, join with the swift running antelope. They could lead any animal into the village to be sacrificed, a gift from The Mother of the Earth to her people.

In his younger days, imprisoned in the darkness of the cave by his white skin and pink eyes, he could visit his people only by bonding with the animals of darkness. First entering a cricket, he scurried to the mouth of the cave to wait for a predator. When the bird or fox ate him, he soared or dashed to the village for the celebrations, his borrowed eyes and skin no longer a problem in the sun and dry sand. His people had told legends of shape-shifters, but in reality his shape had always remained within the caverns, stranded by an ocean of stone.

Since recently emerging from hibernation, he'd merged with other residents of the cave: his spirit bat, the blind fish of the stream that carved the cavern, and the harvestmen spiders, who suspended themselves between the icicles of stone and drew life from gathered moisture. Through these small brothers, he had ventured far enough to discover that the invasion of Wahatoya had taken place, just as predicted by the spirits long ago. But today, he would not be joining any of the cave's usual residents. Today he would bond with the child-demons he'd called with his flute, and begin the process of the trespasser's expulsion.

He sat cross-legged upon a broken pillar, breathing the oxygen-starved air. The air passed through him slowly, deeply, the base of his spine tilting in and out with each breath. The cavern's blackness would render any other man helpless, but the special vibrations he produced through chanting and meditation clarified every feature of the cave.

He concentrated inwardly, stared into his soul and chanted. Soon the rhythm synchronized each cell in his body, every thought in his mind, every emotion and feeling. When his entire being vibrated together—as a ferrous piece of iron that aligns into a powerful magnet, or the lattice of a diamond that orders its molecules into a perfect, clear crystal—the harmony projected his soul beyond the limits of his frail form.

Step-wise, he organized the molecules of the air around him. Still chanting, still reaching, his expanding aura seeped into the rocks. It passed through water-polished stone like ripples on a pond's surface. The cave rang out. The reverberations built and amplified his power, and soon the entire cavern vibrated in synchronicity with Stars in White Cloud.

He was ready to weave his soul with those of the demons.

Nine points of light crouched in the shadows of the cave, the nine who were able to join him so far. He must project himself within their skins. Only after he blended and shared their feelings, gained their knowledge, would he know how to help them.

They must, like all of the world's creatures, find their spirit guide to discover the reason for their birth, their name, their place in Earth's family. Each could have a different path to follow, or they might be as one. The act of bonding would illuminate their path.

His wave of unity reached the first demon. White Cloud's body jerked as his energy consumed its body and forced the living creature into his rhythm. He shared the taste of what lay on its tongue, let himself withstand the hollow squeeze of its hungry gut, gasp for oxygen and grasp for light. Like a human newborn, the demon needed so much. But unlike a young child, knowledge already flowed within the creature. It understood space and numbers and logic and thought about many unfamiliar things. He poured himself through its spinal cord and grew within its brain, in search of the source of the strange, ordered knowledge.

Then he found it. The demon seemed to have two hearts. One beat with warm, life-giving fluid, made of flesh and blood. The other pumped fire in small pulses through its hard metal core. In the fire was knowledge. The fire-heart waited, waited for guidance while urging the body to grow, but not telling it where to eat. Foolish. Perhaps the fire-heart had been injured during its journey from the other world.

Sensing White Cloud's presence, the small demon cried out for mother. It needed soft arms to enfold it, a warm teat against its cheek, sweet milk flowing down its throat and relieving the gnawing cramps in its empty stomach.

White Cloud calmed the baby and walked it unsteadily toward him, feeling the cold cave floor under its tiny toes. It was no longer content to crawl, its development swift as a river in spring. The demon came to White Cloud and sat at his feet, joining him in his trance.

The exchange began.

And endless stream of fire pulses, on and off, fluxed through the fire-heart. The demon's brain and spinal cord translated the numbers into knowledge. White Cloud rested within the brain, absorbing the hot flow.

And learned.

At the same time, he comforted the child with P'ónin legends that told of the tribe's emergence and triumph. He taught the child what to eat and where to find it within the cave. He laid out a map of the cavern's obstructions and the maze of tunnels within.

White Cloud called each demon in turn and repeated the process. Some were angry. Some were in pain and may not live long, but that just made his mission more important—they must find their guiding spirit before death. All were afraid and very, very hungry. In all of the children, their fire-heart waited endlessly for instructions.

White Cloud did not understand. Perhaps they were born in search of their totem spirit, and already waited for the spirit's call.

A sudden burst of energy shot through his pool of ordered, vibrating magma. A new fire-signal, from outside the unity of their bodies. The call cut into his heart—the demons' fire-hearts—and they were glad. This was what they waited for. The call of fire said, "Come, come, come, warm milk, love, mother." Then, "Chocolate, sardines, bananas."

Inside himself, and yet immersed in each demon, he focused on the new call and stumbled, crawled, moved, however he could, toward it.

It promised food. It promised peace. It fulfilled their waiting.

He moved as nine, yet never left the pillar. He forced his demon bodies to hide along the wall as they drifted, not knowing what kind of spirit called to the fire-heart. They must be careful.

Then he heard a scraping, and a voice. The sounds thundered inside his head, much too loud after an eternity of silence. A beam of light, bright as a thousand suns, blanched the peaceful darkness.

Laughter. Talking. *Too loud.*

He recoiled, although the call of fire that promised nourishment came from the direction of the sound. The sound of men. How could a man emit the fire pulses?

He loathed the loud, spiritless men. He stayed hidden behind the stones while he watched and listened.

* * *

Bruce Jawoski covered his nose. The overwhelming smell of ammonia threatened to spill his gut. "What is that stench?"

"Guano," Hog said, as he led the small group through the passageway.

Dressed in coveralls, high lace-up boots and hard hats sporting carbide lamps, Bruce, Stark and Hog each carried a waterproof, nonbreakable flashlight. Extra batteries and candles hung in their pockets, and each man held a palm controller.

Hog was a veteran spelunker and led the small group. Although Stark worked out to keep up the appearance of being a tough guy, he was really nothing more than a computer nerd. But he was one of the only men who had readily agreed to enter the caverns—either because Caesar had ordered him to go, or because he thought of himself as Mr. Universe, Bruce wasn't sure. But he wondered if Stark was having second thoughts, now that he'd actually entered the caves.

Bruce aimed his in all directions, trying to summon the Cybers. The chips imbedded in the Cyber's brains should trigger them to come to the signal. If they were still alive. Bruce hoped they weren't, but just in case, the cages waited at the cave entrance for any Cybers they caught. All they had to do was stun the little monsters and drag them back to the cages. Then maybe Bossidy would get off his back.

Bossidy wasn't the only thing bothering Bruce—his apprehension about working for the company grew daily, and now the feeling skyrocketed. Lately, everything about TransGenesis unnerved him. He hated the wide open spaces of New Mexico, the Indians, their legends. All the Southwest shit. And the worst thing, these caves, left him longing for concrete highways, skyscrapers, the sweet scent of sausage roasting on street corners, smoggy skies and rain-drenched blacktop. The Bronx. He wanted to go home.

Hog stopped and waited, becoming another stone statue in the cave. *Only a damn Indian could stand so still.* Hog had been the only local willing to come into the caverns to search for the Cybers. The rest refused, even if it meant their jobs.

Bruce didn't get it. Caesar had been raised in the Pueblo, had been given a ridiculous name, too, but left it behind to become one of the great technological leaders of his time. Could it be his father's

European blood that had allowed him to leave the mud houses and bread ovens? Why were so many Indians afraid of something as benign as a trip into a cavern? Yes, the Cybers were unpredictable, but the chance they still lived was minimal. Their programming was verbose, but it wouldn't help them find food, stay warm, or provide any of the other necessities for life. Those things were supposed to be supplied by the company. If by some miracle the Cybers had survived, the palm controllers would take complete control of them. That's how the buggers were designed.

It was all logical. But his hands were shaking. He couldn't control the flashlight, and its beam vibrated on each rock, every stalagmite, forming dancing phantoms. The three lights set everything in motion around the small tunnel, shaping shadows that bent and moved and waved. If one of the Cybers crawled right out in front of him, he wasn't sure he'd even notice. Just trip on it, assuming it was another specter darting across the floor.

Sounds were changed within the cave, too. Some vibrated in the rock and amplified a whisper to a shout. At other times the cave seemed preternaturally still, swallowing his words as they left his lips like a greedy, thirsty monster.

The thin air was stuffy, dusty, and ammonia permeated everything. It burned his nose hairs as he struggled for oxygen. His ears rang and his head was light. *Damn these damn caves.*

And even that wasn't all that bothered him. A strange presence, like a giant consciousness, seemed to loom around him, as though he walked inside the mouth of a whale instead of a cave. It was just his imagination, certainly. A mild form of claustrophobia. The legends were dumb. He was a modern man, who lived in a technological world. He wouldn't allow a stupid cave to spook him.

"I've never liked this spelunking shit," Stark mumbled. "Besides, didn't know chasing Cyber-monkeys through caves was part of my job description."

"You wanted to go," Bruce reminded him.

"What Caesar wants, Caesar gets," he replied. "But I'm a computer guy, not a fucking zoo-keeper. I never shoulda taken this job." He shined his light right into Bruce's eyes. "Let's go. This place stinks. They're not here, anyway."

"They gotta be here somewhere," Bruce whispered back, his eyes stinging. *Stark couldn't be as useless as he seemed.* "At least their bodies. If we can just find something to convince Bossidy they're dead, then we can get out of here."

"Cybers, oh, Cybers. Here Cybers," Stark called in his high, squeaky voice.

Damn. Stark was a damned Denace the Menace. "Shut up, you idiot. You'll cause a cave-in or something."

"How're they gonna hear us, if we don't make any noise?"

"They'll respond to the signals from the palm controllers, imbecile. Not our voices. Think, would you?"

Hog paused and ran his light over the wall. He bellied up and ran his fingertips over the smooth stone. Hog's face, as usual, was unreadable. *A damned Vulcan.*

Bruce stood behind him and angled his light at the wall. Small, delicate lines formed a pattern in the stone, almost undetectable. Age filled the deliberate scratches with mold. A chill crept up Bruce's spine. He shook it off, and his flashlight went wild for a moment. "What is it?" he asked in an exaggerated whisper.

"Hunting magic," Hog replied. "My people have come to these caverns for many ages. The pictures are said to trap the spirit of an animal before the hunt begins."

Bruce wanted to laugh, but his heart thumped in his throat. "They're old, then?" He backed up almost to the other wall, trying to make out what the lines depicted. His heel caught something, and he tripped. Panic seized him and he cried out.

It was only a rock. *Steady, Bruce.*

He hadn't been this damned nervous in his whole life. Not even when he got married to that ugly Jewish girl he knocked up. Hog and Stark stared at him, because he was panting.

Pull yourself together, Bruce. You're making a real jerk of yourself.

"Who gives a fuck about pointless Indian mumbo-jumbo?" Stark whispered in Bruce's ear. He flashed a look at Hog and continued down the passageway.

Bruce's gaze followed him, but he couldn't get his feet to come along. His heart thudded so hard he was sure that not only could Hog and Stark hear it, the sound would probably knock some of the rock icicles from the ceiling.

Hog backed up, too, so his beam would take in a larger portion of the wall.

Bruce stared, his mouth hanging open, gasping the ammonia fumes. The scratches. They looked like a kid's drawing. *Of a damn Cyber!* His heart jumped into his throat. He swallowed, trying to understand. "How in the hell did this get here?"

"Come on!" Stark yelled. Bruce could see his light far down the tunnel.

"The legend says that The Great White Shaman lives in the caves of Wahatoya, the caves of the demons. Waiting for the day that he shall lead the uprising against the invaders of the holy ground."

"*This* damned ground?" Bruce asked, pointing down.

Hog nodded.

"This has got to be a joke. Or some kinda coincidence."

Hog looked at him, then through him. Behind the light, his eyes were cold and dark. "Perhaps."

Without another word, Hog continued down the passageway in Stark's direction. The damned fool was still yelling for them to hurry up. Didn't he know anything about cave-ins?

Bruce didn't follow. Not yet. He stared at the drawing. It felt like a warning, saying, "I'd turn back if I was you."

Damn.

He tore himself away and headed down the passageway, sweeping the walls and floor with his circle of light, searching for more pictures. What else could he do? He wasn't going to be left alone in this damned cave.

Relief settled over him when he caught up with Hog and Stark. Three was definitely better than one. In these caves, he was even thankful for Stark.

A scraping, scuttling sound moved nearby. He jerked his beam in its direction and found a large pillar. "I heard something," he whispered. "Did you?"

He stood silently. Hog froze. Stark wiggled a little less.

"No, I don't hear anything," Hog said. "But I feel something. A presence."

"Yeah," Stark said. "I know this sounds fucked up, but it seems like the air is moving. Breathing."

"Maybe there's an opening up ahead. Maybe it's a breeze," Bruce suggested.

"No. It's more like a vibration."

"Maybe a stream."

"Yeah, maybe a stream." They all lingered.

Bruce had enough. He didn't know what waited beyond his light, and didn't want to find out.

"Let's go back," Stark whined.

Bruce wanted to go back more than anything in the world. But he couldn't. Caesar would have his hide. "Yeah? And say what to Bossidy? 'Sorry, we got scared and came back?' Not me, man."

"I'd rather be in trouble than dead," Stark said.

"Come on," Bruce demanded. He couldn't let them stop. He was head of security, and that meant something. He forced his feet to move.

* * *

White Cloud extended his synchronous field around the invaders and searched each one. There was a foreigner, from a land far away. He didn't know about P'ónin laws and rules. He was excusably ignorant.

The next man was one of White Cloud's descendants, bravely entering the caverns to make sure the intruders did not offend the mountain. He followed the spirit of the groundhog. White Cloud welcomed him. The other man, though, was raised nearby, knew of the legends, and laughed at them.

Suddenly White Cloud understood why the demons were led to these men by the call of the fire pulses. The third man, chosen as a sacrifice, was less than a man, no more a man than the animals of the plains. The children would eat. The fire pulses had led them to food.

White Cloud concentrated his field around the chosen one, entered his mind, his heart, flowed through his blood, invaded his body. Letting go of the demons, he let them know that an offering would be made. "Thank you for sacrificing your body for the good of the demon children," White Cloud said to the man's mind.

The demons chittered with excitement and emerged from hiding.

* * *

"You hear that?" Stark asked.

"No," said Hog.

"What, are you fucking deaf? There's something moving. Over there." Stark aimed his beam to the right. A small passageway opened like a mouth. Stalactites and stalagmites rimmed the entrance of the narrow orifice like shark teeth.

Bruce felt as if evil flowed from the dark hole, like blood from a wound. He shuffled his feet. His imagination was sure working overtime.

"Shit!" Stark complained. He shivered and rubbed his arms. "I feel like spiders are crawling through me or something." He lifted his shoulders and shook his head. "I can't stand that vibrating. It's fucking terrible, man."

"I don't feel it much anymore," Bruce said. "It's going away."

"No, no. It's getting worse." Stark dropped his flashlight and clapped his hands over his ears. "Aah! Get it out of me!"

Damn. This is getting way too weird, imagination or not. "Let's get out of here," Bruce said.

He pulled on Stark's arm, but he seemed to have blanked out. He'd frozen. The way Hog had done. So still he seemed to absorb movement.

Bruce waved his hand in front of the expressionless face and got no reaction. "Hog!" Bruce called over his shoulder, panic tightening around his throat. "What's going on here?"

Hog peered up into Stark's face. "Stark," Hog said, putting his hands on Stark's shoulders and shaking them. "Stark!" Dropping his hands, Hog turned to Bruce. "He's in some kind of a trance."

"Is he epileptic? Or maybe it's the damned ammonia fumes."

Hog's face remained impassive.

Bruce felt like a pack of wolves was closing in around him, slipping like lupine ghosts from the coal-black shafts. "Let's get out of here."

"Yes. Now," Hog agreed.

Bruce leaned over to pick up Stark's flashlight. Something skittered through the abandoned beam on the floor. "Damn. I saw something," Bruce breathed. His blood raged through his veins. "There. Where Stark dropped his light."

Hog shined his light over where Stark's had been. A cricket scampered away, escaping from the beam. "I don't see anything," Hog said.

A shadow shuffled between two rocks. "There!" Bruce arched his light across the shaft to the new sound. "See it?"

"Ay ay ay," Hog said, his eyes wide. *"No es posíble."*

"Set your palm controller to *sleep*," Bruce said.

"Done."

"Come on, Stark," Bruce urged. He jerked on a stiff arm. Stark didn't budge. Bruce glanced over his shoulder at Hog. "We're going to have to carry him."

Hog bent and shoved his shoulder into Stark's stomach, intending to heave the big man over his shoulder, but Stark pushed him away. In a monotone he voiced, "Thank you, thank you, thank you," repeating the word over and over, his eyes dead, his body motionless.

Hog, his eyes finally showing some fear, bent and tried again to heave Stark over his shoulder.

Bruce watched, panting. Scratching, scurrying noises sounded all around them, mixed with Stark's haunting robotic speech. Chittering began, primitive jungle-like voices all around them. But he couldn't catch anything in his light. Then, he finally saw them. Panic rose in his throat. "What the hell?" Bruce asked.

Hog straightened and backed up toward Bruce.

Scraping and slapping sounds, then one, two, then all nine Cybers emerged into the light, swaying back and forth, crying, a rhythmic death chant. Stark started swaying too, chanting, and wailing.

"Hit 'em with *sleep!*" Bruce commanded. But his controller seemed to have no effect. He switched the control to *kill*. Pointed, squeezed. Still nothing. The growling, the weaving, the rocking, the ammonia smell and the damned walls closing in, he couldn't take it.

"The legends are true. All true," Hog said.

Rocking his head violently back and forth, Stark began to drift toward the chittering Cybers.

"No. Stark, no!" Bruce reached out and grabbed the entranced man, but was tossed on his butt by a quick shove from his muscular arms. Bruce's tail bone cracked against a protruding stone.

Stark continued toward the Cybers. They encircled him, rocking, chanting. Stark opened his arms in welcome. "Thank you," he said one last time, then was met by the creatures and fell under their ripping swarm. They lifted his body and pulled him into the hole, dragging him between the fangs of stone. The points sticking from the floor carved long gouges in his belly, the sabers hanging from the top scraped along his back.

A short scream, his final sound, and Stark's body disappeared into the tunnel, leaving clothes and entrails caught between its teeth.

Boiling spasms of fear shot from Bruce's stomach to his throat. He didn't just turn and run, he bolted, fleeing back the way he came. Wild-eyed with panic, he tripped over a stalagmite, fell hard and dropped his flashlight. While scrambling to retrieve it, Hog flattened him, and didn't stop to apologize or help him up. As Hog disappeared ahead of him, Bruce found his feet and ran as best he could down the rocky tunnel.

All the way, he felt the fingernails of evil scratching his back, the breath of darkness on his neck, and the warm wetness in his pants.

13

Jeff swallowed his bounding heart back into his chest and crept down the stairway. A wooden step creaked beneath his feet and his heart leapt again. Had anyone from inside his office heard him?

Geez, he couldn't believe it. Chavez was hooked up with whoever had killed Dr. Meaks. Jeff had watched enough television to know where there was one bad cop there was a whole precinct full. Maybe all of them were in on this, whatever *this* was.

The stairway was steep—Jeff could almost reach straight back and touch it as it rose up behind him like a ladder. Probably, this whole area had been sealed off when they remodeled because it wasn't safe. With his luck, he'd break through one of these steps and add a broken leg to his list of troubles.

His eyes had adjusted as much as they were going to, and all they revealed to him was a few hulking shadows. His ears worked fine, though, and he heard the patter and scratching of little things in the darkness. Four legged things.

And there was Eleanor to worry about, too. She hummed an ominously sweet song as she descended the steps. She purred along as if the world was fine and they were descending not into an abandoned cellar, but into a swimming pool on a sunny Fourth of July, with a steak sizzling nearby and family laughing and splashing all around them. Strange. Eleanor was not the humming type. Bitching, moaning, yes. Humming, no.

Finally, his foot found solid ground. He extended his arm and felt for Eleanor. "Where are you?" he whispered. As if the darkness had substance, it lodged in his throat like dry sand, and hung in his lungs like cigarette smoke. He quelled the urge to cough. "Elly!" he said, louder this time.

"Over here."

Her voice came from his left. He looked, but saw only blackness. With his good hand out in front, the files beneath his throbbing arm and the medical bag draped securely over his shoulder, he shuffled toward her, honing in on her panting breaths. He found her sitting on the cold earth, her back against a brick wall, breathing hard.

He dropped to his knees beside her. "You okay?"

"I...don't know," she said, her voice sounding more normal now. "I don't hear it any more, do you?"

"Hear what?"

"The flute. The sound of the flute."

He hesitated, searching his memory. "I never heard a flute."

"Isn't that why we came down here? To see where the sound was coming from?"

Jeff shot a glance back toward the ladder, expecting Rod Serling to materialize from the darkness. "I don't know about you, but I came down here because you said we had to get out of my office, and fast. And boy, were you right. After I closed the door I heard Chavez talking to that guard he had stationed outside my door. It sounded like they intended to arrest both of us."

She gasped. "For what?"

"How in the hell should I know? But I don't plan to go back and ask." He tried to examine her face, but she was just a gray shadow in a pool of darkness.

"Jeff." She found his hand and squeezed it. "I'm scared. There's something really wrong with me."

He held his tongue. Now was not the time for contrite banter. "How long has this weird behavior been going on?"

"I don't know. Months. But not this bad. Not nearly this bad. Meaks gave me medication. But it's at the house."

"You seemed to be in a trance. Zoned out. You talked and hummed, but you didn't answer me. Not really."

"It's like…I'm being possessed. Something calls to me. Something I can't refuse. It gives me instructions. Oh, God." Her voice cracked. "I've really lost it, haven't I?"

He set the files against the wall, dropped to his butt and gathered her in his arms. He held her, the darkness giving it all a dreamlike quality.

He was so tired. He hurt so much. His arm throbbed, each pain like the touch of a hot poker. Above, the police searched for him, for some unknown but malevolent reason. Right now they were probably rifling through his personal things like thieves in the night. The thought raised goose flesh on his arms.

So strange. In the last day, he'd lost so much. Yet he was finding things he'd unconsciously sought for a lifetime.

Chavez and his cronies would turn up his past. They'd dig deep, until they unearthed his history. Like grave robbers, they'd bring the rotting evidence out into the light. The faculty would find out, his new friends would know, and this new town, this new job, this new life of his, would take on the same fetid smell of the poisoned body of the woman his carelessness almost killed. And once his reputation was crawling with maggots, he'd once again have to move on.

Yet here was Elly. He held her, smelling the freshness in her hair, feeling the softness of her skin. And the cold of the damp, unknown darkness. How many times had he wished he could break down her wall? That something, anything, would plow through it and let him find and hold the real woman behind the defenses time had built? He'd wanted her to need him.

Well, now she needed him. She was sick, frightened and needy. Here in this dark place, pursued by the world, she had finally surrendered. But at what cost? At the moment, it seemed they would never be able to appreciate each other. The minute they emerged, they'd be swept into Chavez's plot, drawn down as surely as if they were hit by a desert flood. But they couldn't camp here forever, couldn't freeze time. Eventually, they'd have to grab their boards and ride the wave.

The heaviness in his bones made him wonder if this was the end of the line. There was probably no exit from this basement the police wouldn't cover. If there was an exit. Finally, he asked, "Can we get out of here unseen?"

She sniffed. "I don't know." She moved uncomfortably in his arms, adjusting her feet. "Back before they expanded the university, there was an Indian structure built here, supposedly guarding an entrance into some caverns that had sacred significance. When the university acquired the land, they removed the adobe building from the ground up, but left the basement—expanded it in fact, which is where we are now.

"After they remodeled, this area went to the old zoology professor. He had a grant to study the relationship between skeletal structure and speed, which is where I came in. Engineering-wise, there's not much difference between the human bone and a support beam. That's how I got to work with him, and spend time in his office."

"Which is now my office."

"Yes."

"How many people know about this place?"

"Hardly anybody. It was closed off so long ago."

Hope crept over him. If few people knew about the basement, it might take time for the police to find it. Time enough for them to get away. "Why didn't you tell me about the staircase?"

"I thought you knew. It was in your closet. Haven't you ever been in it before?"

"Obviously not. I opened the door twice to stick some teaching materials in there and spray it with air freshener. The place stinks. Like this whole basement."

"Probably remains from the animals who were here before."

"It smells more like ammonia."

They were silent for a moment, listening. A drip of water. Their ragged breathing. His heart, pumping pain through his body. "I wonder how long it will take the police to find us down here," Jeff said.

Her grip tightened on him. "And what will happen when they do?"

"I've got to know that you've told me everything," he said softly into her ear. "I need to know that you've held nothing back. What exactly are you mixed up in, here?"

"We," she said.

"Huh?"

"We're both mixed up in it." She leaned her head against his shoulder. A shiver went through her, and he remembered she was in boxer shorts. The basement's damp chill was no place for a pregnant woman.

"These...feelings I've had, they started back before I moved here. A couple of years ago."

"I never saw you behave strangely, ever. I mean, not in this way."

"I know." She shifted in his arms, drawing closer. "It used to be more of an idea than a physical feeling. This feeling that I needed to be in the southwest."

He squeezed her chilling arms, trying to keep the circulation going. He needed to take her somewhere warm, quickly.

"My mother was a full-blooded Apache, did you know that?"

"No. We never talked much about those things."

"I know. Anyway, I thought maybe it was that. Curiosity about my mom, I mean."

She faltered, and Jeff realized it was the first time he'd ever heard her at a loss for words.

"Everything about the southwest intrigued me. Frontier women. Wide open spaces. The idea that you fend for yourself. When the position at the university opened up, I took it."

"So you came to New Mexico."

"Yes. Everything fit. My old position was at a dead end, my apartment building went condo. This university offered inexpensive housing, more money, and chances at advancement. It seemed right." She shivered again.

106

"Advancement," he echoed. "The infamous position—Dean of Engineering. How could I forget?" He imagined she was glaring at him in the dark.

"I want to get as high on the totem pole as I can get, and I make that no secret. The further up I go, the more control I obtain."

"So," Jeff said, "being stuck in this damp basement. How high did you have to climb on the pole to get here?"

"This happens to be your screw up, not mine."

"Yeah. I'm the only one who's dumb enough to listen to you." Jeff could have bitten his tongue for the remark, but she seemed not to notice the shovel full of sarcasm in his statement.

She continued, the words spilling out like water from a broken dam. "I thought I'd found my spot, the perfect job. The perfect town. But something was still wrong. I developed this incredible...restlessness. I kept driving out to the mountains. I'd take long walks through desolate areas. I felt like I was searching for something. That's when I met you. I thought—"

"You thought I'd be a distraction?"

She shook her head. "I don't know. Maybe I thought I'd found what I was looking for." Another shiver passed through her. "I guess I needed help, wanted help, but I was scared to death to admit there was anything wrong."

"Gee, and all this time I thought it was my looks that attracted you."

She slapped his arm playfully. Unfortunately, it was the wrong arm, and he covered his mouth to keep from howling like a wolf. Pain shot down through his elbow, up through his shoulder, fanned out across his back. "Shit, shit!"

"Oh, my God. I'm sorry. I'm sorry. I can't really see you, and I forgot."

"That's okay," he said through clenched teeth. "As long as I can tickle your feet with a wire brush."

"Not funny."

"Neither is my situation."

"And neither is mine." She squeezed his leg. "You've got to promise not to tell anyone else about these episodes. The university isn't going to choose a weirdo to head the engineering department."

"Is that why you broke it off the way you did? You were afraid that as a fellow university employee, I'd rat to the bigwigs about their nutty professor?"

She cleared her throat. "You were getting too close. I didn't want anyone to find out. I was afraid I'd lose everything."

"So you sacrificed our relationship instead." He grunted, a new understanding coming to him. "It wasn't just that you were afraid I'd find out about the episodes. It was also that you thought I'd make them worse."

"Something like that." Her voice cracked, and he wondered if she was close to tears. "The episodes were getting worse. But it wasn't you, it was the pregnancy." A whine entered her voice. "I can't control them anymore. When I get the feelings now, it's not just a feeling. It overwhelms me. You saw what it did to me."

He embraced her as tightly as he could, trying to enfold her in his shell. He knew what she must have been going through. Control defined her. Control was her security blanket, her arsenal, the moat around her castle. No wonder she'd become more and more difficult. As she'd lost control over her episodes, she'd tried to exert more control over him. "You should have told me, instead of chasing me off. After all, I have experience with a life gone crazy."

She was silent for a while and said, "I suppose so. But I wanted to fight it myself."

"No problem. I've been there. But it looks like we're kinda stuck together now."

"Good," she said. "I mean, I was hoping you'd feel that way."

"That doesn't mean I'm going to be any easier to live with. I still have all those faults you so frequently remind me of."

"Yes, you do." Strength entered her voice. "But no matter. As soon as we sort this mess out, I'm leaving. I don't know where I'm going to go. Just as far away from the desert as I can get."

Her words brought some of the gnawing anger and rejection flowing back, but he ignored the feelings. Now was not the time to

108

indulge in self pity. Besides, any strength she showed was something to be thankful for. She would need every bit of her stubbornness to get through this, especially once she knew what he'd discovered in the files. "You sound like you're feeling better." He tried to kiss her on the cheek, but his lips grazed her eye.

"Another strange thing. I hear a flute. A distant melody. I can barely hear it. Just barely. It accompanies the feelings. Sometimes, it causes pain. Like cramps."

"And the medication Dr. Meaks gave you. Does it help?"

"A little. I don't know."

He sighed. This was definitely not good news. He needed to tell her about what he'd found in the files, but first he needed to get her someplace warm, and he wanted to see that prescription. He knew of no meds that could block out flute music. If they worked, he'd make damn sure to take a large dose before attending the mandatory staff trip to the Santa Fe Opera. "So none of this makes sense to you either?"

"Believe me, it was a total, unexpected shock that those men came after me. I only knew Dr. Meaks as my doctor."

Fear made the bottom drop out of Jeff's gut. If she really knew nothing about what was going on, then how were they going to fight it? Approaching weariness gripped him, and the pain in his arm competed with the roar in his temples. "You feel up to exploring a little bit? We've got to see if there's a way out of here, or if this is the end of the line for us."

"I don't see how we're going to find our way around down here. It's totally dark. And there's no light outside to shine in and show us any openings."

"Well, that means the bad guys will be in the dark, too."

There was a leak somewhere, dripping, coming faster now. Like the ticking of a clock, it reminded him that time was passing. Outside, upstairs, wherever, the bad guys were looking for him. Every drip brought them one step closer to him. He couldn't rest, not now. If he were apprehended, it would be a nightmare.

"I have an idea," Eleanor said. "When I came in for my interview, I stayed in the visiting faculty apartments. They're not too far from here. If we can get out of here, we could go check them out. One of them might be empty, and we could clean up, maybe stay overnight."

"If one is open, how will we get in?"

"Break in. Everything I learned in those foster homes has to help out sometime, doesn't it?"

A rolling boom sounded from somewhere above then was gone. He listened. The basement sealed them from the world, muffled all light, and up to now, all sound. Only the splash of one drip after another. Then another, softer growl, and he knew what it was. Thunder.

The rain had started, and it would save their butts.

"Come on." He stood and helped her to her feet. "Just hold onto my hand. I'll follow the wall, slowly, head toward that drip. If that's the rain coming in, it could be a way out."

Holding her hand, he pressed his palm against the cold, damp wall. He slid his right foot a step through the darkness. Eleanor followed, hissing in pain.

He repeated the process. His eyes strained to see, to pick anything out of the perfect blackness. He reached out in front of his face, waved his hand around, then touched the wall, dragged his foot. A step. With each movement, he braced himself to hit his head, to twist his ankle. The dripping continued, and he headed toward the sound. It seemed greatly magnified by the attention he gave it.

His mind perceived the darkness as a barrier, told him the darkness was solid, that he couldn't move through it. With every step he ducked unconsciously, as if he might ram his head against the black air. His breath became labored, as if he couldn't breathe the darkness. His senses scrambled for something to perceive, anything, and the smells in the dark hole became clearer, almost gained dimension. A dog-piss aroma soaked into his body through his nose. He could feel the unevenness of the floor beneath his shoes, every rock and crevice, every rise and fall.

He continued on. The dripping sound became louder. More thunder rumbled. Minutes passed. He could smell the rain now, and hear more water pattering against a barrier, something wooden, something still far way in this darkness, but there. A way out, perhaps.

He stumbled. The floor dropped away a few inches. "Be careful. Step down here." Under his hand, the texture of the brick changed. He paused, running his palm over the surface. "Eleanor," he whispered, "this feels like adobe."

"We must be in the old part of the basement."

He took a deep breath of the living darkness. It flowed through him, like cold syrup. It seemed that if he didn't escape it soon, he would drown. It would erase every part of him, inch by inch, until he disappeared, becoming part of it.

A squeak. A patter of feet. He turned his head, right, left, like a blind man, directing his ears. Rats? Thunder roared outside, louder now. The rain pelted against something wooden. The hair on his arms stood up.

Careful now. One foot in front of the other.

The wall he followed angled away from the dripping. Soon, the sound came from his side. He could no longer follow the wall.

"You doing okay?" he asked, turning toward Elly.

She moaned. "What do you think? My feet feel like they've been chewed by rodents."

The picture she conjured up did not make him feel any better about the sounds he'd heard in the basement. "We're going to have to leave the wall. Go across toward the dripping sound. Can you make it?"

"If you walk me into something, I'll kill you."

"So you still trust me, huh? Hang on."

Defensively enclosing her hand in his, he searched the darkness ahead of him, stepped away from the wall and headed into the openness, toward the sound of the rain, toward the sound of the scurrying and squeaking. His heart beat double time, his stomach tightened with tension.

Thunder howled and he jumped, letting out a cry. He gathered his wits and continued on. Now the dripping was just beyond his hand.

His foot found something soft. "Shit!" He jumped back as a rat screamed, and wiggled out from beneath his foot.

"What?" Eleanor asked.

"God damn, shit." He stopped, composed himself. "The rats must be after the water, just like us. I stepped on one."

She let out a keening cry. "I don't have shoes on. I don't want to step on one. Please, scare them away."

"I think I already did." He stopped to listen. "Come on. It's right up ahead."

A cold drop hit his hand. "I found it!" Stepping forward, he reached the wall.

Here, it was wet. Water flowed down the adobe. He could hear the storm above them, the rain pelting against a wooden door. The thunder rolled, far off in the night sky. He looked up. A drop hit him in the eye.

"God, my socks are wet. What next?"

"Stand by the wall. Touch it. I have to feel around for an opening."

"This is hopeless. Let's just wait until first light."

"That's what we want Chavez to do. Not us."

She let go of his hand, and he slapped both palms against the adobe and walked them around, searching for anything. His arms were getting wet. A cold drop ran under his hair and scurried down his neck. He shivered. Then, he found it. The end of a rope. Hanging above him, in open space. "I found something."

"What?"

He pulled on it with his left hand. He jerked on it.

"Jeff?"

He grabbed it with both hands and lifted his feet from the floor, applying his entire weight to the cord. Grabbing the rope caused pain-lightning in his arm, rushing through him and out his mouth in a scream. He let go and dropped to the floor in a heap, regretting the noise and the damage he'd done to himself immediately.

"Eleanor." His voice squeaked. "I need your help here. I think I just really messed up my arm. See if you can open the door."

"Get over by the wall," she said.

He scrambled out of her way. He heard the door creak and it whooshed open. She cried out and fell on top of him. The door banged his shoulder. Pain like none he'd ever experienced flooded through him, followed by pails of cool water. Dazed, he fought to stay conscious. His clothes stuck to his skin, wet and cold.

"It's open," she said, climbing off him.

He sat up, shivering, hurting. Laughing. The sky threw drops at him, but provided a dim glow. City light, beautiful light, flowed in through the opening.

14

The door that tumbled Jeff and Eleanor to the floor rested at an angle against the wall. The worn boards nailed on its surface formed a crude ladder up and out of the basement. Jeff squinted into the rain, then touched Eleanor's arm. "Ready to get out of here?"

She hesitated, shivering so violently he could almost hear her bones clacking together in the darkness. "What if they're waiting for us out there?"

"If they are, they're mighty quiet. I don't hear anything. But that doesn't mean they aren't standing around the opening, guns and dogs ready. You worried?"

"I am way too cold and wet to worry."

"Look, if they're waiting, then they know we're down here. We'll have to climb up anyway, in handcuffs."

"Let's go." She nodded. "I'd rather be in jail than in this hole, anyway."

The rain fell in hard flat drops, the thunder constant. Lightning flashed in the distance. He braced himself to be drenched, glad that today the sky had chosen to pour rain, boom thunder, and drip into the forgotten basement. "Ladies first." Gritting his teeth against his own pain, he stepped aside and motioned her to the ladder. To his surprise, she climbed up without hesitation. He didn't wait for her report about what waited outside. With the files tucked into his pants and his medical bag over his good shoulder, he followed her out of the hole, not saying a word about how much he hurt.

He saw bushes first, then a large, sweeping lawn, and a brick two-story building. All the lights were on, making the building shine like a Jack-O-Lantern. Behind the building, police cars crouched in the rain, although the crowd had fled home to warmer, drier excitement in front of the television set. No one looked their way. He dropped his medical bag next to Eleanor, who crouched behind the hedge.

Reaching back into the hole, he grabbed the rope and pulled, trying to close the door. A searing pain shot through his upper body and the rope slid from his hands like a startled snake. His head emptied and he felt his body tumble into the wet grass, suddenly numb. Rain washed down over him in streams. Then Eleanor was helping him to his feet, her voice soothing. "Come on, this way. It's not far." She pointed along the high row of bushes. Staying hunched below plant level, they hurried along the natural barrier, ducked behind the building, and soon were out of sight.

After a laborious walk, Jeff rang the bell at one of the apartments while Eleanor waited behind the wall. When no one answered, she pushed him aside. "Let me see your bag." She didn't wait for an answer, just popped open the bag and muttered as she dug around its depths.

"What are you looking for? A key?"

"Yes." She extracted a tongue depressor. With her back blocking his view, she fiddled with the lock. Her hands still shook from the cold, but soon he heard a faint click. When Eleanor stepped back, the door was open.

They stumbled through the entryway and to the couch. As their clothes soaked the upholstery, they caught their breath and rested.

Jeff felt like he'd just played a professional football game. And lost. He leaned his head back and closed his eyes, trying unsuccessfully to catch his breath. "This...feels...great."

"Don't get too used to it," she said, her eyes focused on the ceiling. "We have to get cleaned up before we rest."

"I hate to say it." He frowned. His nostrils were saturated with the basement smells and his breath seemed to become more labored, instead of slowing down. His skin was dry. His pulse raced. "But I don't think I can move from this spot. Not even if the entire police department and a legion of longhaired, Uzi-toting murderers break in. About all I could manage is a weak wave with my left hand." The sentence came out in little pieces, cut where he had to pause for breath. "I think we should go to a place with more oxygen." He gasped for breath.

"You always have been a girlie man," she said through clenched teeth. Clenched, he knew, because she'd been upright on her torn feet for too long.

He lifted his head and smiled at her matted hair and mud-stained, soaked clothing. "I refuse." He paused to suck in a breath. "To respond to your jibes."

She gripped his injured arm and gently urged him off the couch. He rose to his feet. "Ouch! Shit, woman. Have you no mercy?"

"No patience." She pulled him down the hall and sat him on the coral-colored toilet seat. She turned on the bath water. He groaned as he saw the bathroom was done in southwest motif—he hated the pale blues and greens and fake Indian designs. No wonder he couldn't breathe. "Shit," he said, for no reason he could think of. She tugged at his clothing. It hurt. He pulled away. Why wouldn't she just leave him alone?

She helped him into the tub, and he felt scalding water beneath his feet, then on his buttocks. He sucked in air—the water was hot against his chilled skin. He was too tired to fight; he'd just have to boil. He watched black spots dance in his vision, entranced by their bouncing, growing and receding, and the ringing in his ears that accompanied them.

Through his limited vision, he saw Eleanor's full breasts near his face. He almost regained his awareness, it seemed important enough, but then his arm's searing pain pulled him back under, where safety and warmth awaited.

15

While he sipped bitter morning coffee, Caesar stood outside the isolation booth and watched Sunflower through the glass. Her movements mirrored his emotions: swinging, bending, running in circles. He'd slept that way last night, up and down, cursing for not going into the caverns himself to retrieve the Cybers. They were creations of his master's hand, his crowning glory, too important to trust to anyone else, even his most loyal employees. And now, with day dawning, there was still no sign of his men or his precious creations.

He kept his attention on Sunflower, looking for any indication that her pregnancy was not going as planned. Her eyes shone brightly, her activity rarely ceased. Her appetite was normal for a pregnant chimp. But still, he had made sure the room was soundproof, and completely inescapable. If anything came springing from Sunflower's womb, she would be the only one in danger and the Cyber would be unable to escape. Barring any unexpected problems, he planned to extract the Cyber the moment it became viable. That should be within the next few days, although the Cybers seemed to be maturing much faster than planned. He had to watch Sunflower closely.

Grunting, he looked at his watch again. With each jerk of the second hand, the tension in his gut tightened. Where was Bruce? As security chief, he had a duty to report to Caesar the minute he returned. Before even taking off his hard hat, Bruce had better be in Caesar's presence with a report.

Caesar's mind sorted through the facts, trying to figure out what could have interfered with his perfect plan, other than his employees' usual incompetence. Why had a Cyber burst from its mother's womb? Why had the others suddenly escaped from the nursery? As he'd told himself endless times, it was impossible. He hadn't programmed the Cybers to emerge from the womb themselves. The idea would be ridiculous—they'd be out of breeding animals in a matter of weeks. Even though they bred the mothers in-house, the animals still had to mature to be able to reproduce, and that process was expensive and time consuming.

On other sites, in the beginning, the distorted Cybers had died only hours after birth, or their vermicular forms had killed the mothers during labor. A series of failures had forced Caesar to program the growth patterns more exactly, but this took experimentation and Cesareans before natural labor could set in.

The first results had been monstrous, horrible, twisted versions of chimp/humanity, not able to live long, or morbid deformities he was forced to kill instantly at birth. With each failure, he'd change the information the superconductor provided to the cells, slowly refining the Cyber's form. Now, the superconductors not only controlled the division and specialization of the cells, they were also able to receive commands from his palm controllers in utero to allow spontaneous programming changes.

He didn't even have to be patient to see them mature. They grew fast. With the gestation period cut to twelve weeks, their journey to adulthood was only slightly longer. In a few years, TransGenesis would have a remote control army of slaves that held entire maps of countries, histories, and personnel files in their heads. Each would be able to think and reason like a human being, move like a chimpanzee and store and access data like a computer. Plus, Caesar would control them—although they'd be almost superhuman, they would remain unable to resist any instructions given to them by the nanochip embedded in their brains.

Each progressive generation carried more human genes than chimp genes, and the newest experiment contained a high percentage of human characteristics. The new Cybers were too human, in fact, to use the chimp mothers. Now TransGenesis needed human hosts, and the first three had been implanted by Dr. Meaks. Caesar's heartbeat quickened just thinking about it.

The mountain provided the isolation he needed to create and study the improved Cybers. Several pregnant chimps had carried their altered cargo to completion and the extractions had worked perfectly, filling the nursery with model Cybers. Here, the Cybers lived and prospered. Super transgenic beings with superconductors in their brains, they were completely manipulated by whoever held the palm controller.

Why bother to learn to control the average person's thoughts when Caesar could create Cybers to do anything for anyone? With a palm controller in his hand, he held the key to the future.

His own personal army.

He wasn't after power or money. His motivation was pure. Noble. Caesar Bossidy would single-handedly improve the human race. His army would not fight wars in the traditional sense. His Cybers would be his slaves, and fight the war against human error. They would not make mistakes. They would not cause delays with unnecessary disagreement. The race Caesar created would be different from the one that presently populated the world. His new race would have no free will, God's biggest mistake. First, they would become his new staff, and the Cybers would work to improve their own race. Cybers designing Cybers. When the design had been perfected, everyone would want to give birth to the superior Cyber-children. Or be forced to. Until the last traces of human vulnerability were erased from the Earth.

But his mission had hit a snag. *How? Why?*

A memory, buried deep within him, elbowed its way to his conscious mind. A flash of clarity lit the remembrance, and for a moment he knew the answer. It smelled like adobe mud, sounded like tribal drums, tasted like fresh bread. He cursed the thought, pushing it away.

He would never let his mother's archaic legends and superstitions rule his life. One of the reasons he'd built TransGenesis inside Wahatoya, as they called the mountain, was so he could beat the tradition out of himself once and for all by succeeding in high science right inside this sacred hill. He would win. There was nothing to the old P'ónin legends about the mountain. Nothing at all.

Caesar felt a hand on his arm and jumped, sloshing coffee over the side of his cup. "Hog!" Caesar exclaimed. He'd been so deep in thought while watching Sunflower that he hadn't heard Hog's approach.

"Sorry, sir, but you weren't answering me," Hog said, looking from Caesar to the spilled coffee.

Caesar put down the cup and wiped his dripping hand on his pants. "Where are the Cybers? Where's Bruce?"

Hog shook his head. "Sir, Stark's dead. The Cybers got him. In the caverns."

Caesar stood up straight, shock striking his spine like a whip. "What do you mean, got him?"

"They…consumed him."

Caesar stared in astonishment at the man, not believing his ears. "Why? You had the controllers with you."

"Didn't work. They didn't work," Hog said.

"That's impossible," Caesar said, nose-to-nose with Hog. The Cybers couldn't make their own decisions. Hog was obviously tired and confused.

Hog shook his head. "The Cybers were unaffected by the controllers."

Caesar saw that several men had noticed their heated conversation, and he didn't want to start a panic. "My office," he said, and placed his hand on Hog's shoulder. They walked in silence. Unspoken anxiety hung in the air around them like dark, swirling clouds. Caesar shut the door and locked it, then sat behind his desk. Leaning back in his chair, he laid his elbows on the armrests, resting his fingertips together in front of his mouth. "Now, tell me. Everything."

Hog stood by the door. His face was lined with weariness, his eyes dark. "The Cybers were all there, at least a good portion of them."

"Where?"

"In the caverns."

"More specific, please. A room? A tunnel?"

"About a hundred yards down the main tunnel."

Caesar gritted his teeth and tried to appear friendly and patient, although he wanted to throw this man against the wall and beat the information out of him. "How did they look?"

"They've grown. Some are walking upright."

A thrill of triumph gripped Caesar. The project was a success. They were growing, prospering, his little army. And these were the chimp Cybers. Imagine what the human Cybers would be like. He rose from his chair, his mind racing, excited. "Why didn't they obey the signals?" he asked himself aloud.

Hog leaned against the wall with one hand. He looked at the ceiling, his braids falling over his shoulders.

Caesar leaned forward, pressing his palms on the desk. "Do you have any idea what went wrong?"

Hog's eyes traced over to Caesar's. His gaze burned. "You went to the pueblo day school."

Caesar fell back in his chair and sighed. "So?" he asked, throwing up his hands.

Hog crossed to the desk and leaned on it with both hands. "You read the legend of the Great White Shaman. All the children did."

"Your point, please." His heart picked up, banging in his chest. He couldn't seem to tear his eyes away from Hog's. He felt like he was back at the one-room schoolhouse with Hog as his schoolmarm.

"Although history claims our pueblo did not join in the Rebellion of 1680, legend states our pueblo actually organized it. We provided the communications hub, so to speak."

Caesar scowled as Hog drifted back into his native tongue, Tiwa.

"The Great White Shaman, the shape-shifter, carried the message of the rebellion to many of our pueblos over a vast land in only a day. Now, that land is divided into four states. He flew with the wings of eagles, ran on swift coyote's feet and climbed with the mountain goat. Our people could not join in the rebellion or the entire nation would have lost their communications link." Hog threw a long braid over his shoulder. "The people of our pueblo had to act as if we supported the Spanish invaders, so they would not suspect our involvement."

Caesar didn't like the way Hog said "our people."

"That is when the legends of the demons, the dark spirits in the mountain, began. Many heard the screaming, the screeching of the demons, condemned to the underworld."

Caesar began to shake. He was not afraid. His racing heart pumped anger through his veins. *Superstition!* Stories to keep children tethered to the old ways, to keep technology at bay.

"According to legend, although the Great White Shaman had to remain in the caverns or die, he attended feasts and celebrations in the forms of many different animals. As a child, didn't you ever look into the eyes of a lizard, and wonder if—"

"Stop!" Caesar interrupted. "Get to the point."

Hog leaned forward and spoke quietly. "It is the Great White Shaman himself. He still lives. He controls the Cybers."

Caesar threw himself back into the chair, exploding in furious laughter. "Impossible. Even if he ever did exist, he would have been dead for centuries."

"His spirit controls the Cybers. The flute…he plays the flute of his spirit guide, the bat. He calls them with it. He ordered the Cybers to him. They are the promised demons. Don't you see?" Hog asked, his voice haunted with legend. "That's why they killed Stark. The Cybers are the demons, and the Great White Shaman is their leader. The whole point of their existence is to make sure the sacred caverns stay sacred, and that means running all those not part of our tribe out of these caverns."

Caesar concentrated on snuffing out his fiery anger. Exploding would not help, would not stop Hog from believing. He'd tried a million times with his mother, tried to get her out of the adobe, into an apartment. Tried to get her to buy her bread instead of slaving every day to make it in the *hornos*. Tried to get her to speak English and leave the old language behind. Maybe go to a real school. He'd made no progress with her. He would make no more with this poor man.

"There is hunting magic on the walls," Hog continued. "The Cybers are drawn there." He raised his hands in the air. "The spirit of the Great White Shaman fell upon us. Stark offered himself up to the Cybers as nourishment, as the deer or buffalo would have done in the old times."

"Pictures?" Caesar asked. "On the walls?"

"Yes. To trap their spirits."

"I've never seen them." Caesar palmed the table and pushed up out of his seat. Despite his efforts to maintain control, his heart beat powerfully in his temples. "Think about what you're suggesting. You're saying that hundreds of years ago, someone went into these caves," he made a wide gesture toward the caverns, "and carved pictures of the Cybers I hadn't even conceived of yet."

Hog stepped back and crossed his arms.

"This is nonsense," he growled. "Utter nonsense."

"It was there, by the pictures, that Stark was taken. The Great White Shaman's power is stronger than your science—"

"There is no goddamned White Shaman!" Caesar roared, throwing his hands in the air. "No truth to the legend. Anyone who believes this nonsense you're spouting is a backward idiot!" He stepped out from behind his desk. "Computers are logical. They either work, or don't work. Superconductors are not superstitious. If something went wrong in the caves, it was your own idiocy that caused it, not some legendary ghoul!"

"If the nanochips are functioning, then we should send the destruct signal now. Kill all the Cybers before they get stronger, bigger. Soon we will lose all chance of being able to control them."

Caesar shook his head. "They're too valuable. I've waited too long for this!" Caesar tried to slow his frantic breathing. "No. The Cybers must be captured. Studied." He drilled Hog with his gaze. "They do not have free will. They can't." He opened the cabinet to his makeshift bar. His hands shook, and the brandy bottle clinked against the glass as he poured.

Behind him, the phone on his desk rang, the sound piercing the small, enclosed space. Caesar returned to his desk, and lifted the receiver. "Speak."

As he listened, all his tension and anxiety molded together into one solid ball of anger.

There was not one man in this world capable of working with him, of understanding his dream and being able to act it out. No one with his sight, his vision, his intelligence. The entire human race was flawed. Stupid. Lazy.

He pressed his teeth together until he thought his jawbone would pop. He replaced the receiver without a word.

Taking a long draw on his brandy, he let the heat slip down his throat and into his gut. He took a deep breath. "That was Chavez," he growled, not looking up at Hog. He was sure if he looked at the man, he'd want to kill him. "Meaks is dead. But the idiots who killed him were seen by a university staff member." He got up and poured some more brandy. "They lost the Vanguard woman, Number Two. Then, surprise, surprise, she showed up later, back at the office of Dr. Meaks."

"Then the police have them in custody."

"No." He swirled his brandy and watched the patterns it made on the inside of the glass. "Somehow, Number Two and the man who witnessed the murder, a Dr. Clinton, both disappeared from the scene. Together."

"With half the force at the site?" Hog asked, amazed. Then his attitude changed. His features melted into acceptance. "It is as I said. The woman is under the protection of the Great White Shaman."

"Then the bastard had better be everything the legends say he is if he wants to protect her, because I want everyone we've got out after Number Two and this witness." He banged a fist on his desk. "Send every available man over to help Chavez in his search, and order the men watching Numbers One and Three to bring them in, now. I don't want to take any more chances."

Hog grunted and turned to leave, his braids swinging.

"Oh, and Hog," Caesar said, stopping his hasty exit. "Get Bruce in here. He has some explaining to do."

16

Bruce Jawoski got back to his room and threw everything he could find into his gray leather bag. A red sweater, a picture of his wife, computer disks. He was getting out of this damned mountain, today.

Something had gone horribly wrong with the project. The Cybers were monsters with free will.

With free will.

They had escaped by themselves, hidden in the caverns and now laid in wait for the unwary spelunker. They'd eaten Stark.

Oh, God. That last agonizing wail.

Bruce's breath came faster, the nerves in his chest tensing into stone. He'd never get it out of his mind. Never shake the terror.

Something had settled over Stark, turning off his mind. He'd marched to them like a willing sacrifice, and then...the Cybers. Like hungry demons, they'd pulled him into that hell hole. Swarmed him. Had eaten him alive. And Bruce knew that in the last moments Stark had regained his awareness. Stark's scream would echo through Bruce's memory for the rest of his life.

It could have been any of us—it could have been me! Bruce sobbed aloud and covered his mouth with his hand.

He must be quiet. Must think straight. Must get away.

And the pictures carved on the cave wall. *How?* They were ancient, but clearly depicted the Cybers. Indian lore packed a powerful blow for those who believed it. Now Bruce was among the believers.

TransGenesis shouldn't have picked this demon mountain to put the company in. Caesar of all people should know better. He was half Indian. Raised in the pueblo.

What a damned fool.

He zipped his bag closed, leaving plenty of room. Now all he had to do was collect some information before he left, something to prove to the authorities that they needed to come and blast this mountain, and all its demons, to kingdom come. Before it was too late.

There was a presence in the mountain. *I'm a German-Slavic atheist and even I know that.* There was something evil and beyond human in the cave. Something that called the Cybers, controlled them and kept them alive. Bruce knew this to be true down to the marrow of his bones, but Caesar would just ridicule him if he tried to explain.

Yet, whatever lurked inside those damned caves, it was a lot more powerful than Caesar and his stupid palm controllers. That's why he had to get out. Leave now. Because that evil would spread from the damned caverns, through the company, through the city, and no one would be left alive.

He was going to get out of here, somehow. Before it was too late.

17

The sun broke through the morning mist. It warmed the splintered wood of Eleanor's front door and shone through the clinic's windows onto the chair where Dr. Meaks had died. Its cleansing rays removed the taunting darkness from every corner, where the night before only fear and evil had prospered. It even found Jeff and Eleanor, skin to skin, ache pressed to ache, resting beneath a down comforter. Jeff saw the sun's glow through his eyelids. He moaned and turned over.

His gaze fell upon Eleanor, and his heart warmed as if the sun had seeped in through his chest. She slept, still as a Greek statue, without pain or anxiety on her face. He could see the little girl she once was, content and curious, before the world had taken away her parents, her security and her childhood. Before she'd discovered she was alone in the world and had built her defenses.

Dark, thick lashes flickered as her eyes moved beneath her eyelids. She was dreaming, her cheek resting on her palm, her full lips slightly puckered. Loose curls framed her face. The skin of her shoulder, like cream, peeked out from beneath the covers.

She was naked. As, he realized suddenly, was he.

As if someone threw a switch, last night's events came tumbling into his mind. The pregnancy test, the murder. His arm. The ache was there, but duller now. *What did we do last night?* He'd passed out, or something. Eleanor had been chased from her house, and, *oh God!* The police.

His heart started racing again, and he let himself fall limply back onto the mattress and stare at Eleanor. *Amazing.* She'd really come through for them. She'd found the escape route in the closet, thought of this place and made it here on her cut up feet without complaint. Then she must have bathed him, bandaged his arm, and put him to bed. He, on the other hand, had been his usual wimpy self.

He sighed, not even wanting to think about today. Where would they go? What would they do? All he had were the files and his medical bag. She had nothing. They didn't even have clothes.

Deep down weariness pulled him back to the comfort of sleep. He snuggled as closely as he could to Eleanor and surrendered to sleep.

* * *

He flew as the white dove.

Stars in White Cloud felt the wind stroke his feathers, the dry air sting his eyes, and watched the morning sun bathe the city beneath him in soft rose. Cool, crisp air pushed upward on his belly and the warm morning sun caressed his back. The smell of clay and dust and the scent of the fertile land beneath reached up to him, but his eyes burned with the visions ahead. The city of the invaders stretched out as far as he could see, in all directions. Metal beasts roamed hot paths of black oil. As he flapped his wings and soared into the city, the stench of city smoke and human waste slaughtered the clean mountain scents.

No wonder the braves had stopped coming to him for guidance. Their village was small, alone, surrounded by a sea of the invaders and their filth. He had never imagined the total destruction of the land caused by the coming of the strangers from the south. Until now, safe in the caverns, he had thought that when the demons finally appeared, the time would be right to drive out all trespassers from P'ónin land. But now he saw how small and ridiculous the idea was. While sailing over the endless city, he gave up hope of winning back the land of his people.

He'd begun his journey from the caverns by entering a black, skittering insect in the innermost cave and darting to the middle cave where a bat consumed him. Inside the bat, his spirit guide, he'd flapped blindly to the outer cave and had waited. When a dove came to roost in a nest just inside the cave entrance, he'd jumped to the dove and had begun his first flight over the land since awakening from his hibernation.

Two demons lived beyond the cave, and he needed to find them and lead them to their home. He'd connected briefly with the mother of demons last night, as well as another child who lived outside the caves. He could feel its need, desperation and hunger. With these two, that meant there were eleven demons in all. The legend had said twelve would work together to sanctify the caverns.

He left the other demons back in the cave, foraging. They'd learned to snatch the bats while they slept, to grab the slimy blind fish from the stream, to capture any insects that scurried by. Not enough food to sustain them for long, but soon the spirit of the fire-heart would offer another sacrifice, he was sure.

So what was the real mission of the demons, if not to drive out the strangers from P'ónin land? Perhaps to drive them from the sacred mountain, to destroy their invasion into the caverns. To seal the caverns off as a tomb for his people's ways and as a home for the demons, a place where the ways of his people could be housed for all time and passed on to the next generation. Of course the demons would have to hunt, but it seemed there were endless trespassers of which to partake, spread out over the plains like buffalo.

A structure below him glowed. A spark, a need, flowed up from the ground and called to him. *There.* The demon he'd called the night before waited there, hoping for his arrival. Weakening. White Cloud swooped down onto the roof and strutted across the warm surface on his small stick legs.

He felt the call, the need flowing from the house. He sang to it with his warbled throat and his heart heard it answer, but he didn't know the way into the house. For now he would just wait, something his people had learned through battle and drought. When The Mother of the Earth was ready, She would reveal an answer.

* * *

Jeff stirred. The memory of Eleanor's bare shoulder made him reach out toward her. He wanted to feel the soft, creamy skin. His fingertips tingled with anticipation. Maybe, they could take their time getting up today, there was no hurry. Why rush out into—

His hand found an empty bed. He came fully awake and sat up. Where was she?

Sharp words and loud expletives seeped through the closed bedroom door. Eleanor's cursing ripped the last remaining cobwebs from his head. Someone must have found them! Either Chavez and his dirty crew or the brown van guys with automatics. Throwing off the comforter, he stumbled out the door, his heart pounding.

His back against the wall, he glanced into the kitchen and dove to cover to scout the living room. There was no one but Eleanor, pacing in the foyer, alone. Her hair stuck in all directions as if she'd used mousse to purposely spike it. An oversized Lobos sweatshirt hung loosely on her frame, reaching past her knees and casting the illusion that she was eleven years old. She padded on her bandaged feet back and forth across the tiles, waving a piece of paper in her fist. Her face glowed red with anger. She must have found the files.

She spotted him, stopped in her tracks, and stared at his groin.

A warm blush began between his legs and spread through his body.

She stooped, retrieved a pair of red sweat pants from the floor, and threw them at him. "Lord, put these on. I don't intend to look at you swing all day long."

He held the pants up, inspecting their size. They'd fit him a little big. "Where did you get the clothes?"

"There was a sweat suit on the table by the door. Complements of the university."

"Great." He pulled the sweat pants on. "Now we're practically dressed."

Wearily, he leaned back against the wall and rested. Geez, just pulling on a pair of pants had tired him and made his arm flare with pain—he must have further injured the muscle while escaping from the basement. He had to remember to take it easy.

"God damn Bixler," she roared. "The lying asshole." She hissed through her teeth and growled. "I'm going to kill that son of a bitch. Sue him. Someone will pay for this—"

"Wait a minute," he interrupted. Now he was confused. What did Bixler have to do with the files? She should be cursing Dr. Meaks, not the university's president. "What's going on here? I wake up and find you doing laps in the hall, bitching at the Kachinas on the wallpaper. Explain."

"Explain this," she said. She wadded up the paper she'd been waving around and threw it at him. It bounced off his bare chest and onto the floor.

He stared at it irritably. He didn't want to bend over again and have pain shoot through his arm. But he had to know what had lit the fire under her. Groaning, he reached down, grabbed the paper, and opened it. Eleanor stood, feet placed wide, arms crossed, eyes thin slits in her face, her mouth turned down. With feathers, she'd look like an old photo of a stern Indian chief.

The paper was a memo on official university stationary. It read:

Mike,

Welcome to New Mexico! I assure you, you've made the right decision in joining us at UNM, home of the Lobos. Please make yourself comfortable, and take a few days to see the sights and house hunt before you begin working. Sorry I couldn't be there to meet you in person, but I'll be back in a week or so. I'll call you then, and we'll meet and discuss the new direction of the department. Again, congratulations on your new position as Dean of Engineering!

Sincerely, Michael Bixler, President.

At first, Jeff was confused. How did Bixler know Eleanor would be here? Then he looked back at who the letter was addressed to. Someone named Mike. Not Eleanor.

Not Eleanor. The words echoed through his head. Someone else had been given the position she had been working for since she'd come to the university. His mouth got dry. "I...don't know what to say." He glanced up at her. She was a rancorous fireball.

"How about *asshole?* That's a good thing to say." She tore the paper from his hands. "How about *dirty lying asshole?* That's even better!"

"Who are you talking about?"

"Bixler, of course! The asshole who promised me the job. The asshole who told me I was a shoo-in for the position. Shoo-in, indeed. Instead, I'm booted out. I should have known it was taking too long. I should have made him give me something in writing."

"Okay," he said, finally sure he had a clear understanding. She hadn't found the files—she'd found confirmation that someone else had her job. For Eleanor, that was probably worse than carrying an implanted baby.

"I'm going to find Bixler right now, on vacation or not. Gonna give that Judas a piece of what's coming to him."

"No, you're not."

She whirled around. "Stop me." It was a dare.

He grabbed her shoulders. "We have more important things to do here."

"Like what?" Throwing out her arms, she jerked from his grasp. "What's more important than my career?"

"Your life."

She hesitated. Doubt flared in her eyes then was gone, like a hummingbird lighting on a flower.

She narrowed her eyes. "You mean *your* life."

"No. I'm not in as much danger as you are."

"But the police, Dr. Meaks's death."

"Yes, I know. But I can run, hide. Hire a lawyer. You can't get away from..." He stopped, not sure how much he should say.

"From what?" The doubt landed back in her eyes. "What are you saying? What do you know that you haven't told me?"

"Come with me." He took her hand, and pulled her after him into the kitchen. "Sit." Surprisingly, she complied. Gathering up his nerve, he poured them both some water, snapped some soft music on the radio, picked up the files and joined her.

"I pulled these out of Dr. Meaks's office. He was looking at them when he got shot, and maybe when he called you."

She scooted her chair closer to his, and folded her legs up onto it. "Are those the same files you were carrying last night?"

He nodded.

"What are they?"

"This file is on you." He pointed to her name. "It says that you were…implanted…on 8/13." He watched closely for her reaction.

Her eyes opened wide. "Implanted? What the hell does that mean?"

"Well…" He planned to present this carefully. If his interpretation was wrong, he'd have terrified her for no reason. He changed positions in his seat. "Okay. You are six weeks pregnant. You claim that I was your only lover—"

"You were."

"And I'm sterile. So…" He cleared his throat, not wanting to continue, but knowing he had to. "The note in your file could mean that he implanted an embryo in your uterus on this date."

The angry blush drained from her face, leaving her ghostly white. Her paleness frightened him.

"Bastard!" she said. "How in the hell could this happen? I'd sue him, too, if he wasn't dead."

"Before you ride a wild hair, let me ask. Were you in his office then? On August thirteenth?"

"Without my Daytimer, it's hard to say," she said slowly, remembering. "But that would be about the time I had the uterine biopsy." Her gaze snapped to his and held. "Could that have been when the bastard did this?"

"I don't know. If someone was going to implant embryos, it doesn't make sense they'd choose women randomly. Clinics charge big bucks for that, and there is a host of infertile woman willing to try anything to get pregnant. Why draft unknowing patients?"

"Knowing that drunkard Meaks," Elly began, "he probably just botched the procedure. You hear about it all the time. Surgeons amputating the wrong leg, taking out a gall bladder instead of a spleen."

Her eyes rose from the file to his face. "I'm sorry, Jeff. I didn't mean—"

"I know," he said, cutting her off. He put a hand on her knee and watched her expressions change, like a laser light show on her face. "We need to talk about *you* right now." What a nightmare. To be carrying a child inside your body against your will, have to give birth to it, know nothing about it. He wouldn't be able to stand it.

The morning radio announcer excitedly gave the details of a contest. The eleventh caller would win 1000 dollars.

"No," she muttered, gritting her teeth and ramming her fists against the table. "This is not happening to me."

He reached for her hand. She shook it off.

"It's not as bad as it sounds," he said, not meaning a word of it. "As soon as we figure out what happened for sure, we can just abort the fetus. A simple operation. You'll be back to normal in no time."

She looked up. She no longer looked like a little girl, now the Eleanor he knew and loathed was back, and she had murder in her eyes. "*My* job. *My* body." She grabbed the file and slammed it down on the table. "Someone will pay for this. So I can't sue Meaks. I'll sue the university, instead. I'll sue Bixler!"

"I wouldn't count on it."

"Oh, I'm counting already. Ten-million, eleven-million—"

"I mean that you can't prove it," Jeff said. "You can't prove that the baby was implanted."

"What are you saying?"

"Let's say you bring charges against the university. The first thing they're going to say is that you're full of it. They'll claim the baby is yours—and mine. People knew we were seeing each other. Without Dr. Meaks's testimony, without his records, how are you going to convince anyone of his guilt?"

"Tests," Elly insisted. "Paternity tests."

"Yes, but you'll have to either abort the baby or carry it to term. Or near term, anyway. But even that might not help if there is no father to match the DNA to. All they could do is prove that I'm *not* the father, they couldn't figure out who the father really is. Besides, the most successful implantations use the surrogate's egg. You're probably the mother. "

"But...how? How did he get my egg?" Her confusion changed quickly to understanding. Her eyes widened. "No wonder there were so many tests. I thought he was being thorough. I thought maybe he was holding something back, because I was sick and he didn't want to scare me. He was holding back, that bastard, but because he was using me! Oh, God." Her hand fluttered to her heart. "A mother. Me? Oh, God."

"That's no different than when you thought the baby was our love child." He smiled.

"But that's when I knew who the father was." Her hand dropped to the table. "Now, I'm carrying someone else's child. It could be anyone's child."

Jeff hesitated. *Should he tell her more?* "There's something else."

She leaned back in her chair. "Great."

"In the file, it says that you were scheduled for extraction. I think that means they were planning to give you a C-section."

"Of course. Goes along with the rest of it. Didn't know I was pregnant. Didn't know I was scheduled for a Cesarean."

"The weird thing is...it's scheduled for only a few weeks from now. No child would be viable by then."

Again, her face washed of color. She covered her abdomen with her palm as if she were trying to hide something. "How much should I be showing? I mean, at six weeks?" Her voice was almost a whisper.

His heart stopped. His gut clenched. "Show me."

She lifted her shirt slowly, her eyes riveted on his face.

He gasped. What he'd seen of her last night had not prepared him for this. Her abdomen was enlarged, all right. If he didn't know better, he'd think he was looking at a woman in her fifth or sixth month of pregnancy. He tried to keep his voice quiet and calm. "Have you felt any movement?"

"Yes. Just…flutters. Is that okay?"

His attention was grabbed by the radio announcer, who said Jeff's name. They both sat upright.

"*…a professor at UNM, is wanted in connection with last night's brutal murder of Dr. Randall Meaks, a doctor at the university's clinic. Clinton, who was being held for questioning, apparently escaped with one hostage, Dr. Eleanor Vanguard, a UNM engineering professor. A statewide manhunt is under way. Clinton is considered armed and dangerous. In other news this morning…*"

He stared at Eleanor.

She stared back. "My God," she said. "The police. How could they think…I'm not your hostage. And you certainly didn't kill anybody. You're the victim—you were shot." She rose to her feet. "We have to go to the police. Clear this up."

Adrenaline flowed into his brain. His heart sped. His hands began to shake. "No," he managed to say. "The police are in on it. We can't take any chances."

"But your reputation…"

He stood, his thoughts a blur. "What reputation? Looney bird surgeon, lousy professor and now sloppy murderer?" Everything seemed to be happening all over again. He'd heard his name on the radio in Baltimore, too. Telling the world how his botched operation had almost cost the life of a mother of three, and led to a record malpractice award.

Eleanor glanced nervously at the window, then back at him. "Who else was implanted?"

"These are the files." He waved his hand over the table. "Look for yourself. There's a girl named Rita Frederickson, and another named—"

"Rita Frederickson?" she asked, her eyes wide. Her hand flew to her chest. "She's one of my students."

Jeff leaned back in his chair. He reached for his water and took a long sip to open his throat. It was pinched with fear. They had to take action to save themselves, yet right now, he felt like running. "This Rita." He leaned over and pointed at the file. "She was

136

implanted quite a while before you. In fact, she was scheduled for extraction, whatever that means, very soon. We should tell her our suspicions. Find out what she knows."

Eleanor stood, obviously ready to go. "No need to wait around. She might be able to help us. Maybe we could stay there, with her."

"Not if the police are mixed up in this. They'd know about Rita."

"I don't see how. They don't have the files."

"It depends on how deeply Chavez is involved and who's passing out his orders." He looked at her bandaged feet, and at the band of the sweatshirt hanging around her knees. "We need something to wear. Half a sweat suit will look suspicious out there in the real world. Cold, too."

"Let's go see what we can find." Eleanor hesitated. "Wait. Who is the other girl?"

He gestured to the files. "Donna something. A first year student. Lives in the dorms."

"We need to go see her, too," Eleanor insisted. "She needs to know what's happening before it's too late for her."

After going through the drawers and closet, all they found was one white T-shirt. Jeff pulled it on. "Look, you wear these pants." He pulled off the sweat pants and handed them to her. "I'll wear my jeans."

"They're in the bathroom."

They had been rinsed and folded over the shower rod. He pulled them on. He moaned, having to use his right arm in the process. Eleanor pulled on the socks she'd worn yesterday, and he handed her his shoes. "I can get around in my socks better than you can. I know the shoes are too big, but they'll feel better that way."

"Thanks." She pulled them on. Top to bottom, she looked like a girl in her father's clothing. "I wish we had a gun."

He sighed. "What would we need a gun for?"

"Defense."

"Ha. What're we gonna do, shoot a cop? If we win, it will be with our wits." He tapped his index finger against his temple. "We're two smart people, who both want to stay alive. Whoever is after us is under orders, and doesn't care about us half as much as we do." He straightened up. "We out gun them in intelligence."

"Right. I can just see the headlines. *Dead bad guy found in Albuquerque, brain cells imbedded in his chest.* We need street smarts, not the ability to solve differential equations."

"You got some of that."

"I'm glad you noticed," she said with the first hint of a smile he'd seen that day.

"Hopefully, we can find something out. If not, maybe we can help Rita and Donna, anyway." He opened the back door, and they stepped out into the sunshine. It warmed his skin. The birds sang.

The world didn't seem to know it was coming to an end.

18

Leaves, coated with water from yesterday's storm, glowed with a fluorescent sheen. A layer of moisture darkened the tree bark and brought out the varied hues of every stone. Standing pools in the grass reflected sunlight. Although the sun would soon chase off the morning dampness, for the moment the rain had transformed the dry, desert area into a contrast of colors.

The quiet neighborhood where Rita lived was close to campus, a village of boxy houses set in yards of patchy grass and rock gardens. Jeff and Eleanor plodded through alleys, only emerging when they crossed streets. The gravel pathway proved tricky for his stocking feet. Thankfully, the fenced yards were random so they could skirt the chain-link and wooden barriers—neither of them were in a condition to vault fences or climb walls. Dogs barked as they passed, a squirrel flicked its tail and chittered at them, and sparrows splashed in puddles. But no one else took notice.

That was just fine with Jeff. Perfect, in fact. Yesterday had held enough bizarre excitement for two lifetimes. He needed the mundane, familiar sights, sounds and smells of a suburban neighborhood. He needed order.

The surroundings took Jeff's mind off his pain. A little. His fear, alive since he'd heard the glass break in Dr. Meaks's office, still percolated through his blood. It hung in his bones and swam in his gut. He managed okay, as long as he didn't try to visualize the scene of the doctor slumped over his chair, and all that blood...

He fumbled with the strap of his medical bag, making sure it was still slung over his shoulder. *Look at the trees, Jeff. Look at the rambunctious mutts. Don't think about Donna. Don't think about last night.*

Although they saw no sign of a brown van or police cars, and ran across no suspicious men bush-lurking, Jeff was still spooked. They'd gone by Donna's place first, as it was in a dorm close to the faculty housing. Her door had been ajar, the television on, and her purse sat on the table near the entry, where a lamp had been overturned. Apparently, they'd been too late to warn her.

The scene had humbled him. They could easily be next. He could just imagine meeting up with another big gun, or feeling the hand of a policeman on his head as he was shoved in the back a squad car, his hands cuffed.

Then he'd never see the morning again like he'd seen it today. Never again watch the sun come out over the desert and warm the world. Never again wake up next to a soft, beautiful woman. He had to take one day at a time, one minute at a time, and do whatever would protect them the most at that moment. Right now, he had to find Rita and talk with her, find out whatever she knew, and warn her that she was in danger. Meanwhile, he had to keep himself firmly rooted in the present.

Eleanor hadn't spoken in several minutes. Her eyes were getting that glazed look, and worry prickled his skin. The last thing they needed right now was another one of her "episodes."

"Elly." He put his hands on her shoulders, turned her toward him, and looked into her eyes. The sun glimmered a thousand colors in her hair, and sparkled on her dark lashes. "You okay? I don't want to do this if it's too much for you."

"I'm okay." With two fingers, she rubbed her temple. "I think."

"You think? Hey, we can stop and rest. There's no hurry."

Her eyes darted around, looking everywhere but at him. "That's not it."

"Then what?" He waited. A sparrow landed next to a small puddle near them, its beak jerking back and forth, ever watchful. Eleanor's eyes did the same thing.

"I'm starting to feel...something. Close by."

"The house? We're getting close."

"No...something else. A presence. *The* presence." She emphasized the word "the" as if it should have great meaning for him.

Surprisingly, it did. He hesitated, remembering they'd neglected to talk about her medication. He didn't want her to go into one of those *Twilight Zone* trances again. "Maybe you should just stay here in the alley. I'll check out the house."

She finally looked straight into his eyes. Even though the sun bathed his neck and hair with warmth, her haunted stare sent chills skittering down his spine. "I don't want to be alone," she said, almost a whisper.

"I know." He ran his palms up and down her arms, the loneliness in her voice pulling at his heart. "But I don't want you to take a one way trip to la-la land again. Please, stay here."

A blackbird squawked from a phone wire, high above their heads.

She broke eye contact with him and nodded. "Okay." Weariness evident in her movements, she found a chipped stucco wall and sank down against it. She picked a dry sprig of grass. Staring, she rolled it between her fingers. "I'll be here, but hurry. Come and get me— soon."

Concerned, he walked over and hunkered down next to her. "You got it. I'll check it out then come back for you. Okay?"

Without expression, she nodded.

When he started to get up she placed a hand on his shoulder. "Be careful. I have a bad feeling about this."

He wanted to say, "Me, too." Instead, he gave her an encouraging smile, put his hands on her knees and pushed himself to a standing position. "I'll be right back."

Without a backward glance, he hurried down the alley. When he reached Rita's block, he crossed to the sidewalk. Though he felt like the city held a thousand eyes and they were all on him, he saw no brown van, no police car. No one stood on their front porch pointing at him. Just a boy on a bike, who saw only the clear sky and the endless possibilities of the day.

Goose bumps crept across his skin when he came upon the house, as if the structure had consciousness. It just sat there in the sun, patiently waiting. His future.

He marched up the walk and knocked on the door. Shaped like a shoe box, a chain link fence ringed the stucco, salmon-colored structure. Small flower boxes hung under each window. A beige Toyota truck sat sunning in the driveway. He swallowed hard, forcing down the need to turn and run. "Rita," he mumbled to himself. "I'm here. And I don't have good news." He glanced nervously over his shoulder.

Raising his fist, he knocked again. There was no answer. No fresh-faced student came to the door and invited him inside. One hand against the door, he leaned over to ring the doorbell. The door pushed open with a creak, surprising him. "What in the hell?" He staggered backward.

An intense odor stampeded out the door, overrunning him. Reflexively, he spun away, covering his mouth and nose with his hands. A familiar smell, one he knew all too well. A smell that caused everything within him to recoil. The nausea that shadowed his gut rose up into his throat. The fear that lurked in his bones exploded out into his blood stream, alive, breathing, hungry, with an edge like a razor.

He lurched back into the morning air, breathing hard.

Death. Old blood. Sickness, disease, infection.

His fear stalked him as if it had taken an avatar's living form. It had shadowed him, and laying in wait, had ambushed him again.

He should leave and call the police. That would be a new one—a fugitive reporting a crime. He glanced back toward the open door. Whatever was inside, he had to check it out...for Eleanor.

A white dove swooped down off the roof and flew through the door into the house. A vulture would be apropos, maybe, but a dove?

Doves stood for peace, forgiveness, spiritual purity, all that Hallmark card gibberish.

Pulling his T-shirt up over his nose like a makeshift gas mask, he followed the dove's course inside. To his right and left were the formal dining and living rooms, in front of him a staircase. The kitchen lay beyond. He headed there, first.

It was a mess. The cupboards were ajar, their contents splayed out onto the floor. Trash had been spilled and tossed around the room. Every drawer stood open, its contents pitched. The walls were scratched and feces peppered the room. Someone, or something, had ripped through the boxes of crackers and cookies and anything else that could be opened and flung around.

A feeling that he was being observed, watched, lit on the back of his neck. He whirled around. There on the counter was the dove, strutting across the counter, pecking at crumbs it found there. "You are one strange feather-ball," he said. His voice seemed extraordinarily loud.

Instead of flying off, the bird turned its head and stared at him with one dark eye. For a moment, Jeff felt as if he saw intelligence in the creature. Light flashed in its eye as if it snapped a quick picture.

Jeff saw another quick movement and whirled around, his heart leaping to his throat. Something small scampered across the floor and into the living room. "Looks like something that might eat a bird," he said to the dove, trying to calm his racing heart. Probably just a cat. Probably got closed up in the house, and had torn up the kitchen.

The stench was coming from upstairs. A thick, sweet odor flowed down the steps. He wished he had the gun Eleanor had talked about. Holding it out in front of him, his ascent of the steps wouldn't seem nearly as frightening. But he had a feeling he wouldn't really need a gun for whatever he would find upstairs. Just a stomach of steel.

Hesitantly, with his T-shirt still over his mouth, he drifted to the stairs and put his foot on the first step. He could stop and call the police. *Ha. There you go again. You have to stop thinking of the police as good guys, Jeff.* Chavez, anyway, was a bad guy in blue. Or black, in this case. Albuquerque's worst.

Jeff put weight on his stocking foot and pushed up to the second step. Maybe he should get a knife from the kitchen.

No, bad idea.

Go, coward. Go. Gritting his teeth, he forced himself step by step up the staircase, his ice cold fingers squeezing the railing as he went. The smell became stronger until it seemed to penetrate his skin, the filth mixing with his blood. His eyes watered.

Approaching the bedroom, he peered inside. Sunlight shone through the lacy curtains, casting a pastel green throughout the room. Steeling himself, he stepped inside the room.

Totally unnerved by the stillness of the bodies, by the silence of the room, he wanted to scream and dance, just to break the eerie spell.

Come on, Rita. Joke's over! Move. Tuck your entrails back inside and zip up. Stand up, yell, "Surprise!" and laugh.

Starved for air, he dared to breathe, and inhaled the scent of corruption. It entered his mouth, throat, lungs. The foulness flowed through his blood stream, violated him, and a wave of nausea crashed over him, trying to push away the defilement of his flesh. He pulled the shirt off his face and ran into the hall. Unable to control himself, he lost his guts on the carpet. The heaves gripped him until he felt he would turn inside out.

He breathed deeply for a while. After the reek of the bedroom, the air in the hallway seemed almost fresh.

Gathering his wits, he examined his jeans to make sure he hadn't splattered on the only pair he had. They were clean. *Thank God for little things.*

He looked back toward the room with apprehension. The first cadaver he'd ever seen, in medical school, had caused strange and varied reactions in his class. Some braved it out, others made sexual jokes and grabbed the body in intimate places. But most were shocked, sick, and one kid he knew even dropped out of med school and picked up engineering. But slowly, all the remaining students became used to the sight of dead people. Convincing himself that this was no different from class, he stood and stamped his feet to get his circulation going. He had to examine the scene and try to understand what had happened. For Eleanor's sake and for his, he had to look again. He had to look for a clue as to what had caused this madness.

With determination, he pulled the shirt back over his mouth and walked back into the room. Rita was dead, very dead, dead for a day or more. A man lay spread eagle on the bed next to her. His face had been ripped away, leaving just staring sockets and a pit for a nose. His genitals were missing. Sympathy ached in Jeff's groin.

Rita was cut completely in half across the abdomen, as if someone had hit her with a giant ax below the belly button, like she'd fallen prey to the pit and the pendulum. Trailing out from the hole was a placenta and umbilical cord. *Charles Manson strikes again.*

Perhaps the worst thing was that both bodies had been chewed up. Some animal, small from the size of the bite marks, had been at them for hours. Bone lay exposed. Pieces of tissue lay around the bodies, thrown during a ravenous feast.

A shock shot through Jeff like electricity.

Small animal.

The kitchen.

He'd seen something down there. What if the creature was still here, still hungry, still downstairs? What if it wasn't a cat?

Just as he raced for the staircase, he heard a scream. A woman's scream.

Eleanor's scream.

* * *

The Mother of the Earth was surely blessing Stars in White Cloud today. The missing demon mother had just arrived on the pathway outside. She must be a wise one, a woman who understood the plan, who heard his voice, who had a guiding spirit. Perhaps she was one of his people, at least a distant cousin. Why else would she be here, but to gather the other demon and bring it with her to the caverns? He'd called this demon last night, but hadn't told the demon mother where the child waited. He hadn't even known at that time.

There was a man with her, probably her husband, and he seemed to be helping her. This was good, very good. He was willing to sacrifice his wife for the good of the tribe. He was honorable, and would win much respect in the next life.

The man left his wife behind the structure, on the path, and came to find the demon himself. White Cloud flew in ahead of him, and then turned his head sideways to see the man one eye at a time. Bird eyes were strange when used close up. Good for flying, seeing much at a time, but hard to use in small spaces. The man seemed to be searching for the demon. He spoke to the dove. *Could he know?*

There it was—the demon child! It ran by. The man saw it, too, but didn't pursue it.

White Cloud closed his eyes and waited for the chanting, performed by his body back in the cave. The chanting was the power that allowed his spirit to leave the cave in many different forms, although his body stayed behind, safe in the darkness. Finally, he flew around inside the bright structure, looking for the child. He found it, hiding under a table. He landed on its head. The child batted at him. Quickly, he let go of the bird, projected his spirit outward and jumped into the baby thoughts and fire-heart.

He was confused for a few moments, trying to adjust to the new body. The demon's power dazed him. This child was different than the others in the cave. Smarter, more determined, healthier. It already planned to go out into the sunlight to hunt.

But that was not what White Cloud wanted. He fought its desires and moved the demon, intending to take the creature to the man. Then, with the child's eyes, he saw the mother silhouetted in the doorway. The demon's will was strong. Hunger drove it and it rushed up behind the mother. *No!* It didn't understand that this woman must be allowed to carry its brother to birth. This was the mother of demons.

But White Cloud hadn't had time to instruct the child of the legends. Its eyes focused on the ankle that showed beneath the red and white pants. In its mind, it remembered the taste of the salty skin, the texture on its teeth as they sank into the flesh, the pleasure of the juicy red flow. Its stomach clenched with fierce hunger.

White Cloud could almost taste the blood, drowning within the demon's desire. If he allowed the demon to take over, his spirit would join forever with the child's, and he would be unable to exit the body and go back to the sacred caverns. He would be unable to fulfill his destiny.

This demon was stronger than the rest, a far superior child. It used the information flowing from the fire-heart willfully.

White Cloud concentrated on creeping up to the woman, used all of his will to force the creature to ask the woman to take it with her to the caverns. But the child took over in a burst of energy.

White Cloud watched in horror as it sank its teeth into her ankle and held on.

* * *

Stabbing fear sliced through Jeff's chest as he raced for the stairs. If whatever had done this damage was downstairs now, and Eleanor had come into the house, she was in grave danger. She called out for him, her voice breaking. He reached the stairs and plummeted down. His toe caught in the deep carpet and he tripped, but grabbed the handrail and managed to stay on his feet. Eleanor sat on the floor in the entryway, gripping her ankle, rocking back and forth, moaning.

He rushed to her. "Elly!"

"Oh, God," she wailed. "It bit me—its teeth—oh my God!"

"What?" Jeff kneeled down next to her. He should look around the place, but this was more important. He pulled his medical bag off his shoulder and zipped it open automatically.

"I shook it off. I kicked it." She gritted her teeth and shook her head violently. "It took part of my ankle with it."

Jeff squatted on the floor beside her and peeled her hands from her ankle. It bled profusely. He pulled off his shirt and dabbed at the wound. A quarter-size piece of flesh was missing. He pressed the shirt against it. "Hold this," he said, and fumbled in his bag for disinfectant and bandages. He thanked his lucky stars once more for having brought his bag along with him.

"What was it? What kind of animal was it?"

"I...don't know. I couldn't see it clearly. It was...naked. A child...a monkey...I don't know." Her eyes filled with panic as she

147

realized the implication of what she'd said. "I don't know," she wailed again.

He quickly dabbed disinfectant on her wound, padded it, and wrapped it firmly. "Nothing important broken in there. You'll live." He put the supplies back into the bag. "Where did the thing go?"

"Out. Out the front."

Pulling his bloody shirt back on, Jeff ran out the door and looked up and down the flat street, but saw nothing unusual. Then his eyes focused on something he didn't expect to see at all, because he was looking for the animal. Intense sunlight flashed off a vehicle parked across the street—a brown van.

He ran back inside and slammed the door. He locked the knob and threw the deadbolt. "Come on. We gotta go. The bad guys are here. Parked outside." He helped her to her feet and draped her arm over his shoulder.

"Which bad guys?"

"The *B* team. *B*rown van. *B*igger guns. Sons a *B*itches."

She cried out in pain as he led her into the kitchen. "Where are we going?"

"I don't know, don't know. But we have to go there fast."

"Maybe out the back door."

"Right." He turned with her quickly, and knocked her into the corner of a drawer that hung open.

Inside, keys rattled. "Keys!" He lifted the key ring. It held a plastic red and white caricature of Louie the Lobo in a football helmet, two car keys and a house key. "We can take their wheels."

She shook her head and whined. "We'll never make it to the car fast enough."

Shit. She was right—but he wasn't ready to die, not today. "We have to try anyway. It's our only chance."

He headed back toward the front door, supporting Eleanor. With one glance at the van, he ducked outside and raced toward the truck. Before they were three steps out of the house, the men emerged from the van and pointed automatic rifles in their direction. The men moved as quick as hunting coyotes, straight at them.

Jeff looked at the car then back at the men, judging the distance. Even if the men didn't open fire, he and Eleanor would never make it to the car.

19

Stars in White Cloud forced his being upon the demon, making it release its grasp. But before he could withdraw his teeth, the mother screamed and shook her leg so violently he was thrown against the wall with her flesh still in his mouth.

It tasted salty, slightly metallic, and although he wanted to spit it out, he allowed the demon to swallow it, as he needed the sustenance. A kick came out of nowhere and struck him, hard. The demon's head hit the wall with great force, stunning him.

While the creature recovered, White Cloud took charge of its motor skills and scampered out the door. His newborn skin was sensitive to the warm cement in front of the house, and the sunlight burned his eyes.

Staggering, he ducked under the row of bushes in front. Almost instantly, the mother emerged into the sunlight, supported by the man. They moved fast toward a metal carriage. *Come, yes, come. Let's go home.* He ran toward the carriage, too, intending to jump in the back. But then he saw what the woman was frightened of—the other men. They ran toward the mother with metal weapons. He couldn't allow them to hurt her.

He flung the demon into the back of the carriage and took a great leap into a blackbird swooping by on its way to join a flock in a large tree. The birds' simple, spastic minds were already joined as one. What each one felt, the others felt. What each one saw, the others saw. They were a tribe in perfect harmony, stronger for the synchronism. This simple unity was what his people had tried so many years to attain. With the birds it was so much easier. Their minds only reacted, they did not create.

It was no problem to convince them that the men were a threat, and move them as one being toward the advancing men. A rush of air smoothed his feathers as he dove toward a dark head.

A shock wave shook his body as he impacted the first man with his beak. The man howled. The high, squeaky wail intensified the sense of urgency in the flock, and they all began to screech and dive along with White Cloud. For a moment, he thought he wouldn't be able to recover from the shock of sudden impact, but his bird instincts took over, and he managed to flutter his wings just enough to rise back up out of reach. He saw the other birds all diving at the men, too, and his own urge intensified. He had to chase them away. It became the only thought in his mind.

Like a red sheet had been pulled down in front of his eyes, all he felt was the communal anger of the flock, and the need to drive off these invaders. He dove again, this time connecting with a man's arm as it reached up to fend him off, but he opened his beak and ripped at his clothing, pinching him. The man screeched, and at first it startled the birds, but they continued on.

The thrill of the attack, watching the clothes being shredded and the men run and fall underneath the birds' plummeting bodies was the closest experience he'd ever had to being part of an actual hunting party. The other boys in the camp all had been able to join the hunters when they reached the age of manhood, unless they chose to don women's garments and stay at home. Those that hunted would run and work as one, as this flock of birds, to bring down the buffalo. They bit with their spears, and chased with their legs, but they worked as a group. Now he finally had a chance to experience it himself.

Completely immersed in the attack, he was nearly blown from his feathers when one of the men managed to fire his gun. The bullet caught one of the birds, the pain swift but intense, and they scattered to the trees and hid, breathing hard, their hearts racing out of control. All thoughts of attack were crushed by the sudden blast of fear. Hiding in the trees along with the birds, he momentarily forgot the woman and the demon child, and when he looked for them, they were gone.

He had intended to ride along in the demon with them, but now he would have to return to the mountain inside the bird. But all was not lost. They would be as easy to find again as two campfires on the prairie. Without his presence there to control the demon, he hoped the creature did not feast on the two people. Surely, once the child was calm and fed, it would recognize the demon mother.

The birth of her demon would be one of the last sacred events before he banded all the demons together as one, like the blackbirds, to drive the unholy men from his sacred mountain, Wahatoya.

20

Bump. Rock. Toss. Knocked off feet. Sit. Sit down. Can't look out, can't stand up. Sit. Sit down.

Rock, rock, rock.

Yawning. Sleepy. Sound of engine singing. Eyes hurt, close.

Oh, hungry. Still hungry. Growing, growing, must eat. But first, sleep. Lay down, yes, feels good. Forget hunger. Eat later.

Rock, rock, rock.

Still smell blood, blood on woman. Shouldn't have bit the mother. But so hungry. Still taste her in mouth. Eat, eat. Hungry.

Eat later. Now sleep, yes.

Rock, rock, rock.

21

Jeff pressed his foot on the gas and didn't let up until Eleanor's tugging on his arm and her protests broke through his terror.

"Jeff. Slow down. They're not behind us, but the police will be chasing us soon if you don't slow down."

He glanced at the old analog speedometer. He was going sixty in a residential zone. "Shit!" He hit the brakes and dropped his speed. He checked the mirror. "Are you sure no one's following us?"

"Yes, yes. A million times yes."

He exhaled heavily, and forced his muscles to relax. "What in the hell was that back there?"

"Simple. The birds attacked the bad guys so we could escape. Makes perfect sense to me, in an Alfred Hitchcock sort of way."

He glanced over at her questioningly. She had her injured ankle on the seat, applying pressure to the wound. She'd removed his big shoes, and they rested on the floorboard. She seemed calm, maybe too calm.

"It was really the only polite thing they could do, since the neighborhood monkey child tried to eat me." She looked up at him, her eyes flat. "What did you find upstairs?"

"Rita. And her boyfriend."

"Dead?"

"Very."

"Who killed them?"

"I don't know."

"The shooters again?"

"No." He hesitated. "They weren't shot. They were...well, chewed up. Like an animal had attacked them."

After a few moments, she said, "A monkey child, perhaps?"

"Don't know." He wasn't going to give her any details. Just thinking about it made him lightheaded, and he didn't want to taste any of the filth on his tongue. When he turned left toward faculty housing, Eleanor sat up straight. "Where are you going?"

"Back to our hideaway. I'm starving. You're tired, and hurt. We need to rest. We need to think about all this."

"I don't think we should go back there. And I don't want to think anymore."

He looked over at her. Her eyes were glazing again.

"Oh, come on. They couldn't have traced us there. Not yet. It's perfectly safe." He gripped the wheel so hard his hands ached. He needed some normalcy. Just anything. He needed to make a sandwich with American cheese. Watch Jeopardy. Vacuum. Listen to MSNBC talk about terrorism. Anything.

"I'm serious," Eleanor said. "I have a bad—"

"You have a bad feeling about it, right?" He lowered his voice. "You have a spooky-ooky psychic sense that something is lurking for us there?" Angry, he slapped the wheel. "Give it a break. Please. Just give it a break."

They drove silently for a few moments. His heart beat in his ears. A fist tightened in his stomach.

"I don't think we should go back," she said.

"Is this a logical feeling? An engineering, statistical feeling?" His anger was building. Why couldn't she just be plain old logical Eleanor, the computer with a temper? "Is your feeling based on empirical data?"

No answer. Her eyes glazed further. Well, to hell with it. If she was going to zone out again he'd slip her into the apartment and she'd never know. He had to shower and get this filth off of his body, all the foul matter the scene had painted on his skin the minute he'd walked into that damned house. He needed the hot water to cleanse his twisted brain cells and help him make sense out of chaos. Accelerating, he turned the corner that led to the faculty housing.

He slammed on the brakes and they skidded to a stop. Something in the truck bed rolled up against the cab. Waiting outside the apartment where they'd stayed last night was not only a brown van, but two police cars.

No time to think. He threw the truck in reverse, pulled a quick L-turn and sped down the alley they'd hiked through earlier in the day, praying no one had seen him.

"God damn son of a bitch!" He wanted to grab Eleanor and shake the damn demons out of her. "How did you know?" he demanded. "How did you know?" Through her window, he saw the same houses they'd walked past earlier and realized they were headed back toward Rita's. He pounded his foot on the brake and dropped his forehead to the wheel. *What now? Where now?*

Staring at the horn, he gasped for breath. He fought back his anger. No matter what they did they were screwed, everyone was against them, death-spikes were hidden in bushes, land mines were buried under stocking feet. Their options were gone. Eyes were everywhere, evil eyes, nothing was normal, nothing made sense anymore. He was the proverbial goldfish swimming in a blender, darting about the small aquarium, but the moment someone touched the button the metal knives would swirl and cut him to shreds. It was all over. He knew it and they knew it. Whoever *they* were.

He might as well just sit here in this alley and wait for the bad guys to come and get him, because every damn thing he did backfired, ever since Eleanor had come back into his life, *no*, it had been ever since he'd almost killed that woman, made her suffer, that young pretty woman, just because he wouldn't listen to her. Just because he wanted to make money and be a big shot. Because he was greedy and wanted the next patient and the next and the next and wasn't listening to the one under his knife and he'd really killed his own career. Killed his own damned career. He banged his fists on the wheel. He gripped it and squeezed, wanting to crush it.

Then, a hesitant touch on his hand. Soft fingers closed around his, ungluing his death grip. Elly guided his hand to her cheek and he cupped it, warm and soft. Simple sensations. "Shh," she said. A simple word. She stroked the back of his hand, the hand that rested against her cheek. "It's okay. Shh, it's okay."

His head was going to burst.

She turned toward him. Now his other hand was around her waist. His hand rubbed her skin through the sweat suit, round and round, in circles, over her swollen belly. He couldn't help it. He looked at her face, into her eyes. And her eyes, they were full of something beautiful, yes, there was love there, and an offering of strength and...hope.

No. He didn't want to see that. He closed his eyes. If he accepted the hope she offered him then he'd have to go on. He'd have to keep trying.

Leaning over, she gathered him into her arms. Her breasts, so large, so soft. Too soft. They pressed against his bare chest and again it felt right. Normal. Her hand rubbed his neck under his hairline. She murmured. She kissed his cheek.

He wrapped his arms around her so tight he pulled her right off the seat into his lap. His tears flowed over her hair, all over her, and he didn't care. His heart swelled, everything was purging from his mind now and he shuddered and held her.

The motor purred beneath them, and he held her. His life poured out of his eyes, and he held her. *Damn it, if she isn't just what I want.* Just something normal. Something simple. Something real.

She was humanity and life and love. That was all he needed to go on.

During the time they held each other there in the alley, they could have been in space, traveling to a distant land at light speed. He felt that when they were through embracing, generations would have come and gone on Earth, and the forces they were up against would have already turned to dust. Certainly then, no one would remember Donna, Rita, Eleanor or Jeff. The only thing left of them would be the record of their unpaid bills, and perhaps a mention of their unexplained disappearance.

Funny. In actuality, no one would miss them. The only person who cared enough about him to even report if he'd been kidnapped by aliens was in his arms right now, and the same was true for Elly. It was reason enough to go on. He wanted, someday, a wife, a daughter, a grandson. People who loved him.

It had been so long since he'd admitted this to himself that it left him breathless. His life *did* matter and he hoped it wasn't too late to save it.

He stroked her hair, kissed the top of her head. "Eleanor. I don't understand how you know these things, but I don't care anymore. I just want to get us somewhere safe. Where? Where can we go?"

She leaned back and looked up into his eyes. The vulnerability he saw there made him even more determined that they would survive. "Bixler's house," she said in a whisper. "He's out of town— remember what the letter said? Let's go there."

Jeff nodded and without another word, they strapped themselves in and drove to the heights, to the home of Michael Bixler, President of the University.

22

Bruce's feet trembled when he walked. He could barely place one in front of the other. His tailbone ached where he'd bruised it in the cave. A band of fear tightened around his chest and he had to fight for every breath. He had never been this scared.

What he used to think of as genius in Caesar Bossidy was actually madness. The man was a raving lunatic. Finally, Bruce understood his own fate, and could grasp the importance of what he was about to do. It was his job, his duty, to get out of here and report Caesar to the police, the FBI, the government—anyone who would listen. Caesar needed to be put away, and someone had to bomb this mountain out of existence, and quick, before the damned Cybers got any bigger or smarter. Before they headed out into society to do to other people what they'd done to Stark.

Bruce had to get the hell out of here, but first he needed some protection, and some income. Some evidence. So far he'd been lucky. He'd managed to get back to his quarters and pack just the essentials he wanted to take with him. Unless one of the men had already reported back to Caesar, the boss wouldn't even know they'd emerged from the caverns yet, and he'd have time to catch a van to town before he was even missed.

He was running, but he wasn't a coward. He was a soldier of righteousness. A world savior. Certainly, he'd been born to save the world, so escape would be no problem. He could see the road to greatness paved in front of him clearly now, and there were no obstacles.

A deep breath eased the tension in his chest. There was no reason to be afraid. All the forces of right were on his side, so he would win. Escape. Prove Caesar a madman, and become famous to boot. A real damned hero.

He could see it. *60 Minutes, Oprah,* lecture tours at universities. He would be the greatest authority on the genetic engineering procedures Caesar had pioneered, but he'd also have a great story to tell the world. *Damn,* he could probably write a best selling novel, *The Mountain of the Demons,* and make millions. Then the government would hire him on a top secret project to create Cybers for them, and he would become an honorary general or something, working for the people who ranked the highest in the country and therefore in the world. He would become one of the most powerful men alive.

All he had to do now was just get the evidence and sneak off the property. The tape cabinet in Caesar's office contained the entire computer record of everything that had occurred in the facility since the beginning: the design and layout of the nanochip and the palm controller, the scientific process of transgenic implantation, all the proof of what was happening here. With that, he could go to the police with clear-cut evidence, and his new life would begin.

Caesar stormed out of his office with two men in tow, almost trampling Bruce. Reflexively, he stepped back and pressed his body against the wall. *Damn.* He'd been daydreaming instead of sneaking around, like he was supposed to be doing. His pulse pounded in his head. He could have been caught, right then! After a few moments to rebuild his courage, he ducked into Caesar's office through the open door.

He took keys out of Caesar's desk drawer and unlocked the tape cabinet. Tossing his duffel bag on the floor, he looked through the hanging row of marked computer tapes until he found the latest complete backup of the computer system. This would have everything on it. He threw it into his bag and noticed VHS tapes stacked on the floor. The video tapes! That would do it. Not everyone could understand custom semiconductor layout schematics, but anyone could watch a film of Felipe Jojola being eaten by a Cyber and understand the danger of what Caesar had created. He smiled, filled with confidence, his fear fading. Why hadn't he thought of this before? He shouldn't have stayed here so long, enduring Caesar's holier-than-thou crap. If he had thought of this years ago, he'd be famous by now.

Zipping shut his bag, he started for the door then changed his mind. Caesar may have something else in his desk, something worth taking: personal records or a diary, something he could use to further his case or enrich his story. He began searching through the drawers, power surging through him.

"Bruce."

His head jerked up at the sound of his name. Caesar stood in the doorway. Bruce had been so busy he hadn't heard Caesar come in, so full of thoughts of his fame, he'd forgotten that he was still trying to hurry, to get away. Anxiety gripped his chest like a vise. Sliding the drawer closed, he breathed out his last bit of confidence and inhaled pure fear.

Caesar slammed the door shut behind him. *Damn,* the man looked angry.

Bruce attempted a grin. He must control his fear. Caesar would be able to smell it. Besides, he could still get away with this. Caesar couldn't possibly know his traitorous intentions. "Looking for your schedule," Bruce said, unnerved to hear a shake in his voice. "I've been trying to find you, to give you a report on the trip into the caverns."

Caesar hesitated. "Glad to see you," he said. Bruce allowed his tight knot of apprehension to unwind a little. Caesar had no reason to suspect him, after all.

Caesar remained in the doorway, his body stiff. "So what happened in the caverns, and where have you been since the men returned?"

"We just got back," Bruce lied. He glanced at his bag, wondering if Caesar could see it. "Like I said, I've been looking for you."

Caesar slunk further into the room and closed the shutters on the only window to his office. "Is that so?"

"Yeah," Bruce said, watching Caesar warily. He should have left when he still had a chance. His eyes darted around the office, searching for a way to escape.

Caesar turned and faced him. "I think not. I think you've been hiding. I think you're spooked, Bruce, and are planning to run."

Bruce managed a sheepish grin, though his blood roared through his ears. "Come on. That's ridiculous."

Caesar's voice droned on like a mechanical robot. "I think your bag is full of secret company records. You're trying to steal them, and use the information to destroy me. Destroy TransGenesis. You're running scared, Bruce."

The way Caesar spoke his name, with a hiss on the end—Brucccccce—unnerved him. The guy sounded like a snake. "Hey, I admit the scene in the caverns scared me, a little. Would have done that to anyone. But I'd never cut out on you. Who's Caesar's number one man?" Bruce asked, trying to sound lighthearted.

"Brutussss," Caesar answered. Hissing. Still hissing.

The blood rushed from his head. He leaned against the desk. "So, I'm spooked," he started. "You should be, too. You should put a stop to this whole thing. Those monsters ate Stark, right before my eyes." His voice shivered, his hands trembled. Pain pulsed through his tailbone. He had to work himself toward the door. Make a run for it. *Forget the damn bag.* "I'm not going to be next, damn it." He eased out from behind the desk.

Caesar spoke in a monotone. "This research is the most powerful, important thing to happen to genetics and engineering in the history of mankind. I can't stop it because some of you have made a few mistakes."

His eyes clouded with his madness, like the inner eyelids of an alligator. Why had Bruce never seen it before? He swallowed down his terror. *Two more steps toward the door.* "You call murder, multiple murders, mistakes?"

"The deaths of the innocent are just further proof of the great flaws in the human race. The deaths were unnecessary, but if a few people must die for the sake of the rest, it's worth it."

"What gives you the right to decide who lives and who dies? Who the hell do you think you are, God?"

"No. Not God, Bruce. But soon the most powerful man who ever lived."

Finally. Between Caesar and the door. With his back to the door, he inched toward it. "You're insane," he spat at Caesar, sure now he'd make it out.

"Throughout the ages, all great men have been called insane by those who cannot comprehend their greatness," Caesar said quietly. Einstein said, 'Great spirits have always encountered violent opposition from mediocre minds.' That's you, Bruce, a mediocre mind."

Caesar kept saying his name. *Bruce, Bruce, Bruce.* And he was too calm.

"Don't you see, Bruce?" Hissing. "I am helping evolution along by providing stronger, healthier, smarter beings than it ever had to choose from before. From now on, no one will have to worry whether their babies will be smart, or healthy. I'll have freed everyone from that concern."

Just feet from the door.

"No more nine months of wondering," Caesar continued, as in a trance. "A woman need carry her baby for only two months, three months at the most. Just think! And then, nothing wrong with it. In fact, the child will be perfect, will grow to maturity in a matter of months. No more terrible twos, or horrifying teenage years. Parents will finally be able to control their children, with their own palm computer. They'll be able to control everything they know, everything they do. We'll be able to get rid of all the years of schooling, all the jails."

A couple of steps backward. *Almost there.*

"We can make people designed to play basketball, to be engineers, to be soldiers. Soldiers without fear, without pain. Whole armies that can be controlled with one handheld device. Brains that are designed to be denser than Einstein's. Packed with neurons. They'll be able to improve their own design, and the concepts they'll come up with! A whole race of people with genius like mine, changing the world."

Now! Bruce bolted for the door.

"Stop," Caesar ordered to his back. "Turn around."

Bruce heard a click, and his heart pounded like gunshots booming through his chest. A warm trickle traveled down his leg. Turning slowly, he saw the barrel of a small pistol. He swallowed. Cleared his throat. "We aren't allowed to carry weapons here." After he said it, he realized how stupid it sounded.

"No, you aren't. But because of the overwhelming incompetence of the human race and the head of security specifically, I was able to sneak this in. Too bad, Bruce. If my Cybers were guarding this place, you wouldn't be staring down this barrel right now. With a chip in your brain, you would never have been born the sniveling little weakling you are today. You're living proof that what I'm doing is right."

Bruce raised his hands. "I give up. I'm sorry. You're right."

Caesar didn't seem to see or hear him any longer. He was off in his own world, talking to some unseen person. "No more backwards religions that preach things like the legend of Wahatoya, or spirits that guide you. Everyone will be smart, as smart as me. Imagine what the world would be like. Ten million Caesar Bossidys. They're all my children, you know, all of them." A serpentine smile stretched his mouth, but his eyes stayed cold, misted, far away.

"Please, Caesar," Bruce begged, trying to get Caesar to look into his eyes, to see that it was just him, Bruce. "I'm sorry. You're right."

Caesar focused on Bruce briefly, then back into the void once again. "Good," he said. "Then you understand what I'm about to do."

"No," Bruce said, pleading. "I'll leave. I won't say anything, I promise."

"You're not necessary any more. People like you will be trampled by the Cybers I will create."

"No," Bruce begged. "You don't know what you're doing."

"It doesn't matter if you live or die." Caesar pointed the gun at Bruce's heart.

"No!" Bruce felt a fist punch through him, another one. He fell to the ground. But the blackness didn't come. Just overwhelming pain. Caesar had missed his heart. *Had he? Yes.* He was still alive. Dying, but still alive. He must not let Caesar know. *Play dead.*

Caesar grabbed his ankles and dragged him to the back of the office. It took every ounce of Bruce's remaining control not to cry out. He heard a clicking sound and the whirring of a motor. Air rushed into the office from the back. A stuffy odor invaded his nostrils. *A secret door into the caverns?* He was dragged further, and soon felt cool dirt under his head. His legs were dropped to the ground, sending pain shooting through his back.

"See how long it takes the Cybers to discover their new food source," Caesar said, and laughed.

Bruce heard the panel begin to slide shut. With all the strength he had left, he shoved the tip of his shoe in the door, wedging it open a tiny crack.

He stared into the cavern and groaned.

So dark and empty.

But he knew they were out there. In the shadows. Waiting.

23

As the truck labored uphill, the houses became mansions, dwarfed by park-size yards and brick walls. Sun glanced off autumn leaves and piñon trees lining the properties. Green landscapes invited bare feet and checkered table cloths, dogs and Frisbees, lemonade.

But Jeff didn't feel comfortable. The neighborhood was preternaturally empty, as if the residents had built an ideal environment and then all simultaneously died in their beds. If the brown van brigade or a crooked cop decided to chop him into a million pieces, only an occasional cat and a nestful of sparrows would notice.

He drove at a snail's pace, wanting to hurry but wanting to avoid the police more. He scanned the area continually, expecting trouble but finding only suburban bliss. He didn't know which was worse.

Eleanor directed Jeff to the top of a steep hill where Bixler's house rose up out of the summit like a giant stretching from slumber. A brick wall encircled the property, stretching off in both directions.

Jeff pulled up to the Jurassic Park-like entrance and stared down the long driveway on the other side. "Now what?"

In answer, Eleanor climbed from the truck. His big shoes flopping on her feet, she limped toward a black box next to the gate. The metal cover squealed when she opened it.

A blackbird dropped from the sky and strutted near her on the wall. The sight of it tightened his gut and he realized lack of sleep was affecting his thinking. In his state of mind, even a bird could be a bad guy. But was that really so strange, considering today's events? It stepped toward Eleanor and squawked. Jeff tensed. But humming and clicking startled the blackbird and the gate slid back with a whir of electronic music. Eleanor climbed back into the truck.

"How did you do that?" Jeff asked.

"Most systems have a backup to open them, in case the owner forgets the remote control or wants a family member to take care of the house or something."

"A backup?"

"Just a code that you type in to open the gate."

"Yeah...but how did you know the code?"

She smiled, satisfaction on her face. "We lucked out. This system comes with a pre-programmed code. The owner should change it after it's installed, but most don't. Bixler hadn't, anyway. Idiot. Hard to believe he's president of anything, isn't it?"

Jeff put the truck in gear and headed up the driveway, vowing to never let Eleanor get a burr under her skin about him. She could be dangerous. She was a Microsoft maven and a mechanical Merlin.

The gate closed automatically behind the truck. "I hope no one is taking care of the house for Bixler. I don't feel like entertaining. Or killing any yuppies."

"I wouldn't mind torturing Bixler himself for awhile. I'd find that quite entertaining. As long as afterward I get a good meal and some rest."

The weariness in her voice made Jeff glance over at her. Although she'd handled the events at Rita's calmly, weariness and pain were now molding her features. Her cheeks were hollow and gray, the lines around her eyes like dry creek-beds.

Shit. She really looked bad. Thank God they had a place to flop for a while. Eleanor needed food and rest. And she needed medical attention, a lot more than he could give her with his little black bag. The urge to strap her down and head to the nearest emergency room hit him. *Why not?* They'd both be arrested, for sure. But that was

167

better than dying. Chavez would throw them in jail, but at least they'd have food and water and a roof over their heads.

But then what? Chances were Eleanor would be dead before the legal system and the slow-to-take-responsibility medical professionals would figure out half of what Jeff already knew. And of course, no one would listen to ex-doctor Jeffrey Clinton.

By then, Eleanor could be dead. At the rate the fetus seemed to be growing, if she didn't stay on a high-calorie vitamin-rich diet, she would begin to sacrifice pieces of her body to the child's development. And she did seem to be wasting away.

His stomach rumbled at the thought of food. He was hungry, too. And tired beyond anything he'd ever known, even in his sleep-poor residency days. But his tiredness didn't even matter now—not until Eleanor was free of the pregnancy.

He pulled up the long circular driveway in front of the house and paused. "Do you think we should leave the truck in back, so no one sees it? We don't want to draw any attention our way."

"No. I'd rather have it here for a quick getaway. Leave the keys in it." She opened her door then turned back. "Besides, who's going to report it stolen?" She climbed from the truck, walked to the front door and surprised him by knocking. After a few moments she rang the bell. Jeff kept the truck in gear, ready to peel out. His heart raced. What would she do if someone answered? He could just hear the five-o'clock news. *Outlaw professors strangle butler. More at ten.* But no one opened the door. Apparently, the house was empty.

Relief washed over him, his bone-aching, muscle-straining weariness increasing with every pain-filled breath. He was not designed for this sort of adventure.

"Now we just have to get in," she yelled back to the truck.

"Want me to bring my bag?"

"Sure."

He retrieved his medical bag from the car and handed it to her. "You do your high-tech criminal thing. I'm gonna keep an eye out front."

He stood tensely by one of the stone statues that guarded the front porch. The street was still quiet beyond the gate. He readied himself to hear an alarm go off behind him at any moment, but prayed she would get in silently. If anything went wrong, he'd stuff her in the truck and blow the gate. He bounced on his toes, ready to run.

"Come on in," she called. He turned to see her disappear inside. The door stood open.

He wasn't surprised, but grateful beyond words. They were good together, damn good. Although right now he was hard-pressed to remember what it was he brought to the partnership.

As he approached the doorway, Elly was already poking at buttons on a small keyboard attached to the wall, the burglar alarm controls. Jeff entered the cool interior slowly, taking his time to look around.

The house reminded him of his mansion back east, and the abundance of self-indulgence he'd enjoyed there. He instantly disliked this Bixler guy, whom he'd never given a damn about before, just seen from afar, at graduation speeches and cocktail parties. This man reminded him of the old Jeff, the man he no longer wanted to be, or cared to remember. The luxury here, the black marble entryway and dancing diamonds on the walls reflected from the chandeliers, the deep carpets and wet bars. All of it spoke of a man who cared about things that Jeff had once treasured, and lost.

Eleanor peered around, an angry grimace on her face. "Nice house," she said, sarcastically.

"Yeah, if you like museums. I just hope his kitchen is well stocked. Race you to the pantry."

They found enough frozen and canned deli food to satisfy a hundred ravenous New Yorkers and sank their teeth into roast beef on rye, salt and vinegar potato chips, and pickles. They chased the whole business with dark beer and ice cream. Sated, they went to the guest bathroom, the size of an average bedroom, where he cleaned and wrapped her feet. Except for the new injury, they looked better. The angry red streaks had faded to pale angry red streaks. The bite wound looked nasty, though. He paid special attention to disinfecting it, and wrapped it carefully.

Eleanor stood, trying out the new bandages, wincing. "My revenge will have to wait a few hours. I'm going to find the biggest, deepest, softest bed in this house, strip off these clothes and sleep until I can sleep no more. Sorry, you'll have to either fight me for it or take second best." She kissed him on the cheek and talked quietly. Her breath tickled his ear. "Boy Scout, take my advice and do the same. I don't know if you've looked in the mirror lately, but you don't look so good." She smiled, said, "Night," and hobbled toward the stairs.

Jeff began clearing the table and stopped, staring at the plate in his hand with amazement. They were playing Goldilocks, here to eat the porridge and break the chairs, not wash the bowls. Why was he clearing Bixler's table?

He set the dishes in the sink. Steaming water rushed over his knuckles and the heat seeped in, soothing him. The sound of the splashing water, the clink of the dishes and the hiss of foaming bubbles, all like music, made him realize why he was playing busboy. It was normal. Doing dishes. A normal thing. For a few moments, at least, he wasn't fighting the pain of a bullet wound, running from monsters, or watching Eleanor waste away before his eyes. He was cleaning the kitchen. He decided to hum a country-western song while he worked, just to make the picture complete.

Afterward, he looked in on Eleanor, who'd taken refuge in the master bedroom. Goldilocks in Papa's bed, a little girl lost beneath an oversized comforter and sheets. Although he longed to join her, he had a job to do first.

Throwing open the door of the massive walk-in closet, he dug through the dress shirts, jackets, and ties. He found a pair of jeans, a soft cashmere sweater and a pair of running shoes that would fit Eleanor if she tied them tightly. Then he dug through the drawers and came up with cotton underwear and socks. He folded the booty together on the floor by Eleanor's side of the bed and returned to find something clean for himself.

Next, he headed off to look through the files one more time. Maybe he'd find something, anything, he hadn't seen before. If he could just glean some new information—anything that could lead them to an answer, or some help.

Grabbing his bag from the bathroom where they'd wrapped her wounds, he realized that they were sorely low on bandages. No problem. He went through Bixler's medicine cabinets and replaced much of his depleted stores. *Now they really were criminals,* he thought, as he fought off a vague sense of guilt. They'd broken in, eaten deli food, and stolen bandages.

With the bag in hand, he looked through the rooms downstairs until he found a place where he could sit comfortably and go over the files. Bixler's office. Floor to ceiling windows looked out over the back lot, where a cedar deck ringed a sparkling pool. Inside, the spacious office had a conference table and a huge saltwater aquarium, where brightly colored fish darted from end to end. They were caught in a world they didn't understand, a place that looked like reality, but was just a clever fake. Someone had created the world the fish moved through, and sadly, no matter how hard they swam, no matter how long they searched, the living ocean would always be beyond their reach. They were infinitely vulnerable, and completely unaware of that crucial fact. The master needed only to reach inside and crush them at will.

Although he saw the weekend feeders dissolving and sending up a steady stream of bubbles, he unscrewed the bottle of fish food that sat by the tank, opened the hood and sprinkled some flakes across the top of the water. *Better to die of too much than too little.*

Strung across one wall was an extensive desk, complete with computer and speakers, flatbed scanner and two printers—one color laser and one black and white. A center nook enclosed baskets, files, and a well-lighted study area. He fell into a deeply padded black leather chair that began vibrating.

He sat for a moment, irony overwhelming him. While he and Eleanor fought for their lives, this man sat in a vibrating leather chair making decisions that affected their lives. *Well.* Now he had taken the throne, massager and all.

Jeff assured himself he was not envious of Bixler's lifestyle. He'd been here before and knew the tragic truth—high position meant high responsibility, and few men were equipped with the moral values required. Too many people thought those they were responsible for were fish in an aquarium, not individuals equally important as themselves. The one sure way for a man to bring himself down quickly was to see himself as superior to the rest of the world. That would buy him a ticket on the express train to Fool's Hill.

Jeff sat for a moment and let the chair's hum soothe his tired muscles and sore arm. He laid back his head and relaxed, sinking into the chair. The house was silent and locked tight. For the moment, they were safe. From outside threats, anyway. But Eleanor couldn't lock out what threatened her.

He spun the chair around and eyed the plasma TV. He was tempted to turn on the news to see if he and Elly had become celebrities. But the leather chair would hold him too well, and the drone of the voices would probably launch him into dreamland in moments. Besides, he knew their situation better than any anchor did, and he needed to resolve it calmly, not watch something that might spook him and make him want to sit in the corner with a bag over his head.

With that thought, he lifted the files from his bag and began going over them. They described three women—all being treated at the university clinic. All young. One nursing student, one freshman with an undeclared major, and an engineering professor. How did Meaks pick them? What did they have in common?

He picked up a shiny, silver pen and listed what he knew on the front of the file. The pen was heavy and cold in his hand.

1) Three women implanted by Dr. Meaks without their knowledge. (Why? Who hired him?)
2) Dr. Meaks killed by whoever hired him to do it. (Brown van brigade— BVB. Why? Because Meaks called Eleanor to warn her?)
3) BVB tries to kidnap Eleanor and someone does kidnap Donna. (Why? To keep them quiet?)
4) Rita is killed. (By BVB? By animal?)
5) Strange animal bites Eleanor. (Monkey-child, she called it. What is it?

Where did it come from? Did it kill Rita and her lover?)
6) Chavez is involved. (Why? What possible interest could the police have in the gynecological histories of women?)
7) What do Rita, Eleanor, and Donna have in common? (Pregnancy?)

Jeff stared at the facts until his eyes blurred and stung. He sighed, tossed the files on the desk and rubbed his eyes. There were too many questions and too few answers. Without being able to interview Meaks, Donna or Rita, it seemed they were at a dead end.

It was time to pack up and join Elly in bed. His hand hesitated over a letter setting in the in-basket. The letterhead had a stylized *TG* in the top corner. His heart seized in his chest. It was the same symbol he'd seen on the PDA Chavez had been holding. Excitedly, he grabbed Eleanor's file back off the desk and ripped it open. *There.* The *TG* was in the file as well.

Snatching up the letter, he read it. He stood, his head swimming. No wonder Eleanor had not been promoted. From what he'd just seen in this letter, she'd never had a chance.

At least now he had a new lead to follow. He added one last entry to his list before stuffing it in his pocket:

8) TG

The letter was lighting the path to discovery. But what would he find at the end of the trail?

24

"I know absolutely nothing about this! I never accepted or even applied for a position with this TransGenesis company." Eleanor sat on the edge of the bed, sleep still thick in her eyes. She'd pulled on one of Bixler's white T-shirts and a pair of boxer shorts, not yet ready to dress. Jeff had brought her a cup of cocoa and the letter.

"This letter is from you," Jeff argued gently. "See your signature on the bottom? *Eleanor Vanguard.* Right there." Jeff pointed out the authentic-looking signature.

"I admit, the signature looks like mine, but it's a forgery. I've never even heard of this Caesar Bossidy."

He watched her outrage, concerned. He hadn't told her, but since finding the resignation letter on the desk, he never doubted it was a fake. No one knew Eleanor's dream better than he did, and he knew that she would never move from a university position to one in the corporate world, not unless she could work part time as a consultant and continue her research and teaching. She loved the campus environment.

The forged letter was addressed to Michael Bixler, and not only withdrew Eleanor from the running for the Dean of Engineering position, but announced that she was leaving the university altogether to take a job with a company called TransGenesis, working as an engineer under Caesar Bossidy.

"Besides," she continued, "I'd never work for someone named Caesar." She looked up at him pleadingly. "Look, anyone can fake a signature these days. All you need is a scanner and a printer. You scan in the real signature, print it out on the bottom of the letter in light gray so it's almost invisible, then trace over it and voilà. The real thing."

He fell to a seat beside her. "I believe you. I know how much you wanted that stupid Dean's job. But how do you explain this?"

"I don't know." She shook her matted head and sipped on the cocoa. "Someone wanted to take me out of the running."

"Out of the university, you mean. Maybe out of this town altogether. This not only takes you out of the running for Dean, it resigns your position at the university. I don't understand how the president could get this letter, apparently from you, and not say anything to you. You're sure? No one said anything?"

"Well, Bixler did talk to me a few times, and I had a meeting scheduled with him when he came back from vacation next week. He said things like, 'We need to talk about finding the proper replacement for you.' That's why I assumed I had the Dean's job. I thought he was hinting that I was getting promoted. Some other folks congratulated me on my decision to take up a new challenge. I thought they were talking about Dean, as well." She tapped her forehead with the heel of her hand. "How could I have been so stupid?"

"You weren't stupid," Jeff said, taking the letter out of her hands. "You just got mixed up. Believe me, I know how that works. You think you've gone over everything with someone, talked through every detail. But all you've done is hear what you want to hear, and say what will get you what you want the easiest and quickest. You avoid mention of anything the other person might find irritating or anything they might argue about."

Eleanor searched his eyes. "You're not talking about me now, are you? You're talking about that woman. The one who almost died because of your mistake."

"Yeah. That's who I think about—all the time." He rubbed his temple with all four fingers. "She told me over and over that she was in pain, but I didn't listen. I don't think I wanted to hear anything that might...I thought she was just whining, complaining. If I'd put any stock in what she said, I would have had to admit I made a mistake, so I just didn't hear her. I didn't listen to what she was saying. It took another doctor to hear her, and save her life."

They sat silently for a moment. Eleanor sipped her cocoa and stared at the letter. "So you're saying that I didn't listen to Bixler, didn't listen to what people around me were telling me. That everyone was telling me there was something awry, but I didn't want to hear it. All I wanted to hear was that I was being promoted, that I was finally getting the job I'd come here to get."

"Yup. That's sounds like you, all right."

Her eyes found his. "Then you're full of shit."

He stiffened. "What?"

She leaped to her feet. Cocoa splashed the mattress. The spreading stains had an ominous resemblance to the blood that had colored the sheets at Rita's house.

The roast beef in his stomach churned.

"Bixler purposely kept this from me, the conniving bastard. Don't try to tell me he knew I was leaving and couldn't say something clear and obvious like, 'Why have you decided to leave?' I was listening, damn it." She threw out her arms, cup in hand, and the cocoa splashed from the cup in an arc. "I can hear the difference between, 'Sorry you're leaving,' and, 'Gosh, you've been promoted.'"

"Okay, okay. Fine. Whatever you say." He held up his hand. "Bixler was in on it. Just calm down." His heart raced, his nervous tension back in full bloom.

"You bet your ass Bixler was in on it. And this is our lead, right here." She shook the letter. "This is what's going to get us one step closer to the answers we need."

"I agree."

"Good. Then let's go find him. I've got a few well placed words for that ape. And maybe a knee." She started for the door.

He grabbed her elbow and turned her around. Her eyes were blazing, her face red. "Eleanor, I've got the strange and irrational feeling you're talking about Bixler."

"Who else have we been talking about?"

He tore the paper from her hands and jabbed his finger at the letterhead. "TransGenesis. Caesar Bossidy. That's our clue, our next step. These are the people behind the whole deal. That's where we need to go. Right now your life is more important than your career! Besides, even if you could figure out where Bixler is vacationing, what would you say to him? 'I broke into your home with a wanted murderer and found this letter on your desk?'"

They remained silent, staring at each other, each standing their ground. Jeff's breath came quickly and his heart pounded in his ears. The wind whistled through the windows like the sound of an ancient flute.

As he watched, Eleanor's eyes unfocused. Her gaze turned inward. Her eyes widened. Her lips parted, emitting a soft groan. Was she going to cry? He should know better than to fight with her over this issue. He'd tried before and failed. With Eleanor, her career was her life. He watched in horror as her fingers loosened and the mug tumbled to the carpet.

He stared at the cup lying motionless on the floor as if it had suddenly and tragically plunged to its death. His gaze flicked back to blank eyes. "Elly?" He grabbed her shoulders. Fear bubbled from his gut into his throat. "What's wrong?"

The silence of the house, the music of the wind.

She slapped her hand to her abdomen. In slow motion, her mouth opened wide. A low moan crawled from her throat like an escaping animal. Her knees buckled.

She tumbled over.

25

"No!" Jeff caught Eleanor in his arms and dragged her to the bed. He eased her down onto the mattress, cursing at the fiery pain and weakness in his arm.

She groaned and folded into the fetal position. Clutched her abdomen. "It's moving," she yelled.

Panic gripped him like a crushing fist. "Oh, shit. Oh, shit. My bag." Down the steps, into the office. *Where the hell is the damn thing— there!* He jerked the bag off the floor and fumbled through it until he found a syringe. Quickly, hands shaking like a first year resident's, he filled the syringe with a double dose of a tranquilizing pain killer. He pounded back up the steps. Without preface, he jabbed the needle through Elly's boxer shorts and emptied the contents into her buttocks.

He laid down next to her and held her with all his might. He tried to hide his fear as he spoke. "It's okay." His voice cracked. He cleared his throat, trying to remember the clinical clichés that had helped him through his medical practice. "I've given you something that'll help. Take deep breaths. Relax. You're hyperventilating." Listening to himself, he decided that he might as well throw the doc-speak out the window. He'd never been good at it. "Take deep breaths." He demonstrated for her, placed her hand on his chest so she could feel the cadence. "Come on. You can do it." He continued on and on, talking her through it like a Lamaze partner, except he didn't want this child born, not until he could protect Eleanor. Her thrashing diminished, then stopped. But the child still moved within her.

Impossible. It was too big, damn it. Too big and too strong. Too developed. Too...everything.

He slid his hand up over her heart. It beat, thank God. Too fast, but solid. Strong. It beat against her rib cage like it was trying to get out, struggling to give him an urgent message.

The wind circled around the house like a phantom, whistling its eerie song. Jeff folded around her, drew her closer. Unable to protect her from what was within, all he could do was hold her. And pray.

Finally, the child rested. Eleanor's heart bumped along at a normal pace, her breath came easy and even. She slept.

He unwrapped himself and stood, staring at her for any bad signs, still unable to stop the trembling that shook him from the bones out. Something was terribly wrong here. This wasn't just a pregnancy, wasn't normal in any way. Jeff had just gotten a glimpse of the real reason Meaks had called.

He gasped for breath. *Stop shaking.* This was not the time for fear. It was the time for clear thinking, for action. But good action this time. Positive action.

What the hell had he been thinking, waking her and showing her that letter? How did he think she'd feel, anyway? He knew it would upset her, and yet there had been something within him that had to show her immediately. He hadn't even waited for her to wake by herself.

Had it been his fear, his sense of loneliness that had compelled him to share his discovery with her immediately? Had he wanted to upset her, wanted to see her fail, just as he had failed? Had he wanted, just for a moment, to see Miss Perfect find out what it felt like to have her life stripped away from her? Like his had been, like she never tired of reminding him.

Well, he'd seen it. He'd had front row seats for the defeat of Professor Eleanor Vanguard. He'd thrown her to the wolves and witnessed her fight for survival. It had given him no pleasure. His own fall from grace was nothing compared to the agony of watching her crumble.

A tight band inside of him snapped and he was able to stand a little taller. He'd been such a wimp for so long. Hiding in his office where he'd thought he was safe, never knowing his closet had a door to danger. Courting Eleanor but hating her at the same time, her anal ways. Resenting that she had a goal, that she wanted something enough to pursue it.

In reality, he hated himself, his fear, his apathy. His…cowardice. *No more.*

Before he smashed something in frustration and awakened her again, he left the room. Retrieving his bag and address book, he called David at the UNM Medical Center and reserved a private ultrasound room for them during the night, during light patient traffic in the labs. Tonight, after they slept, he was going to find out what grew inside of Eleanor and what was going wrong.

Now that he'd faced his inner fears, it was time to reveal hers.

26

Jeff's heart banged against his rib cage when the alarm began screeching. He rolled over and pounded his palm on the clock, but the sound had already stopped. Two o'clock in the morning, a half hour before he'd planned to get up. He stared at the clock face with bleary eyes and got to his feet, his heart speeding up as he realized it hadn't been the alarm that had awakened him. Irrational childhood fear stabbed his chest. As a child, he'd often woke up in his twin size bed, hearing his mother's cries, knowing his drunkard father had returned home, ready for trouble.

He stood motionless, listening. Far-off thunder cracked and rolled. A few raindrops ticked at the windows. That must be what had brought him back to consciousness—the thunder. Relieved, he sighed.

He glanced at Eleanor. She was still deep in sleep, nothing moving but her chest as it rose and fell. A chill slithered through the room and he shivered. He felt trapped between the need to return to her cozy embrace and the nagging masculine responsibility to check the house. Remembering his resolve to no longer be a coward, he pulled on his new clothes and tiptoed from the room.

It had been a scream. The memory halted his steps. He was suddenly sure the sound that awakened him had been a scream. He slowed his descent down the stairway, more cautious now. The thick carpet wrapped around his feet, cushioning his footfalls. He crossed to the entryway. The tiles were cold beneath his feet. Pausing by the front door, he listened. Outside, something puled. Then a cry, like the call of a suffering child. His scalp tingled and fear trickled down his neck.

His hand on the knob, he peered through the peephole. Thunder crashed outside, closer now. Claws of raindrops and leaves scratched at the windows. A sudden flash of lightning made him squint. Then just the porch light's dim glow, showing shadows of dancing tree limbs, but no visitor, no one near the porch.

The doorknob was brass, ornate, shaped like a dead man's fist. The fingers of his left hand rested on the bolt lock above the knob. His heart pounded in his ears. Taking a deep breath, he turned the bolt counterclockwise, unlocking it. His right hand still gripped the knob. He turned it with aching slowness. Listened. The hinges squealed as the door rolled open. He looked.

Stepping up to the glass of the storm door, he shaded his eyes. Peered into the yard.

Another flash. He noticed movement on the other side of the glass, near his knees. He yelped and jumped back from the door. Something small darted into the storm and disappeared. A dark shape laid on the porch, fur pressed against the glass. He stared at it, his hands shaking like the storm-blown leaves, his knees weak. His mind tried to comprehend what he was looking at. A dog, maybe, or a cat.

Rain gusted against the glass. He hesitated. This house was safe. And dry. But he couldn't hide here forever. Elly was upstairs, trusting in him, her clock ticking. If he didn't investigate every lead, if he didn't swallow his fear, and… *Oh, to hell with it.*

He unlocked the storm door and pushed on it. The animal was dead weight. Placing his shoulder against the door, he slid the fur-covered creature away and stepped into the night. The door snapped shut behind him.

The scent of ozone and pine hung in the air, and other more earthy smells—wet animals, feces. Raindrops ran over his scalp like bugs in his hair. Cold rain pelted his shoulders. He shivered and bent to examine the animal. His hands found the head. A cat. It wore a collar, with a name tag and address. Probably Bixler's cat.

The rain continued to beat the poor thing like the hammer of an unrelenting killer. His hands roamed down to the front legs, the belly. Something warm flowed through his fingers. His gritted his teeth, tasting bile in his throat. The cat was open from rib cage to groin, its chewed body contents steaming in the rain.

He stood, his hands stained with red. Terror rushed through his veins like ice water as he stared at his hands. Something had run from the porch while he was looking out. Something small and lithe.

Something had killed this cat, intending to eat it.

Something had killed Rita and bitten Eleanor.

Elly.

He raced up the steps and burst into the bedroom. "Elly!" She bolted upright. Her sleepy eyes focused on him and widened as they noticed his bloody hands and his fear. She leaped from the bed.

"We've got to get out of here." His voice sounded desperate. He *was* desperate. "The cat's dead."

Mercifully, she obeyed. Without comment or sharp retort. No questions, just instinctive trust. They pulled on clothes and Jeff grabbed his bag. Together, they ran down the stairs. She paused and looked at the cat. "Let's go."

Jeff clutched the car keys in his hand, wishing the old truck had remote locks and a force field. A Gatling gun. Arm in arm, Jeff hurried Elly across the immaculate lawn. At the sidewalk he detected a tinge of red in the runoff water. The hedges swayed, hopefully from the rain and not some unseen killer.

They made it to the truck. Jeff mumbled a quick prayer as he put the key in the ignition. The old truck jerked to life and they barreled down the driveway.

The sterile, bright corridors of the university hospital made the night's events seem like a harmless dream. Images of the dead cat, the rain, especially the darkness, were all banished by the white tile, white walls, Lysol scents and rows of florescent lights. For the first time since his patient's death, Jeff felt glad to be in a hospital. Safe even. How could any creature of the darkness survive in this sterile environment?

Jeff held tight to Eleanor's hand as they strode down the halls. He'd explained to her on the way over that the ultrasound would give him a good picture of the baby, and maybe he would see something that could tell him what was causing her pain.

They were early for the hour Daniel had set up for them in the ultrasound room, but when they pushed through the door into the examination area, the room was empty. A note from Daniel was taped to the machine's monitor saying they had until 5:00 a.m. before the next patient was scheduled. A blue robe was folded neatly on the examination table.

"Here," Jeff said, holding up a meager blue hospital gown. "Put this on. Leave it open in front."

His hands shook as he handed the garment over to her, and he wondered if he would be able to even run the damn machine. His headache and injured arm flared with every erratic beat of his heart.

Elly took the wraparound piece of cotton from Jeff and held it at arms length. "This is the nicest outfit I've had in awhile," she said, managing a wry smile. "Do you have a matching hospital-blue Brighton belt?"

"No belt." He forced a smile, too. "But I've got some nice slippery personal lubricant to go in the front."

For a moment, a question hung in her eyes, then flitted away. He noticed that her hands trembled despite the tranquilizer he'd already given her. She glanced at the tremor in her hands then clutched the gown close to her body like a young girl would hug a doll. "It's soft," she said quietly. A tear rolled down her cheek.

He gasped as a profound sadness pressed on his chest. He extended his arms. His fingers closed on her soft, rounded shoulders and he gathered her into his embrace. She folded into him, her body nestling close. If he just held her tight enough, close enough, maybe he could staunch this nightmare. "Don't give up." His lips moved near her ear, inhaling her musky scent. "Remember, you're not a quitter."

184

Her hair flowed like silk under his palm, her fragile neck made his massaging fingers feel big and awkward. Feminine warmth surrounded her like an aura he could sense with every cell, permeating him. His sorrow began to melt.

He groaned and repositioned his feet to hold her better. "Hey, this whole…mess, it's going to clear up." His mind raced, trying to think of the right words to comfort her. "We're going to fight. We're going to win." Finally, he spoke from the heart. "No matter what happens, Elly, I'm going to be here for you."

She leaned back and looked up into his eyes. Her gaze was wide and red and damp. "Yes," she whispered. "I believe you will be." Her face drifted ever closer. Her warm breath puffed his cheek. Then her lips touched his.

He tasted tears.

Her mouth was warm and wet. And open.

And it belonged to him.

Desire flared like a lighted match and he deepened the kiss. Images of their past nights together filled his mind. Her pale skin, the curves that always led like a trail to a place he wanted to be. His jeans tightened. His pulse quickened. They were so close, if he could just get a little closer, push up against her until their bodies melted into one.

Elly moaned. A contented moan, but it struck like a tight fist. Only hours ago, she had uttered moans of pain. He knew that the tiny heart beating within her counted away the moments they had left to decide what to do. Gripping her shoulders, he drew back gently. "Put on the robe." He ran his fingertips across the soft downy hairs on her cheek. "We have to get this done, fast."

Her eyes darkened. "Yes. All right." She placed one fingertip on his mouth then turned toward the dressing room.

He watched her go, his blood sliding through his veins like warm syrup. After she disappeared behind the curtain, he forced himself over to the large console and pushed several buttons. The monitor blinked and came to life. A whirring sound rose from the base of the machine.

"I guess I'm ready." She emerged from the dressing room, her arms wrapping the gown around her protectively. Her hair was mussed, static electricity holding strands in the air. She reached up and smoothed her hair with one hand, the other clutching her gown. The pastel blue light of the CRT lit the room like candlelight.

He cleared his throat and tried not to stare at her. The blue robe brought out the vivid cerulean in her eyes, the scooping neckline revealed the fullness of her breasts and the long, elegant line of her neck.

Her hand slid from her hair to her neck. "What?" she asked.

He shook his head and pressed his lips together in a smile. "You just look...beautiful."

"You've got to be kidding."

"Really. You do."

Her voice hardened. "I've got bruises and scratches everywhere. I haven't groomed or dressed in so long I feel like a vagrant. Now I'm wearing this ugly cotton frock." She grimaced at the robe, then up at him. "How could I look beautiful?"

"I was just asking myself the same thing." The machine broke the moment by beeping twice, indicating it was warmed up and ready. With concerted effort, he turned his attention back to the equipment. "Okay. This baby is booted up and calibrated. I guess we're ready to go." He licked his lips, and tasted a trace of salt.

"I need to pee," she murmured, glaring at the machine.

"That's good."

"For whom?"

"It'll make the test more accurate. Come on." He gestured to the table. With one more uncertain glance at him, she rolled onto the table and he helped position her on her back. "Any pain right now?"

"No. Well, a little. But it's okay."

Nodding, he parted the folds of her gown, and tried to think like a doctor as her soft auburn pubic hair and shapely thighs were revealed to him. "Now, I have to spread this jelly stuff over your abdomen. Just relax."

"Improves contact, right?" she asked, lifting her head.

He tried a strained smile. "Right as usual. Now just relax."

"That's easy for you to say." She lowered her head and closed her eyes.

He squeezed the jelly into his palm. Using two fingertips, he touched her swollen abdomen and began moving the silky substance in ovals.

His fingers slipped over her skin, dusted with peach fuzz. A sweat broke out along his upper lip as he reacted to her contours. Her belly was swollen and firm, accentuating the hollows near her feminine places. He spread the oil over her navel, around the sides toward her waist, and all the way down to where her downy triangle of hair began between her legs. His hand trembled. Pain shot through his shoulder as his heart sped up. He wanted to cover her body—with him.

Doctor. Think like a doctor.

He wiped his hands on a towel and tried to concentrate on anything but her body. His thermodynamics class in college. The room in his house that stood waiting for him to paint. The dry sensation of kissing his grandmother.

He lifted an object that looked like an electronic vacuum attachment, tied to the machinery by a cable. "This is the transducer. It'll send sound waves into your body and pick up echoes from the different planes of your own organs and the baby's tissues." The techno-babble eased his arousal even further, and he continued. "It'll translate the information into the form of a map and display it on this screen over here."

He ran the metal object over her oiled skin, watching the screen. He had to keep his eyes off her slick, supple body.

"What do you see?" she asked.

"Nothing, yet. I have to adjust the focus to the level I'm interested in." He turned the dial and a picture like Rorschach inkblots grew and ebbed, bled in and out on the screen. The fuzz became shadow, and a dark image formed.

Not quite right.

He moved the transducer, adjusted the focus again. Numbers ran across the bottom of the screen. The machine's sound seemed to change from a gentle hum to a growl. His heart rate increased. He moved the transducer again.

Adjust. Move. Focus.

A clear image emerged. Large head. Beating heart. Long arms.

This can't be right.

But no matter how he moved or adjusted the equipment, he kept seeing the same impossible image. A miniature, full term baby. He could distinguish fully developed lungs. That didn't occur until twenty-eight gestational weeks. According to what he was looking at, this tiny fetus could be delivered soon.

Impossible. He glanced at her belly. Her abdomen was enlarged, maybe about five months in size.

His eyes darted back to the screen. The placenta seemed to be placed right, but there were strange shadows, too.

"What's taking so long?" She lifted her head again, trying to see the screen, but he blocked it with his body.

He overlaid the screen with an electronic image of a ruler and measured the head of the fetus. Too small for delivery, way too big for the gestational age. He slid the emitter around some more and the fetus moved, flopping over. Jeff gasped. Directly underneath the large fetus was another small embryo. He focused in on it, and read it to be around seven weeks gestational age. It had a separate placenta. Fraternal twins, of different ages. How was this possible?

"Jeff. Tell me what you see."

"Just a minute." He focused back in on the larger of the two babies. Another image caught his eye. Buried in the brain cavity of the larger fetus was a dense dot about the size of a pinhead. Maybe metal or bone. He leaned toward the screen. What could it be? "Did you ever use an IUD for birth control?"

"No. What's going on?"

Implanted IUD's sometimes allowed the bodies of babies to grow in the uterus around them. But this was a very, very, small piece.

Moving out in all directions from the dense speck was an overdeveloped vascular system leading to almost fully developed and muscular legs and arms. He focused closer on one of the arms and blew up the image on the screen. At the end of the arm, its hand looked to be the same density as the child's skull.

He shuddered. *Lord.* What in the hell... The baby was deformed.

I had a hand of bone almost like a claw. *How on earth?* That appendage could tear up the placenta easily if flung around. Hurrying now, he went back to the head and found malformed jaws. They stuck out like the jowls of a bulldog and he could see fully formed incisors, large teeth.

Shock sizzled and jumped through him, like arcing electricity. He glanced at Eleanor on the table, then back to the screen. There was no mistake here, this was real. As the image changed on the screen, he placed his hand on her belly and felt the movement. It was true. This strange monster was inside this beautiful woman.

Suddenly, what had happened at Rita's house slashed through his mind in terrifying clarity. The baby hadn't been ripped from her womb. The creature had emerged from her womb using the claw. It had cut its way out and then feasted on its own mother. And her guest.

Nausea tumbled in his stomach. *Shit!* What the hell had Meaks been experimenting with?

What should he tell her? That within her lived a monster just like the one that bit her on the leg, the one that killed Rita? He'd already told her too much once before and she'd had some kind of attack. He didn't want it to happen again.

Eleanor cursed and lifted her head from the table, trying to see the image on the screen.

He blocked it with his body.

"What are you doing?" she demanded. "Get out of the way."

He pulled a paper towel from a box and wiped the gel off her belly. "Go get dressed. Then we'll talk."

"I want to see the picture. Now."

"I want to talk to you, first."

"I have a right to..." Her face fell. She breathed deeply and he watched understanding creep slowly over her like a cloud across the sun. "I'll be right back." She swung her legs off the end of the table and stood up. With a long backward glance, she disappeared into the dressing room.

Quickly, Jeff printed a picture of the image on the screen, ejected the video tape he'd recorded of the session and turned off the machine. Slipping the picture into his pocket, he marked the tape with Elly's name, Daniel's name, and the date, as well as the words, *TransGenesis test case, 6 weeks gestational age*. He placed the tape in a cabinet with a host of other records and closed the cabinet.

TransGenesis. What a perfect name. Somehow they grew humans that were not human, but crossed with the genes of an animal. They were changed so much that they were no longer human, just humanoid. Even with his medical background he couldn't imagine how something like this could be accomplished. Had research come so far since he'd been in medicine that it now created life instead of preserving it?

My Lord, how long before that thing decided to cut its way out and eat them for lunch? He sat on the table where Elly lay earlier and cradled his head in his trembling hands.

He felt her sit next to him and place her hand on his shoulder. "Well?" she asked.

He looked into her eyes. "You're carrying twins," he said roughly. Wiping his hands down his face, he straightened his back. He was so weary, so tired.

She covered her abdomen with her hand. "Is that why I'm so big? Because there are two of them?"

"No." He stood and walked away, feeling as Abraham must have felt as he raised his sword to sacrifice his son on the mountain. How could he tell her? He didn't want the kind of reaction he'd gotten at the house. He wanted her to be calm, happy. Safe.

"Please." Her voice sounded desperate. "Just get to the point. I'm not a weak little girl. I can handle the truth."

He turned. "I never thought you were weak. If anything, you seemed too strong, almost threateningly so. But now I'm thankful for every ounce of strength you've got."

She paused, absorbing his words, her face changing as she realized his news would be grave. "All right, then. Let me have it."

He cleared his throat again, forming his words in his mind carefully. "One of the twins is...deformed. Very large. Much farther along than it should be for this gestational age."

Her eyebrows knitted. "And the other?"

"I don't know. A normal child, I guess."

"I don't understand."

"The deformed one has what appears to be a piece of bone or metal in its brain."

Eleanor sighed and leaned back on the table, bracing her hands behind her. "What are the abnormalities?"

He turned away again. "Let's just say that we cannot allow the fetus to grow to maturity." He paused, cleared his throat. "You will need a Cesarean section. Within the next few days, if the rate of growth continues."

"A Cesarean? Why not an abortion? I'm not that far along—"

"No!" he exclaimed, whirling.

She jumped as he yelled, and let out a cry.

"Hell. I'm sorry. It's just..." He sat back next to her and took both of her hands in his. He concentrated on pocketing his own fear. "This fetus cannot be aborted. It's too dangerous. It must be taken Cesarean...and soon."

27

Caesar pulled up his mask as he entered the operating room, located deep underground. He'd purposely designed the medical areas to be the furthest back in the mountain, so they could be closed off and made virtually inaccessible when necessary. This was one of those times.

Holding his fingers in the air, Megan stretched skin-tone rubber gloves over his hands. Having put too much trust in others, Bruce particularly, Caesar had decided to perform the rest of the extractions himself, to allow no errors. His heart raced. This morning he was extracting the Cyber from Sunflower. That would put one chimp Cyber in his grasp, and if all went as planned with the human subjects, he would soon have three human Cybers within his control as well.

"Where's Bruce? He's usually is here for security," the vet, Dr. Chung, asked from behind his mask and thick glasses.

Caesar hated people who wore glasses; they displayed their imperfections without shame. "We don't need him," Caesar snapped back, irritated by the question. Dr. Chung had always been too procedure oriented. He wanted everything done by the book and couldn't cope well with change. Part of genius was the ability to adjust quickly. "It's a simple extraction."

"But Bruce has—"

Caesar cut him off. "Bruce will not be joining us today." *Or any other day.* Caesar should have dealt with Bruce long ago, but the man's excuses had been so convincing. "Too soon, we cut too soon," he'd said after loosing the first Cyber. Then, "We used too heavy an anesthesia and were forced to kill it," or, "Too light an anesthesia, it was violent." Several other reasons had followed before he had finally helped deliver eight healthy Cybers. If Caesar had paid less attention to beginning the project with human subjects and more attention to Bruce, he would have realized the man's ineptness sooner. Bruce's stupidity was probably a contributing factor behind losing the first several Cybers.

And now because of Bruce's idiocy, they had lost track of the first human Cyber ever born. His men had discovered the bodies of Number One and her boyfriend. Apparently, the Cyber had run out of patience and cut its way out of the womb, proving once and for all that the Cybers were maturing much faster than expected.

But his men had been unable to find the Cyber, those incompetents. Amazingly, they'd seen Number Two and the doctor at the scene, but hadn't been able to catch two unarmed people. *Idiots!*

But nothing would go wrong today. Caesar had planned everything perfectly. Bruce was gone. The operating room was sealed off.

The powerful creation would soon be in his grasp. He'd personally raise it and fill its mind with visions of greatness. One success was all they needed for government funding. *It begins today.*

He turned to the operating table. Sunflower lay limp on top, like a mangy stuffed animal. Dr. Chung fed her oxygen through a plastic mask and the IV provided drugs and liquids. The scrub assistant, Megan, stood by. Claus was suited up in operating greens as well, looking like St. Nicholas in green, except he ran the palm controller and stood ready beside a cage with reinforced bars.

Sunflower's swollen abdomen loomed out between the white sheets, shaved and scrubbed. It looked unreal, like a brown plastic dome.

Everything was ready now. This was the moment he'd been waiting for.

He approached the table and ran his fingers over the distended abdomen, determining the position of the Cyber. An ultrasound machine waited to be used, but the fetus was far enough developed that he could feel its head easily. He held out his rubber-covered hand and Dr. Chung slapped a scalpel into his palm.

Eager, he slid the blade along the abdomen, making a long vertical cut. *Beautiful.*

Some men avoided the operating room as they moved up in rank and assigned the bloody jobs to underlings, but not Caesar. This part of his work excited him. The flesh separated smoothly and fell away like Jell-O under a hot knife. *Thrilling.* Sometimes he had to remind himself to stop, to only cut what needed to be cut, but sometimes, against all reason, he wanted to just tear open the rest of the body and watch the moving, living organs. Touch them, feel them, immerse himself.

He wondered about his feelings sometimes, but rationalized his strange longings. All doctors must feel the urge to slice, or they wouldn't be doctors. If they didn't like cutting, reaching into a bloody hole, holding a pulsing organ in their hands, then why else would they do it? They could have easily gone into less bloody work. He had studied both medicine and engineering, but he'd never give up his place at the table.

Finishing the incision, he laid aside the flaps of skin, fascia and fat, and slit through the muscle layer. Megan helped him to place retractors to reveal the uterus. "Packs," he said, holding out his hand. This time, Dr. Chung gave him rolls of surgical gauze, which he pressed into the opening to absorb blood and force the other organs out of the way.

He slit the uterus horizontally. A sense of great power rushed over him as the water bag containing the Cyber and it's placenta bulged through the opening like a water balloon shoved through a bloody crack. He had created this being, with the potential for greatness. It was a superior transgenic chimp, having more human genes than any of its older brothers. Perhaps it would even be superior to humans.

The nanochip that had already regulated its growth also had access to an encyclopedia of information for the Cyber to learn. It's brain would have the computing capacity of the fastest computer as well as the flexibility of sentient intellect.

It would be strong, like its powerful father. That was the one most crucial ingredient; it shared Caesar's superior genes.

He had seen too much impuissance. It ran rampant in the world, like the pathetic herds of buffalo who were too weak to even survive as a species. The being within this sack of fluid was the wolf who would hunt the herd—it was Caesar's flesh and blood, and more. It's brain contained large amounts of data, previously only accessible by computers. Using the superconductor, the Cyber could repair itself on the cellular level. It could survive almost any injury, unless the chip embedded in its brain was destroyed.

"Caesar? Is there something wrong?" Dr. Chung asked.

"No," Caesar snapped. How long had he been standing there, staring? "Give me the pump. I'll drain this fluid first."

He reached for a tool to drain off the amniotic fluid and heard a strange sound, a noise that didn't belong in the operating room.

A flute.

The song chilled him. He glanced from person to person in the small white room. Did they hear it, too? Their eyes, their only feature visible between the operating hat and mask, were fixed on him, alarmed.

He held his breath to not miss a note of the floating tones, and time seemed suspended with his breath. The music was familiar. He knew he'd heard it before, and he more than heard it—he felt it. It called to something in him, something deep within him.

Nonsense! He rested his hand on the bulge in his pocket. This was an interruption, an inconvenience caused by some stupid employee. If the flute music caused trouble, he was prepared.

After a moment of silence, voices fired questions around the room so fast he couldn't keep track of who said what.

"What the hell is that?"

"It's that damn flute."

"Where is it coming from?"

"It seems like its right here, in the room."

"That's impossible, there aren't even air exchange ducts in here, this is a sterile environment."

"There are speakers. Is it coming from the tape player?"

"There's no tape in there!"

"It's just like with Felipe!"

"Let's get out of here!"

"Look!" Dr. Chung said, pointing, and all gazes swept to Sunflower.

As though it responded to the music, the fetus inside the fluid-filled bag began to sway and move. As they watched, the movements became faster, more violent.

"Hit it with a tranquilizer!" Caesar shouted, too loud for the small room. The sound of the flute seemed to pump him full of air. He couldn't exhale to draw another breath. Panic closed in around him.

As Megan increased the Valium drip on the IV, Dr. Chung grabbed a syringe prepared just for such an occurrence, and rushed to the table. He placed one hand on top of the wiggling Cyber, pierced the bag with the needle and shot the syringe's contents into the fetus. A thin stream of water shot into the air like a geyser.

"There, that should do it—" he began, but his eyes grew wide and he yelped as a claw pushed out through the bag and pinched his little finger. He jerked his hand back reflexively. The movement tore the Cyber from Sunflower's womb, showering blood, amniotic fluid, and pieces of the placenta onto the scrub suits of the crew.

Dr. Chung bellowed and tried to shake loose the Cyber. It carried his little finger with it to the floor. After it slammed against the tile, it turned, unfazed by the impact, and snapped up the finger like a hot dog, swallowing it in one bite.

Dr. Chung let out an unceasing high wail and dove for the bandages he needed to wrap his hand. Urgent shouts in Mandarin echoed from the walls.

No one else moved. They stared at the hideous monster they had created. It hunched on the floor and stared at them for a moment, then turned and began to consume the placenta ravenously.

Caesar stared, didn't breathe, didn't move, just stared—amazed. He was overwhelmed with respect for this creature. His knees shook. Pride overwhelmed him. *Phenomenal.* He was truly a genius to have done this. "Claus! Bring the cage over here."

Claus moved slowly, stiffly, his gaze never leaving the creature on the floor.

"Is it responding to the palm controller's signals?" Caesar barked.

Claus set the cage on the floor beside him, unwilling to get any closer to the thing. "No...maybe it's the flute." His voice shook.

"Someone, find the source of that music and kill it!"

No one moved.

"Claus, grab it while it's eating, God damn it! Throw it in the cage."

Claus took quiet steps toward the Cyber. He reached down to grab the Cyber. Slowly...too damn slowly.

When his hands were only an inch from it, it screeched and vaulted over his head onto Dr. Chung. Dr. Chung hadn't been watching, because he was busily wrapping the stump where his finger had been. The impact knocked him back a step.

Dr. Chung screeched and hammered wildly at the Cyber, trying to knock it from his face. His bandage loosened and blood pumped from his hand rhythmically, seemingly along with the beat of the flute's song.

Caesar watched, fascinated. Better to sacrifice the vet than lose the Cyber.

The newborn creature held fast to Dr. Chung's face, its right hand and foot digging into the flesh of his temple and neck. Its jowls snapped off his nose, the flesh from his cheeks, ripped away his lips like Caesar pulled skin from a chicken, then used its claw to snap the carotid artery. It drank.

Caesar fumbled for his gun. If he shot the Cyber, just to injure it, it would be slowed down enough to get into the cage and into an isolation booth, where it could repair itself. He pointed the gun and pulled the trigger.

Dr. Chung's knees folded underneath him.

The report of the pistol bounced off the walls and temporarily deafened him. Both man and Cyber fell to the floor in a heap. When he could once again hear, the flute music had stopped.

Caesar, panting, dropped the Derringer into his jacket pocket. He slipped on the slimy mess on the floor as he rushed to the Cyber. He cursed. He'd shot while Chung was falling. The bullet had passed through the Cyber's head and embedded itself in Dr. Chung's brain.

The Cyber was dead.

Disabling the chip in the brain was one of the only ways to kill a Cyber and he had inadvertently done it. Curse Claus's slowness and Dr. Chung's fear. If they'd kept it together, they would still have the Cyber. Curse Bruce and his incompetence. And curse Hog most of all, for taking his time finding Number Two, for not being here when Caesar needed him most. This was the last chimp-carried Cyber and now it was dead because of his stupid employee's mistakes.

Caesar waved his hand over the dead man and Cyber. "Clean up this mess," he said, taking one more disgusted look at the carnage that had been Chung and a Cyber. "I'm leaving."

"But...how about Sunflower?" Claus asked, whining.

His fear and weakness repulsed Caesar. "Disconnect her. Try to sew her back up if you want. I don't care."

He pushed out the door of the operating room, anger eating him alive. He was running out of chances. No one had recovered the Cybers that had escaped into the caverns, and now Number One's human Cyber was gone. They had managed to capture Number Three, a nursing student named Donna, and lock her safely away, but she was not showing any signs that Dr. Meaks's last implantation had been successful.

So Number Two, this Vanguard woman, had become his last, greatest chance at success. She was on the run, and he couldn't afford to lose her.

He would stop at nothing to be successful. He was going to find Hog, his best man, and send him after the Vanguard woman immediately. The woman had to go under the knife, and soon. The Cybers were maturing too quickly, and Caesar refused to allow another human Cyber to escape.

No matter what it took, Eleanor Vanguard would not get away.

28

Folding into a full lotus, Stars in White Cloud lifted his flute and ran his fingers over its delicate carvings. His fingertips explored the niches at the end, carved into the shape of his spirit guide, the bat. The bat symbolized the inner fears of his people, fears that lurked in the dark corners of mind and spirit, where Stars in White Cloud lived. But when he, the shaman, played the bat flute, the music spoke these fears. The music carried them through the caverns, where they were eaten by the blind fish and the insects, where the rock formations absorbed the vibrations. The remains of his song were pure music—floating, swirling, lifting—singing of his people's rising hopes, raised from beneath fear by the spirit's cleansing melodies.

His dry lips found the end of the flute. He inhaled, and his lips vibrated as he began to blow the calling melody. At first, the full sound rose like the howling of a lonely wolf, calling his family home. Then like the meadowlark, the sound trilled and danced. Then the music, free of the bonds of fear, took flight and carried the song of hope to the demons, wherever they were, no matter how far away.

As he played, he sensed a connection with one of the children, close by, possibly even within the caverns. It heard him, answered, responded. It danced with the anticipation of joining its family. It came closer, gained strength, and then—

With a burst of light and pain it was gone. Even its fire-heart had been silenced. Its dying scream for mercy and its sad plea for life pierced Stars in White Cloud's heart. Pulling the flute from his mouth, he roared with anger. The demon was gone.

The child had been destined centuries ago to help sanctify demon mountain and now it had been allowed only a few breaths before being silenced for eternity. Surely it would run in the fields with his people in the next world, but it would never meet its earthly spirit guide, because it had no time to search.

Again, fury rumbled through Stars in White Cloud's being like lava within a volcano. His eyes moved back and forth wildly under the fused eyelids as he tried to control his anger and frustration.

Without all twelve demons, his destiny could not be fulfilled.

He fought off his own longings, his own needs. There was only one goal, only one thing to accomplish, before he could once again join his people and run in the sky. Before the powerful totem of the bat could act. He must concentrate. The legends could not be wrong. There must be another demon child.

He settled into his body. Here there was only old flesh strung across brittle bones. Only dry, cracked carcasses within him maintaining his life force, so like the crumbled adobe and ruins of his old village. The scattered crickets in the cave were like the remains of his people, darting about in the darkness of the new world, trying to find their way, but hopelessly and utterly lost in the obscurity that closed in around them as sure as the stone enclosed him now.

Upon awakening, he'd thought that he and his people would be able to once again join in uprising to run off the invaders from their land. But he'd had no inkling as to how countless they were, or how fruitless any attempt to resist would be. When he'd left the cave and flown over his land, he'd seen the extent of the ruin. Time could not be reversed.

But he would follow the plan that had been laid out for him by the tribal leaders, anyway. He would pass on the knowledge of the tribe to these demons and leave them behind him to keep the mountain clean, sacred and free of outsiders, until the day when somehow, they could restore the knowledge of the P'ónin and again overcome.

White Cloud felt his heart quicken at the thought of passing on the heavy burden that had always been his. When he traveled to the next world he would actually be joining his tribe for the first time. He had been chosen by the gods and had handled his burden for centuries, but now longed for a chance to let go. To fly like the mammal that flew, like the bat, up, up, up into the land of freedom.

Before his long sleep he'd often imagined what it would be like to play in the sun, to have it caress his hair and his shoulders. He let the dream unfold in his mind like a map on deerskin, in full color.

After he passed to the land of the dead, he would move in the light. He would feel not only warmth, but cold. He would walk through the snow and feel the tingle on his feet and his legs. He would reach down and pack the white powder in his fist and let it fly, running with his brothers. He would hunt the animals provided by the Mother of the Earth, Wahatoya. He would, first hand, stand on mother mountain and look as far as the eye could see, be in the great openness. He would hear the birds sing, and let their tune tickle his eardrums like the strains of the flute, but instead of echoing in the rock, it would join the wind and sail away. Ah, the wind. It would blow against his skin and lift his hair—*his* hair—not feathers, or the fur of an animal he inhabited. His hair.

He would no longer have to flap in darkness like the fears of his people. He could drop his bonds, join the birds, and sail into the sunlight.

The day was near. The day when his dry bones could be immersed in a fresh, cool lake, where his mortal eyes would never again have to strive for the light.

Only a few things had held him back before today. Now, another burden had been added. He still had to find the demon child who would make the legend complete. He had three hundred years of waiting to motivate him, to give him the strength to overcome the few obstacles in his way.

The only way his demons would have enough time to be taught and to meet their spirit leaders would be if he led them to slay the invaders soon, before they killed any more of his children. It was too soon, because the demon mother still cared for two of the children outside the caverns. But he would bring them here, preparing their path by massacring the men who violated the sacred mountain. Soon. Whether they found the twelfth child or not.

The second revolt of the P'ónin was about to begin.

* * *

The lights in the hospital parking lot created darker shapes in the darkness. It seemed to Jeff like the landscape of his heart—black patches concealing the good and the bad, and hanging above it all, points of hot anger and fear casting the shadows. He grasped Elly's hand tighter as the glass door swung open. "So I figure this. We go back to Bixler's—"

"But the cat," she objected. "Something killed the cat, probably whatever was at Rita's. We can't take the chance."

"Screw the damn cat. It's dead. We shouldn't have run. I just freaked out. We're people, not pets. We can protect ourselves." Elly's hand was cold in his. He squeezed it. "You need rest. We both need rest, and we know we can get into his place. He's got food and clothing and he won't be back until next week. It's the logical place to go. Then in the morning, I'll head over to TransGenesis and demand some answers. I'll shake that fake resignation letter in their faces." *And show them the ultrasound picture,* he thought, but didn't say. *And tell them I made a copy of the entire procedure. That should definitely get their attention.*

"If they're behind this, don't you think that might be a little dangerous?" she asked. "They could have you in custody before you have a chance to do any letter shaking."

He stopped and faced her, taking both her hands in his. The rain had stopped. The parking lot gleamed like oiled skin, pieces of him reflected in a thousand mirrored puddles. A blackbird landed near him. It poked at the water and lifted its beak toward the moon to swallow. A breeze nestled Jeff's hair and filled his nostrils with the scent of wet yucca. "What are our options? Running won't help this."

He patted her belly. "We've got to find out more about what they did to you and how to fix it."

"Look, bozo. Don't you think I know that?"

He smiled at her in surprise.

Her face twisted in a determined scowl, but there was amusement in her eyes, too. "I'm worried about losing *you*," she purred.

His heart warmed.

"It hurts to admit this, but I need you right now. If the TransGenesis jerks nabbed you, or called the police and they took you away for a long vacation in a jail cell, where would that leave me?"

The warmth evaporated. "Gee, I didn't know you cared so much."

She suddenly perked up. "Do you feel that?" she whispered. Her eyes darted all around them.

The hairs on the back of his neck prickled. He looked around him. A woman pushed a stroller toward a van, each turn of the wheels uttering a squeak. Two men in purple scrub suits leaned on the bricks by the front entrance, smoking. No one even glanced in their direction. "What?" he asked, seeing nothing unusual.

"You're the sensitive one," Elly whispered, an intense look on her face. "You used to tell me I wouldn't notice if an elephant sat on my head."

"I take that back. Lately, you've been more than sensitive. In fact, you've been very perceptive. The extrasensory type." He examined her face, looking for signs of one of her episodes. She looked normal, though hyper-alert.

"Well, my ESP tells me we're being watched."

Jeff turned in a slow circle, peering into every shadow. Listening. He saw nothing threatening, smelled nothing more than the scent of recent rain and fragrant yucca. He slipped his hand through her arm and pulled her closer. Even though he sensed nothing, he'd learned to trust her instincts. "Let's head for the truck. We can continue this discussion later."

The stroller squeaked by. The men by the entrance laughed. His heart thudded. His steps splashed on the wet blacktop. The blackbird flapped past them and settled on the cab of their truck. It tilted its head and cawed.

Huddling closer, they moved on. The muscles in his arms and legs tensed. His eyes strained to make out any shapes in the darkness.

Their steps quickened as they approached the truck, then Elly stopped suddenly. She gasped and pointed. Jeff's heart came to a screeching stop. He saw it, too.

Two glowing eyes stared out at them from underneath the truck—gold eyes. Panic clenched his stomach.

"Jeff," Elly whispered frantically, "under the car."

"I see it. What is it?" he asked, although he figured he already knew. He'd just seen an ultrasound image of a monster inside of Elly's womb he wouldn't soon forget. Certainly, these eyes belonged to a similar creature. Before Elly could even answer, it crawled out from underneath the car and stood erect.

At first, relief flooded over him. The eyes belonged to a toddler, a harmless child. But then he looked closer, and his relief exploded into terror. The thing stood on two feet, about the size of a newborn. But it definitely was not a normal child. Its head swelled out in back as if its brain had bloated. A growl emerged from its elongated jowls, showing razor-sharp teeth. Its arms and legs were heavily muscled, hands hanging near its ankles. At the end of its left arm an oversized hand gleamed, as if covered in bone instead of skin.

Its eyes focused on Elly. It held out its arms and keened.

She took a step back.

It lumbered toward her with its arms outstretched, crying like a hungry infant.

An unbidden cry escaped Elly's throat. Her loud shriek startled the creature and it sped up. Elly was rooted to the spot. It ran faster than Jeff could ever imagine the stubby legs could move, saliva dripping from its jowls, the cry of a human baby in its throat.

He saw it all in slow motion. Elly still hadn't moved, weighted down by the pregnancy, tranquilized by fear. The thing scurried with a child's singular purpose and would be on her in moments.

M.F. King

She screamed again. She slipped on the wet blacktop trying to back away.

Jeff saw his chance and took it. There was still a small gap between Elly and the creature, a space he could fill with himself. Hunching down, he threw his arms out and vaulted into the gap. The thing charged into his chest, knocking his breath away and spiking pain through his arm. His back crashed into Elly, knocking her down. *Had he hurt her?* He grasped the thing to him like a football, wrapping his body around it, shielding her from it. It screeched and wailed. Feelings of horror shot through him as he felt the naked body of a newborn child wrapped in his arms.

What was he doing? Crushing a baby, *Lord,* what had he become? Then he heard the growl and was reassured—this was no baby, this was a monster. A killing machine.

He scrambled to his feet, the ten pounds of creature in his grasp. It bit his arm and held, slashed its bony claw at his face. Bellowing in pain, Jeff grasped its wrist like he was handling a snake and pulled the hand away from his face. He dug his fingernails into the tiny arm, unable to believe the brutality he used on the baby's delicate wrist, but it wasn't a baby, it just looked like a baby, and the thing cried out from the pain and let go with its mouth. Summoning all his strength, he heaved it as far as he could, moaning with revulsion and horror as he watched the baby topple end over end into the street, and then the van was there. The brakes squealed, but the brown van slammed into the child full force and bounced it across the street. The small frame lay motionless.

"No!" he yelled, although he'd intended to throw the baby, he couldn't believe it as he watched the mangled body ricochet from the windshield. He ran toward the child; he had to save it. *What have I done?*

The van's door popped open. Elly screamed a warning, but he ignored it. He'd just killed a child. He was a doctor, who had sworn an oath to heal and protect, never to harm. *He'd hurt someone again.*

"Stop!" an accented male voice boomed from behind him. "If you want this woman in one piece, stop now!"

Jeff's feet halted, along with his heart. He turned around slowly.

Whimpering, Elly was caught in the grasp of a man, her arm pulled up behind her back, a gun muzzle pressed against her neck. The man was small but muscular and wore long braids that hung over his shoulders.

"Don't," Jeff shouted, his hands in front of him, reaching. "Don't hurt her." Elly struggled in the man's grip, her eyes swimming with anger and fear. "We'll cooperate," he said as much to Elly as to the man, nodding his head.

Elly's eyes stayed on the street where the child lay. "Let me go," she said between gritted teeth.

The man gestured with his head toward the van. "Move that way. Toward the back." Jeff's hands, the hands that could work miracles in the operating room, hung useless at his sides. His wrist howled with pain where the creature's teeth had dug into it, but the voice wasn't nearly as loud as his fear for Elly's safety. Jeff stepped toward the back of the van, his gaze never leaving Elly. The man met him there. "Open it."

Jeff flipped the handle and the door opened with a snap.

"Get in."

Jeff hesitated. If they got in the van, they were as good as dead. *Think, think!* There had to be a way to overpower this guy. There were two of them, only one of him. But was there another man in the passenger seat? These guys always traveled in pairs.

The man tightened his grip on Elly's arm, and she yelled out in pain. The sound pierced Jeff's soul. How much more could she take?

"What are you waiting for? Get in!" the man growled.

Ducking his head, Jeff climbed into the small cargo area. The man shoved Elly in behind him and slammed the door.

29

Stars in White Cloud sat cross-legged on a broken stalagmite. He chanted, projecting his essence throughout the caverns. His spirit vibrated through icicles of rock, rippled dark water in the hidden pool, and mesmerized the demons huddled around him. They rocked slowly back and forth, humming with his chant.

Their growth was as fast as a running deer, and they consumed his teachings like wild fire on the prairie. White Cloud fed them spirit lessons, P'ónin legends, and always reminded them of their destiny— to drive the invaders from the sacred caverns and eventually from the land. And of course, to carry on the collective knowledge of his people.

One drop of water formed on a stalactite's tip and trembled like a plucked string when his spirit passed through it. His awareness permeated everything in the cave, had *become* the cave.

To the ignorant, his surroundings would seem dark, devoid of life. The air would seem stale and oxygen starved, the pool stagnant and infected. But White Cloud could absorb oxygen through his thin skin and see with his echoing spirit. He felt the underground stream's refreshment as it trickled in, bringing life from the outside; it carried seeds, guano and tidbits for the fish to eat. Each flick of a blind fish's tail registered in his mind like the touch of a fingertip to his cheek. He knew every tap of the water bug's feet skimming the surface and the snap of a feasting glowworm when it caught a cricket or fly on its luminous fishing line dangling from the ceiling.

His mind expanded, seeking a clicking bird. He must journey to the outside world to find the demon child whose calls pierced his heart. The need of the child, intense and cruel in its strength, was like thunder on the horizon. When he found the child, he would enter it, comfort it, and bring it home. It was time.

The clicking bird was his favorite to inhabit. A fellow cave creature, its three-foot wingspan was far superior to the bat's.

Unity vibrated out from him in waves, flowing from his innermost cave to the transitional caves where the bats hung like storm clouds on the ceiling, their guano dropping like rain to the cave floor beneath. He found the rhythmic sounds of a clicking bird and reached for it.

His spirit pierced the body. It startled and screeched. His people said the bird's voice was like the scream of a thousand devils. Their banshee-like wails and cries sometimes floated as far as the mouth of the cave, making the cave entrance sound like the gate to hell. But the birds, like himself, were just parables for the real demons that waited around him now.

He stretched within the bird, pushing his hands out to the wing tips, his legs down into the large talons. He snapped his head into the bird's and wiggled the eyes, trying to adjust to sight once more, sight that was divided in two directions. He tested his ability to maneuver through the cave, sending out clicks to guide him past the walls and formations, and finally burst from the cave entrance into the cool, dry night.

Mother mountain was creating wind, and the sweep of air caught his feathers and lifted him. He sailed. The coolness, open space and his great anticipation all helped to overcome the anger that had been boiling within him since the demon child had been killed. The moving air stroked him like the hands of freedom itself. Temperature currents engulfed him. These were all strange but welcome feelings to a man who had always lived in the stifled environment of the cave.

Only during the great rebellion had he remained outside the cave, flying between the tribes, organizing the time and place that his people and the villagers around him would rise up and kill the invaders. But even then, he'd been within a bird's body, not his own, and by the time he'd returned to the cave he'd been almost lifeless, dehydrated and starved.

Using the new eyes, he looked at the lights below him, and screeched. The invaders had stolen the stars from the sky and spread them out over the ground, just as legend had predicted. *No man could be so powerful,* his people had argued. Now when they looked back from the next life, they would see the legends had been right all along. These men were greedy enough to even claim the stars as their own.

He suppressed the bird's own need to hunt, and concentrated on finding the demon mother and child. He let the child's need guide him, and drifted on the currents. Urgency pumped his wings harder.

A wave of fear and pain crashed against him, almost knocking him from the sky. He forced the wind through his wings then folded them back and aimed the bird toward the source of agony.

He swooped low over a few heads that bent toward a heap on the ground. *His demon child!* He tried to enter it with his spirit, but the pain was intolerable and he had to pull back. At least it lived. The fire-heart beat strongly, already rebuilding the body. The demon would recover quickly, but White Cloud's renewed anger would never die.

A man stepped toward the demon. White Cloud could not allow this. He screeched, startling the man, and dove toward the child. He caught one small arm in each talon and struggled back into the sky, barely able to reach an altitude above their heads. He fought for breath and strength. He must save his child. Men's yelling followed his ascent, but he knew he would get away. It was his destiny.

Where was the mother of demons? How could she have allowed this to happen to the child while it was in her care? Was she also hurt, or captured? As soon as the demon was safely home within the oasis of Wahatoya, he would use his flute to call the demon mother and her unborn child. He must find them and bring them home.

Stars in White Cloud propelled the heavily laden bird through the night sky, pumping the wings, forcing the bird's body beyond its limits. Now the wind was his enemy, driving him back. He flew only a few feet off the ground, forcing his claws to hold on to the demon. The child hung, limp in his talons as they dug deeper into its soft flesh, finally scraping against bone.

Fury propelled him harder and further than physically possible for the bird. How could this have happened? The mother of demons had not returned to the mountain although he had called her, and then she had allowed the terrible mutilation of this little one.

White Cloud saw the entrance to the cave at the same time he felt the bird's life begin to fade. He gripped hard with his talons and glided the dead bird down to a rough landing directly outside of the mouth, where the rest of the demons waited. Abandoning the bird's lifeless body, he enclosed the demons with his own spirit. Working as one, they lifted the injured child and carried him back toward the innermost room of the caverns, where White Cloud himself waited.

After nearly an hour, the demons arrived with the body. White Cloud abandoned his chanting and lifted the small, limp form. He walked through the total darkness to a raised platform of rock and laid the child upon it, like a sacrifice on an altar.

The fire-heart within it was already knitting the broken bones and healing the inner trauma. This child would be the smartest of them all, the strongest. He counted on it to become their leader.

Leaving the demon safe above the route of the insects and rats, White Cloud returned to his meditative position. There was one demon child still out in the world, with the mother of demons. It was time to call him home.

30

"Oof!" Jeff said, as Elly landed on top of him, knocking the air from his lungs. He scrambled out from underneath her and gripped her arms, turning her so he could see her face. "Are you all right?" he murmured urgently.

"I don't remember what that means any more," she whispered back.

"Right now it means you're not gonna die soon."

"Okay." She breathed out hard, and steadied herself as the van hit a bump. "Then I'm all right. How about you?"

Relief flooded over him. "God, I was so scared for you. That gun in your neck."

"Me? I wasn't the one fighting with Rosemary's Baby."

"Yeah. You got the devil instead."

"Let me see your arm." She took his hand and turned it over to examine the bleeding wrist. "Damn, that's ugly. That baby had teeth. Where's your bag?"

"In the truck."

Her shoulders fell. "Great. Now what do we do?"

Jeff sighed. "I'm not sure it matters. These guys are gonna kill us anyway."

"We have to at least stop the bleeding."

"Okay. What do you want to do? Lose a sock or a sleeve?"

She thought for a moment. "I think you should lose a sock. I've got the messy feet. Mine need their socks."

"Too bad you're not into scarves or wide ribbons," he mused, pulling off a shoe, then a sock, then slipping the shoe back on. "Damn. I was just getting used to having a full set of clothes." He handed Elly the sock and she tied it around his wrist, tucking the ends under.

"Good job. You're a regular Hoolahan."

"Gee, thanks," she said. "What was that thing? My God, what was it?" Her face became grave.

Jeff winced as the van's motion knocked him down, sending sharp pain through his wounded arm. "This is awful. Come over here. Let's get more comfortable." Jeff leaned up against the back seat and Elly scooted between his legs. He stretched his arms around her and they settled into each other.

For a while, they rode silently. The wind rose around them and the sound whistled through the cracks in the van. "You know," Jeff started, "I used to think work drove me crazy—relating to the administrators, handling the billing, scheduling, and complaints. Don't even mention the stress of surgery. Then, when I lost my insurance and was forced to close my practice, I thought it was just a matter of time until I lost my mind as well." Bright headlights sliced through the van, causing him to squint.

The van made a sharp turn and Jeff tightened his arms around her. "But you know what? I didn't. I didn't go crazy, didn't lose my mind. And now. If I heard about anyone going through what we've been through, I'd expect them to have Post Traumatic Stress Syndrome, or be comatose or something. Hell, even David dribbled on his beard when Saul went after him."

"Your point?"

"My point is this. I'm not crazy. You're not crazy. I guess the human mind is a lot more capable of handling crises than we think it is."

"I don't know about that," she said solemnly. Too solemnly, as far as he was concerned. "My episodes. How do you explain them? That's not rational, logical behavior. And before you pipe up with a load of blarney, I want to tell you what I felt back there. Then you can waste your breath telling me how balanced and sane I am."

"You don't have to tell me what you felt back there. You were petrified. Anyone would be scared with a gun pressed to their neck and their arm pulled behind their back."

"No. I mean before that. When the…child…crept out from under the truck."

"What do you mean?"

"If you would stop asking stupid questions, I'll tell you. You jumped at the child because you thought it was attacking me, right?"

"Of course. It was."

"I didn't feel that way. It seemed to me it wanted me to care for it." She shivered in disgust. "And this is why I say I might already be out on a limb, 'round the bend…" She lowered her voice. "I wanted to hold it. I wanted to pick it up, wrap it up, and take it home. For a moment, I felt it was my baby."

"What?" A shadow of insanity settled around him. The wind rocked the van and whistled. The sound reminded him of flute song.

"Only for a moment. But I did."

"My God, didn't you get a good look at it? Didn't you see the claw? The deformed head? I couldn't see all the teeth, but I saw them on the…it was hideous." *Shit. Bad recovery. He'd gone too far. Did she catch it?*

"Oh, no." Her voice was full of fear and pain. "No, no."

"Don't."

"You wouldn't show me the ultrasound. You said we had to talk first." Her voice grew louder, more desperate. "You said the baby was deformed. Oh, my God! It looks like that, doesn't it? My baby? It looks the one back there. And oh, God, that's why I felt something toward it, because, because…" Her voice faded off. Her body was rigid in his arms.

He petted her hair and hugged her closer. "I'm sorry, Elly. I didn't want to scare you. I—"

She wiggled out of his grasp and turned on him, slapping his hands away. "Don't *Elly* me. Don't even try your bedside-manner-lying-physician crap with me. You've always been a bastard, don't get sweet on me now." She rose to her knees, face to face with him. "Just tell me. Is that what I'm carrying? Inside?"

His teeth seemed stuck together. He reached his arms out to her. She slapped them away again and shook her head. "It is, isn't it? That's why you didn't let me see the ultrasound. Isn't it?"

They held there for a moment, Elly on her knees, hands in the air, face so close to his he could feel the heat of her breath. He stared at her wild eyes, rolling like those of a panicked horse.

His heart beat in his arm, his wrist, his teeth where he'd been clenching his jaws. His mind raced. What would happen to her if he told her? Would she lose it again? He didn't have his bag. Hell, he didn't even know where they were. But he couldn't see any way around the truth. "Yes. That's exactly what the ultrasound showed."

She seemed to melt like a hot wax—her butt to her feet, her hands to her knees. Her head bowed, her shoulders drooped. She covered her face with her hands and her body stilled.

He expected to hear sobbing at any moment, expected a long cry while his heart puddled around his feet, but she stayed still, moving only with the bump and sway of the van. Then she pulled her hands away and pressed them to the floor to steady herself against the van's movement. "I guess we know what happened to Rita and her poor boyfriend. We have no time to lose." She crawled past him to the van's back bench seat and stuck her head over the top. "Where are we going?" she yelled at the driver. "Come on, asshole. Let us out of here, and we'll let you live."

"Shut up back there!" a deep voice yelled.

Jeff yanked on her shirt. "What the hell you think you're doing? Trying to get us killed?"

"Look, you might want to sit here like an obedient child, but I don't. That asshole just forced us into this van against our will, and that's a crime. I'm not going to veg-out back here, waiting for my fate."

"There's only one of them?"

"That's right. One asshole with a gun."

Jeff flipped onto his own knees and peered over the seat. Sure enough, there was only one short guy driving. "And two of us."

"The doctor can do arithmetic." She flung one leg over the seat and before he could stop her, she rolled onto the back seat, then into the center aisle of the van. He watched, astounded, as she hunched over and stumbled up the narrow path toward the driver.

"Sit down! I'm warning you," the deep voice demanded.

She dove at the wheel, jerking it to the right. Jeff tumbled over and his shoulder struck the side panel. He screeched and scrambled back to his knees, throwing his own leg over the seat. All he could manage was to hold on, pain shooting through his arm, as Elly and the asshole fought for the wheel. She grabbed and they swung left, the man pushed her away and the van straightened for a moment, she pulled back and Jeff's grip was ripped from the seat. He landed on his bandaged wrist and howled. They stopped like they'd hit a brick wall, and Jeff rolled, his body impacting the back of one of the captain's chairs. Intense pain shot through him and he was momentarily dazed.

"I'm outta here," Elly announced.

Apparently gone mad, Jeff heard Elly pull up on the passenger seat door handle and throw her shoulder against the door. Before he could even see the result, with a great effort, Jeff dove to the sliding door and tugged the handle, using his whole body to give it a good shot, and only succeeded in increasing his pain. The van was locked down as tight as a prison cell. He melted to the floor of the van, groaning.

Their captor grabbed Elly's arm. "Stop. You don't want to do this."

"Seems all you can do is give us orders, General Asshole," Elly snapped back. "How about some answers?" She shook off his grip.

"I saved your life." His accent seemed thicker. A tumbleweed hit the windshield and held for a moment, as if watching them, before rolling off into the darkness.

"How do you figure?"

"There are more vans than just this one out looking for you. And they were closing in. If I hadn't picked you up when I did, you'd be with one of them right now, and they aren't as nice as I am."

"You could have used the magic word," Jeff mumbled from the back seat, rubbing his arm.

"Not to mention the Cyber that attacked you," he continued. "They don't die easily. It would have come back to finish you off."

Elly gripped the man's arm with both hands, excited. "Cyber? That's what they're called?"

"Yes."

"So you know about them. Is it TransGenesis, then, that's after us? Caesar Bossidy?"

"Yes."

"So…you're on our side?" Jeff asked.

"Again, yes." His long braids swung as he nodded.

"Then why all the drama? Why grab Elly and stick a gun in her neck—"

"I told you, there wasn't time to have a long conversation with you. If I'd pulled up and said, 'Let's go' would you have jumped in?"

"Nope."

"No way," Jeff said.

"So where were you taking us?" Elly asked, "if not to TransGenesis?"

Sand pelted the windshield like crystallized rain, as if the earth itself rose up and flung itself against them to slow their progress. Jeff clung to the seat as the wind rocked the van.

The man raised his voice. "I'm taking you to my home, at Isleta. You will be safe there until we decide what to do."

"Why should we trust you?"

"They are looking for you, Miss Vanguard. And your doctor friend here. They have orders to capture you, and kill him." He nodded toward Jeff.

Alarm shook him. *The men in the brown van were under orders to kill him!* "What? Who are these people?"

"I will tell you all I know. But first, we must get away from here. You are in grave danger. Every minute we waste brings us closer to death."

Jeff took a long look at Elly. Their eyes met, held. Then she sighed, took a sideways glance, and nodded. "Okay. But I want to sit up here. Give me your gun." She held out her hand.

The man stared at it then met her eyes. He glanced at Jeff, then pulled his .45 from his belt and handed it to Elly. She stored it in the glove compartment. "Any other weapons?"

"Just a knife. In my boot."

"Hand it over."

He pulled it out, slapped it into her hand and glanced at Jeff again. Jeff shrugged, his fear melting to amusement.

"Go ahead and drive," Elly said. "But I want to know where we're going, and why. I want to know your name and how you're involved in all this. I want to know about the Cyber. Tell us everything."

Jeff settled into the captain's chair behind Elly, where he could keep an eye on the driver, and hear every word. He strapped himself in, just in case things should get wild again.

Soon they were out on the road. "We're heading south on I-25," Jeff speculated aloud.

"That's right," the Indian said. "Isleta is about fifteen miles south of Albuquerque."

"That's all?"

"Yes. It's about 300 square miles. I was born there."

"So you're a Pueblo Indian?"

He laughed sarcastically. "That's what the metal chest Spaniards called us when they 'discovered' us. We call ourselves P'ónin. Isleta is very old, thousands of years old, steeped in tradition. My name is Peeping Ground Hog. I was named this because since I could walk, I explored the caverns around my homeland. My grandmother said that I was always peering out of some hole like a ground hog. I've always been good in caves. Most people call me Hog."

"Okay, Hog, so how are you connected with this Caesar Bossidy? He runs that company, TransGenesis, right?"

"Yes. It is built into the mountain that borders our land. I work with him."

"Hold on. If you're his buddy, and he's got a price on our heads, then why are you helping us?"

"Anyone who has seen his handiwork would understand why I would want to help you."

A gust of wind jostled the vehicle and sang through any opening it could find, reminding Jeff of the wind at Bixler's house earlier that day. "We've seen the buggers. And we've seen what they can do."

"Then you understand."

"Damn straight we understand," Elly said, strapping herself in the front seat. "What is a Cyber, anyway? How did you make them, and for God's sake, why?"

"And why did you pick Elly to try it out?" Jeff added. "Certainly you could have hired some wacko off the street to become the mother of Frankenstein."

Hog's drawn expression hinted at a grin. "You obviously don't know Caesar Bossidy."

"And I won't for long, either," Elly said. "When I find him, he'll be living his last moments."

Jeff grabbed the back of Elly's seat and leaned up closer to her. "A guy like that might be hard to kill. Especially if that baby's claw came from Bossidy's side of the family."

"Caesar is a ruthless man," Hog said. "And you should pray you will never meet him. If you are ever face-to-face, he will have on a surgical suit and you will be flat on your back, on a gurney."

"Don't count on it," Elly said. "I can be rather formidable myself."

"I know," Hog replied. "That's why he chose you."

Elly stared at Hog. Her eyebrows dropped and she pursed her mouth. The wind outside howled and whistled.

"Dr. Meaks screened his patients. He brought Caesar files of the women that met the first criteria—healthy, the right age, and no family to interfere if they ended up missing. Then Caesar screened for other things. Did thorough background checks. You were chosen as most likely to succeed."

"Ha. At what?"

"Carrying this child to term. Giving the child a high IQ, good health and an indomitable spirit."

Disgust wriggled like maggots in Jeff's heart. He'd never looked at Elly as a physical commodity, a sow who could produce bacon or a thoroughbred who could win a big purse. Certainly never as a genetic prize with a waiting womb. To Jeff, Elly had been an example of strength. She'd been a challenge, his challenge. A stubborn, sometimes sarcastic, always difficult, but brilliant and mysterious human being.

He was surprised again at the depth of feeling he had for her, and the anger he felt, knowing that this bastard, Caesar Bossidy, had violated Elly. She wouldn't have to worry about ever running into Bossidy. As soon as Jeff was sure Elly was safe, he planned to find him and give him a taste of his own scalpel.

"Why did he forge my resignation?" Elly asked.

"He intended to hire you on after the extraction. He didn't think he could get you on the staff if you became Dean of Engineering first. So he stopped your appointment the only way he knew how."

"Why didn't he just ask me in for an interview? Why all the covert bullshit?"

"Caesar doesn't ask for anything. He takes." Hog pulled into the right lane. "He honestly thought you would want to join his staff once you saw what he could do. He wanted you, Miss Vanguard. That is a very high compliment."

Before Elly could react to that one, Jeff broke in. "Enough about Caesar. What about these Gremlins? What are they?"

Hog sighed heavily. "Caesar calls them Cybers."

"Genetically engineered?"

"Yes and no. Their genetic structure has been changed, but not only through genetic engineering."

"How is that possible?"

"It's quite a fascinating process. And brilliant."

Elly leaned back and gazed out the passenger side window.

"How long until we get there?" Jeff asked. He didn't like the look on Elly's face, and the wind's moaning made him tenser by the minute. He wished for his medical bag. The wind's sound warped itself, seemed to wrap around the van. It wheezed over window cracks and door hinges, and below his feet where the highway rushed by.

He held his breath and listened.

Hog started to speak, but Jeff held up his hand to silence him. "Did you hear that?" he whispered. He glanced fearfully at Elly. The interior of the van was dark, except for the occasional street light that flashed over their heads. Far off in the distance, silent lightning played in the clouds. Elly's face had a gray tinge. "Elly?"

She sat straighter in her seat. "No," she groaned. "Not yet. But I feel it."

The flute's woodwind voice separated from the wind's random melody, and soon it crooned in their ears.

Hog pointed at an exit sign that rocked in the wind. "The exit is coming up. Look. There it is, exit 215." His voice held a new-found desperation. He pulled the van to the right and onto the exit. Once off the highway, they raced past a pueblo-imitation convenience store painted with a bald eagle in a circle of feathers. People outside the Isleta Gaming Palace looked up as they whizzed by.

"It's starting again, Jeff," Elly said, wide-eyed, her hands over her protruding belly. "My God, what are we going to do? We don't have your bag!"

31

Jeff gripped Hog's shoulder. "You don't understand. This flute. It hurts Eleanor. The baby." Jeff felt close to panic. If he was scared, how must Eleanor feel? She sat rigidly, her hands pressed against her bulging abdomen. *Calm down, Jeff. Think like a doctor.*

"She will be safe at the village." Hog pushed on the gas. The van leapt ahead.

"No. She needs medication. When the flute plays…" Jeff didn't want to say any more. He didn't want to cause it to happen. He snapped open his seat belt and crawled up between Hog and Eleanor. He took her dry, cold hand. It seemed too small, too fragile, for such a strong woman. "Okay, babe, breathe. You know the drill. Deep breath, hold, exhale. Don't get nervous."

"I'm not nervous," she said, then groaned. "I'm pissed off."

"There," Hog yelled. "They're waiting for us."

"Who?" Jeff rose up on his knees and looked out the windshield.

Hog smiled. "My family."

Like out of a history book, the pueblo lay dead ahead—stacked adobe blocks, tied ladders leaning from openings like straws in boxes, *luminarios* lining the multilevel structures like suburban Albuquerque imitated during Christmas. Nearby, people milled around a huge campfire. Hog jerked the wheel and headed over ground toward the gathering. The bumps and holes pushed Jeff around like invisible bullies.

Hog hit the brakes, jumped out and ran around to Eleanor's side. He popped open the door and helped her out. She bent like a hunchback, her features drawn. His heart racing, Jeff hopped out, too, and helped Hog drunk-walk Eleanor toward the group. "What are these people doing out here at this time of night?" Jeff asked. He moved quickly over prairie grass, rocks and sandy soil, hoping he wouldn't step in one of the holes that had bounced him to bruises in the van.

Greetings sounded, even some cheers, and the air grew noticeably warmer as they approached the crowd. Jeff saw the faces in the surreal light of the fire, orange splashes on dark skin. Five or six people ran to greet them, talking loudly. Backlit by flames, they were just black forms until they came closer. Teenage boys, Jeff finally realized. Their hair was long and ebony, stroked by the flickering light. Excited, they patted Hog on the back, stared wide-eyed at Jeff and Eleanor, then escorted them into a quilt of muted colors and ages.

Mothers plucked young children from their games and held them close. The adult men gathered near drums and instruments on the far side of the fire. The older generation sat like statues on mats close to the fire. A young woman, swollen with pregnancy, froze and stared at Eleanor solemnly.

All eyes turned to Jeff, Eleanor and Hog. Quiet now, the people stepped back one by one to allow the three of them closer to the fire.

An ancient woman waited, staring into the flames. She turned toward them slowly. Tiny, yet heavy, the woman looked like the embodiment of time itself. Her white hair hung over her shoulders and down her back, almost to her knees. She wore a gown the color of her hair, and the shadows cast by the fire engraved the deep folds in her face. Her dark eyes fixed on Eleanor.

Behind her, the fire blazed to twice her height, casting her as a Biblical figure, an apparition. The fire snapped its long, luminescent whip and spit ashes upward. A baby cried out. The flute's song seemed to hesitate, then continued.

The woman moved her hands as she spoke, her gaze following her gestures. Hog translated. "There was once one great rushing river that fed all the peoples of the Earth. Then the Earth pushed a great rock up into the river, dividing the waters. The branches were named Old and New. For many generations, the river changed, until Old shrank to just a trickle, and New rushed unabated over the land. Earth cried out for balance to be restored. To do this, New and Old must be rejoined into one great flow. The time has come. You," she said with fluttering hands, motioning to Eleanor, "carry Old and New within your womb. They, too, shall be separated, and when they are brought together again, balance shall be restored."

Eleanor, watching the wave of the tiny woman's hands with fascination, suddenly bent over in pain.

The woman raised her hand in the air and howled, the sound sending chills down Jeff's back. A drum beat began, a few random thumps that escalated into a rhythm. High, inhuman chanting joined the beat then a new song split the air. Another flute. It floated over the roar of the fire, drowning the haunting tones that seemed to feed upon Eleanor. She relaxed and stood erect, amazed. "Jeff," she said hoarsely, "It's stopped. The pain is gone."

The woman lifted her hands again. "You are my daughter," she said through Hog. "Come."

Eleanor hesitated. "What does she mean, Hog?"

Hog glanced at the tiny woman. She nodded approval. "You carry her grandchildren within your womb. The two of you are now related by blood. She is Caesar Bossidy's mother," Hog said, "although he is no longer her son."

32

In the caverns, and inside the buildings huddled within, there was no day or night. No car horns, lawn mowers, birds, or barking dogs. Caesar heard only the faint hum of the lights, the cameras, the ventilation system and the VCR.

He sat utterly still in the conference room. The video of Felipe's death provided the only light, flickering across his tight, angry features like flames, lapping at his skin.

He listened to the flute sounds that emerged from the speakers. He watched the Cyber emerge, with all its power, and watched Felipe freeze as he witnessed his first glimpse of Caesar's glorious new creature. He watched Felipe die because of his inability to react. He watched the Cyber devour him and slither away. He watched no one, not one staff member, do anything about it.

The anger within him boiled. He embraced it. It belonged to him, and was his, the fuel he used to become greater. He watched the video over and over, letting his anger seethe through him like hot lava, creating his strength, giving him what he needed to continue on—the power to create an equal. The power to create *his* equal. Someone who was not incompetent, like the rest of the world of men.

Caesar had just gotten word from Dr. Claus. Number Three's implantation had not worked. The nursing student was not pregnant.

The failure set fire to his blood. Here in this naturally cool mountain, away from the heat of the desert and all of its inhabitants he loathed, he still felt the heat of the village fire as if it burned right now. Right here.

Dr. Meaks. The fool. Unable to successfully perform a simple implantation, just like all the other morons in this pitiful world he lived in. If the man wasn't dead already, Caesar would drag him here and feed his organs to the Cybers. Then, at least, his existence would have meant something, would not have been a waste of time and energy and creation. He would at least have been as good as a pig, born and raised to die, to feed another. The inept Dr. Meaks hadn't even accomplished that.

Caesar's chances of success had fallen to one. All of his dreams, all of his purpose, depended on one host. Number Two—the Vanguard woman.

He slammed his fist onto the table, relishing the pain that followed. The pain meant he was still alive, that he still had a chance to realize his dream within his lifetime. He still had a chance to be more than the animals that roamed the earth, wasting their lives for no purpose.

But mankind wasn't really at fault. The human race was inherently inferior, and without a superior intelligence to guide men, they would always be inferior.

So what now?

He would keep Number Three alive. Killing her would be a waste of a valuable womb. And he obviously couldn't let her go, she knew too much.

But that was the least of his problems now.

The Cybers were loose in the caverns.

Number One was dead and the most advanced Cyber ever created was missing.

Dr. Meaks was dead, so Caesar had lost his University connection to implant more women.

Stark was dead—worse than dead—he'd panicked the rest of the staff before dying.

Bruce was a traitor.

And then there was Number Two, the Vanguard woman. The confounded female continued to evade his best efforts to locate and capture her. She'd escaped his men and his police. Was there more to this woman than he knew? Was she receiving help from somewhere? He knew she was smart. He knew she was street-wise and stubborn and strong, of course, that's why he'd chosen her to bear the Cyber. But Caesar was stronger and smarter. Her continued escapes made no sense. He had an army to chase her—all of his men in TransGenesis vans, and the eyes of the police force, all networked.

Perhaps they hadn't been thorough enough in their background check of her. Someone had to be helping her. But who?

And there was something else. Something malevolent. Something wrong, terribly wrong. The key to that something was in this video, in the damn flute music, and it all connected to Number Two somehow. Vanguard.

What in the hell was going on? None of this had been predicted by his forecasting programs. Caesar himself had run every scenario he could think of through the programs and come up the victor every time.

By now, they should be getting the first human test results. The Cyber chimps should be far enough along to allow the refinement of the palm controllers, and Caesar should be well into training them. He should be close to celebrating a great leap for mankind, the leap into immortality and invulnerability.

He covered his face, and smelled the residual black powder, like metal, on his skin. The flute's sound teased his ears, his mind, his memory, with the insidious visions of his childhood that wouldn't let him go. The sound jerked him back to the village, to the smell of freshly baked bread, wet clay, sweet tobacco. Something whispered that the answer to the mystery of the flute lay not only with Number Two, but in the past life he denied.

Yet that couldn't be. His people knew nothing about him, the company, the project. Sure, the people worked on site, but Caesar kept them confined as part of their job requirements. No one came and went at will. Even when they returned home, what information could they provide that any of their people would care about? They wouldn't be able to understand even the most elementary principles of nanotechnology if they were gathered in one of his conference rooms and tutored.

And how could his mother's people understand true power? They were the cowards who had stood by and let the Spaniards overrun them, followed by the United States government. They'd finally submitted to their own ignorance. Most of the pueblos had fought back in the pueblo uprising. All the pueblos. All but Isleta, where his family lived.

His mother had said that a man could not gain invulnerability or immortality alone. She used to twist Caesar's ear until he fell to his knees, where she would softly remind him that the only path to strength, to immortality, was through humility.

Oh, he'd been humiliated plenty of times. By her. The first was by her rutting with a man who wouldn't claim him, a man who left him a half-breed in an impoverished clay hole. Oh yes, he'd been humiliated, but not humbled. He'd gained no strength from that.

He'd built his strength with his anger, from studying medicine and engineering, from gritting his teeth and working more, more, more. Giving up all other cares, all the other pursuits of young men. He'd done it all, all by himself. And soon, he would pass it on to mankind, and take his place in history.

But first, he had to figure out what had gone wrong and fix it. And his gut, his base feelings, kept leading him back to this video, back to the flute. It had been present at every one of the mishaps.

There had to be a logical explanation for it all. He would find the key.

He'd given the order to seal up the mountain tight. No one was going in or out of the building or the caverns. The entire staff that wasn't out searching for Number Two was looking for the flute player. He would find the bad weed, and pull it. Burn it. Destroy it.

An operating room was waiting for Hog's return with Number Two. He and Hog had prepared it personally, stocking it with equipment, drugs, and even a computer with a webcam for security. The camera would also record the historic operation. The room was waiting, locked down tight. The instant Hog returned with the Vanguard woman, Caesar would perform the extraction himself.

Then he would lead a new crew into the caverns to find the Cybers. After their retrieval, it would be a simple matter to get the company back on schedule.

Someone knocked at the door. The sound sent bolts of irritation through him. The Cyber in the video hadn't asked for permission to enter the world. He'd taken the initiative. Caesar demanded respect from his employees, but when they rolled over and exposed their soft belly to him, begging for a pat, Caesar wanted to slit it instead. The idiot knocking on the door couldn't even enter a room without permission.

"Sir, you in there?" a male voice called from the hall.

Caesar longed for someone who could stand up to him, like Sunflower's Cyber had done right after its birth.

The door cracked open and Claus stuck his head in. "Sir?"

Caesar bared his teeth. "You better have good news for me. The man with the flute has been found?"

"No sir."

"Number Two? Have they captured Vanguard?"

Claus paled and shook his head.

"Then why are you here? Why are you bothering me?"

Claus hesitated. His dark eyes shined with apprehension.

Caesar rose from his chair and slapped his hands on the table. He could bare no more weakness. "Tell me. Speak!"

"It's Hog. He's broken off communication."

"Hog?" Caesar glanced back at the monitor that was still playing the grisly scene. The last time he'd talked to Hog was after Sunflower's operation, when he'd sent the man to lead the search for Number Two.

"And it's not only Hog. Stark's gone, too. And Bruce. The three you sent into the caverns."

Caesar riveted his gaze on Claus.

"The men are frightened. They think…the legends are coming true. The three that went into the caverns didn't come out."

"What are you talking about? Of course they came out."

"But no one has seen them since. They've disappeared."

"You sealed up the mountain when I asked you to?"

"Yes." Claus swallowed. "But most of the natives are gone. There's only a handful of men left inside."

Shock spilled through him. Another unpredicted occurrence. "What? How could that happen?"

"Maybe they left as the mountain was being sealed. The word is that Hog snuck them out."

Hog. He'd broken communication, sworn all exits were guarded, and yet the locals had escaped. Had Caesar misjudged Hog's allegiance? Caesar rubbed the bridge of his nose. "The entrance to the caverns—sealed too?"

"Yes."

"Then what's the problem? Get back to work. The men should be coming back with Number Two any time. When they report in at the gate, I want word immediately."

"But…what do I tell the other men? They want out." Claus glanced over his shoulder, then back at Caesar. He lowered his voice. "They're real nervous. Hog kept everyone satisfied, you know? Calm. Now that so many have gone…"

"Did I ask you to secure the facility?"

"Yes, but I'm not a security guy, it was Bruce who—"

"Let me repeat," Caesar said slowly. "Did I ask you to secure the facility?"

He straightened up, as if finally realizing his own fear was showing. "Yes." It sounded more like a question than an answer.

"Then go make sure it is done right!" Caesar growled. "No one is leaving this goddamned mountain until the Cybers are found. The Cybers are our whole purpose for being here. They are our company's goal. This superstition is nonsense! If we need more people, we'll hire them. Let the scared fools run."

When Claus stared at the monitor still replaying Felipe's death scene, Caesar snapped it off. Shadows fell over them like the warning of things to come. "Assemble the men and tell them I need more volunteers to go into the caverns. We must return the Cybers to isolation before they die out there. And this time, get me some men with spelunking experience. Tell them I'm leading the expedition myself. "We'll meet in the cave room. Tell me when you're ready to go."

He leaned against the table, pointed at Claus, and lowered his voice. "And if you value your life, you'll find the man with the flute."

* * *

Stars in White Cloud traveled through the caverns, his spirit inside the strongest demon. It hadn't been hurt as badly as he had first thought— its developed muscle structure had protected it during the collision. Although it still felt some pain and limped slightly, it was the strongest creature he'd ever inhabited, and had nearly healed itself completely. White Cloud used its eyes and his own memory of the caverns to navigate, going farther than he'd been since awakening, closer to the invaders' bastion.

The men behind the walls were big, strong, with weapons, but White Cloud had surprise and stealth on his side. And destiny was with him. He must sanctify the mountain so the mother of demons could return.

He would enter the fortress within his demons. There, they would pick off the sacrilegious men one by one until the rest fled in fear, no longer able to violate the sacred hill.

There was one man in particular, their leader, a man of his own blood who knew the legends but led the invasion anyway. He must die. With this man gone, the rest would flee. Yes, kill the chief and the rest would retreat.

As he moved toward the structure built in the caverns, the temperature rose. He recoiled. Heat meant light, and light would burn his real body to soot in moments. His skin was transparent, his bones ancient and weak.

Then, remembering the dark skin and strong arms of the demon he occupied he continued on. He hadn't toured the caverns in many years, longer than he had a memory for, and the demon's eyes were like the wolf's, able to transform deepest darkness into afternoon.

Decorations of rock hung from the ceiling, so numerous they looked like rain, frozen and solidified by the awesome power of time. Huge pillars of stone rose up like trees whose foliage had been stripped away. Along the way, he saw a frozen waterfall and stopped to touch it. Cool, slimy water still trickled down the surface, although the rippled rock underneath was just a memory of the water that had been there before. The cascade of stone reached up higher than he could see, disappearing into the darkness. The water made a slight rushing sound that combined with the dripping to make melodious music, almost as beautiful as his courting flute.

He'd used the flute just a few hours ago to call the demon mother and child, and this time a great power had blocked his summons. Only his people had the technique and will to block his shaman's power.

That's when he'd understood. The demon mother and her unborn child would not come to him until the caverns had been purified. They were too holy to step foot within the sacred mountain until it had been cleansed.

Now, he led the little group of demons through the caves, seeking out the intruders. His children had matured, progressed, grown. He occupied the lead demon, mostly healed now, and the rest followed willingly, needing only a nudge from his spirit once in a while to stay with him.

The group tracked the heat of the invaders and the light they produced. Soon the infidels would sacrifice themselves to cleanse the mountain and begin to fulfill the prophecy of Wahatoya.

33

A rock underneath the woven mat he sat on was gouging a dent in his butt, so Jeff adjusted his position. Elly sat next to him, twirling a blade of grass in her fingers. It seemed she was talking, somehow, with the old lady who'd given the history lecture in sign language—Ruffles. Go figure, a woman named after a potato chip. Hog was off mingling with friends and doing whatever groundhogs do.

Unending song filled the night. The ground trembled with each drumbeat, tickling the skin on his legs. When one chanter was ready for a break, another would start up before he even finished, so the music had a consistent monotony. The fire was as hungry as he was tired, and the teenage boys worked to feed it nonstop. Jeff had to wonder if the wood was trucked in, as he didn't see many trees close by, just scrub and grass. If so, this fire was costing plenty of pesos, or whatever these people used for money. The flute had stopped a while back, maybe when the ghost flute had, well, given up the ghost.

The most important thing was that Elly was okay, and for the moment at least, they were safe. Jeff had a powerful urge to curl up in Elly's lap, soak in the fire's warmth, and let the chanting lull him to much-needed sleep. But they were in the middle of something big here. These people saw Eleanor as part of a prophecy, a fulfillment of their pueblo version of scripture. This whole party, it turned out, was for them. Well, it was for Eleanor, anyway. He'd been disappointed to find out that he hadn't even been mentioned as a bit player in their legends. The purpose of the gathering was to protect Eleanor and to plan the final destruction of Bossidy and his weirdo transgenic monster production line.

These folks were going to help. Even Ruffles, whose son was involved, seemed excited and ready to go.

But would their help be enough? And would it come soon enough? Though the fire was warm and the flames mesmerized his weary soul, he couldn't shake the fear and sense of urgency that crawled under his skin.

Jeff leaned over and touched Elly on the shoulder, pulling her attention away from the old woman. "Do you get the feeling we've been dropped into a bad western whose writers should have been working on Alien?"

She looked over at him, distracted. "What?"

"Nothing," he grumbled. "I was just wondering when we get to put on the war paint."

Both women looked at him with confused looks. "We were just talking about Caesar Bossidy," Eleanor said, obviously giving up on trying to understand Jeff. "Can you believe his real name is Little Creeping Lizard? Ruffles said she gave him that name because when he crawled as a child, he moved the right arm and leg then the left arm and leg, like a lizard. Instead of alternating."

"Great. Sounds like a real winner. How did he get from reptile to emperor?"

"She says he could never understand the elders' wisdom. He was very impatient and angry. He resented that his father escaped the village and left him behind. Little Creeping Lizard ran away when he was only fourteen, not only turning his back on his people's ways but vowing to destroy them someday. She disowned him and he changed his name to Caesar."

"Wait a minute," Jeff said. "You keep saying 'she says.' I thought she didn't speak English."

"Oh, she speaks English very well."

"Then why did Hog have to translate the history lesson she gave us?"

The woman leaned over toward Jeff and touched his hand. "Tradition," she said. "And Caesar is not an emperor's name. It is the name of that chimp who overthrew the humans. Didn't you see that movie? It's one of my favorites."

Jeff had to stop a moment and consider this statement. This woman, who lived in an adobe pueblo, had seen *Planet of the Apes*? Well, it was the 21st Century. She must go to into town sometimes. For a moment, he'd been lodged back in time. Right now he couldn't afford to forget where and when they were, and that they were in imminent danger. He cleared his throat. "So he actually went from lizard to chimp?"

"He is more like a lizard in my opinion," Ruffles insisted.

"Ruffles," Jeff said. "How do you know about Eleanor and everything that's going on with us?"

"Legend."

"Yes, of course." He sighed in frustration. "But how did you know the legend was about Eleanor?"

"Hog has been inside TransGenesis since that angry boy built it. Hog got very close to The Lizard. When Hog told us the company had begun human experimentation, we knew it was the beginning of the fulfillment of the legend. We just needed to wait for the woman to appear." She patted Eleanor's hand again and leveled a serious brown gaze at her. "Now we know it's you. Only you are left."

A streak of alarm shot down Jeff's back. He touched Elly's arm. "Do you realize how valuable that makes you to Bossidy?"

She nodded.

"How do you know Bossidy won't come back here with his army?" Jeff asked. "He could ride in here with his warriors, kill all of you, scalp me, and carry off Eleanor. He knows these legends, too. He could figure out where we're hiding." He said the words with humor, but the underlying tension was apparent.

Ruffles threw her head back and bubbled with laughter. "No, no. Peeping Ground Hog says the Great White Shaman is keeping that angry boy quite busy."

"Of course," Jeff said. He slapped his leg. "The Great White Shaman. How silly of me."

Ruffles nodded energetically. "Yes. He has that angry boy chasing his tail."

"Do chimps have tails?"

"No," Ruffles said. "But lizards can grow as many as they need."

Elly interrupted, a hand held out to Jeff and Ruffles. "This might all make sense to you, but personally, I'm confused. Ruffles, Hog might have told you I was pregnant, but there's no way you could have known I was carrying twins. We just found out about that ourselves. So how did you know?"

Together, Jeff and Ruffles said, "Legend." Jeff decided that he liked this old woman more every moment.

"How's it going over here?" a voice interrupted. Jeff looked up and Hog squatted beside them. "Getting acquainted?"

"Ruffles was just about to tell us about the Great White Shaman," Jeff said.

"Ah, well." Hog grunted as he fell to a cross-legged sitting position next to Ruffles. He rubbed the woman's back vigorously. "I wouldn't want to miss that."

Ruffles nodded to Hog. "I told them The Shaman will keep them safe."

"Yes," Hog said, one arm over Ruffle's shoulders, "that's true, kind of. Right now he's protecting you from Bossidy, but is putting Elly at risk in his own way."

The crawling fear became heavy, holding Jeff down. He didn't want to hear that. He wanted Elly to be safe and unafraid. Elly, however, seemed saturated in interest, not a bit fearful.

"The flute?" she asked.

"That's right." Hog looked impressed. "The shaman is the master of the Cybers, and calls them with his bat flute so they can work to—"

"Uh-uh. Hold on. Start over." Jeff held up his hand. "Bossidy engineered the Cybers. He's the 'master', right?"

Hog let out a long breath, a weary sigh. "Okay. Let me start at the beginning."

"Yes. Do that. Without the confusing parts this time."

Elly nudged Jeff with her elbow. He frowned at her.

Hog continued. "In the 1600s, the Spaniards came from the south into our lands. Slowly, they forced our people to worship their god and took over our fields, our villages, our families. We became no more than slaves. The Spanish did not understand our religion, the beliefs they called 'heathen', and this was to our advantage." He picked up a small smooth stone and tossed it in his palm as he talked.

"Although we picked off patrols and a few mountaineers around that time, the pueblo peoples united to overthrow the Spanish forever. Timing was very important, so all the people in what is now four states had to turn and slay their Spanish invaders at the same moment as they slept, so that none could escape and none could be warned."

"How could you manage that?" Elly asked. "There wasn't even a telegraph here at that time."

"At Isleta we have an old tale, a story that only our people remember. Thirty years before the uprising, a white child was born into our village, with snow white hair and pink eyes."

"An albino," Elly said, thoroughly engrossed.

Jeff wanted to laugh. What in the hell did this have to do with Elly's condition? As far as he was concerned, old Indian legends were just that—legend. Modern day people couldn't be affected by them. Stories. That's all they were. Not prophecy.

"The birth," Hog said, "was seen by our elders as a warning, that our land was to be overrun by invaders."

"How brilliant," Jeff snapped, unable to stop himself.

Hog threw Jeff a dark look and continued. "He was named Stars in White Cloud, because his eyes were so transparent his soul could be seen through them, and his white hair billowed around his face like a cloud. He couldn't live in the village because the sun burned his eyes and skin. His mother tried to help him by packing his skin with clay, but finally gave him up for dead. The elders took him into the caverns and there he lived comfortably, though alone."

Elly wrinkled up her face. "That sounds awful."

"For us it would be, yes. For him, it was survival. He found his spirit guide at a young age and the elders, seeing his potential, went to the caverns to work with him every day. Soon, he became the wisest and most powerful medicine man our people had ever known. He could do amazing things."

Ruffles interrupted. "My grandmother was carried to him as a child, so weak with fever she could not lift her head. She walked home with pink cheeks. People still talk about it."

Ruffles gathered her hair in back, twisted it and moved it over one shoulder. "The caves where he lives are inside a mountain. We call that mountain Wahatoya, the Mother of the Earth. All things come from her. Mother mountain creates the clouds that bring rain, the rain that feeds the crops. The crops that sustain our people." She smiled knowingly at Eleanor. "Does that have some meaning for you now?"

Eleanor opened her mouth as if to answer, but Hog said, "Although Wahatoya was the source of all things to our people, to the metal chests and miners, it became known as The Mountain of Demons. Many settlers, troops of the Spanish, and anyone who came near to the caves lost their lives. They reported hearing the screaming of demons within."

"This is where Bossidy built his company? In a mountain filled with devils?" Jeff asked, astounded.

"Yes," Hog continued. "The mountain was feared by some but was revered by our people. It held the secret of our continued existence. As the Mother of the Earth, all things came from her. Including the P'ónin." Hog rubbed Ruffles' shoulder and looked at the stone in his other hand. His voice lowered. "To build in that mountain was the ultimate sacrilege. It was the ultimate—"

"Fuck you?" Jeff asked, breaking in.

Hog smirked. "Yes. Exactly."

Elly shifted her weight on the mat. Jeff's gaze snapped back to her and searched her face for signs of pain. She was just adjusting to the hard ground, he decided. But her discomfort increased his rising anxiety. This had been an interesting stopover and a convenient escape from the bad guys, but what was next? Legends were for history class, but they were living in reality—in the now, not in the 1600s. He wanted to run; it was hard to sit still. But he wouldn't allow himself to forget that although he could run as far as he wanted to, Elly could not. Wherever she went, the horror within her would be along for the ride. They had to find another option, and soon.

Hog cleared his throat, bringing Jeff's attention back to the present. "Because of the White Shaman's power, our people no longer had to hunt. The animals came to our village and offered themselves for sacrifice. Stars in White Cloud controlled them. He could enter the creatures with his soul and lead them to the village."

"What does that have to do with the Pueblo Rebellion?" Elly asked.

"And why should we care?" Jeff snorted. Something across the fire caught his eye. Something small, skirting the edge of the flames. He squinted, but couldn't make it out.

"Isleta, where you are sitting now, became the communications hub for the uprising. Stars in White Cloud entered blackbirds and flew from village to village carrying the news. It was so secret that not even the women were told. The word traveled from blackbird to elder. The rebellion was all set. Then, in one of the villages, a pueblo boy who assisted the elders overheard the news. He was in love with his Spanish teacher and told her to escape. The word was out.

"So we had to change the time of the planned uprising and let every pueblo know within a few hours. The Spanish believed they had stopped the rebellion. After all, what man could run between four states so quickly? But Stars in White Cloud flew the distance and we moved up the time by three hours. The Spanish hadn't even reached the next pueblo with word of the rebellion before we had completely reorganized."

"Thousands of metal chests were killed," Ruffles said, the fire dancing in her eyes.

"But not here," Hog said. "Isleta did not join the rebellion because if something had gone wrong here, all communications would have been cut off. So we let the Spanish here live on, and they thought we were loyal. We even got more privileges."

"But that was all the way back in 1680," Jeff said. "Surely you can't be insinuating that Stars in White Cloud still lives."

Silence fell on the group. Jeff searched the perimeter of the fire for the shadow he'd seen. Where was it? What was it? His heart beat faster. *Run*, his mind urged. *Run.*

Finally, Hog spoke. "Stars in White Cloud still lives. Because he hasn't yet fulfilled his destiny and cannot step into the land of the dead with pride until he does. For many years, he has been in hibernation. Like his spirit guide, the bat."

Elly's voice was husky with interest. "What is his destiny?"

"Yes, that is the key, is it not?" Hog paused again.

Jeff's pulse spiked. Something emerged from the shadows. He jumped to his feet as a Siberian Husky trotted toward Ruffles, its tongue lolling. It plopped down next to her and she stroked its back.

Jeff fell back to the mat, expelling his breath. His heart pounded in his temples. How much longer could he go on like this?

"The White Shaman's destiny," Hog pondered. "We do not know all. But we do know that he must keep Wahatoya sacred. He must keep the caverns free of those who do not respect our legends, traditions, and law. The mountain must not be defiled. The caverns have always been our holy meeting place, and the source from which all things come. The rest of our lands may be defiled," he said, sweeping his hand in an arc, "but the mountain, the Mother of the Earth, must remain pure."

"Again, I ask you," Jeff said, "what does this have to do with us?" He stared at the dog, the pounding in his head becoming anger. A dog. He had jumped out of his skin because of a damned dog.

"Jeff. Be patient." Elly took his hand.

"I'm getting to that," Hog continued. "Bossidy had planned to create thirteen Cybers." Ruffles mumbled something and shrugged Hog's arm off from around her shoulders. She stiffened then rose to her feet. Snapping her fingers, the dog got to his feet also. Together, they walked away toward the other side of the fire, without so much as a glance back.

They all watched her go in silence, until she had joined the shadows beyond the flames.

With his eyes still on the place where Ruffles disappeared, Hog murmured, "The Cybers are created with a combination of medical science and nanotechnology. There are only a handful of doctors in the world who dare to play with recombinant DNA, and even fewer who can understand the way nanotechnology can be used in medicine. Bossidy understands both, uses both, to make the Cybers."

His eyes came back to meet Jeff's. "When the new life is created—the egg meeting the sperm in specialized conditions in the lab—that's where the nanochip comes in. The fertilized egg, now a human life, is put into a conducting solution with the small, programmed superconductor, a nanochip smaller than the head of a pin. This nanochip helps to control the growth of the embryo. If DNA from another species is part of the mix, it is added here. Like a virus, the nanochip reprograms the DNA, making decisions about how the cells will differentiate and how the DNA will recombine. The brain grows around the nanochip, which becomes a functioning part of the fetus's brain. Once the brain has developed far enough, the superconductor stops telling the body how to grow and begins to program the brain itself. The fetus not only has its own brain to use, but has access to all the data available to the superconductor. It gains a great amount of knowledge while still unborn."

"But we're years from that technology," Eleanor said. "Years. I've read about nanotechnology and superconductors with great interest. And people are experimenting with recombinant DNA, but so much goes wrong. How did he accomplish it?" she asked, her voice trailing off into thought.

"Since Caesar first got this idea, he has been working on it with low overhead, and someone, unknown to all, has provided him with almost unlimited funding. He's been able to keep his work secret from the government and other competing companies. He's had the advantage of not having to explain his mistakes, of being able to kill the monsters he produced for years. His research could fly ahead, unabated by law or morality."

Jeff's attention was captured. As a doctor, he knew the genetic side of this story well. It seemed incredible, yet he had seen it firsthand.

"Caesar started with chimps. Many died. Many were born freaks. Each time, he changed the programming of the chip and the ratio of chimp DNA to human DNA. After a few successes, he began the plan to experiment with human subjects. Three women were chosen from the university where Meaks worked on his payroll."

"I saw how Meaks got paid," Jeff commented, rubbing his sore arm. "I got tipped myself."

"His plan was moving ahead, everything working. Eight transgenic, chimp Cybers with human DNA had been born by Cesarean Section. Meaks had implanted three women. Then…"

Hog stared into the fire. The orange light from the flames lit his face and danced in his eyes. His face seemed older, every wrinkle in light and shadow. "Things started going wrong. The Cybers began to…" Hog broke off and looked apprehensively at Elly.

"It's okay," she said gently. She reached out and touched his knee. "We saw Rita."

"She was the first subject." His gaze returned to the warmth of the fire. "Anyway, about twenty-four hours ago, all the Cybers in the nursery suddenly escaped into the caverns. One actually tore its way out of the chimp who carried it, and joined the others, as if they were in contact. The whole thing was captured on tape."

Jeff shivered. This was horrible. How could they stop this from happening to Elly?

Hog continued on. "After that, Meaks got an attack of conscience. Or fear. He made plans to leave the country and called Number Two…I mean…Eleanor. Caesar intercepted the call, took out Meaks and sent men for Eleanor. He wanted her to be incarcerated on the compound so she could be controlled.

"But still he had great problems. Why had the Cybers escaped? We watched the tape of the chimp Cyber who emerged on his own until we noticed something odd. Right before the Cyber came forth, there was a sound. A flute."

"The flute," Elly said, satisfaction in her voice. "This shaman guy plays the flute, which calls the Cybers."

"Wait just a minute here," Jeff objected. "I can believe the technology stuff even though I don't understand it, but I can't swallow that this shaman can play his flute inside the caverns and we can hear it in the van thirty miles away."

242

Elly continued as if he hadn't spoken. "And when the Cybers hear the flute, they want to come home. That's why I feel pain when the flute plays. The Cyber I'm carrying is trying to go home."

Hog grunted and leaned back, as if all had been explained. "Yes. And our flute confused the child."

Elly was intrigued, almost excited. "How do you control them, I mean, at TransGenesis?" she asked.

"With this." Hog reached into his vest pocket and pulled out a PDA, a twin to the one that Sgt. Chavez had used the night of Meaks's murder.

The memory disturbed Jeff. "I've seen one of those before. In the hands of the police."

"Ah, yes. Sgt. Chavez, no doubt? He's too fond of flashing the technology around."

"Let me see that," Elly said, extending her hand. Hog handed it to her and she turned it in her hands, inspecting it. "This is good engineering. Very good."

"I knew you'd be impressed. That's why Caesar expected he'd be able to hire you on."

"But where's the receiver?"

"In the superconductor implanted in the Cyber's brain. The frequencies emitted by this palm controller will control the Cyber's behavior, growth patterns, everything. Even network with the whole system."

Eleanor leaned closer to the PDA, examining it by the light of the fire.

Remembering the ultrasound picture, Jeff pulled it from his pocket. "Elly. This is the picture of your ultrasound. I didn't show you because, well, you'll see why."

He handed the picture to her. At first she held it distractedly, still interested in the small computer, but then the reality of what the image meant washed over her. She set the computer on her mat and grasped the picture with both hands, bringing it close. Her lower lip trembled. Her eyes shone. When she spoke, it was slow and deliberate.

"This means we should have no problem with the birth," she said. "All we need is this computer to kill the Cyber before we extract it." Her eyes seemed riveted to the picture.

Hog glanced at her and then Jeff, speaking slowly. "I'm afraid it's not going to be that easy. The Shaman interrupts the frequencies with his flute. Right now, he's in control of every Cyber that's been born within the facility. None of them respond to the palm controllers."

Elly glanced up from the picture. "Are you sure?"

"I witnessed their attack on one of my men. They killed and devoured him while I stood helplessly by, palm controller in hand."

Unbelievably, Elly smiled. She tapped her finger on the palm controller, a look of utter resolve on her face. "I have an idea. I think I know how to solve all of our problems. I just have to get into that mountain. Inside of TransGenesis."

34

The rising sun slashed across the desert, pale yellow melting to rose as it splashed the pueblo walls. Jeff stopped packing the van for a moment and looked east, drinking in the warmth of the gentle morning sun.

Would this be the last sunrise he'd see? The last day he'd have? If so, the scene before him was idyllic. Isleta, laid out in light and shadow, was truly a haven where the soul could rest.

"Jeff?" Elly came up behind him. "You all right?"

"Yes. I was just looking at the sunrise."

She slipped her arms under his and around his waist, resting her chin on his shoulder. As one, they watched the sun climb and color the adobe walls, changing shadow to gleaming pastels.

"I know what you're thinking," she murmured in his ear. "You're thinking I'm wrong. Like you said last night. You don't think we should go."

Jeff was silent for a long moment, searching his heart. What was right? Last night, actually just hours earlier, they'd concocted a plan, if you could call it that. First, Hog had taught them in detail how to operate the palm controllers. They'd decided they would sneak into TransGenesis through a secret entrance, where they'd enter one of the operating suites inside TransGenesis that held a computer. Elly would re-program the computer, which would in turn update the palm controllers so they would use a new frequency to communicate with the Cybers' nanochips. Once that was done, they'd use the palm controller to kill the Cyber and extract it from Elly. They'd have to leave the caverns carrying Eleanor, right out the front door.

It was a shaky plan at best, but Hog had talked with four trusted men who had come from inside the bowels of the mountain, and now they had a team. And a chance to save Elly. Perhaps, their last chance.

"We haven't decided anything for sure yet," Jeff said. "Nothing is set in stone. You should make the decisions, every step of the way. You're the one taking all the risks here."

But he didn't want to lose her.

She gently turned him to face her. Dark ringlets lay against his forehead, and sunshine tinted the rest of his curls with blood-red highlights. His eyes fixed on her, his concern deep as an underground river.

This guy could not be scared away. She'd treated him like she dealt with everyone else, in a hands-off way that let them know she didn't want them close, and with everyone else they got the message. But not Jeff. He actually seemed to enjoy her coldness, like ice in warm tea. Thank God he had stuck it out with her. Because like it or not, she needed him now. Not just to be her support, her best friend, and her companion. She needed him to save her life.

The sun shone on his face, and his eyes squinted. Slight crow's feet appeared next to his eyes. She sighed.

There were two distinct, opposing forces in her future. On one side, she had Jeff. He offered her a future filled with promise and companionship. Perhaps, even with love. A future with warm kisses, pressed sheets, and fresh squeezed orange juice.

On the other side was TransGenesis. No matter how much she wanted to ignore it, it was a future she couldn't run from. Within the rock tunnels waited the slash of a knife, the hot flow of blood, and perhaps, the empty darkness of death.

But she couldn't run now. The danger grew within her, but now she could admit that her love for Jeff grew right along beside it. Glancing over at the van packed with spelunking supplies, she saw

Hog waiting, a questioning look on his face. "We go in," she said. "Now."

Hog stopped the van behind a clump of scrub oaks. Jeff climbed out of the car, shielded his eyes and looked around. Birds cawed and soared overhead, a counterpoint to the constant background buzz of black flies. Not on the flats anymore, they were surrounded by rolling hills. They'd parked at the bottom of a hill, near an outcropping of rock that was repeated like the vertebrae of a great beast's spine into the hill. He smelled the earth cooking, the sun drawing out any moisture left in the red soil.

Hog, squinting against the sun, joined Jeff. Elly leaned against the van, drinking from a plastic bottle of water. "This is the way my men escaped from TransGenesis last night. They exited the building and went into the caverns. They followed the caves to this hole where they came out. This entrance is on pueblo land, so Caesar can't guard it."

Jeff searched the powdery dirt for tracks, the needle-like yucca for breaks, the sparse army-green grasses for any sign of trampling feet. He saw nothing, no clue that a group of men had moved through the area recently. "Doesn't seem like we're close enough to the mountain to get in from here," Jeff said.

"The caves are underground. Don't need mountains for caves." Hog squatted and began drawing a picture in the sandy soil with his finger. "There are three entrances to the caverns I know about. One is here," he said, enlarging an area in his diagram, "by the bat caves on the north side of the mountain. "One is inside the main gate, here, several miles east of where we stand. We will leave from that gate."

"But the entrance will be guarded," Jeff said. "And it's so far away." Jeff looked over at Elly. How would she ever make it? She'd have to drag herself through caves—that would be hard enough. Then it would depend on him being able to operate successfully in less than ideal conditions. She was trusting him with her life. He'd been running from the operating room for years. The last time he'd opened someone up...well, the last time wasn't worth thinking about.

247

Hog raised his eyes to Jeff. "The men we talked to last night will make sure they have the front gate under their control when you come out with Eleanor. They will take you wherever you want to go.

"And this," Hog said, going back to his drawing, "is the third entrance, the one we stand near, on Isleta land. It is the oldest, and has been used by our people for hundreds of years."

"Where is it?" Jeff asked, searching the scrub and sand for clues.

"The entrance is hidden, and small, but leads to a big room where our people used to take refuge from the Spanish. And, legend says, where we went to meet with the Great White Shaman. A passageway leads off the big room to an entrance into the labs. If we go in that way, there should be no guards. We will make our way through the labs to the operating room. There should be only a handful of men left inside, if they haven't left already. We should be able to seal up in the operating suite, access the computer from the terminal inside, and operate. There may be some medical personnel still there. If necessary, I will make sure they assist you."

"You think if we take out Bossidy, the people left inside will help?"

"I can't guarantee it. But I suspect so."

Elly spoke up. "Where are they keeping Donna?"

"When I left, she was in isolation, near the operating suites."

"We have to take her with us."

"Of course."

Hog stood and looked at Jeff, then Elly. "This won't be easy, but it can be done. Are you ready?"

Jeff felt like he was on roller skates, and destiny had just tilted the world down forty-five degrees. They were going in. Into the caverns, into TransGenesis.

He just didn't know if they'd ever come out again.

He looked at Elly. She nodded and lifted her face to the sun, soaking in its warmth.

This was it. "Okay," Jeff said. "We're ready."

"We walk from here," Hog said. "The entrance is behind the rocks."

They approached an outcropping of sandstone and Hog ducked under an overhang, disappearing. When he reappeared, he carried two backpacks. One seemed to be made of two white gallon bleach bottles with their bottoms cut off and forced together, their tops pointing out at the two ends. A strap had been attached to the two handles. The other bag looked like a small army pack. "This should be enough equipment to safely get us where we're going. It is only thirty minutes by foot from this entrance to the TransGenesis lab. During that time, my people will secure the main gate."

"And what if the door is still guarded when we get there?"

"Then we will handle it. I am still in their employ. I can say I was in the caverns looking for the Cybers. I can distract the guard. But as I said, most of the employees left are unhappy with Caesar. They think he has gone too far."

Jeff's sense of anxiety intensified as a vision of the Cybers he'd seen flashed across his eyes. "Oh, my God. I forgot about the Cybers. What happens if we run into them?"

Hog looked pensive. "I have no answer to that. Hopefully, Eleanor will be able to get to the computer and re-program our palm controllers before we see one." He hesitated. "And I have this."

Reaching into a long pocket hidden in one of his pant legs, he withdrew a flute and held it out in his palm. Made of a single branch, so small it was almost a twig, holes were burned into its length. The top was carved intricately, shaped like a groundhog. Long feathers whipped back from its face like an Indian headdress.

"I'd rather have a stun gun," Jeff said.

"Right behind this rock." Hog darted behind a waist high sheet of stone that stuck out of the ground like a wall. Behind, he threw aside some dried tumbleweeds, revealing an oval shaped rock about the size of a manhole cover.

Jeff and Elly stared. "You've got to be kidding. That's only a few inches around larger than my belly. You want me to crawl through there?" She held her palm over her belly. "You're insane! I'll take my chances at the hospital."

"It is only the opening that is so narrow. Pueblo people are naturally small. The Spaniards were not, especially in their armor. My people did not want to widen the entrance and take the risk of discovery. Right inside it opens up, tall enough to walk."

Hog bent his knees and sat on his heels. He opened the packs and sorted through the equipment.

"For who to walk?" Elly asked. "You or Jeff?"

"He can walk." Hog looked Jeff up and down. "Hunched over."

"What is that thing?" Elly pointed at the bleach bottle assembly.

"We call it a pig. We use it to carry all supplies we do not want to get wet."

"Wet? Why? You expecting rain in there?"

"We try to plan for all unexpected occurrences. There are underground streams, of course. They are the artists of the caverns. If it rains out here," he held out his arms to encompass the desert, "the ground does not expect it, so the water runs to lowest ground. If we are in lowest ground, the rain finds us there."

Elly squinted, checking out the cloudless sky. "Hog, it's not going to rain in the next thirty minutes. I'll bet my life on that."

"I will not," he said, and actually flashed her a smile as he patted his pig. He recapped the equipment and stood. "I will enter first, pushing the supplies in front of me. Once we're through the first crawl hole, I will turn on a flashlight. You will follow me. Quietly, please."

Jeff saw that Elly's peaceful mood was threatening to change. He couldn't even imagine what she must be feeling. Soon, not only would she have a monster within, but more of them around her, plus human enemies that were just as dangerous. She was looking forward to someone cutting her open in the next few hours, if she wasn't killed first.

Her lips were pursed, her jaw set. She still squinted slightly and for a moment he could see the fear she hid just under the surface. Jeff took her by the shoulders. "You know what I admire most about you?"

She looked at him as though he was her little brother, bothering her again. "What?"

"Ever since I first met you?"

"What?" she snapped at him, impatiently.

"Your courage." When he said it, he meant it from the deepest part of his heart, from the darkest depths of his own dread. It was as much an observation about her as it was a confession about his own place in life—how he teetered over the edge of a canyon of fear, ready to fall. He also meant it to encourage her, to remind her that she needed her mettle now more than ever. To remind her that he, too, needed her example.

She knew all of this. Understood what he felt, what he meant. Her face melted into an expression of love so obvious and sweet that he would forever remember the moment. He leaned his forehead against hers. "Are you ready to steal the witch's broom, see the wizard, and go back to Kansas?"

Without waiting for a answer, he kissed her. His lips melted into hers. She purred. He cupped her head and deepened his kiss. *God.* He really wanted more of that. It was a kiss of promise, of hope. It was a kiss that foretold happiness, that suggested there was a future for him, that his life was just beginning. It stirred him, in many ways.

He pulled back, just a little, and looked into her eyes. One tear ran down her cheek. He wiped it away, leaving a track of red dirt. A fine layer of dust covered them all.

"I'm starting to think," she said very quietly, that I don't want to go back to Kansas—"

"Let's go," Hog interrupted in the loudest voice Jeff had ever heard him use. "We must get moving before someone spots us and realizes something is up."

Together, Jeff and Hog slid the slate cover from the entrance. Hog laid on his back, stuffed the packs in the hole ahead of him and pulled himself into the bowels of the earth.

Jeff's stomach crawled as he watched him. Jeff wasn't claustrophobic, but he wasn't an idiot, either. What he just watched Hog do definitely bordered on lunacy. And they were supposed to go next. He looked at Elly. "Ladies first."

"How did I know you were going to say that?"

"I know it's cliché. But right now, it's important."

She stared at Hog's feet as they disappeared into the hole. "I want you to go first," she said quietly. "Please."

Jeff could tell she was scared, but only because he knew her. Only because it made sense she would be scared. To the casual observer, she'd look as if she were ready to enter a business meeting, after working out at lunchtime. So not to make her admit her feelings, he agreed. "Okay. But you better stay close behind me."

Jeff gave her one last kiss and walked to the overhang. He laid himself down and used the heels of his running shoes to propel himself into the hole, and for all he knew, into hell.

35

Bruce opened his eyes. Darkness surrounded him like a funeral shroud. Only a small glow of dim yellow from the emergency light in Caesar's office lit the cavern where he lay dying.

He felt the life oozing from him but was too weak to do anything about it. He couldn't open his mouth to scream, or move his body back into Caesar's office where someone might find him. Help him.

Each fluttering beat of his heart pumped more of his life-giving blood from him, each beat marking the last seconds of his life. He floated, painlessly. All he could do was listen. He knew they were out there, and he knew they would come for him.

Then he saw it. One pair of gleaming yellow eyes, eyes that Caesar had designed, peeked out from behind a stalagmite. It made a sound like a squirrel, but more human. The chittering seemed to be arranged in rhythmic patterns as if it used language, not just made random noises. Bruce knew they were talking to each other, knew they were communicating. What had he helped TransGenesis unleash upon the world?

Bruce waited until all the points of gold glowing eyes surrounded him. His breath came short and fast, sweat pouring from his brow. He gritted his teeth and put all his remaining energy into pressing the button on his palm controller labeled *kill*. His finger pushed the button and froze in place. Pressing, holding, demanding.

There was no response. Nothing.

The Cybers shuffled closer, chittering and moaning. The one closest to him stepped into the weak light from Caesar's office. His tongue flicked out, in. Out, in. Like a party blower. Then it jumped onto him, its horrible face burying itself in the open wound in his chest.

Bruce's scream echoed only in his mind. His body wrenched and pulled in all directions as the monsters attacked. Why was he still conscious? *Why?*

When the darkness finally came, it washed over him like a desert sandstorm. He sank gratefully into the emptiness.

36

Jeff smelled dirt. The scent seemed to fill his nostrils, his lungs, his mouth. Like being underwater, he was under dirt. He struggled for breath.

The hole was a long tube. The dirt ceiling hung only inches from his nose. Instead of crawling, he was on his back. To propel himself forward, he'd bend his knees as much as the inches would allow, which wasn't much, then reach over his head and find a handhold in the rock. He'd pull with his fingers on the top of the cave and push with his feet on the bottom, dragging his back along the floor. Each grasp sent pain through his injured arm and bruised wrist.

Hog had not said it would take long to crawl through the small hole. He had not warned them that they could run out of oxygen. Was it all a trap?

Panic made each breath shallow, made his fingers shake as they scraped the rock for purchase, made his mind reel. In here, the real world seemed as far away as Mars.

With stark certainty, he realized that he had been wrong to trust Hog. Hog could be on Caesar's side. This could be the final attempt on his life. They could trap him here in this hole.

Elly! She was supposedly behind him, but like a prairie dog in a hole, he couldn't turn to see if she was there.

Darkness, complete blackness. Dirt. He spat. He breathed deeply and coughed. No more air, just dirt. Dust. The faint smell of droppings.

Putrid, rotting things.

He pushed with his feet, dragging his back over rocks.

His arm pulsed with pain. How much longer would it hold out? His lungs burned. The large hand of Earth pressed down on his lungs and covered his mouth.

But if Elly could keep going, so could he. This was horrible for him, but how much more terrible for Elly? Her belly must be dragging along the top of the tube, if she wasn't already stuck. He tried to call to her, to tell her to go the other direction, that they should both get out, but his calls were absorbed by the cold rock as soon as they emerged from his throat.

Don't panic. Not enough oxygen to panic. But his heart beat against his chest, against the earth that pressed down on him.

The cave angled sharply down, he was on his head, on his back, he couldn't breathe, couldn't breathe! He'd made a mistake. Hog could not be trusted.

He had to turn around. How? He stopped, stopped reaching, stopped sliding. If he stopped, he would trap Elly. The hole was too small to turn around in.

Go on.

His fingertips dug into the earth above him. It crumbled into his face. He cried out, but there was nowhere for the sound to go. He coughed again. He needed more air. *He was going to die in here.*

He had been a fool. Of course Hog wanted him dead. Hog didn't find them accidentally, he had been sent as Jeff's executioner. Jeff had been such a fool.

Elly.

He swallowed. His air was almost gone. He couldn't see Hog, couldn't hear him, could hear nothing.

Down, down. He was almost vertical now. He knew he was stuck—he would die and molder here, inside the belly of the Earth. The hole was still getting smaller. *He wouldn't make it!* The roof dipped almost to his nose.

256

Then, a smell. *Ammonia. Coolness.*
Oxygen.

He reached above his head, felt a ledge and grasped it with both hands. He was at the edge of the passageway, at the end of the tube. *Thank God!* He pulled, bending his arms and trying to pull his entire body from the hole. Pain shot through his arm and down his back. He pulled harder, trying to drag himself free. His head poked into a larger passageway and he saw a glow, a beautiful light. Resting for a moment, he gasped for air then wiggled out to his waist and pulled his feet free. He fell from the hole and collapsed to the floor of a cave room.

He heard a muffled cry from within the hole above him, and scuttled back, crab-like, out of Elly's way.

"Hog!" Elly cried. "Aim the light over here."

The light found Elly. With the flashlight in his mouth, Hog pulled Elly from the small tunnel. He grabbed her hands, pulling, then under her arms, jerking. Her feet fell down onto the ground and she stood. "Shit," she said. She turned around and brushed dirt from her sweat suit. "Shit, shit."

"Agreed," Jeff said, too loudly. The sound bounced around the cave's walls like a ping-pong ball. "How did your people ever go through there the first time?" he asked Hog, quieter. "How did they know it would go anywhere, and they weren't just moving on to certain death? A person would think they were dying in there if they didn't know better." He didn't mention that was exactly what he'd thought. Now that he was safe, he felt the usual embarrassment that resulted from his fear.

"Our people didn't need to discover this cave," Hog said. "They've always known about it."

Still catching his breath, Jeff stared at Hog. He should have expected some vague response like that. Elly leaned against the wall near him, her hand on her abdomen. She made no comment.

"Are you all right?" he asked.

"Of course not. Do I need to list my injuries for you? I'm not fine, and I won't be until we're out of here. So don't bother to ask again."

Jeff grinned. Elly's motor was cranking along just fine.

He looked around. They were not in a large room, as he'd first thought, but a small room that led to another passageway. It, too, angled sharply down into the earth. "How far down does this go?" He stared into the gaping darkness, unable to see more than a few feet from the flashlight's glow. "Is TransGenesis built this deeply in the caverns?" The walls absorbed his voice, swallowed it up, yet left a high ringing sound in the rock.

"Only the labs. They are deep. So nothing can get in." He thought for a moment. "Or out."

Hog shined the flashlight beam around the passageway. A few stalactites and stalagmites remained, but most had been broken. The ground had obviously been trampled by many feet.

"Kinda beat up in here," Jeff commented.

"This cave has been used by my people since the beginning of time. No matter how careful you are, the cave decorations are very fragile. Just the vibrations from your shoes can crack them, sever their lengths."

Elly started toward the passageway. "At least we don't have to crawl in this one. How long from here to the labs?"

"It depends on how fast we move. If we do not enter, we will never get there."

"Right," Elly said. "Let's go, then."

Hog walked quietly to the opening, drifting like a spirit. The glow from his flashlight cast him as a silhouette. Elly followed him next, this time without complaint, then Jeff.

She stepped into the passageway bent over, and wrinkled up her face. "What is that smell? It's like old dog piss."

"Ammonia," Jeff said. Almost unbearable, the smell was the combination of everything his mother had ever told him to stay away from.

"Guano," Hog said, back over his shoulder. "It will get worse when we pass the bat cave."

"Great," Elly said, then ducked in after Hog.

Jeff followed. The thought of being left alone inside this cave was too horrible to contemplate.

The scent was repulsive but the passageway was far superior to the first. He could see Hog and Elly and at least six inches remained between his clothes and the walls on both sides. Hog had been correct, though. Jeff had to bend over to walk. Still better than slithering like a sidewinder.

Dampness, the rustle of their footsteps, and a faint dripping noise hung in the air. Calcified patterns adorned the walls like marble sconces. The floor angled down and it bothered him to even think about how far underground he was going or how they could get out, so he tried to concentrate on each step and each breath. The air was humid and stale and the scent of ammonia intensified.

"I thought bats lived in the outer caves, in large rooms," Jeff said. "Not this far in, or in the tiny passageway we came through."

"You are right. The bat cave we will pass connects to the outside world," Hog said.

"Through a big room?"

"Yes. We are near the mountain."

"Then why didn't we enter there?"

"The guano is very deep," Hog continued. "Sometimes to your knees. You must wear a mask to pass through. The last member of my people to go through there came back with white hair. A sign."

"Right," Jeff answered.

"Besides, that entrance is guarded by TransGenesis guards. It opens to their property. It is inside their fence."

"They won't be able to see us, will they?" Jeff asked.

"No. To enter the cave from here, one must be a spider. Or a fish."

"Oh."

Stillness reigned. They picked their way to a crossroad in the passage. Two tunnels went on, a large one stretching off to the left and a smaller one angling to the right. In the silence, Jeff heard only their labored breathing and water dripping somewhere.

"Which way?" Elly asked, her voice swallowed by the cave.

"Look." Hog shined his light into the large passageway, the one Jeff had hoped they would take. Two steps in but hidden in shadow, the cave floor disappeared. The hole swallowed the beam of Hog's light. "If your light runs out, do not walk in these passages. Only crawl, chanting and praying. If you chant, you can hear the change in the pitch of your voice when a hole opens up. If you pray, you might understand what it means before you fall in."

Jeff's stomach clenched. The idea of being without a light in the caverns was unfathomable.

"I guess we're going right," Elly said.

"Yes. Again, I will go first." This time, he got down on hands and knees to crawl through. Although the passageway was small, it looked like cake compared to the initial, much smaller hole they'd muscled through.

Elly followed. Jeff was glad for it. If she was in front him, he could make sure she was all right. Not that he could do anything if she wasn't. Within these caverns, he was as out of control as a caged animal. His fate was completely in Hog's hands.

A strange sensation settled in his stomach as he thought about Hog. About the flute he carried. *What was it?* And then it came to him. During their planning outside the cave, Hog kept saying *you*, not *we. You* will reach the entrance and the men will take *you* wherever you want to go.

A strange mix of suspicion and fear accompanied Jeff into the cave. Hog was guiding them in, but he wasn't sure he would ever leave.

* * *

Stars in White Cloud moved in a cave without decoration, through a room with no natural form or beauty. Everything was square and colorless, shiny from being touched too much. If this was what he missed while hibernating in the caverns then he had nothing to regret.

Inside the lead Cyber, who grew stronger each moment, White Cloud led the others from their feasting into the light, into the ugly room filled with shiny objects and square shapes. A strange hum came from the room, as if these metal objects lived.

White Cloud was living his fate, and excitement strengthened him. All the demons were now within the caverns. The mother of demons was approaching. White Cloud felt every breath she took as if each exhale carried the promise of life and the music of destiny. He breathed back to her, calling her to the next world where she would be honored. He encouraged her on, inviting her to join their family.

As one, they searched the room for food, for weapons, for people. And then, for an exit. There seemed to be no doorway. But White Cloud sensed the Cybers accessing their fire-hearts. Maps. They had maps to these bright caves of dead things.

He allowed the children to forage, letting them discover. He closed his eyes and called to the demon mother.

* * *

Elly paused, a strange sensation overwhelming her. For a moment, her constant pain and fear abated, and she felt the peace of a sunny day, laughing children, and family close around her. She'd never had a family. The picture filled her with joy.

She smiled. The same trancelike feelings that had been molding her, calling her, changing her life, were strong here. So strong, she was inside the ringing bell instead of answering its call. But it no longer frightened her. She felt willing. She could offer herself up to the power, to the voice, and let it take her.

A hand, Jeff's hand, pushed her from behind, jolting her back. She had stopped in the tunnel, trapping him behind her. *Not good.* She couldn't give in and let the call control her. Not yet, not ever. The power was strong, overwhelming, but she couldn't give in to it.

She had Jeff to think about. She took a deep breath, exhaled heavily, and crawled on.

With every motion, more of the scabs on Elly's knees ripped and crumbled, packing the ridges and holes in the rocks, and fresh blood wet her sweat suit.

Her belly hung beneath her like a heavy sack of potatoes, pulling on the small of her back, straining the muscles. Her shoulders ached as she crawled. Blisters formed on her palms where they scraped on rock.

Okay. That's okay. As long as the fetus didn't start up its wild agony dance again. She couldn't even allow herself to think about it: giving birth in this dark, damp hole with a man on either side and murderers stalking her.

But since she'd entered the caves, she no longer thought of them as murderers. Instead of dreading what waited for her at the end of this passageway, she felt a dreamy attraction to it. She knew that death could still await her, but somehow it no longer mattered.

Wrong. Damn it! She had to fight the strange call that filled her head and heart, that persuaded her to give in. But she was so tired of fighting, so tired of being strong.

But now there was Jeff. She didn't have to be strong, not by herself anymore.

Now there was Jeff.

He was so unpretentious and helpless, but she trusted him. He didn't pretend to have all the answers, or even attempt to act the macho male role. He stumbled around like a boy in a department store, well meaning, caring, but without any of the answers or tools to find his way out. Elly knew that if he could, he would hold her hand all the way, to the very end. If they remained lost, at least they'd be lost together.

That was the real deal. The thing that mattered most. She didn't really care if he was the American hero. She didn't care if they stumbled through this like mice in a maze. All she wanted was Jeff's hand in hers, his voice in her ear and the knowledge that even if he couldn't save her, he'd never give up trying.

A slice of rock, sharp as glass, cut into her right palm. She winced and lifted her hand to suck off the blood.

This time, Jeff poked her with a finger. She smiled and moved on.

Now, there was Jeff.

37

Caesar's steps echoed in the long hallway as he marched back to his office to collect his Derringer and ammunition. The building was empty. *Never mind.* He'd gone to the cave room to assist Claus and the others in retrieving the Cybers from the caverns, but had found them gone. Like the weak bastards he knew they were, they'd fled at the first sign of trouble. So now it was time for him to go into action, and he was ready.

Artificial light gleamed on polished tile and off whitewashed walls, bright enough to make him squint. So different from what he knew he'd find in the caverns. The thought sent a shiver up his back. He'd brought light to this mountain, and more. He'd brought science and the future. He'd given the backwards people a chance to take their place with him in history.

Cleanliness, technology, and fame. Even then, the people couldn't seem to embrace the dream. They couldn't leave their pueblo ways behind them. *Why?* He'd never understand it.

Well, if he wanted anything done right, he'd have to do it himself. *The story of his life.* He would go and capture the Cybers, himself. He'd lock them in the isolation rooms, himself. Then he'd comb the buildings and caverns until he found the man with the flute.

After he made sure he locked the company down tight, he'd go out and find Number Two. He'd bring her back here and extract the Cyber. If there was no one to assist him, he could still accomplish the job. He might lose the Vanguard woman without someone to close her back up while he examined the Cyber, but he couldn't let that matter now. The Cyber was his all-important step into the future. The woman knew way too much about his operation, anyway.

Then he'd start at Number One's house and search until he found the missing Cyber. It was hiding in the house or close by, it had to be. There had been no reports of strange sightings, so it must have gone to ground, probably somewhere with a food supply. Caesar had an new idea he cursed himself for not putting in place originally—he would try to track the Cyber's nanochip. If he could find the specific signals—frequencies—given off from the nanochips made by TransGenesis, he could find the Cyber. Some brainstorming and some tinkering was all it would take. And any future design would have GPS as a basic standard. He just hadn't anticipated that the Cybers would escape the secure mountain.

His heart beat along with his steps, forming a rhythm of progress. He ground his teeth and walked faster. Caesar would triumph. He wouldn't let the stupid fear of legends stop him after coming this far. He would make his own history, become his own legend. Never would he bow to fear and suspicion. He'd known since he saw his first *homo* that he was destined for greater things. He just had to push on. Leave the weak behind. Keep his goal well in mind.

A flash of light interrupted his thoughts. His office lay ahead on the right; he was approaching its darkened windows. The spark seemed to be coming from there.

Flash.

Caesar slowed his steps and moved closer to the right wall, instinctively. He saw a glint, a glimpse of something through the smoky glass. A reflection from the hallway?

A warning flared through him and settled in his gut. His jaw tightened. He examined the hallway. Empty. No one anywhere. He listened, pressing his back against the wall.

Yes. There was a sound. Scraping, like a drawer opening. Closing. And something else. Talking, chittering.

Although he knew he didn't have his gun, he patted the pockets of his jacket with both hands instinctively. He found his palm controller in his back pocket, pulled it out and shuffled closer to the windows, back against the wall, arm extended. He glanced toward the doorway. The door was closed. Locked, if it was as he left it. If it was still locked, then that meant someone had come in through the caverns.

Caesar replayed the scene in his mind. He'd rolled Bruce through the back door into the cave, slid the door shut then had locked this hallway door before leaving his office. If Bruce's heart had still beat then, he'd certainly be dead by now.

Had Bruce survived? The .22 didn't pack much of a wallop, but Caesar had watched the blood roses open on Bruce's chest. Had he somehow been able to crawl back into the office? If so, he wouldn't be on his feet searching Caesar's office. That made no sense. Caesar pressed his ear against the window. Things were being shifted in his office, moved around. Something was being dragged. There were utterances—animal sounds, yet not quite animal. He could almost understand them.

There was something else, too. Caesar could feel it, both emanating from the room and echoing within his own chest. A cloud of power, an aura, a jumble of childhood memories.

And then he knew, just like that, like a flashlight switching on in the dark.

The Cybers. They were here, had come to him. The power he sensed in the room must be his own. They knew their creator, and had come to him. Had come home.

The Cybers must have sneaked in through the back entrance into his office. They were probably searching for food, and Bruce's stench had led them right to the doorway.

Brilliant! The Cybers were brilliant, just as he had designed them to be. They didn't huddle in the caverns and die like helpless cowards, they had come searching for food, for warmth, and had found a way in.

This was perfect. He had his palm controller. If they were all in his office, it would save him a trip to the caverns. He could grab them, in his own territory. No darkness, no stinking guano. The Cybers were already, even in their extreme youth, superior to men.

Caesar wanted to see, had to see. He slid along the windows, palm controller extended, toward the office door. His heart pounded. He wished he hadn't tinted the windows so dark.

Hog's words skirted through his mind before he could stop them. *The spirit of the Great White Shaman fell upon us. Stark offered himself up to the Cybers as nourishment, as the deer or buffalo would have done in the old times.*

Nonsense. Ridiculous. And yet, as he approached the door, the hand holding the palm controller began to tremble.

The palm controller would function. The computers were up and running; his design of the palm controllers had been flawless. But Hog had claimed they had become utterly useless.

Hesitating for just a moment, Caesar aimed the palm controller at his office, set on *wide area sleep,* and pushed the button. He held his breath, listening, his ears straining for any sounds within the office. Nothing.

He lowered the palm controller, and still wanting to be cautious, inched toward the door. Grasping the doorknob, he twisted. It wouldn't budge. Still locked. He backed up against the wall again, fast.

He'd have to use his keys and that would make noise. Not only that, he'd have to stand directly in front of the door instead of shielding himself to the side. And he'd have to use both hands, meaning he couldn't keep one hand on the palm controller. So far, he hadn't heard a peep from inside since he'd fired the palm controller, but he had to be sure the signal had reached them and that it had put them to sleep.

Should he call for help? *No.* If he retreated, the Cybers might return to the caverns and he'd lose his chance to catch them. He wanted to trap them in his office, and he wanted to do it now.

He swallowed hard, his heart beating in his throat. He'd unlock the door as quietly as possible and sneak it open. Then, if his steel door had blocked the signal and the Cybers were still active, he'd use the palm controller to put them all to sleep. Then he'd lock both doors and they'd be trapped. All he'd have to do is go get the cages and transport them to an isolation room.

It would work...it *had* to work.

38

Jeff saw the light ahead of him change. The steady yellow glow became erratic then disappeared. Elly's shadow evaporated with it. He tensed and stopped crawling, trying to get his bearings, trying to let his eyes adjust to a blackness too deep to allow sight of any kind.

Darkness seemed to bury him alive. Had the flashlight burned out? Had Hog left them behind? But how? The tunnel was too small.

Then he heard Hog's voice. Instead of a muffled sound, like in the tunnel, it echoed. "Keep coming, slowly. You will be able to stand soon."

He crawled ahead in the tunnel, only to find Elly blocking his way. Fighting down his rising sense of panic, he placed a hand against her body and gently pushed. She moved, thank God, she moved. He poked her with his finger for good measure and within a few seconds, Jeff felt Hog's grasp on his shoulders, helping him to his feet. Jeff's muscles groaned. His knees protested as he rose to a standing position.

He could see nothing.

"What happened to the light?" he whispered.

"We no longer need it. And we don't want to be seen. Look."

Jeff strained his eyes, looked around him, searching for something, anything. He was truly blind. "Look at what? I can't see a damned thing."

Then his gaze found it. A line of light, standing flagpole straight, maybe eight feet high. It was too straight, too bright, to be real. For a moment, he didn't understand what he was seeing. Then he knew. It was the frame of a door. Looking more closely, he could see two other lines of light running horizontally above and below, forming the frame. A door. It seemed totally out of place in the wall of the cave. It was higher than they were, probably up a rise in the cave floor.

"I see it!" Elly whispered, excitement in her voice.

"It's the entrance to the cave room. That door will take us inside TransGenesis."

Jeff felt his stomach tense. He reached for Elly, found her arm and pulled her closer. They had arrived. Now, into the belly of the beast.

39

Caesar listened to the chittering coming from inside his office, fascinated and yet horrified. They were using rudimentary language, he was sure of it. The palm controller had had no effect, probably because the reinforced steel door blocked the signal. He hadn't expected to ever have to use the palm controller against Cybers in his own office. He'd have to open the door before the signal could reach them. He took a breath, dropped the palm controller into his jacket pocket and reached for his keys.

His hand came back from his back pocket empty. He didn't have his keys. Rapidly, he patted himself down again, each pants pocket, his jacket, his shirt. Nothing. Anger rose inside him. First his gun, then his keys. In his hurry to get away from Bruce, he must have left them in his office. There was no excuse for such carelessness. He was being distracted by the ridiculous behavior of—

A chair crashed through the window next to the door where he stood. Safety glass flew like sparkling confetti out over the floor, covering Caesar's pants. He blinked and stepped back, astonished. Was a man in his office after all, had he been mistaken? Had Bruce survived? But then, why not just open the door from the inside? Why break a window?

He froze, staring at the glittering pieces of glass as they came to rest. He raised his gaze to the window. His heart pounded out of control and his mouth was dry. The question banged in his head—could the Cybers have gotten big enough to throw a chair through a window? He took two steps back, his mind racing. What would come through that window? His eyes were glued to the opening. He was motionless, waiting.

It jumped through the opening like a deer. It landed lightly in front of Caesar, but didn't look at him. It turned back to the gaping hole and called through it to the others.

Caesar slowly backed away, keeping his eyes locked on the thing, his breath silent. Maybe it hadn't seen him. Maybe, *oh God please*, it hadn't seen him. It was huge. Maybe three feet tall, and almost as wide. It held its claw hand aloft, like a flag of victory. Its legs bowed only slightly, rippled with muscle. *Impossible!* How could it happen so quickly? The nanochip must function better than he had ever predicted.

Caesar's fear bent into a kind of hysterical excitement. He had done it. He had created a master race.

The claw gleamed, and shock spilled through him with such strength he almost cried out.

It wasn't a claw.

It was metallic. It was a fist, holding a letter opener! This was not a Cyber chimp. *This was Number One.* The first and only human Cyber in existence. The one he'd planned to go looking for.

It couldn't be. How had it come to the mountain, how had it found him? Last he'd heard, it was running loose somewhere in the city, hiding and possibly dead.

This was impossible.

Number One held the brass letter opener high, raised his chin and let out a piercing cry. The sound, alarmingly human, echoed through the halls and touched something inside him, something basic and familiar. Caesar watched, stunned, as another Cyber leapt through the window and landed beside Number One. Then another, and another. Number One led them, and they seemed to be organized. *Amazing.* Half of them split off and ran down the hallway, on a mission. They were a team and they were here to kill.

His palm controller! He'd been so lost in the sight of his creations that he'd forgotten. Ripping it from his pocket, he made sure it was still set on *wide area sleep.*, He aimed it at the leader and pushed the button.

His thumb depressed the button again. And again.

As if it could hear the signals coming from the palm controller, the leader's head slowly turned in his direction. The eyes found Caesar's. *Oh, God, the eyes.* They were intelligent. They held the fierce determination of a hawk diving toward its prey. The Cyber stared at him, unblinking.

Caesar turned and ran.

* * *

One by one, they jumped through the hole into a tunnel. The tunnel, too, was bright. Everything here amongst these trespassers was too light, as if the light would scare away righteousness. It could not.

White Cloud raised his face to the heavens and let out a war cry. He filled the cry with his joy, his excitement. Quiet for 300 years, but no longer. He was finally living his destiny.

His plan was to divide up. While White Cloud and his four best found and destroyed the leader, the man who was once one of his people, the others would find the demon mother, birth the child, and kill any remaining invaders. Quickly, he searched his mind for the mother of demons and found her close by. After giving them instructions, the remainder of his children, hopping with eagerness, turned and fled down the tunnel.

As he watched them go, wishing them well, a disturbance arose. A sound, but not a sound. A thought, perhaps. A call. *Yes,* another call to the fire-heart, like the one that had offered the sacrifice. This one, instead of promising food and warmth, demanded sleep. Ignoring the instructions, Stars in White Cloud turned to look in the direction of the signal.

* * *

The light inside the building was so bright Jeff had to snap his eyes shut and cover his face. Even then, an orb of light danced in his head like the memory of a flashbulb.

"You must allow your eyes to adjust slowly," Hog instructed, too late. "The absolute darkness of the caverns can blind you to any real light."

First squinting then slowly allowing his eyes to open, Jeff looked around the small room they had entered. Only the size of a storage closet, it was filled with spelunking equipment much like their own. Shelves of packs and tools ran up the right wall. Some of the equipment was tossed randomly on the floor as if discarded in a hurry.

"These people aren't exactly neat nicks," Elly said, looking around at the disarray.

Hog moved through the room with purpose, looking for something. "That's not it," he said. He bent down and turned, holding up a smoldering cigarette butt. "Someone was just here. They left quickly."

"Why?" Jeff asked, a tight feeling in his gut. He thought he might know why they had left so fast and he didn't like the idea one bit. "Why would they do that?"

Hog stared, the answer in his eyes. *Cybers.* The Cybers were inside.

"What is this place, anyway?" Elly asked.

"The cave room. We use these supplies for trips into the caverns, through the doors we just came through. It is the only entrance into the caverns from TransGenesis itself." He crushed the cigarette butt between two fingers and tossed it into the corner. "Someone must have been in here, preparing to go into the caverns. Perhaps to retrieve the Cybers. Perhaps to try and escape."

"And they were interrupted," Elly said.

Hog's eyes met hers. Their worried expressions matched. "Yes," he said. "Or they just took off."

Jeff broke in. He didn't want Elly to be upset. She needed a clear head and a steel determination if any of them were going to make it out alive. "Hey, it seems like this is a good thing. If we'd come in a few minutes earlier, when the guy was still here sucking on that cancer stick and shooting the shit with his friends, they would have had us." He looked from Elly to Hog, trying to garner support. "That's good, right?"

Elly and Hog stared at him in silence.

"Let's continue on," Hog said. "The operating rooms are close, because they, too, are far back near the caverns, where we stand. There should be a computer in the operating room itself."

"Great. Let's go," Jeff said, starting toward the door.

"Wait!" Hog said, holding up his hand. "I go first. Then Eleanor. Then you."

"Okay."

"Move quietly. Stay against the walls. Jeff, you look behind us as we go. Warn us if anyone is coming up from behind."

Jeff's stomach tensed as he looked at Hog and Elly. The sense of danger in the hallway beyond seemed as thick as the darkness had been in the caverns.

* * *

The conference room. It was open. Caesar ducked inside, breathing hard. He locked the door and leaned against it, trying to catch his breath.

His eyes searched the darkened space, lit only by the glowing screen of a flat computer monitor set into the conference room table. He dared not turn on the lights, but he wanted to assure himself that he was alone.

He waited until his eyes adjusted to the darkness and breathed a sigh of complete relief. The room was empty as a tomb. There were no windows here. For the moment, he was safe.

He walked to a swivel chair near the monitor and dropped into it. What had happened out there? What had gone wrong with his plan? The Cybers seemed to have taken over their own programming. They'd not only learned to ignore the frequencies coming from the palm controllers but had joined forces with Number One and were working as a team.

Number One's presence in the mountain was unexplainable. How had it known where the other Cybers were? Had the nanochip somehow guided him back to where he'd been created? Even if that were so, how did he get into the company itself?

Swiveling to face the screen, Caesar tapped in commands that would give him access to the company's crucial data. He had to backup everything, immediately. He would upload all his data through the web to his private server that only he knew about, where he could get to it later. Meticulously, he found each folder and began copying. He watched carefully, making sure each copy was made without errors. This data was the sum total of everything he'd done here. With this information, he could escape to his alternate lab and continue his work.

As he watched the filenames scroll by, he had a thought. Since the Cybers had learned to ignore the established frequencies of the palm controllers, why not reprogram the frequencies? He could access the program from the node in this room. He could send the updates out on the wireless network to all the controllers within range. The Cybers wouldn't be immune to the new frequency and he could take them by surprise.

His confidence returned like cool water rushing through his veins. Things were not over here yet. Not yet. He was Caesar Bossidy, they were the Cybers. He could still win.

Opening another window on his computer, he accessed the palm controller program and cursed. The thing was so complicated, made up of millions of lines of code. No front end had been built to easily allow frequency reprogramming because no one had anticipated the Cybers' ability to overcome commands. He hadn't looked at the code himself in years, and his $C++$ was rusty.

A sound. Scraping. Under the table. Over by the wall.

His imagination? His heart leapt and he jumped up out of his chair. Where was the sound coming from?

He walked cautiously around the table toward the far wall of the room. On the floor in the corner, an air conditioning vent silently laid in wait. Anxiety shot through him. *No.* They couldn't have figured it out. Smashing a window was one thing, but discovering the venting ducts and knowing where they led? How? Then he remembered. Programmed into the nanochip in each of their brains were the architectural plans of TransGenesis. He had to move quickly.

Grabbing the edge of the heavy table, he hauled it over to the corner, its feet scraping like fingernails on a chalkboard. He rested one of the big legs on top of the vent. Breathing heavily, he decided the weight would keep the vent closed. Certainly, the Cyber couldn't overturn a mahogany conference table through a vent in the floor.

Standing near the table, he bent closer to watch the progress of his files as they were uploaded to his private server. He realized now that he didn't have time to translate the program, change it, and recompile it to alter the palm controller frequencies, not with the Cybers hunting him.

After the files were done copying, he'd have to sneak out of TransGenesis somehow, avoiding the creatures. He'd have to be more clever than they were to make it out alive. That should be no problem. He'd designed them.

The noises beneath the floor increased. Now he heard the chittering language of the Cybers. They were there. Right under the floor.

* * *

Leaving his own equipment on the floor in the cave room, Hog turned the knob and opened the door slowly, peering through the widening crack. He listened. "Okay, this way."

He darted out the doorway and into a narrow hallway, lit by high florescent fixtures. He flattened himself against the far wall, as did Elly. Jeff followed. Together, they moved down the hallway.

At each turn, Hog would stop and listen, then move across the hallway, again to press himself against the wall. Jeff's anxiety turned into amazement. Where was everybody? The doctors, the computer people, the janitors? The place was completely deserted.

Hog came up against the wall near a door and tried the doorknob. Locked. He pulled out a set of keys, sorted through them and inserted one into the lock. He wasted no time pushing open the door.

This time, he didn't stop to listen or enter carefully. He ran into the room. Elly followed. Jeff heard a question, a muffled yell. Heart pounding, he entered the room.

It was small. A cell with a bed, a toilet, and padded walls. Hog stood in the corner grasping a woman, his hand over her mouth. "I am your friend," he said into her ear. "You must be quiet." He lifted his hand.

She rubbed her mouth and glared at Hog. "I recognize you," she said with venom in her voice, "and you're no friend of mine."

She turned to Elly. "Who are you?"

"I'm in the same situation as you are, Donna." She covered her belly. "Dr. Meaks was my doctor, too."

"What...did he do?"

"He implanted an embryo in my womb, but it's not normal. It's one of his...experiments. I need your help to remove it before it's too late. We were hoping to find some medical staff still here to help, but they seem to be gone."

"Remove it?" Donna, amazement on her face, looked from person to person. "You mean...operate?"

"Yes."

"Oh, my God."

Hog stepped forward. "We don't have much time. Please come with us."

* * *

Caesar, determination and fear battling in his mind, watched filenames scroll down the screen. He gasped as the table lifted from the floor, pushed from beneath. *What amazing strength they had.* He stood, his heart in his throat. *Amazing.* They were pushing on the vent from beneath hard enough to lift the table.

Desperate, he climbed onto the table and crawled to the corner that rested atop the air conditioning vent. Hopefully, his added weight would be enough to slow them down. He gritted his teeth and gasped for breath. He was so close. He had to succeed.

The noises ceased and he breathed deeply, relaxing his muscles. Good. Maybe they were giving up.

A scratching sound like nails on wood made him whip his head toward the door. More noises. His heart beat harder and he looked back toward the monitor. He only needed a little more time.

He breathed fast, but still had trouble getting enough oxygen. The Cybers were all around him. Even if he could hold them back long enough to allow the files to copy, how could he escape? His mind raced.

Something crashed against the wooden door. *No!* He had to get out of here, and now. The files didn't matter if he wasn't alive to read them. But how? The only door was guarded by Cybers.

He sat erect on the corner of the table, straining to hear. The scrolling filenames reflected light on the ceiling tiles, but he heard nothing. Were they gone? Had they given up and gone to find easier bait? His breath came in huge gasps.

Boom!

The table lifted beneath him.

Boom!

Something hit it hard again, this time lifting the table a foot in the air.

Boom!

He slipped, the table rolled on its side, he tumbled down, striking his head on the table, falling, stuck between the table and the wall. He struggled to free himself. His weight pinned his arm beneath him, his legs sprawled above, his head below. The table rose like a polished cliff. He couldn't right himself. Couldn't see.

He stopped struggling and listened. They were in the conference room. They were here, inside. And he was helpless, upside down, pinned in the corner by the table and his own body.

40

Jeff sighed with relief as they pushed through the swinging door into the operating suite. Elly immediately sat at the computer and Hog stood beside her, leaning one hand against the monitor. He pointed to icons on the screen as he helped her to log on and access the palm controller program. They spoke in whispered voices, Hog's eyes darting up to the door every few seconds.

Jeff examined the room, going through equipment and supplies. It was more than he could have hoped for. The supplies were well organized and in easy reach, set up for a minimal surgical team. He ticked off the supplies in his mind as he set them up: catheter, epidural kit, IV... "Donna, look through the supplies on the table over there." He pointed to a white-draped steel table where shiny instruments were laid out. "You're a nursing student, right? Sort through that stuff and tell me what you find."

As Jeff hung an IV bag on the bedside pole, he noticed his wrist had stopped bleeding and now was developing a deep bruise. That was good. But his hands were shaking, and that wouldn't do. He had to maintain his cool. Since his big mistake, when he'd punctured a woman's bowel and she'd almost died from blood poisoning, he hadn't been able to lift a scalpel. Hadn't been able to face the idea of cutting. *Deep breaths, Jeff. This is all up to you now, and Elly needs you. Be cool.*

Donna fumbled with the instruments. Her face was white and she looked as if she might pass out. "I've got sponges, scissors, retractors, clamps, scalpels—"

"Good, good," Jeff interrupted. "And in the drawer underneath. What's in there?"

Donna jerked open the drawer too hard and boxes hit the floor. Her hands flew to her face. "I'm sorry," she said, her anxiety clear. "I'm just first year."

Jeff spoke in a gentle voice. "Whoa, slow down." He picked up the dropped materials. Intravenous Valium and Demerol. "Don't worry. This will be no sweat."

"This program to change the palm controllers is too complicated," Elly called out from her place at the monitor, her voice rich with frustration. "There's too much code and it's not organized in any obvious fashion. I don't know if I can change it."

The anxiety in her voice stabbed through Jeff. Under the bright fluorescent lights of the room, Jeff could see dark circles cupping her eyes and a tinge of gray coloring her skin. He knew that every second was a battle for her to maintain control, but she had to remain calm. He moved to her side and put his hand on her shoulder. "Take your time. You can do it, just take your time."

"It's too long," she said with a whimper, scrolling through lines of mumbo-jumbo Jeff couldn't begin to understand. "I can't find…there!" she said triumphantly, laying a fingertip on the screen. "There it is. I think I found it." She typed frantically, her right hand rolling the mouse back and forth, clicking. "If I just change this part, I think I can reprogram the frequencies. Yes," she said, strength returning to her voice.

Hog placed his hand on Elly's shoulder and mumbled something in her right ear. He handed her the palm controller. She nodded, put it on her lap, and continued to work at a furious pace.

Standing erect, his body stretching to full height, Hog penetrated Jeff's eyes with a stare. "Sometimes," Hog said pointedly, "important parts are left out of the telling of a legend, to not tempt fate." As Hog held Jeff's gaze, all time seemed to stand still.

Hog nodded to Donna and pushed out through the swinging door where he stationed himself as hall guard.

Momentarily frozen in place, Jeff glanced through the small nose-height window in the door. Hog. Their friend, their protector. Jeff wondered if he had just said goodbye.

Elly fought for possession of her thoughts. The power that pressed upon her since entering the cave squeezed harder every moment. Concentrating, she found the routine that would change the palm controller's frequencies. She selected it, started to make the changes, and—

The sun warmed her shoulders and bounced off crystal clear water. Her family was there, her children. Warm peace beckoned her to come, come, come.

No! She shook her head and fought it. She was anywhere but home, any place but safe. She must fight the power that invited her to her death.

The code came back into focus. She made one last change, saved the program and started it compiling.

She swiveled in the chair toward Jeff. He talked with Donna and they both worked at a frantic pace. "Prep me while it compiles," she said. "The moment it finishes successfully, I'll run the program and broadcast the frequency change. We'll zap the entire mountain."

She stood and Jeff walked her to the table. Before he could help her up, she grabbed him in a bear hug. Pulling back, she looked into his eyes. A drop of sweat ran down his forehead and hung from the end of his nose. She wiped it away with one finger and kissed him. "Dr. Jeffrey Clinton," she said, "I am in your hands. And there's nowhere on earth I would feel safer."

41

Blood pumped through White Cloud's young veins, fueled with the hunger of revenge. Two of them had come through the small tunnels and broken into the room, and three were at the room's door. The leader, the defiler, lay beyond the upturned table, trapped.

The worst thing, the awful truth, was that the infidel was his brother, a member of the P'ónin tribe. The sacrilege this man had committed was almost too much to bear. He would die, slowly, his suffering the only way he could be redeemed.

As White Cloud began to chant, to ask for victory and peace, he felt a call from one of his brothers. He'd found the mother of demons! Using the tight bond he'd established with the demons, he deserted the leader's body and projected himself out of the room. His soul followed the line of the call, whooshing through halls, around corners, through wood and metal until it found the source of the summons—a demon child, who absorbed his soul.

Stretching into the new body, looking out the new eyes, he came face to face with another brother, a P'ónin. This man was the last barrier between White Cloud and his destiny.

* * *

Caesar's neck ached. A warm drop of blood ran down his forehead and seeped into his eye. He rubbed it away with the back of his free hand. He had to get upright somehow.

Something tickled his bare leg between his pant leg and socks. He cried out and jerked back his foot as far as it would go. He panted with fear. He would not be beaten! There was still a way. There was always a way.

He arched his back, trying to dislodge himself and turn over. Little by little, he maneuvered into an upright position. He loosened his arm and pulled it free. He planted both shoes on the carpet behind the table.

A Cyber crowed, and the cry filled Caesar with fear. Were they about to attack?

He wanted to look over the side of the table to see them, but was afraid he'd get his head bitten off. He stood, crouched behind the overturned table, his heart beating wildly, still feeling pressure inside his head from having been upside down for so long. He saw his palm controller near his feet, and snatched it up. But what good was it? He should have anticipated this occurrence—made the process of changing frequencies a part of the basic function of the palm controllers. If he ever got out of here, their design would change dramatically.

He could hear the Cybers in the room, moving around and conversing. Bracing himself, gritting his teeth, he peered over the side of the table.

He gasped and ducked back behind the table. It was Number One, all right, leading two other Cybers. He truly was magnificent. His long, black hair almost made him look like a human child, except his muscle development went way beyond any child's. The hand that had become the claw on the chimps now appeared to be more regular, but Caesar knew the fingers were strong as steel and the nails were every bit as dangerous as the chimp Cyber's claws.

The eyes. If anything in his appearance set him off from other human children, it was the eyes. They reflected light in the small room as they magnified it five times over, giving him the look of a feral cat.

Why hadn't they attacked? The leader seemed confused, unsure of what he should do. They must have something else in mind.

Sitting with his back against the table, using it as his shield, Caesar tried to keep his mind off the creatures and on the problem—escape.

Unless the Cybers could be distracted, Caesar didn't have a chance. The palm controller didn't work. They had strength, numbers, weapons and complete knowledge of the plant.

An idea wove its way through Caesar's frantic thoughts. Could he communicate with it? They were talking with each other. Number One had returned to the mountain. Maybe, all the Cyber wanted was to meet his creator. Maybe it—he—would respond to him if he rose with his hands out, in surrender. He had to try. There was no other choice.

He stood, slowly. Upright. He faced the Cyber.

He waited until the Cyber looked directly at him. He said, "Hello."

The Cyber stood still. A magnificent sculpture. "Heddah," it replied, its voice hoarse, its lips unused to forming sound. Caesar's heart froze in disbelief and wonder. It could talk.

It leapt at Caesar. Swinging the letter opener, it struck him across the face with stunning force. The blow snapped Caesar's head around, sending pain down his spine. He fell into a lump behind the table. Pain filled his head, neck and back, as if someone poured it into his body through the top of his head. Caesar struggled to move. He tried to stand, then changed his mind and stayed hunched behind the table. The Cyber wailed that piercing cry again, the others chattered, and something began clamoring up the side of the table.

Caesar braced himself for torture, and death.

* * *

White. The white tile gleamed, white paint bleak and bright. The instruments shined. Artificial light, artificial air. The silence in the room was almost complete, just their breathing and the hum of the computer's hard drive.

284

Elly lay on her back, catheter in place, IV successfully inserted, epidural administered. Although she was numb from breast to toe, she held the palm controller tightly in her fist.

Donna assisted Jeff and watched the monitor. As soon as the program was done compiling, Elly would send the signal and kill the fetus, along with any other Cybers within range.

Jeff wiped the back of his hand over his forehead, momentarily forgetting the waterproof gloves he wore. He glanced up at the monitor, too, willing the program to finish compiling and become operable.

"Elly," he said. "We're through to the muscle layer. Under that is the uterus. I don't want to open it until we're sure the Cyber will be under control." He hesitated. "How much longer until we can use the palm controller?"

She lifted her head from the table and twisted it around, trying to see the monitor. "I don't know. I thought it would be done by now. It must be connected to some larger programs that are taking longer." She dropped her head back down and sighed.

Jeff felt his stomach cramp with anxiety. He held a sponge in his right hand. Her surface tissues were cut and pulled back with retractors, and he mopped up blood as it seeped from her open tissues. He couldn't leave her open like this much longer, she'd lose too much blood. But he couldn't risk removing the Cyber without assurance that it would not attack them.

For the time being, the Cyber within Elly's womb remained quiet, unmoving. Jeff prayed it stayed that way.

"Come on, come on," Donna urged, her eyes on the screen. "There!" she exclaimed. "There's a message on the screen."

"Hurry!" Hog yelled from the hall. "They're coming. I see them coming."

Donna's eyes widened. She gasped and dropped the scalpel she'd been holding for Jeff to use on the muscle layer.

"What does it say?" Elly demanded. "The message, what does it say?"

Donna rushed over to the computer and leaned in close. "There's a whole bunch of stuff." She whimpered. "I don't know what to do."

"Read the end, what does it say at the end of the message?" Elly's voice was dry, hoarse.

"I don't…okay, it says *no match for Node & != const int &*. What should I do?" Donna sounded panicked.

Jeff watched Elly think, the gears turning.

Something slammed into the door. Hog yelped.

"Elly, think!" Jeff encouraged her.

"All right. I think I know," Elly said.

Flute music came through the door. Jeff raced to the window. Outside, in the hall, Hog was backed against the door. Five Cybers squared off against him. Hog's left hand was bloodied. He played the flute as they had at the pueblo, and the Cybers seemed momentarily entranced.

"You gotta hurry," Jeff said.

"It's just missing a node, a computer it's looking for. That's why we're getting the message. I think it will still work."

Jeff walked back to her, laid his hand on her shoulder. "Okay, Elly, do it." Elly lifted the palm controller, set it on *wide area kill,* and pressed the button. She aimed it at all corners of the room, pressing it over and over. Still holding tight to the palm controller, she dropped her hand down by her side, and stared at Jeff. "Your turn."

As he made the final cut, another cry came from outside the door and the flute music was abruptly cut off.

42

Caesar gasped for oxygen, his breathing way too fast. He wasn't ready, wasn't ready. He had too much left to give, to do, to build.

He covered his head with his hands, unable to think of any way out of this. He whimpered, hidden behind the conference table where he'd sat and made his plans for greatness.

His heart beat wildly, visions of his childhood at Isleta randomly appearing in his mind like old photographs. His mother, whose ways had inadvertently given him the motivation to begin his work. His secret room, where in the darkness of the cave, he'd kept his books and planned his escape. The log near the beaver dam, where he'd learned about the power of one well-designed creature, where he'd sat and listened to the snowbirds, learning about their communication. The malamute that always followed him, tongue lolling, ears perked up, eyes shining. The eyes he had copied for his Cybers.

Straining his ears, he listened. *Nothing.*

Was it a trick? Were they flattened against the other side of the table, ready, claws extended?

Nothing.

He heard nothing but ringing in his ears. Amazingly, the monitor still showed scrolling lists of filenames as his records were uploaded to the web, the records of his accomplishments, the proof of his greatness. He would not cower behind this table any longer. He had to risk it. Carefully, slowly, he stood on shaking legs, one inch at a time, to peer over the table. He wiped blood from his eye with the back of his hand.

The Cybers were lying on the floor as if asleep, or dead. How? Taking another good look around, Caesar swung his leg over the table, ignoring the pain, and came down on the other side, the division between him and the Cybers now gone.

Shakily, he approached Number One. Its chest rose and fell. It was breathing. He checked the other one. It, too, was alive, just unconscious. Someone had used his idea. They'd reprogrammed the palm controller frequencies and put the Cybers to sleep. But who?

Caesar glanced around the conference room.

This was his chance. With a glance back to where the monitor showed its progress, he lifted the human Cyber into his arms. He'd leave the others. Where could he take a chimp Cyber without questions being asked? With the right clothes, the human Cyber would look enough like a child to pass a brief inspection.

Making sure he still had the palm controller, he carried his son to the door and headed back to his office, where he could escape through the caves.

Now, his future waited beyond the confines of TransGenesis.

* * *

Stars in White Cloud's spirit continued to leap toward the man as the body of the Cyber fell uselessly to the floor. The fire pulses had ordered the demon's fire-heart to stop functioning, had ordered the demons' heart of flesh to stop beating. The fire pulses, instead of helping the demon children this time, had wanted the demon children to die, and now were so strong the children could not ignore their call.

White Cloud had only an instant to save the children, to tell them not to die, but to sleep, and then find himself a new host. He continued his leap up, up, and possessed the man he'd just attacked, who now played the spirit flute.

In his new host, he became a man, a P'ónin, a warrior. He was brave and honorable. Stretching into the body, he turned and peered through the window into the room beyond. A miracle unfolded inside. The child was being lifted from the demon mother's womb. All of the people inside were part of the legend, so there was no one he must kill—he just needed to take the child, call the others, and go back into the caverns. The mother was not screaming in agony, although she had been eviscerated. She lay still, calm. Truly the legend's demon mother, she was brave and self-sacrificing. An honor to the tribe and a fulfillment of the legends.

* * *

Jeff made the final cut and there it was. Huge. Way too big for the gestational age.

He pushed his hands under its head and guided it out, trailing the cord. Black hair matted its head, its body covered in blood and fluid. *It was breathing!* The palm controller hadn't killed it.

Donna gasped and backed up, her hands covering her mask, her eyes wide.

"Take it," Jeff demanded. "We don't have time for drama."

Hesitantly, she stepped forward, holding out her hands. "Wh-what do I do with it?"

"Hold it while I cut the cord."

Donna whined as she cupped the thing in her hands. The smell was strong. Jeff turned back and removed the afterbirth, tossing it into one of the steel sinks.

The door opened.

Hog stepped in, his face fixed in a strange, serious mask. He walked toward Donna like a zombie, stiff and focused on the Cyber.

"Hog?" Jeff asked. "We're not done here."

Hog seized the Cyber and backhanded Donna across the face. She fell in a limp pile to the floor, weeping.

"Hog! What the—" Jeff demanded, the relief of the Cyber being extracted melting into panic. He stepped in front of Hog as the man turned toward Elly. Cradling the Cyber in one arm, Hog pushed Jeff aside with amazing strength. He stared down at Elly.

Elly, unable to do anything but lift her head, stared at him fearlessly. "Mother of Demons," he said. His speech was in a strange language, Tiwa perhaps, but they could all understand him, as if he spoke straight into their minds. Hog's full attention was focused on Elly, as if the rest of them didn't exist. "Thank you for the child. You have earned your place in the next world. We will take care of your child until you return."

After a moment, he turned and walked purposefully to the door and disappeared down the hallway. Within moments, they heard the light tones of a flute. Racing to the door, Jeff saw Hog walking slowly away, the Cyber in one arm, playing a flute. Other Cybers rose from their sleep and followed him.

"Donna, help me close."

Donna remained on the floor, making loud, sobbing sounds.

"Donna!" Jeff insisted, keeping one eye on the door to watch for Hog. Or worse, anything else that might emerge from the halls or caverns.

Donna climbed to her feet, and together they began the process of saving Elly.

$$* * *$$

The halls all looked the same. This was good because there were no people, Cybers, or monsters laying in wait for them. This was bad because Jeff had no idea how to find the front gate.

"Damn Hog, anyway!" Jeff said. "What happened to him? Was he just using us all along, always planning to take the Cyber and run?"

"No." Elly's voice was reedy and weak. "He could have just killed us before."

"I think I recognize this hallway," Donna said, excitement in her voice. She stopped the stretcher, putting her hand on the rail. "There," she said, pointing. "That way."

They took a left down a hallway that was wider than the rest. Pictures and plaques hung on the walls. A history of Caesar's accomplishments, pictures of the facility, articles describing scientific breakthroughs.

This had to be it. The hallway opened into a room, adorned with couches, a reception desk, plants.

A glass doorway opened to the outside.

"Yes," Jeff exclaimed. "We found it."

"Wait," Elly said, her voice dry. "Don't. Donna, go out first. Look."

"She's right," Jeff said. "We can't trust what Hog promised. Look at what he did."

Donna's hand reached up and touched the growing welt on her face. "Right." When she glanced toward the doors, Jeff saw some of Elly's determination reflected in her. Donna lifted her chin and walked purposely toward the doors, pushed them open, and went out.

"She's brave," Elly said.

Jeff gave her a sip of water from the plastic water bottle he carried. "How are you doing?" Jeff asked, feeling stupid. He knew how she must be doing. As the spinal wore off, the pain would be unbearable. He'd taken a box and filled it with antibiotics and painkillers, as much as he could carry, but it wouldn't last long enough. Abdominal surgery was one of the most painful procedures, and had a long recovery time. He should know. It was what he'd specialized in before he'd quit.

"I'm feeling okay," she said weakly, attempting a smile. Then she grimaced.

"Don't talk. Don't do anything. Just relax."

"I just want to know," Elly asked. "Did you save the other baby? The normal one?"

Jeff hesitated. "I don't know, Elly. Everything happened so fast. We'll just have to wait and see."

The doors burst open. Donna raced in, leading two men Jeff recognized from the pueblo.

"Where is Hog?" one man asked, searching the room with his eyes.

"I don't know," Jeff answered.

The men glanced around the lobby. "All the other men have left. They freed the animals and came out this way. They said they heard fighting, screaming."

Jeff looked at Donna. "Everything went as planned." He hesitated. "Except for Hog. He took one of the Cybers. I don't know what happened."

The men exchanged glances, then seeming to come to a decision, each took one side of the stretcher and pushed it out the doors.

The day was brighter than in the operating room, natural, beautiful, real. Jeff was out of the caverns and out of the nightmare.

Donna jumped in the back of the van and helped move the stretcher up into it. Jeff followed. The doors slammed, putting him back in the darkness.

The men jumped in the front seat, wasting no time. The engine roared to life, skidded, and they were off. Jeff watched TransGenesis shrink behind them.

"Where are we going?" Donna asked.

"Isleta?" Jeff asked Elly.

"Yes," she replied.

"Isleta," Jeff called to the men in front. "We're going home."

43

There had been light. Danger. Loud sounds and touching, pain and wrongness.

He'd hidden from the light. Now he was tired, so tired.

But the mother carried him still, and he knew he was safe. Safe and warm.

He listened for his brothers, but heard only whispers, far away. Had they survived?

Sleep now.

He'd still have time, much time, to fulfill his destiny.

About the Author

An award-winning author, M.F. King has spent time as an electrical engineer and technical writer. She writes regularly for Texas Highway Patrol Magazine and is published in magazines such as Woman's World and Fate. Her most recent speculative fiction story, "The Jacket", was released in May 2005 in *The Elements of the Fantastic* from Coscom Entertainment. She lives in Colorado where she is working on her next thriller. To contact her, visit her website at: www.mfking.net

Printed in the United States
38241LVS00003B/115-135

9 781897 217184